MAGIC ACADEMY

J.E. & M. KEEP

CONTENTS

CHAPTER 1

Her father worked nights, but that suited her just fine. After all, he took her with him to hang out in the dark corridors of the Arcane Academy. It was a place so few humans had ever gone, and at night she didn't have to deal with so many of the sour stares of the high elves.

Instead she could simply wander, admiring the history and architecture of the great buildings.

But she always went back to one in particular. The Grand Library. It contained more knowledge than she could ever hope or dream of, and the young woman felt truly alive there. She'd spent her childhood poring over heavy tomes of spells and secrets.

Yet her ambitions were growing with every day.

No longer was she content to simply read the night away, practicing harmless spells that served so little purpose. The moment she had found the dusty, hidden black book she knew it was calling to her. Begging for her to learn its contents.

For months she'd studied it in detail, the yearning to know something of true value, beyond the mundanities of her self-taught tricks, driving her to a near-religious fervor. Finally, the evening had come that she would cast her first ritual from it. No one she knew of had been able to handle such a spell, and it was just what she needed to get into the Academy. To make the elvish sorcerers sit up and take notice of a desperate human.

Her black hair was pulled back in twin pigtails, her bangs swept out of her expressive blue eyes. Her peachy skin felt flush with excitement as she settled in.

She'd blocked the door of the library's study room, and had everything prepared to see her through to the end of the casting. Yet as the first word of power passed her lips, she wondered if she could ever be prepared for the high she received.

It was something she'd never truly experienced to the same intensity. *"Fush-nea klixak hlinta,"* she continued, and with each word her body trembled.

This wasn't the stuff of parlor tricks that she'd toyed with before: simple twists of light and sound to amuse and confound viewers. Each word tapped into some dark plane of existence and the raw magical energies there coursed through her veins and made her skin buzz with electricity.

The closer she got to conclusion, the more reality seemed to warp before her. It was as if the walls changed shape, angles took on impossible dimensions that were not of her world.

Gradually, it was as if a lightning storm were brewing at the heart of the room. Crackles of energy stabbing out from black wisps of nothingness that grew to consume the air there. It was terrifying to watch, and a sense of foreboding followed in its wake, but the high… the high of that power coursing through her with each new word was so sweet. Too sweet to give up.

She wouldn't. She was so close. She could feel how close she was, and her excitement made her stumble on that final word. *"Punummra,"* she shouted, praying to be heard over the crackle of power at the heart of the word.

Her skin was flush and her light, white shirt clung to her slender body. The black skirt felt sticky around her thighs and calves, and she shifted to try to get the fabric off her.

The tempest before her writhed and swelled with a fury that belied the earlier display. Black tendrils seemed to lunge out at reality itself in random directions! It wasn't long, though, before they began to take on some form, and as if from through a gateway to hell itself, she witnessed the ruddy-black visage of a man that was not a man, both step through to her side and tear it open.

He was wrathful. He was monstrous! He was beautiful, even in his fury.

Sleek muscle, he was bare. Not a stitch of clothing, only the wisps of blackness that still clung to his form gracing his body as he clenched his fists and let loose a cry that beat at her ears. Hooves struck the floorboards, and his mighty, obsidian horns nearly scraped the ceiling.

"Kral'kron krizzixt varuj!" he exclaimed in his demonic tongue, almond-shaped eyes that burned like cinders darting about the room before he realized there was nobody to turn his rage on... nobody but her.

His bare chest heaved, his nostrils flared. Tall and mighty, he was broad at the shoulders and dwarfed her in every manner.

She'd never felt so small and insignificant, physically.

Yet at the same time, she felt larger than life, powerful beyond belief, and a smile spread across her lips. Fear still coiled in her stomach and she took a step backwards, away from the hellish thing she'd summoned.

That *she* had summoned. By herself. Without any aid of elves and their haughty attitudes. He was hers, bound to her alone.

Her body tingled with such perfect disbelief.

The look upon the demon's face said he believed otherwise. Though some strange amusement tickled his fancy.

From out of his chest his words rumbled forth, dark and ominous, so full of masculine menace. "It was you who summoned me?" he asked, part disbelief in his voice, part amusement. Though she could see the strands of darkness flicker out and fade, they swept away from his body, leaving him more apparent to her. Her eyes able to see his reddish form, the dark hairs of his chest that formed a V-shape on down to a trail across his stony abs, that ended in a tuft above his loins. By the gods! Those monstrous loins of his were enough to snap her in half!

It struck her dumb for a moment and her voice came out as little more than a squeaked "yes." It was an odd sensation, of feeling utterly powerful and utterly insignificant, all at once. Yet she controlled him, so shouldn't she feel unstoppable?

The small, young woman forced her eyes away from his massive package and looked instead to his face. "You are here because of me."

The mighty demon before her snorted with derision and then unfurled his fists. She saw then the long, hooked nails that looked perilously sharp. "Because of you," he repeated, touching one hand to his chest, letting the dagger-tips of his claws scrape over his own dark flesh, raking across abs as he eyed her with curiosity.

"Why?" he demanded more than asked, brushing back some of his long, black hair with the other hand. The glossy pitch strands flowing about his neck and shoulders, framing his face.

"Because I could!" she replied, trying to sound strong and brave but feeling anything but. She should have felt that same high she'd experienced casting the spell, but instead, fear was beginning to turn her blood cold.

He was too large. Too unwieldy of a weapon. How could she hope to have the mental fortitude to hold him back? Greater mages than her had tried and failed.

Her eyes narrowed at her negative thoughts and she forced herself to stand straight. No. She summoned him and she would control him.

The towering beast before her smirked and a low rumble of a chuckle emitted from his chest as he rubbed his hand up and down across it and his hard belly. "Is that it then? You tore me from my realm, my home, simply because you could?" He stepped closer to her, his hoof hitting the ground noisily and as if time meant nothing to him, he was suddenly several steps closer to her, looming barely two inches from her body.

She couldn't help but inhale the scent of cinders, sweat, curiously alien aromas and masculinity with him up in her face like that. He pricked beneath her chin with one of his hooked nails, pointing her face up at him slowly. "Nobody summons one of my kind without a reason. Maybe you don't know it yet," he mused aloud.

How was it possible that she felt like her pulse was racing and her heart stopped, all at once? His touch, his nail was so sharp and unpleasant, yet his scent was nearly intoxicating in a strange way. "I have to prove myself. You're my proof."

Something flickered in those fiery eyes of his. Mischief? Perhaps, she couldn't tell, for he looked full of wickedness no matter what he did.

He bent down, which was quite a journey. He towered up to nearly seven feet! And was built wider and stronger than any man or elf she'd seen with her own two eyes.

She saw him up close, the pointed patch of hair on his chin. The hard lines of his jaw. The handsome yet frightening features that made him so alluring and scary all at once.

It was so bizarre an experience, especially once he shut his eyes and sniffed at her. Actually sniffed at her! Letting his eyes shut as his nose grazed her hair, tasting her own natural human scent off the air. "You're young," he said, continuing his investigation. "Too young for such an accomplishment to be believable."

That was what she'd always been told. That humans did not have the lifespan to learn magic – true, powerful magic – yet she'd done it, hadn't she? She'd proved those snooty elves of the Academy wrong, right?

"Without proof it wouldn't be believable! But you're here. I summoned you on my own, and there's nothing they can say to take that away from me." She couldn't believe it. Even *he* was doubting her abilities, and she'd brought him here!

His thick lips spread wide across his face in a wickedly handsome mockery of a smile. The pungent aroma of his masculinity so strong still as he tilted her head one way, then the other. He inspected her delicate female form, and though his manhood twitched and swelled before her, he was slow. Methodical.

Thoughtful.

"You aspire to be a sorceress then," he said, taking the prick of his finger from beneath her chin and stroking his hot thumb across her cheek, as if he were a lover or a doting parent. "And you summoned me to prove you are better and more worthy of that title than your years attest." He nodded slowly. "Daring. Or foolish."

"They don't let humans in here," she hissed bitterly. "So I either carry on in my family's footsteps or I do something daring and foolish. And in the end, I get more powerful than any of *them* are worthy of."

"None of them could have summoned and bound me," he responded with wry amusement on his face, his private joke not shared with her. "Only one other ever succeeded in doing as such, and he was great and powerful by the standards of mortals." He let his gaze slip down over her full body, and she couldn't help but notice the frightening creature's massive girth was stiff and jutted out directly towards her. "You've dared big, little conjurer. Dared big and won, perhaps."

Her body stiffened and she tried to take a step back, but instead she bumped into a bookshelf, keeping her pinned between it and... *it*. That wasn't something any text had prepared her for, and even in her fury and power-drunk sensation, that throbbing phallus was distracting her from her victory.

"Don't they have robes where you're from?"

He looked down at his own lewdly displayed manhood. "They do. But you summoned me through the void," he said simply. "I would assume a clever young sorceress like you would know that one doesn't travel through the void with clothing. Or anything else for that matter."

He grinned unevenly at her. "Does it bother you, little human?" He took hold of that massive length, gripped it in his hand and began to stroke it—actually stroke it!—right in front of her. He stared down at her petite form, mouth hanging open, fangs on display as he tongued his lower lip.

"You're disgusting," she breathed. Fear had been replaced by annoyance and anger at his taunting, and she pushed herself away from him. "You're mine now, and I command you cover that foul thing up!"

His mouth widened in his amusement, and though he didn't stop the slow, firm motions of his hand along that thick, bulging cock, he asked, "With what? I have no clothes, sorceress." He arched his spine back, but kept his fiery eyes glued to her as he pleasured himself so disgustingly. "You must provide me with such things. You're aware of that, surely."

He gave another inhale of the air in her direction, tasting her scent with his tongue even, as that monstrously sized appendage swelled in his grasp visibly.

Wasn't he supposed to be under her thrall? Why did he taunt her so?

"Stop touching yourself and I'll provide you with something, then!" There had to be something nearby.

He obeyed, but only gradually. "Yes sorceress," he said in his gravelly voice, amusement rich on it as he finally took his hand from his shaft. "I'll be waiting here."

She turned her back on him angrily, clearing the entrance and heading deeper into the building.

It didn't take her long to find a wardrobe with a spare robe in it, though it was more her size than his. Still, it would be enough to cover up… that. She knew that demons could be disgusting, but she had no idea it would be like that.

When she returned, however, she didn't see the massive creature. Which was odd, as he towered even above the bookshelves in the room. Was he hiding? It didn't seem in his nature to do so; he'd been so haughty and cocky.

For a moment, terror took her as she feared he had abandoned her somehow, against the power of the spell.

New fright took hold, however, when the figure of another man—this one significantly shorter than her conjured menace—stepped out from behind the bookshelf, covered in shadows. One of the library mages had caught her!

Why were they even out at night? She stood still, her hands going behind her back and her head falling demurely to her chest. The young woman seemed every bit a chastised child, and she waited for his punishing words to rain down upon her.

He approached her quietly from the shadows, no scolding following as she expected and was used to from the elven masters. He stood there in the dark side of the room beside her, until his hand came up beneath her chin. It was bare, and dark. Few of the elves had so dark of skin.

With a careful touch there he tilted her head up, and her blue-eyed gaze moved across his ruddy-brown flesh—bare, just like the creature she had conjured, but man-sized, not monster-sized—to meet his face.

Her heart skipped a beat. For unlike the terror created by the thing she had brought forth, he was simply gorgeous. His long silky black hair reflecting a bit of the candle and moonlight, his face smiling as he leaned in and... and kissed her lips. So mysteriously, he held her chin in a moment of confusion and tenderly kissed her.

She was locked, smitten and unable to even flinch, until he broke the touch and gave her a charming look. "Thank you for the robe," he said, that voice so reminiscent of earlier, though with much of the hellish edge gone.

She barely knew what to make of it and felt her head grow light. She'd never spoken to someone so attractive, and she knew full well why. She felt tongue-tied and scared and embarrassed all at once.

For all her years she'd avoided boys her own age. She got too tongue-tied around them, tripping over her words when she felt they were too attractive to be interested in her. And he definitely was.

At least like this.

How was it possible for him to look like this anyway?

She felt a tremor run through her and she begged herself to speak, to demand answers from him, but nothing would come out.

With smooth, deft movements, he took the robe from her arms and pulled it around behind him. He was in no rush, and she had time to glimpse at his form. He was still taller than her, but no longer inhumanly so. His chest was smooth now, no longer coated with the dark hairs. And though his manhood was on display—and still erect— it was no longer something so horrific. Especially since he covered it up and it vanished from sight, only to linger in memory.

"The summoning process takes a lot from me," he said, tying the robe shut. Though even as he spoke she could see the cloth shifting, the fabric changing shape, becoming something more exotic. Foreign. It hung open at his chest, showing some of his shoulders, the cuffs billowed out around his wrists and on down she could see it slit open up towards his groin, stopping before displaying anything lewd. And his feet... he had feet now too, she noticed. No longer cloven-hoofed.

She was rendered speechless. Where she had grown so confident and commanding to the demon, she was struck mute in front of the attractive man that had "replaced" him. Her lips hung open and she forced them shut, inhaling deeply.

What had he said? She knew he'd spoken, but she hadn't heard a word of it.

The dashing man pulled his hair from beneath the collar of the robe, and let it fall back down to settle around his neck and shoulders, which were so much more slender now comparatively, that he looked to be about her age. It also drew attention to the fact that he still bore horns, but much smaller, and now swept back instead of spiralling high. They blended with his hair rather well.

"Would you tell me your name, madam sorceress?" he asked with every pretense of cordiality upon his charming voice. He sounded—and looked—like a foreign prince. A foreign prince in a lavish bath robe, perhaps, but nonetheless.

For a moment it seemed she'd forgotten her name. It was on the tip of her tongue but she was too flabbergasted to fully recall it.

Her tongue worked over her lips until finally it came to her.

"Firia," she whispered.

"Firia," he repeated in that curiously accented voice. He leaned forward and took one of her hands, lifting it as if it were made of delicate porcelain, then bent forward and kissed the back of her knuckles. "It is a pleasure to have been summoned by so beauteous a conjurer, Firia." He smiled to her, his ruby eyes glinting as they met her gaze. "I am Varuj," and the name rolled off his tongue so appetizingly, as if—she imagined—it would taste delicious to merely say. "At your service."

She actually thought she might faint. She willed herself to remember that he was still the vile demon that was pleasuring himself moments ago, just to make her uncomfortable, but it was so hard to think. He was too handsome for words, and she shifted from foot to foot as his skin touched hers.

"How did you change? You shouldn't be able to."

"It is no worry," he said again as if merely a foreigner with an enchanting accent and a curious grasp on her language, rather than a demon from some dimension of damnation. "I know many things. Many tricks. Many spells," he said with a smile, rubbing his thumb over the back of her hand. "Things that even the wizards of your world do not."

"Teach me them."

Her blue eyes widened in shock, astounded that she'd been able to speak, and with such a commanding tone. Her need for that power, those magics he knew had even outweighed her nervousness of being around him.

And that somehow made her more nervous.

His smile lit up his handsome face, and he kissed the back of her hand again. "I can do that," he said at last. "In less time than the teachers of your world could instruct you, too." And that was what mattered most, wasn't it? For as she was reminded so often, a human's life was not long enough to learn such power. And she'd already lost so much of it on the outside, looking in.

Her head nodded, and suddenly she was hit with the more pressing concerns. Where will he stay? Perhaps she hadn't as much confidence in her skills as she believed, for she certainly hadn't thought so far ahead. Yet he'd made it easier and harder on her all at once.

Her father would never let him stay with them.

She'd envisioned it so differently, her stomping into the Dean's office and demanding fair treatment.

Now she wanted something more.

The beautiful man before her continued to smile and rub her hand. "There is something you must understand first and foremost, madam Firia," he said in his deep, smooth voice. "You cannot expose my existence to anyone. Not the teachers you wished to impress, not loved ones. No one."

"How am I going to explain you? How will I get ahead?" Her voice was so small and meek compared to the accomplished and commanding woman who had summoned him.

"You can't explain me," he said simply, not losing that charm or smile. "Not yet, Firia." He brought his free hand up to her face, cupped her cheek gently. "You can hide me, if you let me show you how. And when you are able to sneak away, I will teach you. Better than any tutor of your world ever could."

It was creeping her out just how much she wanted that. How much she longed for that.

She hadn't realized just how lonely and isolated she had let herself become. Her shyness around men her own age had led to her hiding in libraries, and she'd never even seen one so good-looking as him.

It's an illusion, she reminded herself, but that only made her remember the sight of him stroking that horrifying organ and her breath hitched.

He leaned in close, so that their foreheads nearly touched. "I will be your secret," he said quietly. "Yours and yours alone." His palm cupped her cheek and his fingers moved through her hair delicately. "And after time training together in our secret moments," gods, he made that sound so tantalizing, despite knowing his true form, "you shall be an unmatched sorceress. Not even those who have trained and practiced for centuries will rival you, Firia."

"Why?"

The word toppled from her tongue, and she scolded herself. Because she bound him to her. Because he belongs to her.

Yet someone so gorgeous could never belong to her, could never be so tender with her as he was trying to play at.

He was a beautiful monster, and it was making her feelings become conflicted. She swallowed and looked at him with those expressive, blue eyes. "You are my thrall." She answered her own question.

His beautiful, almond-shaped eyes hardened just a little, then softened in sadness. "That is a cruel thing to say," he said in a hurt voice.

In the blink of an eye, things changed.

He was the same, but he had faded out of reality in his position and now stood at the opposite side of the room, before the window, the moonlight framing his figure.

"The truth is never cruel," she managed to sputter out, even in her shock. "It just is."

He sat back on the windowsill and curled his legs up with him, wrapping his arms about them. The moon glimmered off his dark hair, and shimmered upon his smooth skin, all the way down to where his robe began at the edge of his shoulders. "Even a bound one does not need to obey all," he said simply, that tinge of hurt still in his voice. "You could tell a bound one to perform an action like… attack a foe. But you could not command him to betray his secrets. No conjurer is that powerful a master."

She knew, logically, what he was. A cunning manipulator, a demon from a hellish place. Yet that wasn't how he seemed, and it was so hard to argue with what she saw. He looked so hurt, and she was the one who had done it.

She took a step forward, folding her arms defensively beneath her petite bust, but she didn't know what to say. She was at a loss for words.

Varuj looked aside, the silhouette of his handsome face outlined by silvery moonlight. "I would not share my secrets with a master. Only a companion," he said almost pouty, in defiance of her attempt to cow him.

"I know what you are," she said softly, but she tightened her arms to stop her hands from trembling. It was taking so much out of her just to not run to him, apologizing.

"You're trying to manipulate me into caring for you."

He sighed. "All I ask is that you treat me as equal," he said so simply. "Is grinding me beneath your boot heel all you can think of? So much so that it blinds you to opportunity?" He rested his head upon his knees. All she could see of him was his glossy black hair rested atop his arms and knees. "Fine," he said with some resignation. "I will teach you something… but just one thing. And if, after that, you do not care to treat me as something other than a slave… no more."

Her throat was so dry and she took another step towards him, taken in by his good looks and sullen exterior. "How can I trust you when you are acting like this?"

Slowly, he lifted his head and rested his chin upon his arms to gaze back at her. The fire had ebbed from his ruby eyes somewhat. "Like what? I sacrificed my mighty form so that I might be more pleasing and less disconcerting to you. It was no easy feat. Nor a small sacrifice. I am weaker like this," he explained calmly. "Though it is the only way I could hope to converse with you."

"You can't change back when you feel like it?" That actually surprised her, and though she was smart enough to know he was trying to manipulate her, it didn't occur to her that he would outright lie. Though she'd always been someone craving power and knowledge, she was always open and honest with others as much as she could be.

Except when it threatened her quest for things greater than herself.

"It is not so simple," he said with a sigh of exasperation. He stood, though, and approached her with slow, languid motions. "Shall I teach you then? Do we have a deal or no? If you only care to expose me to your elvish wizards then spare me the trouble and banish me now. They will only punish you for stealing a tome of dark secrets, and do terrible things to me before expunging me from this plane of existence. Such an outcome would be tedious and painful for us both."

"They wouldn't," she gasped, but somehow she knew it was more likely than them praising her for her cunning. For her success. Her eyes began to fill with tears and she knew she was in far over her head.

Her lower lip trembled as she begged herself not to cry in front of the gorgeous demon, but she couldn't help as the first tear escaped and ran down her peachy cheek.

"I would prefer to stay in your world," he said, and he reached out, touching her arms with his hands, "with you." He was so tender, so careful as he leaned in and spoke to her softly. "I said I will teach you a spell. A secret. And all I ask in return is that you keep me hidden."

"Why would you possibly prefer it here? You said I took you away from your home." It was hard to speak while holding in the sobs, but she managed and swallowed the lump in her throat.

He slowly slid his hands along her arms towards her back, gradually embracing her. "My realm is cruel and harsh," he said softly. "Great suffering abounds. But here?" he said, leaning in so that his cheek hovered near to hers. "There is softness and opportunity for things unheard of in my plane of existence."

What was he doing to her?

She gasped, and for a moment wondered if he had her under a spell of some kind. She felt her body soften to his and she wanted nothing more than his embrace. His affection.

She didn't want him to go either, and she knew it wasn't magic. It was loneliness. Longing.

"Okay."

It wasn't passionate, but he held her tenderly, his arms squeezing her only lightly as their cheeks touched. "Open your heart to me," he murmured into her ear. "Do not hide behind your defenses." The light tickle of his smooth voice on her ear was so tantalizing. "I will slip inside you," he said, his voice as rich as caramel, as soft as satin. "And you will hide me within your heart from the gaze of those who would seek to do us harm."

She didn't know what it meant, but it sounded so sexual.

Strangely, however, it felt... welcomed. She wanted him to long for her. For so many years she'd thought of herself as someone unlovable, but he was being so affectionate. He felt so warm.

It was her isolation, her neediness that made her nod against his cheek, her soft skin brushing against his.

His lips touched just beneath her ear only tentatively, "Thank you," he said, and his warm body pressed to hers as he squeezed her form. It was such a careful, loving embrace, and it shifted and felt so bizarre. So different.

Was this what it was like to feel for someone? To have them touch at you physically and emotionally?

Though as he held her, the intensity of it grew. Without him moving, she could feel something strange, as if he was bleeding over into her very body. Tendrils of his existence—his soul?—trying to find its way inside of her. Not her body so much as her own soul: that hidden, inner beacon of light.

Where hers was pure and wholesome, however, she could feel his was dark and... different. It wasn't like hers. But it wanted in. It wanted to mingle with her essence. That much was pure and true. She felt it.

A tear streamed down her face and her hands clenched.

This couldn't be right. He was going to do something wrong, he was going to betray her.

Yet it didn't feel wrong. Not really. There was some piece of him that felt so... so like her. So similar to her own soul.

She wanted to scream but she bit it back, tugging her lower lip into her mouth.

The walls within her came down, and with a bizarre awareness, she realized he was no longer there. Not physically.

He no longer held her in his arms, for he no longer existed in a physical sense before her at all. Though at the same time, she felt his presence more than ever, for he lingered within her.

Like when she cast that summoning, the tingle of power tickled her skin, and warmed her blood. Though it grew gentle with time as he settled into her being.

His voice travelled to her from within her own being, not needing words anymore. *You are not alone*, he said.

She swiped at her eyes as if trying to be strong and hide her tears at his words. He was speaking to the deepest and most hidden part of her and she felt so… exposed. It was horrible and wonderful all at once.

Yet she missed his physical presence, and that confused and disgusted her. She shouldn't feel so attracted to him, to a demon that had such a terrifying presence.

Still, she missed the feeling of his hands around her.

Instead she got the feeling of warmth that enveloped her very soul. An unnatural heat that filled her in ways she thought impossible. Like moments of her father's love unrestrained, but more intimate.

When the time comes, you will let me out and I will teach you, he said, his voice – which was not a voice at all, but a thought in her mind – so rich and soothing.

There was no need, but she nodded as she looked towards the window. It felt like so much time had passed, but the sun was only beginning to rise, and it cast long shadows on the campus. She had a secret, so large and all encompassing, but she went to clean up the remains of the spell casting.

It was strange how routine it was, and how new it felt, all at once. It was almost as if she were doing it with an old friend, someone who cared deeply about her.

CHAPTER 2

Firia had slept deep the whole morning through. For once in a very long time it was her father that woke her up with a knock on her door. "Honey?" came his deep voice. "Are you okay?"

For years now, she'd awoken before him, began the day with preparing breakfast before heading off to her classes. Though her classes had all but ended, it wasn't that which had interfered with her normal routine.

"Y-yeah dad," she said groggily, face down upon the bed, her blankets twisted about her form. "I'll be right out."

She could hear her father shuffle off, wearily starting his day after another long night of work. Though her mind lingered on other things.

Her whole night was filled with vivid dreams. Curious events of her past, sometimes traumatic, often mundane. She saw herself at her desk in school, shoved to the back with the other humans. Instead of feeling so alone and ignored, however, she felt comforted by a presence. Someone always off to the corner of her vision, but whom she was no less aware of.

She saw herself at her mother's funeral, when her father couldn't bring himself to comfort her. It was one of her worst memories, facing that tragedy alone, so young. Just reflecting on it was enough to make her eyes water, though in the dream she was not alone.

Thick, strong arms wrapped about her, pulled her to a warm chest and cradled her against her misery.

Then there were moments of joy. The lonely moments of happiness, like when she was in the forest and watched two foxes fight over her cloth-wrapped lunch, thinking it prey, only for their struggle to cause the contents to spill out into the stream below, where one desperate fox – then the next – dove in after it, only to come out with a half of her sandwich each, looking like scrawny rats.

She'd laughed then, though at the time it was tinged with mournful loneliness. In her dream, the laughter was shared by that presence, and it no longer held the sting.

For so long she'd pushed all those things aside, hidden under the layers of protection. Even happy memories had been tinged with melancholy and she'd kept herself focused on the future. The bright, wonderful future where people wouldn't treat her like a mousy reject.

They'd know she was someone worth paying attention to.

Yet the past had no such occurrences, and she swiped at the tears she knew were begging to come out. It almost felt like it had all been a dream. Not just the unpleasant drudging up of painful memories, but the demon.

Self-doubt still lingered in her subconscious that she could do such a thing, and as she got ready for the day, she wondered if she was simply going mad with loneliness.

As she pulled up her skirt, she felt that slight tingle of a presence again, and when she arose to stand up before her mirror she saw… him. His beautiful black hair, so sleek and shiny in the morning sun, those ruby eyes alight with a soft smile as he stood behind her.

He lifted his hands and put them upon her shoulders as he kissed the back of her head. She felt it too! It was real! Though when she spun around to see him… nothing. He was gone. Nothing remained to hint it was ever real and more than a delusion.

She went out into their kitchen to find her father preparing a meal for them both. Her dad was a fairly tall man, dark hair, tousled by sleep, with a thick, groomed beard. He flashed her a warm smile as she approached, despite his own weariness. "Up late reading again?" he asked.

"Yea," she agreed as she rubbed her eyes. "Kept having weird dreams." She sat down, rolling her shoulders and trying to work out a kink in her neck. "How was work last night?"

Her father wasn't as good a cook as she was, but he gave it his full attention, which was something she wasn't always capable of with her thoughts so prone to returning to her books and dreams. The fried dough he served up looked appealing though, and was likely a sign that they were out of other food again.

"I need to go pick up some food today," he said sheepishly. That had always been his task, despite how she had more free time than him. She knew he thought it allowed him to hide how tight their finances were, but it didn't work. She was well aware, despite his best efforts.

"Looks great," she rebuffed him, forcing a smile to her face. Her black hair was tousled from sleep and she'd tried to fix it, but the vision of that... demon had distracted her. She pushed some loose strands behind her ear.

"I'm not feeling great today. I could pick some things up until you get some time."

"No, that's okay," he said immediately, smiling to her as he set down the modest helping of amber syrup between them. It wasn't the fancy stuff the elvish families used, but then, few humans could afford that. "I like it," he said, lying to himself as much as to her, she was sure, "gives me time to think."

She didn't have classes to attend. They had ended for all intents and purposes for the human students. That is, she hoped, all of them but her. The weeks following graduation were spent amongst the top tier students – almost exclusively elvish – competing in displays to earn the attention of the Academy's professors, or independent wizards, in the hopes of getting a billet at the school, or if not that, then an apprenticeship with someone of some renown.

The human students mostly went on to apprentice under their own mothers and fathers, carrying on their family's role from generation to generation. Her father was a night time groundskeeper because his mother was one, and she because both her parents were.

It was a less auspicious career than Firia had hoped for, scrounging for meals and lying to herself about her life. It was misery. She could see what her future would be just looking into her father's eyes. So often he tried to look away, but she knew why.

He was just as lonely as she was.

"Alright, dad. If you're sure. I'm just going to rest for as long as I can today."

He cut into his fried dough-cake and smiled. "I'm sure sweetie. You make the most of this time," he urged her with a smile, though she knew the unspoken undertone of that was: *Make the most of it, because after this, you're future is like mine.*

CHAPTER 3

It's funny how being utterly alone, being so far away from civilization in the heart of the forest made her feel somehow less alone. It always had, but now it was even more comforting. She sat on a fallen log, her eyes closed as she breathed in the mossy scent of her surroundings.

Finding peace and silence was a big key to her abilities, her success. Everyone else was so busy with so many thoughts and worries that they never got anywhere. She took time to do nothing so that she was focused when she did work.

When finally she exhaled and her blue eyes fluttered open, she spoke to no one in particular.

"Are you real?"

His charmingly foreign voice came to her so velvety: "As real as you." She immediately traced it back to him, sitting beside her on the log. She hadn't noticed how he'd done that; there was no warning as such. He was just… there. Smiling at her handsomely. Still garbed in that luxuriously exotic robe, coloured in burgundy, brown and gold.

She took in another breath.

"When I was a kid, I used to make up friends. And that's really embarrassing to admit to, so I almost hope I made you up too."

He screwed up his lips in one corner, looking across at her with a perplexed expression. "That is an odd thing to say," he remarked, standing up and peering about her reclusive forest glade. She noticed then he wore not only the robe she'd given him, but a set of tall boots that went to his knees, and were capped with metal at the toes. It made him look all the more like some foreign prince out of a storybook.

"If I didn't make you up, then I actually summoned you. And it doesn't even matter because now it just makes me feel crazy to think about."

She'd put her hair back in pigtails, and brushed her bangs so they lay flat along her forehead, swept to the side. The sun filtered down through the trees and played against her peach-toned skin.

Pivoting upon one heel, a thumb hooked in his fancy belt, he gave her a curious smile. "Why do you fear it? What is done, is done. And you still live to tell the tale." He shrugged his shoulders and moved back to her, dropping to one knee, his robe parting as he reached out and touched her wrist with a gentle, warm hand. "My lovely young summoner, you have grander things to worry about than the past."

"Right. Such as the future." She sighed and her shoulders slumped even as her body warmed to his strange touch. She didn't know whether to scream and run or roll around in triumph, but she didn't feel much like celebrating.

She'd done something so great, yet she knew he was right. No one would give her this accomplishment.

No one would let her do anything but go to work as a grounds keeper.

"Do not look so sad," he said softly, lifting his free hand and delicately brushing her bangs back just a bit, his fingertip grazing her forehead just momentarily. "While I was inside you," those words felt so significant with how he said them, "I felt your apprehension. Your fear. Not the details, no," he remarked, looking upon her with a mix of warmth and happiness, "but what drew me most was your ambition."

Her button nose crinkled slightly as she looked away. "That sounds weird when you say it like that. Those things are private. Those feelings."

He laughed delicately, "I could not read your thoughts," he said gently. "I felt them, as I can feel them now." That notion made her worry, though he continued, clarifying. "I can read your emotions through your expressions, sweet dear. They are as plain as day to me."

She wasn't to call him her slave. He told her to see him as an equal, but it was tearing her in two directions. She wanted to revel in her power, at her success, but she was unable to with him... lurking. Being a part of her. She hadn't understood what she was agreeing to.

And at the same time, the sense of being... with someone. Of having someone that cared, close at hand, was so nice. It was something she'd longed for since she was a child.

She swallowed. "Then what am I feeling now?"

The wry smirk he gave her might've been construed as something less wholesome, but for some reason it only felt playful to her as she gazed on that smooth, blemish free face of his. "You are conflicted," he said, and he rose up from his knee and retreated back a couple of steps, twirling in such a casual way that caused his robes to lift and spin, showing a glimpse of his bare knee and thigh. "You need to impress the masters of your world, no?" he asked with one brow cocked high.

"If I didn't, I wouldn't have summoned a demon from some hellish place into our world," she agreed with some sarcasm.

"And time is of the essence," he added as a statement rather than questioning.

Casually he began to move his fingers in the air, meticulous little gestures like she'd seen wizards sometimes do, though his seemed so much more fluid than theirs. His whole body, with every movement, had a fluid sort of grace to it that was captivating to watch. "Only by showing them powers you were denied the knowledge of, do you stand a chance to rise above your station, hmm?" Conjured from the air before him, she watched wisps of light begin to form, like crackling fire.

"And something that they couldn't chastise me for stealing a book containing it," she added on, remembering what he had said last night. She was captivated by his motions and she felt that lingering power in the air come alive.

The billowy sleeve of his robe flowed back as the air churned, and she watched as the tendrils of flame took shape before him. He was silent, but she saw as strands of his glossy black hair whipped about his face. It took some force of will to accomplish on his part, but before her eyes the visage of a fiery fox took shape.

It was orange with the embers of fire, but it was unmistakable. It's large, triangular ears perked, and when Varuj at last finished, the flames died down, and the creature before her looked like a beautiful rainbow of lights, taken on animal form.

Her lips parted, and she was rendered speechless. The young woman was blown away by the sight and wasn't certain what to make of it. He made it seem so easy. So graceful.

"How?"

"The how is the hardest part," he said, brushing back his hair and fixing it after his display. Though as he smiled, the prismatic fox sniffed at the air, then bounded over to her, its large tail swishing in the air as it buried its nose into her lap. "I will teach you the how, but it will take the rest of the day."

For the first time since she'd met him, she found it hard to focus on his words, for the beautiful familiar before her licked at her hands, its tongue warm, but pleasant.

Her eyes watered, and she cursed herself for being so easily moved to tears. She tried so hard to hide it, that sensitive, needy part of her, but it was so much harder around him. She was exposed to him, and even the fox reminded her of that memory he'd dredged up the night before.

As if in response, the fox lifted its paws up onto her lap and it licked at her face, as if chasing away the tears with its smooth, warming tongue.

Varuj moved back to her side, sitting upon the log as he leaned in close and pet the creatures head. "He is your familiar now," he remarked. "I created him, which is not how it is usually done, but he is linked to your soul. A mirror of your essence in magical form. And shall not leave you lest you wish it so." He smiled warmly at the fox first, then her. "My gift to you."

Her entire body trembled as she held back the crashing waves of affection, rubbing behind the fox's ear. "How can I trust you? Aren't you... linked to me as well?"

He pondered her question a while then said, "No. Not as you think." He turned his ruby-eyed gaze towards her. "I am tethered to you on this plane of existence. Like..." he searched his head for some metaphor appropriate for their cross-dimensional understanding, "like an anchor tying a boat to the seabed." He nodded, satisfied with his effort.

She crossed her legs, her hand still petting at her new familiar. "And, what? … This is all in thanks for me bringing you here?"

Varuj's hand brushed hers as they both toyed with the chromatic fox, the creature eagerly licking at her face and making soft little yipping noises that sounded so happy. "It is my thanks for your agreeing to my terms," he said softly. "It is not often one of my kind can meet a mortal who will entreat with us fairly."

"Maybe I'm just stupider than most mortals, then." She looked at him sidelong, trying to read his expression but seeing that gorgeous visage just made her more distracted and uncertain. She'd seen him for what he was. A monstrous demon.

She cursed him for looking so attractive.

"No," he said, sounding so sincere. "You are clever beyond your years. That much is true," and she could detect none of his deception, none of his charm put to work in that compliment beyond what he exuded naturally.

"Now I will teach you to command and use your familiar," he said to her, his eyes moving back to the fox with a smile. "He may be more than a mere pet if you know the proper incantations and methods. He may be a fierce ally. A cunning tool."

She pet the fox again, staring at him curiously. "And I'm allowed to call him a tool, even with his cunning?"

She wished he didn't choose to look as he did. Her barriers were being chipped away and she had to keep reminding herself of what he was.

It was so easy to forget.

"Do not confuse he and I," said Varuj to her softly. "You summoned me. You did not create me," he explained. "I existed, thought, lived a life of my own, long before you tore me from my place across the gap between dimensions to aid you. Him?" he looked to the fox. "He did not exist as separate from you. Not even for a second. He is made up of the aether, crafted from the blueprints of your soul." He shrugged his shoulders casually. "You may call him what you wish. It would be no more insulting than saying your toe is an instrument unto you."

She nodded, putting her hands on either side of the log. "Where will he stay?"

He gave a wry smile, "That is what I shall teach you first." He reached out and took hold of her wrist, turning her hand palm-up and unfurling her fingers. "He is linked to your soul. Not merely tethered as I am," he explained, though with his delicate touch upon her palm it was not as easy to focus as it should have been. "A simple magical gesture is enough to dismiss him, so do as I instruct…"

With gentle care he guided her through the motion, the gentle swish of her hand in the air, from left to right, the light wriggle of two fingers, then curling her hand into a fist as a strong closure. "Memorize that. Then repeat."

She was keen with magic and memorized it instantly. How else could she have summoned him if she hadn't any skill or natural grace with it, after all?

Yet even though she followed through with the motion with such diligence and interest, she couldn't stop focusing on him. On his touch, on the way he felt against her. On what he truly was.

The sparkle in his ruby eyes caught it, and he smiled. "Try once more," he said, demonstrating for her with that fluid grace.

It was enough, and she got it on that try. The kaleidoscope of colours that was her fox-familiar, drained into her palm then vanished into her flesh. Though truthfully, similar to Varuj, she felt the thing settle against her very soul. Unlike the dark monster, however, it felt quite… familiar. Nothing was odd about it at all, it felt as if a piece of herself was merely returned.

It took her breath away and she closed her eyes, letting herself enjoy the sensation. When at last she managed to open them again, she looked to him.

"Are you using me?"

His beautiful face did not falter in the face of that question, though he retorted. "A curious question for a woman who unquestionably is using me for her own ends." He arched a singular brow – the dark hairs so perfectly sculpted – as if challenging her to deny it.

"I've never denied that," she argued. "But… I'm not a being of… evil."

"And I am?" he responded, looking slightly insulted, though he brushed it off quickly. "Why do you presume I am evil, hm? Because I am different? Because I come from a realm that abides by different rules of order than yours does, Firia?" The challenge was delivered smoothly, and he crossed his legs, some of his bare, chocolatey dark thigh showing from beneath his robes.

"Because you're a heathen and the first thing you did was start looming over me and touching yourself?" she retorted. "I can feel it." She touched her chest, overtop of her heart. "In here. You're not like me."

"Precisely," he said, back arched, shoulders out, that well-shaped chin of his pushed up in the air. "I was born of another realm. Where the laws of the universe were different. Do you expect otherwise any more than you would expect a foreigner to eat the same food as you or dress likewise?"

"I pretty much expect all strangers not to touch themselves in front of me."

"Where I come from it's simply a display of interest," he stated, his eyes dipping down over her form for just a moment. "We don't hide such things as your kind do. I ceased as per your wishes, however."

"Interest?" She almost laughed as she thought back to it. "You looked more like you were just trying to scare me."

He sighed a bit. "See how pleasant you would be if you were ripped between realities from your home without clothes or items by a powerful summoner. It puts you in a rather sour mood, and leads to you feeling defensive. I got over it," then added, "with you."

"You said you were glad to be rid of that place," she stated, trying to sound confident but the blush of her cheeks gave her away. She looked aside, hiding her face from him as she stared into the forest depths.

"I am," he confessed, "now." He watched her quietly. "Were it some cruel summoner who intended to only use, abuse and toss me back when done, however, I would not have that sentiment. When I realized how pure of heart you were, however?" He shrugged his shoulders. "I thought I had found someone who might deal with me. And help me to stay. As a free man one day."

Her gaze fell to the forest floor and her heart thudded loudly in her chest. She was sure he could hear it, but then, she wasn't entirely certain what he could sense within her. What he experienced in kind.

Her tongue pressed from between her lips and dabbed them thoughtfully. She'd let him in so quickly, so eagerly, and she wondered what that said about her. What that said about how lonely she was. How much she desired someone in her life, even if he was a demon.

"I see."

"Your world is softer than mine," his words delicate. "Existence is not so cruel for those who live here." He reached over, gently laying his warm hand upon hers. "I wish to help you become a great sorceress. Powerful and respected. That one day you might use that power to free me, and let me live here as one of you." She could feel the hope on his voice, it was palpable. The gentle touch of his smooth hand against her flesh; it was exquisite.

Her heart stopped and her breath hitched. She wanted so badly to believe him, to feel close to someone. To know someone.

Yet there was still that wall of defensiveness, of caution, and she withdrew her hand from his. "We don't have a lot of time for me to get into the academy."

He retracted his hand slowly. "I can teach you some useful skills with your new familiar today," he remarked matter-of-factly. "Perhaps that shall be enough to get you into the academy. Perhaps not," he shrugged his shoulders. "I have much more to teach you as well, but we can discuss that later. One step at a time."

She nodded, looking at him curiously. He hadn't tried to betray her or harm her, but then, perhaps he hadn't the power now. He could be biding his time, waiting for her to let her guard down.

So she wouldn't. She'd take his lessons and succeed in her bid to get into the academy. She controlled him, she reminded herself. Not the other way around.

CHAPTER 4

She had gotten so wrapped up in her lessons with the demon that she hadn't noticed the day slip by. When hunger finally began to overcome her excitement at learning how to change her familiar's shape to better suit it to different tasks, Varuj merely smiled and taught her to send it off to fetch food. The ripe berries it returned with were enough to keep her satisfied and delighted.

Though all good things had to come to an end, and with night so advanced, she knew she had to get back home, or else her father would finish work and worry at her absence.

They walked together through the woods, the town still a ways off, her new pet fox prancing at her side.

She hadn't felt so… excited for life in such a long time. All her hopes and dreams of actually becoming someone of value, someone of note, were coming true. She knew her father didn't want his job for her any more than she did, and now she finally felt she knew a way to break the cycle.

To show those elves up, once and for all.

"I didn't even know these things existed. Not like this."

"There is much more," he stated casually, his hand gently touching the base of her spine as they walked. "This thing is relatively simple," he explained, "though it would take one of your competitors many years of tutelage to learn and do what I have done for you in but a day, Firia. It is a good start. And one they will not be too likely to suspect."

She nodded and a smile actually began to creep to her lips. "Well, I hope so. But… thank you. Just knowing these things is a joy, even if it gets me no further ahead with my goals."

"It shall," he said with infectious confidence, though he came to a halt as they neared the edge of the forest, facing her. "I must hide within you for the night again, Firia. Though know my offer stands…" he tilted his head down and let his warm gaze meet hers. "Treat me as companion, and I shall show you more." He looked back over his shoulder to where they'd come from, "Go there when you wish to learn, and I shall come forth and help you. Our bargain set."

"Just… Please don't go hunting for more memories…" she pleaded, her body stiff from the long day of practice.

The moon reflected off his hair, and the sleek little black horns hidden amongst the strands, its silver light making him look that much more appealing. "You mistake what happened," he said. "Two souls mingled, that is all." He gave her a deferential bow of his head, though. "But I shall not meddle or play the voyeur this eve, madam," that alluring foreign accent of his so rich, "I promise."

"Thanks." It was so weird. All of it. His behaviour, his looks…

But the strangest was how he was making her feel such affection and longing to be around him. To have someone who actually shared interests with her and yearned to find out more about her. She stood up straighter, her large eyes becoming heavier as her mind began to quiet down for the evening. "So good night, then."

Varuj leaned in, his arms moving up about her in that warm gesture. He embraced her again, as he had the night before. "Goodnight," he said softly, head tilted, her dark, foreign prince of the damned looking about to kiss her as he leaned in, but then…

He was gone, she felt him settle within her. His essence mingling with hers. So foreign, so unlike her own, yet feeling so warm. So comforting.

The soft yip of her familiar tore her from the moment, however, his tail swishing as he gazed up at her.

She smiled warmly at it before repeating that motion the demon had taught her, calling her familiar to join them. To make her whole once more.

31

CHAPTER 5

Firia had resisted the urge to turn to the demon for help again. It would've guaranteed her success, she knew that for certain, but she feared for herself. Feared what she might do if she were exposed to his smooth charms and stunning good looks again.

He wanted more in exchange for further favours, she knew. The thought of what it might mean to treat him as equal scared her.

She instead practiced with her new familiar, honing her use of the tricks she'd learned, and trying to devise new ways to impress with her mastery of him. She also practiced the little cantrips she'd learned on her own over the years too. The ability to control flames – albeit tiny ones – and freeze water upon her touch.

It was impressive work for a human such as herself who'd never been tutored, but all the same they were meager tricks for a potential apprentice, and she knew the true road to success would be her stunning new familiar.

It consumed her thoughts as she ate her meal in front of her father, her hand repeating some of the gestures the demon had taught her – without actually casting the spells – as she prepared for the day ahead.

Her father, however, had been watching her. "You okay, hun?" he asked with concern. He knew what day it was. How the elven students would begin their competitions for recognition. She hadn't told him of her new tricks yet, and as far as he knew her chances were still so very slim.

For her part, she was distracted with not only her spells. For though the demon had kept her word and not probed into her memories, she had dreamed of him quite frequently. Natural dreams, she felt. They were not tainted by his actual, meddling presence, she believed; it was just hard not to think on the newest addition to her life. Her great gamble.

"Yea, dad." It was a lie they both saw through, but they were so used to these little white lies. The denial that anything was wrong in their life. The denial that they were both so unhappy.

But this was something new. This was excitement that lay beneath the dread and fear, and her mind kept wandering. She had to be focused and sharp, but it was so hard with him on her mind. She wanted to see him again, to feel his smooth hand caress her wrist, but she had to resist.

He ate quietly, though she knew he was aware of the significance of the day. He had gotten up early to prepare her a rather lavish meal of "brain food", as he called it. He knew she would compete, and whether it was hopeless or not, he would do all he could to help her see victory.

"I was thinking," he said, not looking up from his own meal. "Those elvish children have a lot of advantages over us folk," he was beating around the bush, she realized. "What with their money, trainin' and years. Heck," he said with a chuckle, "when you were just a girl competing on the exams, you were up against ones twice your own age."

He wet his lips and didn't pause long enough for her to speak, "So I was thinkin', Firia... why not give you a lil' advantage of your own, huh?" He put down his fork, and she watched as he reached into the pocket of his old, frayed beige sweater. What he pulled out then surprised her, for it was something human families never really provided for their children. No, it was far too rare and expensive to be spoiled on their kind. Even ones who could afford it rarely could find a seller willing to deal with their kind.

Yet there it was, embedded in cloth: a crystal ring.

"Dad…" she couldn't help herself from saying, shock written all over her face.

Crystals, real crystals, were so rare. They helped focus a caster's abilities, gave a great edge to anyone who wore one and focussed their efforts upon it. No real professional magic user ever went without one.

She cursed herself as her eyes blurred and she swatted it away. Was this why he never had money for food? "I don't know how you got this." Her voice quivered as she stared at it, then at him, a new affection warming her heart. She'd never felt so… loved by him. So cared for.

Her kindly father couldn't help but smile, and he got up from his seat and walked over to her. He put his arms around her and hugged her, as he hadn't done since her mother had died. "Do it, sweetie," he murmured to her. "Show how much potential you've got, and make 'em have to claim you."

She managed to hold in her sob as her hands went around his arms. "I will. I promise," she murmured softly.

She had no idea how much he was rooting for her, how much he wanted for her, and she was even more determined to succeed.

With a kiss to her dark hair, he pulled back, and she saw his own eyes, red with moisture. "You'll do it. I know you will," and she knew he had supreme confidence in her.

CHAPTER 6

The competition – for that *is* what it was – had the look of a county fair. The great tent that swelled up to tremendous proportions, the banners that flowed in the air representing the various academies, companies and interests. It had a spirit of joviality about it. At least, elvish joviality.

They were more formal than humans in the day to day, but when they celebrated they were full of laughter and song that was not tethered to sadness, as the lowly humans were.

Firia had to press on towards the scene, her heart beating fast. Though the elders were all in high spirits from what she saw, the other students were mostly grim and determined. Their elaborate elvish clothes – reminiscent of what Varuj wore – looking so stiff on them as they all eyed the competition.

This would be but the first day of trials, but she knew that the magical academies made their picks on the first day then left, not wishing to make any further waste of their professors' precious time. The remainders were left for lone sorcerers and trading companies to barter with. Or to simply go home in defeat.

The very first thing she couldn't help but notice was how so many of those long, ovaline elvish eyes were upon her. She had been the only human they'd seen thus far, and she stuck out.

Yet she held her head high, despite the fact that she wanted to run and hide. To get away from their stares and scrutiny. She'd been such a loner for so long, though, it was hard to be in the limelight. To know how closely she was being watched.

And how quickly they'd laugh at her failure.

She could see it in them. Curiosity, sure. But also a desire to see her fail. To know that they were better than even the best the human world had to offer.

She was grateful she'd gotten loan of such a fine robe with flowing sleeves that showed off her wrists when she cast. It felt like a safety blanket, something to protect her from the cruelty of others, and she tried to calm her breathing as she took it all in.

From out of the sea of watchful eyes, one of the elves approached her. He was tall, lanky, with wheat-coloured hair that was cropped close to his head. He wore not a robe, but a cloth tabard, bearing his family crest. It wasn't one of the ones she recognized, though after the elf nodded and spoke his "Greetings," she recognized him from her class. He was not a wealthy or influential elf. He couldn't have been, to have gone to school with humans.

It was almost like he was an ally, but she wouldn't go that far. She knew that those with as dismal futures as she could be more cutthroat than any, and she gave him a reserved smile. "Hey, ah…" she paused, struggling to remember his name. She'd never bothered to even learn that about her classmates.

"Mae'lin," he said without taking offense, giving her a respectful bow that in elvish society was reserved for equals. "You're going to compete then?" he asked, his emerald eyes alight with curiosity.

"Well, I didn't come here to see how the better half live," she agreed with a sarcastic smile. She had pulled her hair back in a single ponytail and it swished against the back of her neck as she glanced around. "I guess you are too? And… I'm Firia," she added, just in case.

"I know," he said with an amused smile. "There was always talk of the quiet human girl in the back of class," he remarked, standing more casually then, comfortable it seemed with her greeting.

"Some of the other kin –" and she knew elves all thought of each other as kin "–speculated you were plotting some violent act of rebellion," and his ovaline eyes flashed with amusement.

She laughed, and her blue eyes sparkled. "Well, we'll just have to see what happens here. I'll say no more." Even though her words were dark, she smiled at him deviously and gave him a wink. The thought of the others talking about her – her! – came as a surprise, though.

Mae'lin smiled at her, almost bashfully really. "I always told them they were foolish. Truth be told," he remarked with a shrug of his shoulders, "they never react well to humans who make them wonder or strike their interest. It bothers them."

"Well... I suppose that's good." She wasn't doing it for them, or to embarrass them. She simply wanted to do what she was best at. Always. "You never answered if you were competing."

"Oh," he said, brushing a hand back over his blonde hair. "Oh! Yeah, of course," he remarked, a bit of a blush forming on his own pale cheeks. "I'm giving it a shot ... My family has enough sorcerers of our own working the business, so... it's make the cut at one of the academies or else..." he shrugged his shoulders again.

"It's not often humans compete," he blurted out. "I mean... that makes you pretty special... is all... I'm sayin'." He gulped.

Was he nervous around her?

Suddenly her stomach tightened, and she felt nervous too. It was as if all her forced confidence slid out of her and was replaced with the heat of her blood rising to the surface. She finally really looked at him, not just through him, and a lump developed in her throat.

She tried to swallow it down. "I'll be special if I get picked."

He was handsome in his own way. Though all elves were, his long, lanky nature gave him a curious look that contrasted his kin. It made him stand out more, she realized, for the others tended to be so perfectly uniform humans could hardly tell them apart. "Either way..." he began, but then nodded firmly. "Same boat as me then. Well... kinda." He knew it wasn't. No human could be competing for such recognition on the same level as an elf, of course.

She forced a smile, but it was lopsided and awkward as she scuffed her black shoes into the ground. "Well... goodluck. I mean..."

she trailed off, her tongue tied. She had no idea how to talk to these elves, even if they did seem genuine.

But then, did she know how to talk to her fellow humans that well either?

The longest conversation she'd had with anyone in her life might've been with a demon.

"To you too," he said with a boyish smile, though she knew he had to be well beyond her years. Elves always were somehow.

The horn sounded signalling the call for competitors to assemble, and Mae'lin gave a bow and gestured for her to go ahead. "I shall see you in the fields then, Firia. Goodluck," he remarked genuinely.

CHAPTER 7

Inside the grand tent Firia couldn't help but be amazed at the staggering scope of the area it covered. It spanned the entire field, and housed within it dozens of house-sized enclosures where different groups, each showing their own banner, prepared for the festivities and competitions.

The boom of the organizer's voice carried over the crowds, clearly instructing the young hopefuls on where the competitions would be held.

Firia had only two real tricks up her sleeve: her ability to manipulate heat and fire, and her familiar. She still held some small hope that the familiar wouldn't be necessary to impress the academies, so she wanted to keep that one in reserve. Though she was at a distinct disadvantage.

The competitions were mostly highly regulated things, where the hopefuls competed on a series of tasks that were laid out. These were contests that basically only wealthy elvish families could aspire to, as only they could afford to give their children the private tutors necessary to master so many little introductory spells to numerous schools of magic.

When she heard the announcer declare the "general aptitude display competition," she knew that her best chance lay there. As she shuffled through the crowd towards the indicated area, she saw Mae'lin doing the same and knew he was in the same boat.

Upon arrival, however, she saw the competition would not be small. The crowd of young hopefuls was enormous! The ring where they would display was large, but as she saw they were only filtering through a couple at a time, she realized the wait would be long.

It wasn't fair. They had all the advantages, and still they couldn't cut it in the specialized fields. She was here because this was the best she could aspire to as a human from meagre means. They had every advantage and still they thought themselves to be on the same playing field as her.

No. They thought they were better than her.

Her head lifted high and her eyes narrowed as she looked around, seeking some way to move ahead. To catch the gaze of someone important.

The contests began in the meantime, and she realized, even as she scanned for some way to get ahead, that the reason they were being filtered two at a time was for the sake of comparison. The first pair off was odd, only one of them seemed to get that fact, and while the other did her best to impress the judges, the more prepared one simply did his best to outdo her.

It was a short match for that reason, and quickly they shuttled them off, one towards one of the academy's area, the other towards the edge of the tent-dome where she'd doubtlessly be forced to wander home defeated.

It only heightened her sense of urgency, and as the contests continued – growing more fierce with time – she wedged her way to the front as best she could.

Once there, she got a good sight of the next competition. The tables arrayed with components for ease of display. There were sconces for fires, which she noted first and foremost, there were basins of water – quickly refilled from the last competitors – and an endless assortment of wooden fixtures, practice dummies and all sorts of spell components.

The pair-off began with one performing a dazzlingly elven display before conjuring forth fireworks-like explosions from their fingertips. It was small, but it looked intense with how concentrated he was.

The other countered with her telekinesis, throwing a blanket over his hand and dousing out his display with merely the power of her mind. It not only won applause but laughter, and the young elvish woman was taken away with a grin on her face to be haggled over by the academies.

Firia saw then, in the midst of watching the furor in the centerfield, a curious sight. A brown-haired man. A human. He was dressed well for not being an elf, and looked determined. Confident.

She tried to move towards the kindred spirit, but before she could get anywhere near him, he was ushered through onto the field and she was left standing behind the academy students, blocking off access during the competition.

Still, she was where she wanted to be, and with a prime view of the most intriguing fight of the day other than her own, as far as she was concerned.

The tall, brown-haired human strode up to his place, facing off against an elvish man at his side. He didn't waste any time, and flipped his overcloak back before moving his fingers in a hypnotic gesture. As his competition began his own spell, she couldn't help but notice the elf was having a hard time with his own chant.

Curiously, the crowd tittered here and there, watching the elf get tongue-tied and begin to sway.

It was confusing to her; she didn't quite get what was happening, because you weren't allowed to cast spells upon an opponent in the competition, so he surely wasn't hexing the elf or else he'd be disqualified. She looked around and saw only some of the other competitors seemed to understand, but all of the students and professors in the stands were openly amused.

There was something going on that was clearly lost on the less educated.

Before she could decipher it, however, the elf fainted. Not a single spell cast as he hit the ground.

Applause broke out in the stands from some select few of the senior academy students and professors who could overcome their racial bias, while the unconscious elf was carried off, and the triumphant human brought to be negotiated over.

It was her chance then, and all the world was abuzz with what would happen. The whole trajectory of her life would be set then and there, and –

She watched as the elvish guards picked some others behind her, sending them on ahead of her.

He stole her thunder!

Damn it, she cursed, her blue eyes turning cold as her hand shot up in the air as if she were in class. "Hey!" Her shout could barely be heard over the din of the crowd, and she repeated it, louder.

How dare another human compete, just before her. Distracting them from her.

She didn't know where the animosity came from, truly, but her frustration was making her skin buzz and he was the only target she could think of. She expected to be treated poorly by the elves, but for them to usher him along and ignore her?

It was an insult!

The head "usher" glowered at her. "Wait your turn," he snarled, keeping her back as the contest resumed.

The other beside him turned her gaze upon Firia, "We've had one token-human for this year, and that may be enough if you don't watch yourself.

It was my turn, she pouted, unable to hide her anger.

Her breath was quickened and she wanted nothing more than to show them all, to impress them with her demonstrations.

Yet she couldn't even understand what the token human had done.

She was out of her league.

The competition went on, the ushers passing her up again and again. She wanted to lash out and say something, but the look on their faces said they'd relish the opportunity to retaliate and maybe cost her her chance entirely.

When Mae'lin came up by her he looked to her with some surprise. "Firia?" he said as they moved to take him and another, holding her back yet again. The elf looked surprised, "Why is she being held back?" he asked.

"Take your turn or shut up," he retorted.

It was the only time since being passed up that she was able to feel anything other than hatred, and she stared at him intently. "You win this, alright?"

Mae'lin didn't take the opportunity though, the tall, lanky elf hesitating and refusing the tug of the usher's hand. "What's going on here?" he asked stubbornly.

It got him exactly what she thought. "Fine then," said the usher, and another elf was taken and the competition went on as before. "You two can wait," he growled, pushing the confused-looking Mae'lin over towards her.

Firia sighed as she looked up at the elf, her arms crossed beneath her small bust. "Why'd you do that, huh? You know why they're holding me back. They already have a human, they don't need another."

Mae'lin's ovaline eyes looked truly baffled, then saddened. He didn't have any words for her, but she could read the sadness in his gaze. Not for himself so much as her.

Still, the competition carried on.

CHAPTER 8

There were so many surprises that day for her, but by the time the pool of candidates was whittled down and evening was drawing near, she saw that the not only was the competition thinning, the viewers in the stands were too.

A sickening feeling began to sink in: she might not even get her chance to compete. She might be denied her shot at that one slim hope.

The thought of that was sickening to her. It made her stomach – already roiling from being empty – turn and sicken.

Mae'lin seemed to want to comfort her, but he didn't know what to do or say that wouldn't make matters worse. So he stood beside her, arms folded, anxiously hoping.

How was it possible she felt so alone, even in the bustling crowd? So hopeless, even on the cusp of her great chance?

She felt it then, the slight tickle of his presence within her. It was faint, like the brush of his warm hand against hers. Just a thin strand of comfort.

It managed to steel her resolve again, but she felt lost and frustrated. What was she supposed to do? If she drew any more attention to herself, they'd just throw her out. If she waited patiently – obediently – then they'll never even look at her.

Either way, she wasn't going to win any favour. She wasn't going to succeed.

Her blue eyes narrowed as they scanned over the remaining crowd, over the "competition". There had to be something she could do.

All she saw was the gloomy reminder of how few remained. Less than a dozen, herself and Mae'lin included. Though as she nearly lost hope, an odd motion caught her sight: someone returning to the stands to sit and view.

It had only been the opposite for hours: people leaving. So she looked and saw a most strange thing, an old, human wizard. He wore voluminous robes, fine and decked with symbols of accomplishment and power. He was no minor wizard, he was an elder sorcerer even by the standards of the elves, dressed as and seated where he was.

As he stroked his grey, trimmed beard, he looked out over the field, and she swore for a moment he locked eyes with her, even across the near-endless span of the fields.

The ushers held up their hands. "That shall be all the competition for this evening! Sorry, but the rest of you will have to return on the morrow."

Tomorrow. Firia knew what that meant.

She was seething. There were so few of them left. It would barely take any time to see them through. She wasn't even being afforded the dignity of losing to someone better.

She was just being passed over.

She felt terrible for Mae'lin, for the fact that he'd thrown away his chance just to try to help her. Yet she wasn't selfless, and her blue eyes went back to the strange human in the stands.

It was a strange sensation. It was as if his steely eyes bore through her to her soul from across the field. The moment dragged on, and it felt as though tendrils probed her inner-being, prying and prodding.

Then with casual purpose the elder human stood, his voice carrying out across the field, magically amplified. "One more competition for the evening, don't you say, Yae'ra?" he addressed one of the other professors, who was in the process of leaving.

The elf turned his gaze upon the wizened old human, a glare for him. Something went on between them, but she couldn't be sure what. The elf didn't broadcast his words back.

"If you don't care to see what comes next, then perhaps I'll take on a new apprentice myself," retorted the human wizard, which stiffened the elf's spine. Meanwhile she felt a faint buzz of excitement from that demon soul that inhabited her being. Excitement and something else.

Was he truly rooting for her that hard?

The elven wizard's voice carried out then at last: "One more competition for the evening then. Those two," he said, and she knew then she would be facing off against Mae'lin.

The two ushers didn't give her time for much, as they grabbed the two of them and pushed them forward onto the field towards their respective spots.

"Goodluck," she murmured to the only friendly face she'd seen all day, and hated that she'd been pitted against him. The man who had only tried to help her. The competitions were fierce and caring about others only got in the way.

At least, it did for her.

She'd spent so much time isolated and putting up walls between herself and others, but his tiny act of kindness had edged its way under her skin. She licked her lips thoughtfully and fluttered her eyes, concentrating.

There was no time for compassion.

Mae'lin acted first. The lanky elf, despite his concern, held nothing back.

With a flourish of his hands, he sent up a column of water from the basin, that formed a curtain of crystal liquid. He motioned his hands and the water formed the shape of fish, crabs, and even some serpentine, dragon-like creature. It was masterful, and more than she had expected from the low-rung elf.

She couldn't be outdone though. With her own elegant display that was beautiful enough to counter any elf, she sent the flames from the brazier up, creating a dazzling display of her own.

It far exceeded anything she'd done in the past. The flames licking at the air, reaching so high that she wondered if the grand tent itself was in danger! But with the power of the augmentation crystal her father got her, she not only wielded the flames bigger and higher, she contorted them into fanciful shapes.

Great and mighty birds! Phoenixes that soared through the air. Hawks that dove to the crowds! She amazed even herself with what she could do with the help of her father's crystal!

That amazement almost made her miss what was happening, however. She saw the glum look on Mae'lin's face, and even as her heart skipped a beat she knew he felt sad about what he was doing.

He shaped the water into a semblance of a whale, and it chased after the source of her fire, to douse it out.

What could she do against that?!

The warm comfort of Varuj's presence became a burning at her heart. She mistook it for pain at first, pain at her failure. But then he did something curiously strange: he whispered his counter to her.

She made a sweeping gesture with her hand and the flames formed into a great dragon that roared – literally roared! – its fury against the approaching whale. The two collided, and she watched, amazed, as her beast of pure flame contested with water and... and was winning!

It was startling to see, and the crowd around her was holding its breath! Though she was beyond noticing such things. She had a contest to win despite it all!

Steam formed between the two conjured giants. Dragon battling whale as flame licked at water, steam rose and each tangled and destroyed the other.

She willed her creation on, and as the struggle intensified – her thing of fire miraculously outdoing a creation of water! – she noticed the burning on her finger as the crystal ring glowed red-hot, nearly searing her flesh.

The pain made her want to cast it off, but she couldn't! Not without forfeiting the competition and losing it all. So with a final bout of tenacity, she pushed herself into the spell again and watched as the dragon expanded and with its mighty jaws doused the last of the great water-whale into steamy oblivion.

Exultant victory should have taken over then, but the force of her spell couldn't be stopped so easily. The dragon pushed on, and though the pain urged her to cast off the ring, she saw that its fiery jaws were swooping in on Mae'lin himself.

She had to do something! It was all playing out in a split second, but she reigned the thing in just in time to spare Mae'lin a horrible searing. Although he fell back into the grass, his clothes were smoking in three places from his close contact with the fire.

She was breathing hard, the lingering smoke of her dissipated dragon filling her lungs as she raced to the basin of water, dousing her finger. The scalding pain slowly dimmed, but it still felt raw and tender as she ran across to Mae'lin, trying to help him up.

For all intents and purposes, Mae'lin looked far better off than her. Only merely stunned by the intensity of her power. "Wow," he mouthed to her, looking on her with great awe. "That was… that was amazing!" he said, and only then did Firia become aware of the applause that carried across the field to them, quite impressed by the late display of such power and technique.

"You were great," she smiled to him, but there was a hesitation there. It wasn't that she thought she was being a good winner.

She just knew she had an unfair advantage. Or, well… as fair of advantage as any other. She'd summoned the demon, after all. It was her cunning that she'd invited a powerful… ally… into her. It wasn't as though she'd bargained with him for that win.

She'd earned it.

Mae'lin stood up with her help and, smiling, the pair faced the applauding crowd. She even noticed the old, human mage giving a dignified, but standing ovation.

The booming voice of the elven master carried out over the fields, however. "The human girl is disqualified for assaulting a fellow contestant," came his stern words. "Gaul'di-mere Academy shall take on the other impressive young hopeful."

It all came crashing down then.

She couldn't even cry. She was too stunned to do anything but stare ahead, dejected and confused. Assaulting him?

She blinked and looked to Mae'lin, pain clear on her face. Pain for herself. She struggled to be happy for him, for his success, but there was no amount of goodness in her that could combat the fact that her dreams were snuffed out.

Just like that. In an instant.

The applause had ended, and in the silence of the hushed crowd, she could hear the familiar, masculine voice of Varuj in her mind, calling to her. "Plead," he urged. "Tell them you've got more tricks and can compete again," his words forceful, persuasive, holding all of their charm as he sought to comfort and assure her.

Her hand tightened around Mae'lin's for a moment, as if in congratulations, before she stepped forward. "Let me compete again. Send me against another. I won't even use fire!" Even the mention of the word made her finger sting from the searing of the ring. "Mae'lin is fine, right?" she asked as she turned to the lanky elf.

He was surprised, but immediately turned and shouted towards the stands, "I am! It wasn't an assault at all! Just our competition getting out of hand." His future was assured, it seemed, and he was more than willing to go to bat for her. "Give her another chance, she's worth it for any academy!"

Time seemed to slow so much, and the elder human looked to the elven master. Words were exchanged, but not through the magical amplification, and she could not make them out.

They debated, paused, the elvish master and his entourage debating amongst themselves.

Mae'lin gripped her hand tightly, and she could feel his own hope for her through that tight hold.

At last, a decision had been reached and the loud voice boomed out to them. "Tomorrow morning, the young girl shall face off against a more worthy contestant." Her heart skipped a beat with renewed hope.

He paused, and she swore she could see a smile upon his face. "Bright and early, someone who can handle her recklessness will give her the chance to prove herself… again."

The human wizard spoke up again, his voice carrying over. "Who?"

The smug elven master delayed then said, "She will display her powers alongside a senior student." Suddenly the chance seemed that much less hopeful.

"Tomorrow morning, then," she said with every ounce of confidence she could muster and didn't feel. She knew what teachers thought of troublemakers, and the only reason she got as far as she did was because she kept her head down and her eyes on her goals.

They would do everything they could to humiliate her.

But she would be prepared.

CHAPTER 9

Mae'lin had been ushered off to meet with the academy who had taken him in, and truly he deserved it; his display had been so very impressive. But then again, she deserved it too. She wouldn't let herself think otherwise.

She had walked off after that. She needed food and rest for the coming trial. More than that, she needed an edge.

She had her ring to amplify her spells, but her repertoire was woefully low. There was little else she could do but manipulate heat and flame, and whatever senior academy student they put her against would be prepared for that.

That only left her with her familiar. The demon's gift.

Would that be enough?

She was reminded of how at that moment of seeming defeat, the reassuring voice of Varuj had come to her salvation. His suggestion of a strategy she would never have thought of – for she had no idea she could've managed so impressive a feat, even with the power of the ring! – had saved her from failure then and there.

He had suggested she cry out for this new chance when sorrow threatened to doom her to silence.

He was making her stronger. Both magically and emotionally.

And she wasn't sure how she felt about that. Yet when she grabbed something to eat, she didn't go to rest like she knew she should.

Instead, she went into the dark of the forest.

In the clearing, that special place that was hers and hers alone until she'd introduced him to it, she stood in the dark, waiting. His presence was felt before seen.

He put his hand upon her shoulder, and turned her towards him so she could see his smiling face. Pride written on it. "You did well, despite refusing more of my help in preparing these past few days," he said.

"I wanted to do this on my own. Clearly they have better ideas. They want to humiliate me, and I want to make them wish they'd never tried to." Her voice was stern and confident, and she was trying so desperately hard not to get caught up in his touch.

"They're pitting me against one of their students, who has every advantage. I need something… controllable and safe … Something that will make me a shoe in."

He pondered that, his glimmering ruby eyes moving down as he mulled it over. "That won't be easy," he said truthfully. "Certainly not in a night," he admitted, his strong hand rubbing her shoulder reassuringly. "I would need more time to teach you a spell of that sort." It was as if he was running down a checklist of the impossible.

His hand slid down from her shoulder, over her arm until he was holding her hand. The same hand that now had a black ring about one finger from the searing heat of her spell battle.

"I'm not going to just give up. Please, just… give me something. Something that will make them see me. Need me."

Her large, blue eyes glistened but tears wouldn't fall. She wouldn't let them. She needed this too badly, needed her strength too much.

His warm hand soothingly rubbed hers as he thought, then he lifted it up and inspected her burnt finger. "Poor girl," he murmured, and with a gentlemanly delicacy, he kissed her hand softly, again, and again. Somehow the warmth of his soft lips soothed the burnt flesh.

It was intoxicating. To watch that beautiful man, his robe hung open, revealing a tantalizing display of his hard, smooth flesh, on down to the edge of his groin with him bent over to kiss her so. "I have an idea," he murmured softly.

"Tell me," she pleaded as she tried to keep her eyes trained on his face. The sight of his body was just too distracting, and it made her forget who he really was. What he really was.

He rose up, still holding her hand. "First," he said delicately, "I want you to promise me you'll forego your mastery over me. Treat me as an equal. And command me no longer… only work with me," his almond-shaped eyes widened, and she read some hope there in them. Hope she would relent and let him go.

"When did I last command you?" she asked, her eyes narrowing a bit in scrutiny. She thought she'd been treating him rather well, especially considering what he was. She'd come to him for aid, hadn't she? She could have made him help, but instead she'd asked.

Even in her desperation.

"That is my condition," he said with a gentle finality, not quite letting her hand go, but leaving their grasp tenuous. "It's only a simple promise. A few words and I will help you again to ensure you receive your just assignment." He made it sound so simple. And she was reminded of that pang of emotion she had felt, his excitement for her at the competition. His urge to see her victorious. It had felt too genuine to be faked. Too close to her soul to be deceived, she thought.

Her teeth drew in her lower lip as she looked at him, her breath held as she chewed it. He was hers. He was supposed to be hers.

Yet everything had turned out so wrong, so differently than she anticipated. "What will you do if I say them, then?" she finally asked.

"I will keep my word and help you win this," he said smoothly. "The rest? Well…" he deferred to her softly, lowering his eyes. "I would be free to do as I wish, no?" his curiously accented voice so lovely on her ears. "Trust must be involved between us."

"And you won't even tell me what you plan to do with this… freedom?" She was relying on him, needing his help. She'd almost give up the world for it but his eagerness to be free of her meagre rule made her suspicious.

He knew how desperate she was. He could surely feel it just as she had felt his joy for her.

The moment dragged on, he made her so unsure of herself! So she couldn't trust her own judgement.

Perhaps he felt the conflict. The tough corner he had backed her into with his desperation. He brought his other hand over and clasped her between the two of his. "I will help you," he said, a flick of his head causing his hair to spill backwards over his shoulder. "And trust that when you are selected, you will overcome your doubts of me."

He hesitated for just a moment, "Give me your ring."

Her head tilted as she reached for the scorched metal, pulling it off her red and inflamed finger. It stung and she was worried about being able to use it tomorrow, but she was still reluctant to hand it to him. She did it, though. Slowly.

It was a gift – the gift – from her father, after all.

The demon Varuj took her most priceless possession in hand, and held it up to the moonlight for study. He took his time, his beautifully masculine physique outlined in silver as he studied in silence.

She could never decide what to make of him. He was so strange, so alien to her. Could she trust her eyes with him? No. Her heart? She had no idea.

Without doing anything to the ring, he took her hand again, and slipped it on her finger. "Say after me," he stated, stating the words in his own tongue so very slowly. *"Ta'ruk, baum, veesh, kor'ano'tier. Alu'for, mala'kech."*

She mimicked him, uncertainty etched in her brow.

Nodding to her in approval, he said, *"Wa'roosh,"* in finality, and she had no choice but to repeat it after him.

Varuj bent down, he kissed her hand again in that gentlemanly fashion, she saw the cloud of blue fill the clear gem, as if matching her eyes in colour. He gave a soft blow of warm air across her ring and she witnessed as tendrils of red snaked through the shimmering azure until all motion ceased and the colours locked, the ring changed. Forever, she felt.

She swallowed nervously, once more astonished by how much she trusted him. That's why she didn't want to release him.

She was afraid he'd know. That he'd learn just how much she'd grown to actually trust a demon. It wasn't right.

It was her deepest secret.

"What did we do?"

"When you need it," he said slowly, affectionately, "help will come." He smiled softly and leaned in, kissing her forehead so tenderly. Lingering there until she could only shut her eyes and shudder.

When they opened again, he was nowhere to be seen.

CHAPTER 10

Firia went to sleep once she arrived home, it was before her father finished work so she didn't see him. Nor did she when she awoke the next morning, as he still rested from his night of work.

She didn't need to guess what he thought. If she had good news, she would've told him. He had to know that.

As she ate her breakfast though, she couldn't help but be grateful for the restful sleep she had. She'd dreamt, yes, but it was soothing. That warm sense of companionship accompanying her through beautiful, pastel dreamscapes. She knew *he* had a hand in it. Though it was hard to be upset with him when she'd asked him for help, and getting rest for this day was something she worried about immensely.

Firia set off as quickly as she could after eating; she didn't want to bother her father. Not until she had good news for him, if she could help it. And she wished to get to the competition ahead of time so that she might get an idea of what was to come.

When she arrived, however, the first thing she noticed were the constables waiting.

For her it seemed.

"Firia Tunst?" said the elven constable, undoubtedly in charge of the other two humans in lesser uniform dress.

Her hands went behind her back submissively as she tried to stand up straighter. To look confident. "Yes," she answered rigidly but her heart was in her throat and she nearly felt like she'd choke on it.

One of the human constables stepped in front of his boss and interjected. "We heard tales of a competition out of control the other day," the elf muttered "assault" behind him, though it didn't interfere with the man's speech. "When we investigated we came to believe there was not enough evidence to charge anyone with assault, however..." he took a deep breath and looked hesitant to continue.

"There were tales of a human woman with a crystal ring. Most... peculiar," the elf said, his words rich with implication.

"Yes," added the human, giving a bit of a harsh look to the elf before peering back to her. "Was that you? And do you have the ring?"

She blinked and her head cocked to the side, surprised that this was what they'd stopped her for. It hadn't even occurred to her that her ring...

She'd never asked her father how he'd gotten it. She just assumed he'd scrimped and saved...

"It... was a gift. For the competition."

The elf looked about to scoff, but the human constable nodded and looked understanding. "Of course, miss. Can I see it?" he asked cordially.

The elf added in, "There was a crystal ring reported stolen but three days ago."

"From where?" she asked even as she looked to the human, her dark brows knit in a plea of compassion and fear. They were going to take it from her. They'd never let her keep it, and that was the only thing that she had left.

It was her only way to succeed today.

"Can I see it please, ma'am?" the human reiterated, and she realized she wasn't the one able to ask questions here. Though within her she could feel the warm glow of Varuj, comfortingly tingle, so much like his warm embrace.

She slowly withdrew her hand from her cloak, her flesh still raw beneath the band. Her hand trembled and her eyes were filling with tears even as she tried to speak. "He would never steal. Never. Not even for me."

As the human constable gently took her hand and inspected the ring, the elf questioned abruptly, "Who? Who wouldn't? A relative?" his questions so insistent.

The kindly man gave her a gentle smile. "Was it your father, a brother perhaps?"

She was almost grateful that the human's palm calmed the trembling of her fingers, but she looked up at the elf with a pitiful stare.

Her lip trembled but still she couldn't bear the thought of turning her father in. He'd never do that. Never steal for her.

A darker thought occurred to her, then, and her gaze moved to the elf. What if this was all a ploy to take her out of the running? The ring wasn't stolen at all. She felt confident in that, and her shoulders squared as her free hand brushed away her tears.

"This wasn't stolen."

The elf's face hardened and he looked about to tear into her with his mean spirited words, though remarkably, the human held up a hand and silenced him before addressing her again. "Please miss, we need to investigate, and refusing to answer us will only increase suspicion. On yourself and whoever you're trying to protect." He looked genuinely bothered by the notion. "Just tell us who gave it to you. We won't jump to any conclusions."

"You already have by stopping me," she whimpered. "Almost every other elf around here has a ring, but I'm the one being questioned because I'm a human. But I was given the ring by someone who would never steal. Please … Please, this is my only chance."

She was trying so hard to be strong but her slender body was battling sobs of frustration.

The elf butted in: "Confiscate the ring, hold her under suspicion as we –"

The human cut him off again. "It's too late for that," he said, the elf looking startled and surprised.

"What?"

He held up her hand, showing the azure ring. "It's been bound to her soul," he said simply.

To which the elf stammered, "That's not possible... she's not even an acolyte."

The human shrugged his shoulders and smiled, though she could tell he tried to resist it. "She's more skilled than she looks. It matches her eyes, see?" he held her hand up higher, that shimmering azure that Varuj had set in her ring being some sign of the powerful jewel being bound to her soul.

"We couldn't take this from her even if we wanted to," he remarked, and she could almost hear Varuj inside her, assuring her he'd taken care of it all for her.

She tried not to look surprised, and forced her gaze to the ground.

Had the demon known this? How could he have?

She took a deep breath in, trying to steady herself, but it was pointless. She felt like a trembling leaf about to fall.

"I would have won the competition yesterday. Even you said there wasn't enough to warrant an assault charge. I'm..." she paused. "I have an aptitude for magic."

"That much is clear," said the kindly officer. "Very well, miss. I won't keep you from your contest, but know this isn't the end of this. Not entirely." He gave her a cordial bow: "Good day. And good luck," he added with a smile. He gestured to the other two, and she noticed that that despite the fact the elf wore a more fanciful uniform, it was the human who was the higher ranked one. The subtle pips on his collar displaying it even though the ostentatious garb of the elf had drawn her attention at first.

She felt like she was going to faint, and she leaned against a tree to steady her nerves.

How did you know?

I didn't, came his soothing voice. *It was merely a part of the greater plan. I told you, I would be there when you needed me, and so I was, and shall be.*

Her thumb ran over the ring, as if caressing it thoughtfully before she pushed herself up on her own two feet. She wore the same robe she had the day before, but she'd left her black hair down, leaving it to curl lightly at her shoulders.

Wish me luck.

You shall not need luck if you embrace me, he responded in that smooth voice, which translated even in her mind so seductively.

When she went to the same arena as the day before, she found a much smaller setup, though the elves from the academy the previous night were there still. Ready and waiting. There was, however, no sight of the elder human wizard. Which meant it truly would be her last chance.

The elvish master spoke, and his booming voice carried. "Show us something new today, young miss. And this time, we have one of our own students to display some true mastery. In case you get carried away again."

The beautiful elf that strode out in the field beside her wore an uneven smirk that marred his handsome features. Though he looked ready to humiliate her the first chance he got.

She tried to match his look, but she was certain it came out more as a fearful grimace. That forced confidence was wrestling with her insecurities and she forced herself up straighter. "I won't get carried away."

The only response she received was a flourish and a twirl, as the elf created a display of lights that shimmered and sparkled about the tent. It drew more of the attention from the great crowds, the pop of the explosions, the beautiful imagery of human-sized dragonflies cavorting with fawns and floating tufts of white seeds on the air.

She didn't know how to create illusions like that. It was an advanced skill that required great tutelage, and couldn't be picked up on your own, not like she had to do.

However, she did have something nearly as good. With a bit of added style, she made the hand gestures she practiced so hard, and from out of her came the shimmering form of her familiar, the iridescent fox bounding from her chest and onto the grass to prance and cavort excitedly.

As she made it perform tricks and alter its form – from a fox to a snake, from a snake to a great shelled tortoise – her mind worked on other things. She didn't know how seriously they expected her to compete against a far more learned magician than her, but she didn't want to stop at this.

The brazier was lit nearby as the day before, and an idea sprung to mind. They didn't wish to see her tricks with fire again, but perhaps they wouldn't mind using that to achieve something else.

She redirected the fire from the brazier to beneath the basin of water, and as her opponents impressive light show continued, and her familiar went from fox to antelope, she made the water boil. It was that steam she wanted, and with great concentration she was able to redirect it through the heat that coursed through those miniature water droplets.

Her knack for such things didn't just end at controlling flames, she could remove heat from objects. So she drained it from the steam, and with the aid of her ring she created a crystalline lightshow of her own. The sparkling snow and ice flakes glimmering and reflecting the light from not only her proud antelope familiar, but the neighbouring competitor's show as well.

It was like those pleasantly cool flakes were serving as a magnifier, taking what the elf did and making it into something a little more special.

She found herself laughing a little, not maliciously, but at the miracle of her own little trick, which she'd come up with all on her own.

It almost caused her to miss the work of her competitor, who was subtly turning her work against her.

The evaporated water was forming into great crystalline shards, that began to fall and impale the earth around her. Each one bigger than the last. She knew it wasn't her handiwork, but his, though she had little idea how to counter it.

The fire, she thought, and tried to redirected it back to the air to end the icy presence. Though when she did, something strange happened. The elf had interfered yet again!

Panic took over as the flame, instead of going into the air to melt the crystals, was instead careening directly towards her. Nothing she did could make it change course or alter! It was a ball of death that was on an unalterable course for her!

It seemed as if time slowed down in that instant, her life flashing before her. She had time to appreciate the look of deviousness on her opponent's face. The smug derision on the elven master's.

It was surreal.

She was going to be defeated by her own fire – or maybe worse! – and it'd look like it was her fault.

She bent her will to stop it even then, but nothing could alter her destiny it seemed. Nothing until…

The ring on her finger shifted, and she saw the red lines hidden in its azure depths grow. It was no longer just amplifying her powers; it was working with Varuj. She could sense that fact.

When the fire hit her, instead of hurting or harming her, it instead absorbed into her, much like her familiar did when she desummoned it. She could feel the heat within her! Or was it Varuj again?

She wasn't certain, but when his voice echoed inside her mind to *Exhale!* she had to obey.

A great plume of fire and smoke erupted from her mouth in the shape of… of Varuj! Though it was only an instant, and then it took on a more explainable outline of another antelope, that then cavorted with her familiar.

As she finished exhaling the smoke, it joined the other two. Three beautiful, magical animals prancing as the crowd erupted into applause.

Never had she felt such gratitude for that demon. For his prowess and ability.

And for showing up the smug elf.

She smiled brightly as she spun, her robe flowing about her ankles as she took a moment to revel in the spectacle. It was the first time since she got there that she truly felt… enjoyment.

The elder student fumed quietly, eyes darting about and feeling bothered by having been outdone by a mere hopeful. Though once she'd finished her spin she saw one of the entourage around the master beckon her over.

She complied, and once there the master said to her in an even tone, "You've a great deal of promise. And we can turn that into something great at Gaul'di-mere Academy." He simply turned and left then, no more time to spare for her or the event it seemed, though one of the entourage with him spoke up.

"We'll be in touch with details. You'll come start soon," he stated, "so be ready." Then he turned and left with the rest too.

She couldn't believe it.

Her dreams were actually coming true.

Her face flushed red and for a moment she felt faint. Gaul'di-mere Academy.

Her.

Firia's smile damn near broke her face and she had to force herself not to leap for joy. One of the best Academies in the land… and they wanted her! A human that they weren't even going to let compete!

Best of all, she'd actually be going to school with Mae'lin, one of the few people who had ever been kind to her.

And all it took was a little help from her new demon… accomplice.

Okay… a lot of help.

She could feel him inside of her, the demon's excitement so high. It was like he wanted to rise up out of her and join her in her celebration, but knew better than to do it there amidst the ongoing events.

She needed to get out, to be alone and celebrate.

She had to tell her father!

Firia was giddy as she began to leave, needing to get away before anything else went wrong. Before they tried to steal this moment of happiness from her.

CHAPTER 11

Firia was jubilant as she made her way back home. She even found herself hopping and skipping as she made the journey.

Not only had she done it, accomplished her life's dream of being accepted to an academy, but she'd been fortunate enough to get into one of the most prestigious magical academies in the land. And not even that far from her father! It was beyond what she could've thought realistic for a human without any training!

When she arrived back to her father's small cottage, she almost didn't see the notice tacked to her front door. Though at the sign of the constabulary, her heart froze.

She knew what it said before she even tore it off and read it. Her father had been arrested for theft of the ring, and they'd taken him in to the constables office for questioning and jail.

Her heart could barely take the constant ups and downs of her rollercoaster life the past week.

"Noo," she cried out, to no one and nothing. She swore her heart was breaking and her eyes filled with tears. There was no way that they'd believe someone like him was innocent...

Yet the human, the one in charge… he'd been kind, hadn't he? The way he looked at her had been sympathetic. She had to speak with him, alone. Convince him.

CHAPTER 12

Firia arrived at the constable's office nearly breathless. It wasn't a large building, for they operated outside the town and serviced the rural areas around where her father and she lived. Though the moment she abruptly set foot in, all eyes turned to her.

The familiar constable rose up from his desk in the back and he came forward towards her. "Miss Tunst," he said, "your father is fine. He's safe, don't worry." He was so quick to reassure her.

Her body trembled despite her best efforts at keeping calm as she looked up at him. Her blue eyes were rimmed with red and she knew she couldn't hide the fact that she'd been crying from him.

"Can I speak with him?"

He hesitated but smiled to her. "Sure. Follow me," he said, leading her in around the barrier and into the back.

The rows of cells were all empty, but for one, and her father looked so sad and unhappy. She'd not seen him in such a state since his bout of depression following her mother's death. His shoulders slumped. His face seeming to sag with sorrow.

"I'll give you some privacy," the constable said, shutting the door and leaving her there.

"Daddy, please tell me this isn't true," she said as she went towards him, reaching out for him. "I know it's not, but you have to tell me."

He stood up from his hard-wood bench and went to the bars. "Oh sweetie," he said, his own eyes looking so reddened. Not with tears, but the stress and strain that she knew so intimately he felt. She'd seen it in him in those long, hard days. "I bought the ring," he said, reaching out through the bars limply, "but... but I suppose I should've known the chances were high it was stolen. I just... I just didn't want to think of that. Not when you could use it."

She felt a rush of anger at whoever had sold her father the ring, and she brought his hand to her lips and kissed it. "Daddy, who did you buy it from? Where were they? What did they look like?"

He shook his head and let it hang low. "They know who it is already," he said sadly. "They knew before I even said it. He's a known crook and con man," he said, and she knew he felt so stupid. "They said I'll probably be free to go soon. I just... I just wish it had been enough... enough to get you through the contest," his face hung downwards, but she could tell, for the first time in so many years, her father was on the verge of tears.

"Daddy... Dad. I got in. They accepted me into Gaul'di-mere. It worked." She was trying so hard to hold back her excitement, but she realized then that it was all he wanted to hear. He didn't need her to save him from this place.

He needed her to give him hope.

Her father was slow to lift his head, but when he did, she saw the wide-eyed look on his face. "You... you made it?" he asked, and though there was surprise on his voice, she knew he'd had complete faith in her. Just not in the circumstances that bound them. "Gaul'di-mere?"

"Yes! I.. they had me back today. They... put me against one of the students. A student, dad, and I still did it. I still impressed those..." she lowered her voice, "those elves."

Her grin spread across her face and her brows went up in the centre. "I couldn't have done it without you."

She realized just how right she'd been. Nothing could have cheered him up like that news. Not a single thing she could have said or done would've made him smile like he did then. Nothing else could've brought the joyous tears to his handsome, dignified face. "My girl…" he murmured in disbelief. "By the gods… how could I have raised such a girl?" he shook his head and laughed, clutching her hands so tight. "You are more than I could have ever imagined a child of mine could become, Firi."

She caressed his knuckles, kissing them tenderly as she tried to hold back her tears. "So now we gotta get you back home so we can celebrate. Now that they know who the thief was…" she smiled, but it was tight.

The ring was hers now. It couldn't be returned to the original owner. Someone was going to pay for it and she prayed it wasn't him.

He shook his head, grinning like such the foolishly proud father he was. "Don't worry about that. It'll sort itself out sweetie. You've got bigger things to worry about then some silliness with your old dad." He hadn't stopped squeezing her hands. "You go home tonight and make yourself a fine meal. Okay? There's something I was saving in the cupboards for when you did this. And I want you to enjoy it to the fullest."

"Dad," she whimpered and her lower lip trembled. She was so happy and so worried all at once. "You've done so much for me. They… couldn't take the ring from me. It's mine now. Bound to me."

He blinked in surprise and looked down at the azure stone, the faint traces of ruby so hard to see, she didn't think one could make them out unless they were looking for it. "How…" he shook his head with surprise. "You never cease to amaze," he said with a smile. "Good. You deserve that ring more than anyone, sweet child. I'm glad of it." He gave such a defiant smile, she knew he would be glad to accept any fate as long as it meant she kept that edge to help her succeed.

"You didn't know, dad. I'll do what I can, okay, but know how happy I am. How much you've done for me, alright? You've… You've done so much for me and now I'm really going to the Academy. All because of you."

She was being emotional. She knew that.

But at that moment, she loved him more than anything.

He had not cried since that long-ago time when both their lives had been irrevocably changed forever. Though now it was so much better. "I only helped bring out what was in you, Firi. And I'd gladly pay any price for that little bit of help I rendered."

The knock came on the door, a courteous reminder from the friendly constable outside.

"Go home and celebrate, sweetie. I might be in here a day or two, but you've got big events ahead, and you need to be ready."

She nodded as she kissed his hand again. "Be strong, dad. I love you, and don't think I don't still need you!"

She was still crying as she went to the door and swiped away the tears quickly before opening it. "Thank you," she said as she slipped out, then looked up at the constable. "Can I speak with you in private?"

The constable took a look around then nodded, "This way, miss Tunst." He guided her to a small office in the rear, shutting the door behind them. "Sorry for the interruption, but there's rules about how long you can visit with prisoners, ma'am." He sounded so sincerely apologetic.

"That's okay," she sniffed and tried to force a smile at him. "I just... What's going to happen now?"

"Well," he started cautiously, rubbing a hand back over his own dark hair. "We're looking for the man your father implicated to corroborate the story. Now, if we can get him – and we know this man and what he's like, so I believe your father, personally – we can hopefully clear your father of all suspicion. If we can't? Well," he frowned just a bit, "we'll hold him briefly, but I don't think in the long run we have anything to hold him on, and he'll go free regardless, miss."

Such a wave of relief crashed through her and she leaned against the wall to hold her balance. It was better than she could have anticipated. Hoped for.

"Is there anything I can do? He's... Dad's never been in trouble like this before and after he lost mom he's been... sad. This is hard on him."

He gave a wan smile, "Even if we had the man right now, miss, he's too wily to just confess. And we'd have to hold your father a bit longer anyhow. There's nothing left for you to do but go home and wait."

"Will you tell me if anything changes, Mister...?"

"Alderon," he said pleasantly. "Darby Alderon. But a new student of the Gaul'di-mere Academy can simply call me Darby." There was a certain sort of shared pride in his look for one of his own people's accomplishments. "Congratulations, Firia."

She smiled genuinely at him and felt her cheeks grow red. "You heard, huh? Thanks. I'm… I'm really excited."

"You should be," he said. "But you earned it from what I hear. Don't ever let anyone convince you otherwise," he said with a light touch to her shoulder. "You do us all proud."

She bit her lower lip to keep it from quivering. "Thanks, Darby. Let me know if anything changes. I really appreciate you taking care of my dad."

He nodded. "I'll treat him as well as the law allows. So rest easy, Firia." He moved to the door and opened it up for her, the noise of the outer office filtering back in.

CHAPTER 13

It felt so good to be alone for a moment. To be able to let the joy and sorrow and anguish simply flood through her and not have to explain why she was laughing one minute and sobbing the next. She was just processing everything, and it was coming at her so fast.

The fact that her dad should be out, though, helped build her up a bit, and let her enjoy her success. She'd worked so long and so hard for this chance, and finally it was hers.

She'd really done it.

Firia was used to her home being quiet; her father worked so late, and though she liked to follow him to the academy he worked at as often as she could, it wasn't always possible. Not with classes and her own chores.

As she took the quiet time to deal with the aftermath of the explosive last few days, she was slow to notice the new presence. It wasn't until the sound of cupboards opening and closing reached her ears that she was aware she wasn't alone.

With care she crept out, though the visage she found rooting through her kitchen wasn't what she expected.

In the light of the orange setting sun, Varuj's dark skin was like bronze, his hair a metallic sheen to it. His robe hung low, and she could see his shoulders beneath his long strands of hair.

"How'd you get out?" she asked, curious as she wiped her face free of the happy and sad tears. She felt like she'd been crying for days, but the emotional rollercoaster was really putting her through the wringer. "And are you… hungry?"

He turned, and the smile that lit his face was both beautiful and infectious. "Starving," he said. When he bent down and reached into the pantry he pulled out a large, brown-paper wrapped package. "Mmmm," he said, unwrapping the rare elven-bred venison that her father must have bought special for her victory celebration. "This smells… simply divine," he remarked.

She took a step forward and pushed her bangs off her forehead. Why was she so concerned with how she looked around him? He was just some… disgusting demon that she owed a lot of her success to. Yet looking at him, the way he was, it was so easy to forget the disgusting part. And the demon part.

She blinked her large blue eyes and tried to stare past him instead of at his beautiful skin. "I didn't realize you got hungry. Have I been starving you?"

"Mm, a bit," he remarked, laying down the package and looking about ready to bite into the large flank of meat raw. "Luckily when I shed my old form, it freed up a lot of excess energy for me to consume. In other words," he said with an endearing smirk, "I was a bit bloated for a while. That kept me sated until now."

The idea of him cannibalizing his own body was strange, to say the least.

"Ew," she whispered as her nose crinkled. She smoothed back her hair and tucked it behind her ears. "So I guess it's time to talk again, hm?"

He arched a brow and peered at her sidelong as he took hold of a knife, holding it a bit awkwardly as he began to cut the meat. "I enjoy talking with you," he said, slicing the meat into smaller cutlets. "You're rather pleasant to speak with."

She snorted and then flushed in embarrassment, watching him slice the delicacy. "I'm glad a demon thinks I'm pleasant. Must mean I'm higher ranking with your lot than the elves."

It was strange watching the beautiful yet alien man work away. He was such a mix of the primally attractive and the fearsome. He had shed almost all of his bestial appearance, but still, she knew some of it must still lurk within him.

He lit the stove with magic rather than match, and began to set the frying pan down, laying out the cutlets to sizzle. "Well, we are partners now, are we not, Firia?" he asked casually, apparently knowing his way around a human kitchen with the same sort of familiarity he showed with their language: capable but a bit stilted. "How do you like your meat?" he inquired with a pleasant smile.

"I… don't really know." It wasn't something she had a lot of experience with, or choice of. She shifted awkwardly under his gaze, embarrassed at her lack of knowledge. "However you have it, I guess?"

Her blue eyes went to him and she thought of his statement. That they were partners.

He'd given her so much, gotten her so far.

"What will you do with your freedom?"

He picked through the assortment of spices, taking a sniff of each one. Finding some interesting, others repugnant, and a few tantalizing. "Your journey is not over yet," he remarked, applying some to the frying meat. "Elven academies are tough. And exhaustively long even for their kind I hear," he said, sticking his nail into the cutlet then licking his finger for a taste of the red juices. "Perhaps you might have use for a partner still, hmm?" He arched a brow and peered over at her almost innocent-looking.

Her brow arched. "Who do you hear these things from? Was there a lot of gossip about elvish academies where you're from?"

She couldn't take her eyes off of him. He moved with such purpose and grace, and everything he did just seemed so smooth. Meanwhile she felt awkward and even though she was goal-oriented, well… she certainly didn't have the easy confidence he did.

With a flick of his wrist he expertly flipped the meat cutlets over. "The fel plane from which I come is a solitary place," he remarked as the flames licked up over the sides of the pan. "There is nobody to trust. You may make momentary alliances with someone, but it never lasts. You never expect it to," he remarked, tossing in a dash of something she didn't even see. He was so quick and fluid with his motions!

"That doesn't answer my question," she sighed, but she knew she hadn't answered his either. She was still cautious. Worried.

Frightened.

"What if I set you free and you turn on me?"

"Why would I do that?" he asked with a furrowed brow. "I've nothing to gain from seeing you dead or injured," he stated simply, serving up the cutlets and immediately beginning to fry up more, seeming intent on frying the whole slab of meat up. "No, beautiful Firia," he said with a sigh, and a gentle smile, "I will not turn on you. On that I promise."

"I don't know how much promises mean to demons, though," she admitted meekly. "I don't know much about you at all."

He smiled pleasantly at her, taking out the cutlery for her and him, handing her a fork and knife. "Would you like to find out more about me?" he asked in that wistfully charming way of his that lit up his striking face. "I have never had someone curious of who I really am before."

Her nose scrunched up again: "Really? Why not?" She was rather fascinated with him and only held back her questions out of... fear? Was that what it was? She wasn't entirely certain, but she knew she didn't feel wholly comfortable bombarding him with questions.

After she took the cutlery from him, he began to slice up his own, eating the rather rare meat with a certain relish. "Mmm, where I come from," he said, chewing while he spoke but managing to retain at least some dignity while he did so in his hunger, "one does not share such things with others. For it might betray a weakness to exploit." He smiled. "This is quite delicious, is it not?"

He was even managing to distract her from her father's second gift, and she took the time to finally savour the first bite. It was exquisite and unlike anything she could ever recall tasting. She licked her lips as her eyes fluttered closed and she nodded.

"You did really good," she agreed as she cut off another bite. "And that makes sense. People do that here, too."

He nodded, devouring his at a faster rate, then taking time to flip and season the next cutlets on the pan. "And when one of us is summoned, the summoner does not care for who we are. Only for what we might do for them. So, you see? It is a curious thing for me," he remarked, biting into the tender meat. "Exquisite. We have nothing like this back where I come from."

"So… why don't you tell me about yourself, then." She was beginning to devour hers as well, enjoying the taste and feel of it. Her demon dinner companion even managed to distract her from the fact that her father should have been there, appreciating the food with her.

Varuj smiled pleasantly, serving himself up more, his appetite simply ravenous it seemed. "I am something of a sorcerer in my own right," he said with no small amount of pride. "I live alone, as I said, but I have many minions. Similar to your familiar," he remarked with a charming look. "They keep me company, guard my dwelling. They are very nearly pleasant to be around," he said with a light chuckle that sounded almost musical.

"Hopefully they're very good guards, then. Since… I stole you away from it, I mean." Why did she feel bad about that? He wanted to be here. He told her that.

And why wouldn't he? A hellish place would be… terrible. Worse than her world.

She finished her cutlet and pushed her plate away. She'd been on such a lean diet for so long that she was already feeling full.

Despite his own pleasantly fit physique, he had a far greater appetite, and continued to eat, tossing the last of the meat onto the pan. "It is hard to say," he said with a shrug. "If anyone is aware of my absence, then minions or no, it is too late, and my dwelling is lost. With all I have accumulated." He grimaced a bit. "So you see, stay or return, I start with nothing. At least here," he looked around then pointedly to her, "I have some connection to this place." He kept his ruby gaze locked upon her as he continued to chew.

She felt so uncomfortable under his stare, as if he could see right through her. And maybe he could.

She chewed her lip as she pushed her bangs back awkwardly, fidgeting as he watched. She was strong. She summoned him here, didn't she?

So why did he make her feel so nervous?

"I just don't want to make anything bad happen."

He was quiet a while, eating more of the venison until it was all gone, and he wiped his lips with a certain foreign elegance.

"You brought me here," he said delicately. "You tore me from all I had and knew. And asked favours of me," he took a deep breath and pushed the plate away. "I like you," he confessed. "You are a far better summoner than I could have envisioned. But we all chafe beneath servitude, do we not, Firia?" He stepped around the counter and reached out, taking her hand with a gentle, warm touch.

She felt steadier with it, and that simply made no sense to her. She should have felt something - anything - but comfort at his touch.

"I'm not saying I'm not going to... honour... my promise. I'm saying that I'm scared you're not what you seem. That... you're a demon."

He gave a sweet, almost amused smile. "That is your word for us, not ours," he remarked softly. With one hand in his, he used his other arm to put around her shoulders and guide her back towards her room. "There are no guarantees, sweet Firia. I cannot say or promise you anything that would change that fact." He shrugged lightly as they went to her bed and he sat her down upon its edge before joining her, sitting beside her quite closely. "I wish it were otherwise, but it is not so."

Her hands rested in her lap, her shoulder pressed against his arm. She wanted to trust him, to be confident she hadn't brought something terrible into the world.

"What's the first thing you'd do if I wasn't... If you weren't under my service?"

Varuj moved a hand up to delicately cup her chin and tilt her gaze up towards him. "I would set out to woo a beautiful young lady and aspiring sorceress. To make her a partner and together make ourselves a place in this world worthy of remembering. Of celebrating." He leaned in so close, his eyes partially lidded as he spoke those delicious words before wetting his lips. "I would propose to you. An arrangement that we might cooperate. As partners. And more."

She didn't breathe. She felt like her heart would stop and her head went fuzzy.

How could she even want that? How could his words make her feel so pleasantly warm and comforted?

This was the same vile beast that she had summoned to her aid, who she had seen so nude in all his demonic glory.

Yet all she could think of was how badly she wanted to feel his soft lips on hers once more.

His head tilted, and he hovered so near to her lips without touching. "Say you will release me, and I shall hold you this night through. And tell you of things I can teach you. Of things we might do as partners. Sorcerers without compare."

He lifted one leg up and pulled her to his chest as she sat between his legs, his nose rubbing against her own pale peach skin as his succulent lips hovered near.

It was like she was suffocating under the weight of her choice, and even as she began to nod her head she wondered if she was making the wrong decision. She should keep him to her, be a proper master. Force him to serve.

She already had all of his knowledge. She could force it out of him.

Yet she wanted so much more than that.

His beautiful, masculine lips lit up in a smile, and he nuzzled his nose to hers as he reclined back on her bed, keeping her body close to his with his strong arms. "That's all I needed," he said softly, holding her petite form against his nearly bare chest. "We will go far together, sweet Firia. Much farther than any master and demon ever went." He kissed her so lightly, just a soft little prolonged peck on her forehead, "I promise."

"Please don't make me regret this," the small woman whimpered, already feeling so tense. Yet he'd been freed, hadn't he? And still his sweetness, the warm feel of his lips remained. She found herself more and more thinking of him in this form, forgetting the terrifying visage that she first drew through the portal.

It was hard to remember that first impression with how his beautiful male physique now held her so tenderly. Even with her control broken – she assumed? – he was delicate. Caring. Holding her against him, letting her rest herself to his chest, laying between his legs as he stroked her dark hair and kissed her peached skin.

"What is there to regret?" he said softly. "You are on your way to being recognized by your peers, and together… together you and I shall do great things, sweet Firi. Great things indeed." His warm lips skirted hers, but came so tantalizingly close. "You performed brilliantly today. Worthy of the woman who summoned me from across the void."

"Firi," she whispered. That's what her dad called her. It was filled with such familiarity and warmth, and she wanted that more than anything. She needed his comfort.

"Varuj... Where will you stay?"

"Beside you when I can," he said to her softly against her ear. Then his one hand went to her chest, resting softly above her breast, over her beating heart. "Here when the situation calls for it." It was so strange, that touch, so casual, yet intimate. So near to her breast, yet warm and comforting over her beating heart.

It wasn't necessarily sexual, and yet it made her skin prickle with excitement and she had to look away from him. Her pulse quickened beneath his touch and she prayed he wouldn't notice.

"Will you always exist like this?"

"Will you always exist as you are?" he replied in his usual enigmatic way. Though he relented without her pursuing it further and murmured softly, "More or less. I won't change significantly again without a great deal of effort." He nuzzled against her ear. "Would that please you best?"

It had been so nice to have him always there, comforting her. Rooting for her.

She was surprised to realize just how much it had meant to her, though, as she nodded. She liked him like this.

She liked him a lot.

Varuj kissed the corner of her lips and smiled. "Then so it shall be," he stated firmly. "You brought me into this world, beautiful Firi, and I shall respect your wishes, and cherish you for it." The soothing stroke of his fingers through her dark hair was supremely comforting. "There is a long road ahead for you. Even I cannot make magic simple and easy for you, but I will stand by you, beside you... inside you, wherever I may, as you make your journey."

CHAPTER 14

Firia awoke the next day to the sound of someone pounding on her door. The demon Varuj still held her, nestled to his chest as she lifted her head and looked about. "Morning," he murmured to her softly. "You should probably get that. Sounds urgent."

It was startling to wake up in someone's arms, but she found herself disappointed to be torn away. She lingered for a moment, feeling her small body press into his before she pulled away, red-faced and embarrassed. Pulling on her dressing gown over her clothes, she ran to the door.

When she opened up the door she was greeted with the sight of a very official-looking elf, donning a tunic bearing the sigil of Gaul'di-mere Academy in bright gold. He didn't appear to be all too pleased with where he was, at the footstep of a human peasant's home, but he spoke crisp and formally: "Madam Tunst?" he asked.

"Yes, that's me," she said as she stepped aside, allowing him in if he chose. "What can I do for you?"

He didn't take the offering, though he extended a scroll to her. "This is for you. You're not to open it until the time arrives," he said vaguely. "You're to be at the Commons Trade and Tax Office at sundown tonight."

The request didn't make sense to her, for everyone in the village knew the sole government office in their small village shut down before sunset.

"But it'll be closed." She accepted the scroll anyways, blinking her eyes free of sleep. Perhaps she had simply misheard.

He tipped his wide-brimmed hat to her and cracked a wry smile, "Be there, madam. You're allowed to bring one servant. That's all I can say!" He turned with a bit of a flourish then headed off away from her home at a brisk pace, rounding the gates and then… his walking speed became something of a blur as he took off down the road, as if defying time itself.

"A servant," she scoffed as she shut the door. Was this some type of hazing? She put the scroll down and let out a groan as she went to fix her hair. It seemed like her pigtails were in a mess, and she brushed her bangs aside.

As she looked at herself in the humble mirror the visage of her demonic companion slipped behind her, his strong, reassuring hands resting on her shoulders, his charming smile evident as he leaned in, inhaling her scent near her hair. "Beautiful. You slept well?" he asked, and she was reminded of the night's dreams.

The jarring awakening had shaken it from her with the urgency of the moment, but she'd dreamt all the night through. Peacefully, somehow, but she remembered many long, obsessive fantasies acted out in her dreamscape of her and… and Varuj. Walking the forest paths she knew. Sharing stolen moments at her old school house. Her guiding him through the village. Even…

It made her blush to think of it. Of him in his original form, holding her.

She wanted to avert blame for her fantasies onto him, but he had spent the whole night outside of her. Even if he had wanted to… it wouldn't have been possible for him to influence her dreams like that. Would it?

"Yes," she managed to whisper, but she wouldn't meet his eyes. Not with that on her mind.

Clearing her throat, she moved away from him, shrugging off the gown and placing it over the back of the chair. "I'm to go to the government office today after sunset."

"So you've received your summons to the Academy already?" He said with a raised brow, moving casually out into the main room, his two hands upon his exotic robe's belt. "They're prompt at least. I thought they might keep you waiting for a while," he mused as he looked about, his long, sleek black hair shifting with the smooth motions of his head.

It was odd to see him wandering about her home, odder still to see him doing it in the bright of morning. "How about I make you some breakfast?" he said with a cheeky smile, his ruby eyes turning back towards her.

"Sure, though I doubt there's anything good." She slipped into the chair, looking at the scroll but not opening it. "I don't know that it's the summons. It feels like I'm being set up." But maybe it was just paranoia at work.

He held out his hand for the scroll. "Give it to me," he said simply, though she could read the concern on his face as he eyed the thing.

"I'm not supposed to open it yet. Hell, this thing might be a trap too," she said even as the corner of her lip pulled up into a half smile.

"Just give it to me, please," he reasserted, holding out his hand and giving her a pointed look. "I won't open it," he insisted.

He took the scroll and held it delicately in both hands, lifting it up to his face and inhaling along its length with his eyes shut. He went through some series of odd tests, holding it before the morning light that filtered through the window. Then holding it in the shadow of his robe – which also gave her a generous peek at his leanly muscled abs – to give it another look over.

"It's ensorcelled," he stated firmly, offering it back to her. "And there is some faint trace of mischievous intent associated with it. Though not by its original creator. Most likely by whoever handed it to you," he stated. "It is, however, a very minor mischievousness I detected."

"How can you tell?" she asked, staring at it curiously. "I guess he wanted me to open it at the precise point they all come out and douse me in water or something, is that it? Something to make me look like a fool?" She felt her pulse quicken, and her face flushed.

"Perhaps," he said with a light shrug as he turned and went to the kitchen and began to prepare a meal for her once more. "And I told you, I'm a sorcerer in my own right. A very capable one, I might add," he said with an impish grin over his shoulder as he rooted through her pantry. "You weren't kidding when you said there wasn't much."

"Congratulations, now you know what it's like to be poor. Glamorous, isn't it?"

She couldn't understand why she was being so bitter, but being dragged away from him, from her pleasant dreams... She shouldn't lash out at him, but somehow she felt it was his fault. That he could have protected her from the rude wakeup call.

Of course, nothing could be further from the truth. He could not show himself. Even if he weren't a demon he couldn't do it. The talk that would erupt about her if a strange young man was seen answering her door in the morning!

He took it fine, however, and continued his focus upon the food. He finally found something to his liking. "Aha. I thought I smelled some meat," he said, pulling out some older, salted pork and bringing it to the stove. "The scroll itself is magical, as I said," he explained to her as he went about his intricate preparations. He cooked capably, though in a different manner than she was used to. "Opening it activates its powers in part. So doing so before you need to use it could deplete it's power. So... in that regard the timing issue may not be a trick at all."

"Well, I'm sure it will be the first of many trials I'll have to deal with working with those elves." Her words were half angry, but all determination. It was motivation to spite them, knowing how much they'd hate her and her powers. "Until they learn that they cannot trifle with the human girl."

Her words brought a grin to Varuj's face, and his ruby eyes met hers from across the room. "I knew I hadn't chosen wrongly. You make me fancy you deeply with that kind of talk, darling Firi," he mused so sincerely. He tossed back his long hair and beginning to crack open some eggs, frying them as the meat sizzled.

She wish he'd stop saying things like that. She blushed as her gaze fell and she drew her lower lip between her teeth for a moment. "I don't understand you," she admitted. "You're a demon, aren't you?" Of course he was, she chided herself. She summoned him!

"Like I said, that is *your* word for us, not ours," he rooted through the spices and herbs of her kitchen, finding some he liked the scent of and adding them to the eggs. "It's a wholly strange term from our perspective, however," he explained, going to her pantry again and taking tiny tastes of what he found there before he mused over the goat cheese.

He carried it back to the stove and mixed some of the cheese with the eggs as he scrambled them up. "It would be like calling humans, elves, orcs, trolls and all other walks of life on your world simply "angels" or some nonsense. I mean, what do *you* have in common with a troll, lovely Firi?"

"Not much, I'd hope," she shrugged. Those large, brutish things that lived in forests and practiced their strange, superstitious nonsense weren't even allowed to compete for the Academies.

They were too uncontrollable.

"So fine, what do you call yourself? The angel from hell?"

Varuj laughed again. "Once again, that would be *your* term, not ours." He sighed a little, but began serving up the food. He didn't seem to like his food cooked very much, she noted. "Would you call your world heaven then? Even the slums of your greater cities? Or would you say it is simply your world, with bad, good and everything in between?"

He took up the plates and walked over to the table with them, setting them out then pouring some water for them both. He pulled out a chair for her in a very gentlemanly fashion, holding it and waiting for her to sit then pushing her in comfortably.

"You said your world is mostly bad. That you couldn't wait to get away from it. So I'd say that yea, this place is looking alright compared to that," she retorted, her head tilting to the side and daring him to contradict her.

"Certainly not heaven, but we do have some good here."

He went and sat down at the table beside her, very carefully laying out a napkin over his lap like the princely lord he so resembled. "Where I come from it, it was rather bad, yes," he remarked with a faint, wan smile. "It would be like you residing in the orcish slums. You would be far better off than they, certainly, but their sickly state, their poverty and depression would make you ill. Wear away at you each and every day," he said before biting into his own food with some small relish.

"I would take my chances here with you. This world is richer in opportunity from what I've seen," he stated firmly.

"But that still doesn't answer my question. What do you call yourself, if not a demon?" As usual she was slow to begin eating, trying to savour the moment.

The two of them sitting together was reminiscent of a familial bond. Somewhat like warm moments with her parents before her mother died, but on a different level. He wasn't family, or even a friend as such, but there was a warmth there. She felt it. And having him close by, so casually concerned, it seemed right.

"Varuj. I told you that already," he said with a wry smile before eating some more of the fried pork. "But I am of the Xirai'j: a dying race that is withered and strewn about all of existence. No longer united as one, in purpose or place." He sounded almost morose about it, though he seemed to be trying to hide it.

"Xirai'j," she repeated the word, feeling it with her tongue. "I like that. It has a nice sound," she agreed as she finally began to eat the meal he'd prepared for her. "You cooked a lot back home?"

He shrugged slightly, "It was one of my menial pleasures. Whenever my sorcery would consume me for so long that my mind grew blocked and my inventiveness stagnant, I would break to cook. Replenish my energies and reset my mind." She got the feeling there was more to his enjoyment of cooking, both from how he went about it and the way he spoke.

"I never cared that much for it, honestly." She looked across the table at him, staring at his face as he ate. She still kept expecting him to betray her, to be cruel or hateful. She didn't know how to accept his calm exterior, his kindness.

The way he held her through the night.

"That works out fine," he said, giving a small smile to her as he ate. "I enjoy cooking enough to handle it for the both of us, so all's well," he remarked. "Once you're done your studies, we could get ourselves a nice witches lair to hone our craft. Something solitary, in the countryside. So that we might live more freely, and I could make you breakfast each morning before we set about our experiments and magical adventures."

That was getting a little ahead of himself, and her nose crinkled as she tilted her head to the side. "That's, like… years away."

"Yes, well…" he smiled and shrugged, "it shall go fast." He had polished off his plate of food, and he lifted the napkin to wipe his lips before downing the glass of water. "It's best to plan ahead. I know you just accomplished your big dream, Firi, but realize it is just a stepping stone to true greatness for you."

Why did he plan on staying with her so long, though? Or was it just another effort for him to try to lull her into feeling for him? Letting herself fall for him?

She took another bite of her meal, chewing it thoughtfully. "And all your dreams hinge on me?"

He hesitated then gave a slight nod. "In a manner of speaking. Somewhat. We've worked together this much already, haven't we? Why should we stop now?" He looked across at her with a curious gaze. "The Academy shan't be easy. You made it through the trials, but still, you will have catching up to do for the classes, undoubtedly. The other, elvish students have an edge on you still. And I presume that means the students there will have that high caliber of an expectation upon them. Pure power won't be enough. You'll need to know spells, various spells, to start through the rigors of the academy."

She pushed the rest of the meal over to him, never having been a big eater. Not with money so tight. "But why would you want that?"

His eyes moved to her discarded food, and he began to pick at it, eating her leftovers. "Do you imagine or desire yourself to go through life without aid, friendship or companionship? Surely you realize it takes more than one's solitary self to make it through life? Even in your luxurious world," he said with a brow cocked high.

"I know what I'd get out of it…" She paused, stopping herself short. He wasn't talking about her. Her eyes narrowed a bit as she stared at him, "So you don't have a choice, basically."

"That is… not what I was getting at," he said with a bit of confusion. "Do you not have concepts of mutually beneficial, voluntary relationships in this world? I thought you had," he mused aloud.

She'd never really had any relationships outside of her family; she shrugged. "I guess." Why was she so suspicious of him? Sure he was from another world, but he'd only ever helped her. Wanted to give her more.

Yet she'd built up a wall to protect her from something she thought to be inevitable.

CHAPTER 15

Firia had packed up, though she had no idea what to expect. So much loomed unfinished, but her summons had come; what she'd dreamt of all her life was at hand.

The horizon was orange as the sun neared it, though was still not completely set. She saw the stone building that was the sole representation of the state in their whole area. It wasn't particularly big, nor was it much to look at. Despite being made of some smooth, white stone, it was rather boxy, with only a few simple columns etched into the stonework to make it stand out.

It had already shut down for the day, the quiet little nexus of dirt roads silent as she approached. She had only her familiar for company, the shimmering fox at her side at Varuj's insistence. He told her the creature was gifted at sniffing out magical tricks and would help keep her safe from any potential pranksters.

She was grateful for the fox's company anyways. It made the walk a little less lonely, and gave her a boost of confidence. She'd left a letter for her father and taken everything she owned in a small satchel.

It would be a fresh start, and every insult would push her towards greatness, she reminded herself.

She'd dressed in her best, though it was still no doubt shabby compared to what the elves would wear. Her black bangs were styled against her forehead and her hair was tied back in a ponytail, out of her face.

This was it.

The area was quiet, only the light rustling of the grass in the fields breaking the silence. As she sat upon the stone steps leading into the building, her fox perked its ears and went trotting off around the side. With a yip he outed the hiding elf behind the column.

"Who's there?" she asked.

From out of the shadows she saw the tall, lanky figure of Mae'lin emerge. He wore the same thing she'd seen him in at the competition, and he looked bashful as he ran his fingers over his short, spiky blonde hair. "Sorry," he apologized. "I wasn't hiding, honest," he pleaded.

"You were just…. standing behind a pillar and watching me… without hiding?"

His eyes went wide, "I wasn't watching you!" he insisted. "I was…" he tugged at his collar a little, the lanky elf looking so out of place. "It'll sound odd, but I was studying the stonework. It's… actually quite ancient, I think. Yet still so smooth and flawless… obviously the work of some arcane craftsman."

She couldn't help but laugh. "You were studying the stonework by the light of the setting sun?" Her lips quirked into a half smile as she shook her head. "That's new."

He laughed a bit bashfully, and she could see the colour in his cheeks. "There's not much time left before it goes down completely and I couldn't see a thing," he said, sounding quite sincere. "I just never took the time to come by and appreciate this place before." He smiled to her warmly and approached. "I'm really glad you were accepted too. You deserved to be."

"Thanks. Sorry I almost assaulted you," she smiled before biting her lip to hide it. Since when did she get so brazen?

She knew, of course. Ever since she summoned that demon, she'd been feeling different. More herself, as if that layer of fear had been slowly stripped from her.

He waved a hand dismissively, standing a shy distance away still. "Nonsense," he said. "We were both so into it, if I had won I'm sure you would've been a water-logged mess because I couldn't have possibly hoped to control it at that point." He smiled at her. "You showed a remarkable amount of control for wielding so much power."

"Either way, it worked out for the best, didn't it? I mean… we couldn't both get in any other way." She lowered her voice, taking a step towards him, "Best case scenario, right?"

He shrugged his shoulders, "The competition isn't necessarily a win-lose thing. They often choose both combatants if they display great promise. Though yeah, we both got in, so all's well, no?" He said with a smile. "I am really glad you'll be going there. I always thought you seemed pretty special."

Her gaze fell and that newfound confidence dropped for a moment. Her pulse quickened instead and she felt her skin grow warm. It wasn't that she disagreed… She wasn't like most other humans she met, to be certain. But to have him say it…

Mae'lin cleared his throat, "The sun's about gone down now." He peered around. "There's nobody else here yet."

A voice carried down from above, "Except me." It was another one of the elvish students, looking rather disinterested in their whole exchange as he dangled his legs from the ledge above the building entrance.

She inhaled, her eyes narrowing at the elf, frustrated at his intrusion and embarrassed that he'd been spying. Still, she was too flustered to really speak and folded her arms beneath her chest. Her fox rubbed up against her leg in a comforting motion, and it managed to calm her outrage for the time being.

The darkness of the evening descended upon them so quickly, or perhaps it was simply being lost in discussion with Mae'lin that made it seem so. However the tall elf looked around, "It seems strange they'd just have us meet here for no reason. Perhaps we should check around. Investigate."

"I figured they're just… hazing us. Seeing what we'll do," she admitted with a shrug. "I'd be cautious, anyways."

"Do what you want," came the other elf's voice, "but I'm going to wait here. I can see far, and I'm sure they'll be by to get us soon." He stayed stubbornly in place, gazing off along the roadways.

Mae'lin shrugged and turned to head around the side of the building. "It's probably a test, if anything," he said to her as they went around, inspecting the area. There was so little to see though, just the grassy fields that ended with forests on the east and west sides, and hills to the north and south. The area was mostly farm land, and homes were spaced out so far apart.

"I wouldn't be surprised. We're the new ones that are supposed to be, well, bright enough to go there. So if we can't find our way or just sit by passively," she remarked with a pointed tilt of her head, "what's that going to tell them?"

Mae'lin smiled at her warmly. "Exactly," he said. She was beginning to see that the elf's warmth was just a natural state of being for him. He was curious and kind, a rare combination amongst the elvish sorts.

Though she focussed her mind on the task at hand. Try as she might, she just couldn't find anything out of the ordinary. So she turned to her familiar. "Luka?" she asked. "You detect anything strange?"

The swirl of lights that coalesced as her pet looked up at her, then tilted its head about, snuffling at the air. It reminded her of the curious behaviour Varuj had displayed earlier that very day.

What didn't remind her of him, however, was the strange little yips he gave. He didn't direct it at anything though, he just seemed to bark randomly at the air, the building.

"Well that's… something, anyways," she looked around. "Do you think it's enchanted?" She took a step closer to the building, her fingers tracing along it. "Surely they don't expect for us to be able to break into a magical hideaway without preparation…." A lot of preparation. And books she didn't rightfully own.

"The building?" he asked. "Nah. It's just an ordinary structure I think. It was just really interesting, I thought. I mean, it'd have to have been made so long ago. It had to have required a special sort of arcane crafter to…"

He stared at her, realizing his own foolishness. "Oh. Yeah, I get your point."

"Well, since it was the pillar that caught your eye, why don't we start there and work our way around?" It was actually… kind of exciting. Taking charge, trying to investigate and figure things out. She was losing herself to the excitement for the first time since she found out she was accepted and came crashing down to the news her father was jailed.

Mae'lin took her to the pillar he was looking at. "I was just marvelling at how perfectly crafted the stones were. I mean, it's obviously quite old, but yet not a single little nick or scratch in the whole place," he said with some awe and appreciation, running his hand over the white stone.

"Maybe because it's... protected?" She grinned at him playfully. Her hand went to the other side and she breathed in, trying to concentrate. She didn't know if she'd be able to sense anything, but perhaps... some part of her might.

As she focussed on the stone however, she felt... nothing. The fact of the matter was, she had no training with divination. Had not even practiced such things on her own at any length. Without some education on the matter, picking it up then and there was about as long a shot as she could envision.

She didn't allow herself to fall into despair however, so as the two of them felt out the stone she recalled what Mae'lin had said. She looked to Luka, "Find any flaw in the stone. Any nicks, scratches or missing chunks." The ethereal fox perked up its ears then immediately went about the task.

The spry creature moved along on its paws as its eyes scanned the building up and down, up and down as it moved, then around the corner.

"It's amazing that you have a familiar all your own before even going to the academy," marvelled Mae'lin. "How'd you learn such a feat? It's supposed to be our big first term project at the academy, and you're already done and completed!"

"I spent a lot of time reading." She smiled, her hands feeling out the smooth pillar. "What's your most favourite spell you've learned so far?"

The look of surprise on the elf's face was hard to miss. There were not many self-taught magicians in the world. It's why so few humans ever became one, beyond the excuse that a human's life was too short to truly master the craft, that is.

"I don't really know a lot of them," he said with some embarrassment.

Her gaze went to his and she stopped her inspection for a moment. "Well, fine, but I'll ask you again by the end of the year and I'll expect an answer."

Mae'lin smiled meekly, and looked about to say something to her before the excited yip of her fox broke the moment.

"He's found something?" Mae'lin asked.

"He must've!" she said, and they headed off briskly around the building.

She found the ethereal familiar pointing his dark nose at a particular point in the wall, right up against the column, and she went to inspect it. "Here," she said, feeling the faint little indent in the stone. The only flaw they were able to find in the whole structure, despite its ancient status.

She patted the fox's head with a smile. "You did good." She purred happily as she felt out that small marking.

"Now… to figure out how to get in…"

Mae'lin and she both studied the faint markings for some time. Though with the sun gone down, they had a great deal of trouble seeing what they were doing.

An idea struck her then, and she remembered her training with Varuj. "Luka?" she said, *"ignae."* The familiar lowered his head, and his body glowed brighter, illuminating the wall and making the faint tracing stand out all the more. In fact, it was almost as if the markings twinkled in their own right, and she could see the swirls and swoops, as if someone had drawn on the wall.

She was right!

Even through all her search there was a bit of fear that she'd look the fool, that she should just have sat idly by like the elf on the roof. But here she was, looking at proof of her cleverness, and she smiled brightly. Her fingers followed the symbols, licking her lips curiously.

The annoying part settled in shortly thereafter: she had no idea what it meant. "What do you make of it?" she asked Mae'lin.

The tall elf took her hand and gently and guided her away from the wall. It was then he seemed to realize he was holding her fingers and released them apologetically. "Sorry," he murmured, his blush visible in the light of her familiar. "I think it's text of some sort."

"I can't read it, though," she said, her lips pursed to the side.

Why did she feel so warm? She looked up at him for a moment and instantly knew. He was being way too nice to her.

Mae'lin studied the wall a while. "It's arcane script," he said then cleared his throat. "Something old elvish sorcerers used in times past. I hear tell the more affluent families hire tutors to instruct their kids in it before going to the academies. But... I don't know much of it myself," he admitted with some embarrassment.

She sighed.

"Elf on the roof! Guess who needs your help." Embarrassment wasn't the word for it, but he seemed stuck up enough that he'd know it.

It took a while, but eventually she heard him treading across the roof slowly, maintaining his balance expertly with that natural elven grace. "What is it?" he said with some distaste.

"Can you read this script?" asked Mae'lin, pointing to the wall.

The elf bent down, clung to the edge of the building and dipped his head over. His long white hair dangled down as he took a moment. With a snort he said, "Oh gimme a break. You can't even make out *that* word?" his voice full of derision.

"Can you just tell us what it says, please?" pleaded Mae'lin without delay, perhaps trying to spare her the shame, or perhaps just eager.

With a sigh he rose back up and started walking around the building again. "You already know what it says, fools," he remarked as he vanished around the side to the front again. "It says 'read'!"

She rolled her eyes, muttering under her breath, "He's a charmer." She pulled her sack around and opened the top, reaching in for the scroll. "Guess it's time."

Mae'lin smiled, "Of course!" He pulled out his own scroll as well.

Immediately she saw that the scroll too was written in that same script, and her heart began to sink. Though before she could relent to despair she heard a voice – his voice, Varuj's – waft into her mind. *You don't need to read it. Just focus your will upon the scroll.*

It was the sort of simple thing she'd seen written in the texts she'd studied for so many years, and it came natural to her. Almost as soon as she did, the scroll began to dissipate, fading from existence into nothingness.

"What the –" Mae'lin began, expressing her own feelings well.

Though quickly thereafter she saw it: the script vanished and before her in the white stone a doorway appeared. Narrow and just above her height, as if it were made for her. It would've been an uncomfortable fit for Mae'lin by her side, by comparison.

"See you on the other side?" she asked as she recalled her familiar back into her. "Focus your will upon it." She took such pleasure in repeating the demon's words to him, her heart swelling with pride and excitement.

She didn't even think to take a last look around her, her home nearly forgotten already. Though she had no way of preparing herself for what lay ahead.

CHAPTER 16

The rush of portal travel was something completely new to her. It was as if every part of her was broken down to its infinitely small portions, then rocketed through a needle-sized hole only to splatter against some matter on the other side and reform.

She gasped, every nerve, every sense receptor in her body lit up with colour as she returned to normal.

She'd have compared it to dying then being reborn, not that she knew what dying was like. Though once the buzz of sensation died back down she realized she was in a place like nothing she'd ever known.

The stars sparkled. All about her. Not merely in the sky, but to her sides, even below her. It was then she thought to look down and realized she was suspended on a small tendril of some crystalline branch that wound up from some spec of existence below. Her heart panged with familiarity, and something within her – either Varuj or her own instinct – told her that was home, so far below.

There was no time to make sense of it before she noticed one of the stars seemed to grow larger, its glow growing brighter. It made her squint until it flashed and took the form of a person before her.

Neither a human, nor an elf. She couldn't even peg a gender to the unknown being before her, she could only say they were beautiful and luminescent. "Where are you going?" came their voice, so even yet somehow melodious.

"Oh… Gaul'di-mere Academy?" she said, still lost to the wonder of everything around her. She was surprised by that loneliness, though, that battled with her enthusiasm and curiosity. There was nothing there for her but her father…

She had to shoo the thought aside, for it suddenly hit her how lonely he would be without her.

"Very well," came the being's voice. "It shall be a quick and easy journey there. The vines grow strong in that region."

It was as simple as that. Firia had no more time to respond before the crystalline branch grew shoots that coiled up around her ankles and over her calves, writhing up until they coated her entirely.

Suffocation!

The worry hit her suddenly, and she felt a strange sense of vertigo as she struggled to get some air but failed. The vines were smothering her! Yet the feeling of displacement was so strong until…

She went tumbling from her crystal prison and landed upon a smooth stone surface, gasping for breath.

In retrospect, as air flooded back in, she realized she must not have been choked off for more than seconds, but the fright of it and the lack of preparation had made it seem far more.

Once again however, her thoughts were stolen from her as she clutched her satchel and looked up. The sight before her was gorgeous.

A smooth, shimmering crystal walkway led up to a great tree that grew out of the side of a cliff face. That tree formed a path to what was an unbelievably large castle, suspended in the air over a circular chasm. None of it made a lick of sense without the use of magic, for the tree, though immense, did not seem nearly strong enough to hold up so large a structure over such a gaping void.

As Firia stood, she saw that most of the circular chasm bordered the ocean. Rocks lined the other side, where waves crashed before filtering over and flooding down into that pit. The sheer magnificence of the sight illuminated by moon and stars was breathtaking, almost as much as the literal act of having her breath stolen earlier.

She was carried forward on sheer wonder alone, and she noticed the curious trees on her side of the chasm. They were bent in an odd shape. The moment they left the ground they curved towards the chasm, so that they looked almost like thousands of J's on the landscape that blossomed into green leaves and luminescent silver and purple flowers that bloomed fully in the night.

It was all so stunning that she almost didn't notice the sound of Mae'lin crashing to the crystal platform behind her just as she had, sputtering for air in much the same way. "By the weave!" he choked out.

CHAPTER 17

Once more she forgot her loneliness, her worries for her father. All that there was, all that surrounded her and flowed in her veins was wonder and awe. It didn't even register to her, completely, where they were. Just that she was in the most spectacular place she could ever dream of.

Such warmth and amazement flooded her body as she spun about. "Wow…" she muttered under her breath.

Shortly thereafter, Mae'lin echoed her own sentiment, the tall elf rising up and moving closer to her as he gazed all around.

The sight was so breathtaking that she hadn't even really noticed anything about the great castle itself at first. Its sheer white-stone walls rising to such high pinnacles and peaks, so many towers probing into the heavens all about. It was like chaos, but a beautiful chaos. There was artistry to its creation, rather than the rigid science of measured angles that dictated the peasant homes of her village. *Sorcery could defy the need for proper supporting arches and sensical angles*, was all she could surmise.

The crystal vine behind them spat out another, though he landed so much more gracefully, his nimble feet catching him so that he never even fell. It was obvious he must've had practice at it, his cloak twirling as he smiled.

She recognized him instantly as the annoying elf upon the roof.

"You made it, huh?" he remarked.

She resisted the urge to roll her eyes. "Yes, and all in one piece, it would seem." She wasn't sure if she was more bitter at his help or his attitude, but it was likely equal.

With a bit of a twirl he dove in rather close to her – borderline inappropriately so – flashed her a wink and then reached back over his head. It looked like he was about to rip his own hair out, but then she saw a curious transformation take place.

He was no longer the rude elven youth from the roof, but the messenger who had first delivered her the scroll. "You passed the test," he said. "Not with flying colours, but, well…" he shrugged and smiled, "few do."

Her nose twitched as she stared at him.

Definitely being deceived. That was what made her most bitter.

"Yes, well. Give me a year or two in this place," she responded tartly but with a confident smile. Her back straightened as she glanced about them once more. "I'm sure there will be colours."

The impish elf clapped his hands and laughed: "Welcome to Gaul'di-mere Academy! It's a long road ahead," and he gave a politely deferential nod to Firia, "especially for some, but your new life starts right now. I hope you have said goodbye to all you knew, for you shall not have the ability to see your old life again for a very long time. And I wager by the time you do, you shan't much care to any longer!"

He gave a somber smile and lowered his hands. "The road of sorcery has a way of changing you. And you find in the end you have new dreams and aspirations. But don't fear that! It's part of growing up as well."

He certainly wasn't this perky earlier, and it made Firia cross her arms and stare at him suspiciously. With a raised brow she looked to Mae'lin, then back to the messenger. "I didn't have much to say goodbye to, honestly." Except her father. She tried to push the thought away once more. This is what children do, they grow up… and follow in their family's footsteps.

Yet she had to be persistent and escape that lot. He'd been so happy, but what would happen to him now?

She felt herself start to well up and forced her gaze away. "Yes, well. Thanks for the help getting here."

"Part of my duties!" he said with a flick of his wrist. "I'm your senior-student advisor for the next while. So if you two have any questions, you can take them to me." He turned and began to walk, calling out behind his shoulder as he traversed the crystal pathway, "Preferably as we walk!"

Mae'lin's eyes widened, and he looked to her then went off after the other elf. "So you're like… a high ranking student or some such?" he asked.

Firia rolled her eyes behind the other man as she straightened her sac on her back. Still, she was here, and not even a trickster could make her forget that as she quickly trailed after him.

"I'm an assistant professor in fact," the dashing elf said with a smile over his shoulder as they set off across that massive tree-bridge, the wood creaking and groaning beneath her feet, giving her the distinct impression it was less sound than was safe. "I'll officially become a professor in my own right soon in fact," he said with a dashing smile and cursory gaze towards Firia that held a certain curious feel.

She crinkled her nose at it, but tried to relax. Seeing her house from so high had affected her more than she could admit. It was as though she realized just how far away she'd be, the reality of it sinking in, and it was marring the amazement and joy of the moment. She felt like running to her room and hiding in her corner, and she hadn't done that since she was a toddler.

She reached inside herself, searching for some reassurement. Some warmth.

It was faint, so very faint, but she felt the tiniest of responses inside herself. So vague, but yet so familiar. Despite how new Varuj and she were to one another, she couldn't mistake that feeling for anything else.

The chatty guide led them to the immense front gates and before them they swung slowly open, revealing a great courtyard within. The sight of the beautiful trees and flowers, the intricate carvings of the pillars and archways, then the doors to the various sections of the magical academy were all so much to soak in at once.

There seemed no end to the wonders Firia faced in her new life.

A flock of curious birds, with long legs and magnificent beaks fluttered past and out the gates, leaving a wake of glittering powder in their wake.

"You two aren't carrying much," came the voice of their guide again, breaking her enthrallment with the place. "So if you care to I can show you around a bit before taking you to your rooms. Most of the new arrivals are carrying so many bags it's obscene," he said with some amusement.

"Benefits of getting stuck with the poor kids, I guess," Firia replied sardonically, winking at Mae'lin. "I'm up for sight-seeing, I suppose." She wasn't, but at the same time, she wasn't sure she wanted to be alone, either.

Mae'lin hesitated, but when he did smile back it was a warm, tender one.

Their guide carried on, waving them ahead in his finery. "We'll just make a quick trip around to some of the places you'll need to be familiar with in your first semester here," he declared cheerfully, a bit of a hop to his step.

Leading them to a pair of large double-doors that once-again opened without his touching them, he declared, "Here is the most important place of all: the food-a-torium!" A strange name for so magnificent a hall, as the beautiful marble floor was simply stunning, with its seemingly endless pictographed story of ancient magical accomplishments and its great columns of ancient wood, carved into magnificent shapes and arches that she'd never seen done with wood crafting before.

The tables, seemingly endless, in so many different sizes and with seats all about, and booths to the side, seemed ready to seat hundreds.

She was beginning to feel more and more out of place surrounded by such opulence. For so long she'd dreamed of this, envisioned it, but it was never really a place. It was a library, a classroom at times, but it was never so cohesive and amazing as all this.

"Food-a-torium?" she asked after a moment.

"That's right!" he declared with a smile.

Mae'lin broke in with uncharacteristic forcefulness, "You're just trying to make us look silly when we say that to someone."

He looked about to argue but then waved a hand. "You got me!" He rolled his eyes and sighed, "Moving on then!" he declared as he began to turn and take them to the next building.

Firia grinned at Mae'lin, and felt a genuine sort of affection for the man. He'd been so decent to her, not like the other elves. It was a nice change of pace.

She got a bit of a bashful look in response from the lanky elf, but he smiled sheepishly as they were taken into the next grand segment of the academy.

It was less impressive than the rest, but it was still beyond anything she'd known before that day. It was a massive hallway, with stairways leading up and up. At the center there was just a big ovular opening that showed the numerous levels and doorways.

"This is the introductory spell hall. This is where you'll be going for the bulk of your studies for some time to come," he said plainly, looking back at them. "Make sure you remember your way here, because the real challenge will be finding the particular room you're after!" He crooked a corner of his lips up in a mischievous manner.

No matter how much she liked magic, she still had a distaste for pranksters. She took her craft – and herself – quite seriously, and endeavoured never to lose her way. She looked around with revived interest, trying to commit it all to memory.

From there he led them down a narrow pathway and out into a lovely garden area, "And just through here," he stated as she was mesmerized by the cat-sized dragonfly that slowly hovered on by, "we have... the library."

At that she couldn't help but tear her gaze away from the startling beauty of the many exotic flowers, oversized yet harmless insects, and fluttering birds to see the great gates open and reveal something much closer to what she'd dreamt of.

The Academy library was bigger than even the dining hall, so very large and reaching up immensely high, such that it had to be one of the tallest portions of the whole castle structure itself, if not the tallest.

The main hall itself was full of people passing through, great desks and tables about, though even still there were bookshelves, and up above she could see the next level where there were only books on display. It kept going up, though, and she couldn't really make out the end of it all.

This.

This was where she belonged.

It was as though everything had just been filler until she finally arrived at her place, and that broad smile announced to the world she'd discovered it. All her worries and fears slid aside as she found her place to hide. To live.

"Wow…"

"Wow is right," mirrored Mae'lin beside her, gaping nearly as much as she.

Their guide tried to break the moment, however, and shooed them both back towards the door. "You'll have time for this later. The library remains open around the clock. Though introductory students such as yourselves have a curfew. And speaking of… we should head back to your residence so you can get accustomed to it," he said, sweeping in between them and back off through the garden.

"Curfew?" She almost laughed at the thought. She was a perpetual night owl, as much as she could be with school. Not to mention the idea of being so close to the library and not being allowed in seemed a bit torturous. "When?"

"You'll know," he said with another one of his mischievous smirks. "The Academy takes such things very seriously. So it's not something you'd need to worry about until the time comes."

With so cryptic an answer he just continued to trot along, heading towards another building. This one looked almost… quaint, when compared to the rest of the great castle-academy. It had a stone and wood exterior, and looked almost like a great, faerie-tale cabin, magnified many fold, of course.

The wooden doors creaked open and she saw a mighty hearth, surrounded by sofas and relaxing seating areas. "This shall be your residence hall," he said to them, and the inviting warmth and calmness in there was hard to miss.

She still didn't trust the elf and his mischievous manners, but her curiosity won out over her caution, as it so often did. Stepping in, she inhaled deeply, as if trying to acclimate herself to the new smells and sensations of her "home".

No matter how strange the whole place had been, and how jarring the experiences of the day, she couldn't deny how very inviting the place was. How warm and welcoming it seemed.

Until she saw the visage of that well-dressed human she'd seen steal her thunder at the competition. He stood up before the fire, looking so calm and confident, having apparently been chosen for the same academy as she despite everything.

"With that, I'll give you time to settle in," their guide said with a calming smile. "You'll find your rooms at opposite ends of the hall," he indicated, pointing down each way. "And yours," he looked to Firia, "is up on the second floor. You'll know which one, don't worry."

She stared at him with a furrowed brow. "And why's that?"

"Wait and see," he said with a shrug and a half-smile. "The name's Gway'lin. Remember that if you need anything!" He abruptly vanished, as if pulled through some pinhole-sized gap in reality itself, leaving them standing there by themselves.

Though the display brought the attention of the sole other human there and the elvish woman he spoke with, the two moving towards her.

"So you're the one," he remarked, his dark, hazel eyes studying her curiously up and down. "You put on that big show that had everyone talking, hm?"

Why did she suddenly feel like a cornered rabbit? All of her social anxiety crept back into her and her cheeks already started to redden. "I don't know," she muttered, wishing she hadn't put her black hair into a ponytail. She figured it'd be easier for travelling, but now she wished for nothing more than a veil to hide herself.

She leaned her head down a bit and let her bangs shield her eyes. Just a tad.

"She put on an amazing display," proclaimed Mae'lin with a smile, as if her accomplishment were as much his as hers.

"So I hear," he said, brushing back his own hair and scrutinizing her a bit. He took his time, but then he extended his hand, palm-up: "The name is Bran. Bran Thornson."

This was supposed to be her fresh start, surrounded by others just as passionate as her.

Firia's eyes slowly dragged their way up his body before resting on his hand. She forced her own palm into it, surprised by her actions. It was pure force of will that she was able to grasp his hand in hers. "Nice to meet you. Firia Tunst. You almost cost me my chance."

Bran's eyes went wide with surprise at her remark.

Her mouth gaped with shock. Why had she said that? That was the last thing she should have said, and immediately her cheeks turned beet red. "I mean..." She tried to recover. "I saw your show. It was awesome..."

To her remark he smirked gently and gave her hand a gentle squeeze. "Ahh, that explains it then, does it? You had to pull out all the stops to make sure you were noticed after my little show, is that what you're saying?" he questioned with an expectant gaze.

"They thought they met their token human quota," she admitted, but her voice was so much smaller in her embarrassment. She bit her lower lip as if to forcibly stop herself from saying something stupid again.

Bran gave a derisive curl of his nose then reached out and patted her hand in his. "Well done, all the same. I just wish I was there to see it, instead of in the tent negotiating for my spot here." He was a confident young man, she had to confess, and it made his own rugged good looks stand out all the more.

With a clearing of her throat, the elvish woman beside him stepped forward and introduced herself. "Ala'nase," she said in her sing-song voice, so very elvish. She gave a short curtsey. "It's a pleasure to meet you."

What a beautiful name. She couldn't help but smile at it, though she tried to hide it. Still, it was like a song. Firia tried to curtsey in return, though it was hard to be graceful with the sac still on her back. "You too."

She almost patted herself on the back for not embarrassing herself again.

The sparkling smile the young elven woman gave made her more endearing than most of her kind. The long white-hair that framed her face accentuating her lovely, delicate features. "I did not take part in the competition, but I must say I am embarrassed to admit that. It seems all the truly promising young magicians were out there, showing off their abilities with daring-do, rather than taking the humdrum tests with me."

"Humdrum tests?" Firia grinned, "I don't know… I think that sounds a bit better."

Ala'nase laughed musically and smiled at her disarmingly, "Kind of you to say. Though I must admit," she said, leaning in and playfully batting at her arm, "I wasn't expecting the talk of the competition, who nearly turned her opponent to ashes, to be so… sweet."

"That's just gossip," Firia said, a bit too defensively. "I mean… Mae'lin's right here, and he doesn't seem mad so…"

As if just noticing him for the first time, Ala'nase's gaze travelled up to the lanky elf's with some surprise. "It was you she burned?!" she asked with more than a little excitement.

Mae'lin looked a bit taken aback at the whole thing. Flustered, he answered, "N-no! She didn't burn me at all," he stated as he adjusted the pack over his own shoulder. "We both got carried away in our competition, putting our all into it, and then… well, one of us won and suddenly all that power she'd conjured needed a place to go."

Ala'nase's slender eyes went wide and she gasped. "What a battle it must've been!"

"It wasn't really a battle," Firia smiled bashfully, shrugging her shoulders. "I mean… it was exciting but not a battle."

"That's not what I heard," said Bran with a grin.

Mae'lin shrugged and said, "Well… it kinda was. I mean… a battle of wills, if nothing else."

Ala'nase looked to Firia expectantly, as if excitement or disappointment hinged on her next statement.

Too much pressure and attention. Firia's stomach tightened, and she looked down at her feet. "Well, I mean… if that's what everyone's saying…"

The beautiful young elf laughed and put her arm around Filia's back. "I knew it! You're a champion, alright. And you even earned the friendship of the one you defeated. You're brilliant. Both of you!" she added on for Mae'lin's sake.

To which the lanky elf coughed and laughed awkwardly.

"Well he… beat me. I mean, I was disqualified temporarily…" Too much attention. Too fast! She had to take a deep breath.

Wait, an elf was touching her.

She looked to the other woman curiously, as if she was losing her mind.

The sparkling, silver-eyes of the elven woman met hers as she grinned with some excitement, though the curious moment with the eager elf was interrupted when a loud bell tolled and the hall's doors slammed shut. At the same moment she suddenly noticed as several other students were seemingly teleported in without notice, in various states of unreadiness. One spilling their books, another toppling over.

"What's happening?!" said Mae'lin, though they were all looking about in confusion.

Firia groaned. "He said we'd know when curfew hit. I guess this is how."

The three of her new classmates all looked to her and nodded with some appreciation at her having figured it out first. "That makes sense," muttered Bran.

"She's clever as well as powerful!" remarked Ala'nase, her caramel cheeks darkly hued.

It was all so overwhelming. She didn't think she'd ever spoken to so many people in her life, and her entire body felt so... antsy. She wanted to hide under the covers, but instead she forced a smile. "So we're bolted in for the night?"

"I guess so," murmured Mae'lin.

Bran looked around then pointed. "Some of them seem in a rush to get to their rooms."

Firia saw as some of the other students went off to their rooms, and Ala'nase said, "Do you think they'll be locking us in our rooms soon too if we don't go there?" Her silvery gaze falling upon Firia, as if she held the answers.

She groaned. "I wouldn't be surprised..."

It was so disorienting. Back in school no one paid her much mind, leaving her to the back of the class and her books. Now she was front and center, everyone's eyes on her.

"We should get to our rooms then," said Mae'lin, sounding a bit edgy under the new circumstances. "I'd rather not be zapped in there if I could help it."

Ala'nase looked to Firia and patted her shoulder. "I can show you the way to ours. We're in the same wing unless I'm mistaken. I've already found mine earlier," she said with a smile.

"Gway'lin said I'd know it. Whatever that means." She held onto the strap of her sac, waving gently to the other two. "Goodnight, then. Nice meeting you, Bran."

The two men looked to her and bid their farewells, Mae'lin with a simple wave and smile, Bran with a gentlemanly bow that looked like it was ripped directly from an elven manual.

Ala'nase led her on down the hall towards the stairs at the back, "Oh you'll know it alright," she said to her as they climbed up. "It's a pretty neat system, all told. Though," she remarked, looking about, "this curfew thing is a bit much. I mean, we only just got here; a bit of a gentle touch wouldn't go awry, you know?"

"They're probably just showing us their power. You know, make sure we understand what they can do…" And Firia had no idea the depths those would go. The amount of knowledge she wasn't even aware that she didn't know…

As they came to the top of the stairs, Ala'nase led her down the hall, other women – mostly elves – heading to their rooms as they strode on by. "Mine's here," said the elf, gesturing to one of the shut doors. "I'd show you it, but… well, I haven't done anything yet, so it's the same as yours I'm sure. Now… which one is yours?" she asked, not looking around but directly at her.

Firia didn't know what to say, but then she caught glimpse of some light out of the corner of her eye and turned to see a glowing orb of light hovering by the door at the very end of the hall.

"I guess that one?" she asked, her finger pointing towards the door. "They do like to show off, don't they." Her lips tugged into a smirk despite herself.

Ala'nase's lips curved up at the corner, showing just how big a mouth she actually had. "You see the light too, huh?" she asked. "Seems like we only see the light for our own rooms. Cute trick, isn't it?" she said as she guided Firia to her door and stood back half a step, arms behind her.

Firia was paranoid, so far from her own playing field, but she was too excited to hold back as she pushed open the door.

Perhaps an elvish student might've been disappointed, but to her? The room was magnificent.

It had the same intricate carved-wood beams in the corners, the smooth stone walls, but it also had a very comfortable-looking bed that dwarfed hers back home in both size and quality. She also had a desk, chair, chest, dresser, mirror and clear area that looked intended for spell practice. All in all, it was more space than she'd had back at home in her own bedroom, and in much finer luxury.

She almost felt like crying, but she couldn't. Not with Ala'nase at her back.

Firia let the sac down to the floor and turned to look at her new friend, smiling genuinely. Now that it was just the two of them she felt less trapped and overwhelmed. "I guess this is it. Thanks for showing me the way."

The beautiful elven lady gave a salute while backing away deftly. "Glad to help you newbies," she said in a mock-pretentious voice, following it with a wink. "I'll catch you in th–"

With the sound of the bell she was ripped from where she stood, and from out of an open door further down the hall Firia heard the woman's voice carry out, "Aw damn."

She closed the door and smiled to herself, though the sense of creeping loneliness struck her before long.

After so much activity, it seemed odd to stand in the room in such complete silence. Her mind wandered to Varuj, her companion that still dwelled with her.

She tried to contact him without even realizing it.

Waited.

She felt that faint, barely noticeable warmth, but he didn't come. It worried her, she realized. He'd never refused to come to her before.

Maybe he couldn't, the thought occurred to her.

She had to put it aside though. If what was keeping her in her room was keeping Varuj where he was, it wasn't likely to be something she'd solve that night.

CHAPTER 18

The day began with another loud clang of the bell that resonated throughout the campus.

It had been a strange night for Firia, and it had taken a while for her to get to sleep. Despite the rather plush, comfortable bed that so outclassed her own, it was foreign to her, and she felt more than a little isolated where she was.

Though before she could finish preparing she heard a knock at her door. Upon opening it she saw the visage of her new elven associate, Ala'nase, a loose-fitting robe about her as she rubbed her eyes. "I can't believe they want us to get up so early," she groaned.

Firia's sleep schedule was completely screwed up, but her excitement had managed to make her seem a bit more chipper. "I guess we'll get used to it..." She opened her door to let her new friend in, almost nervously at first. "They didn't really go over the schedule very well, did they."

Ala'nase moved into her room with a great deal less finesse than Firia was used to seeing elves move with. She very nearly slumped!

"They didn't go over it with us at all, as far as I'm aware," she groggily stated. "Though I assume with how things are going, any moment now we'll be zipped off to something else without warning."

Firia let out a bitter laugh, nodding her agreement. "They do like showing off how little control we have over our bodies, don't they?"

Ala'nase nearly snorted her amusement. "They probably get quite the kick out of it," she said with a roll of her eyes. "Though I suppose we should make our way to the dining hall as soon as we can, or risk going without. Sounds like the kind of thing they'd love to do to us, to really hammer the lesson home, y'know?"

Firia was quickly getting the impression that Ala'nase was far less formal and eloquent than most elves of her stature.

It was refreshing to say the least, and as she put together the few things she thought she might need, she motioned towards the door. "Hopefully with any luck the food will be as opulent as the... food-a-torium." She grinned, hoping Ala'nase would get her joke.

The elf stared at her.

Then abruptly broke into a laugh. "Food-a-torium," she repeated before standing up and fixing her pale hair. "You want to head over with me once we freshen up then?" she asked.

"Sure. I think I remember the way." She always had been keen with directions, after all.

She could barely believe her luck, though. A friend. Who seemed really nice.

That was almost as exciting as starting her lessons.

CHAPTER 19

The pair arrived at the dining hall together, the taller elf on the lookout as she wore a rather fancy, elegant dress-robe that hung diagonally from her shoulder. "Hey, there's your friend," she said with a gesture, pointing out Mae'lin to her at one of the side booths, eating by himself.

Firia was far less impressive in her simple robe, but she'd done her hair in as elaborate of braid as she could muster. The last thing she needed was to look ratty on her first day.

"He's all by himself. We should join him."

Ala'nase set off without delay. "You two are close then, huh?" she asked with a raised brow as they made their way through the increasingly full hall, so many students bustling about for a table and meal.

"We just met. I mean… we went to school together but didn't talk until the competition. What about you and Bran?"

The elf simply shrugged then immediately turned her attention to Mae'lin, who still wore much the same thing he had on the day before, Firia noticed. "Hey you, trying to eat without us? That's not very nice," she said.

Mae'lin looked up with surprise, the lanky elf seemingly lost in thought as he ate. "Oh hey! I mean, morning!" he managed. "Take a seat or–" he looked, noticing they didn't have food. "Oh, you get your breakfast down there, if you didn't know," he remarked helpfully, pointing to where some of the students filtered to and fro.

"Watch my bag?" Firia asked the elf, surprising herself with a level of actual trust.

It was her chance to make changes, after all, and she really didn't want to be a social pariah. Again.

"Of course!" he said as the two of them went off to get their meal.

As Firia approached the twin doors that marked the coming and going of so many, she saw that there were the occasional familiars – similar to her own, but not quite – taking the place of some students, carrying trays all the way back to their masters at their tables.

"Well that's convenient," muttered Ala'nase a bit enviously.

"And lazy," Firia retorted. "I suppose everyone's trying to show off today. Make sure people know how great they are."

Her new friend laughed. "Maybe," she said as they made their way into the serving room. "Though if my parents were anything to judge by, magicians just tend to use their magic in place of everything after a while. Becomes a real pain to watch when you can't do the same, let me tell you."

The line moved quickly, and within mere moments, Firia found herself looking at an assortment of appealing breakfast dishes, all looking meticulously prepared and quite rich. Though, they were all behind glass and all single servings.

A glance ahead showed her how it was done, when she saw one of the senior students simply take a tray, hold it up and make a hand gesture at what he wished with it then forming upon his tray.

Firia had a passion for magic, for learning new spells, but the fact that it literally seemed that everything was done magically was jarring. She was so used to having to do everything herself that it was quite a culture shock.

She elbowed Ala'nase gently, motioning towards the older students.

Together they made their selections and ventured back to the table with Mae'lin. It was only her second day – her first day, really – at the academy, and already Firia had better accommodations, far better food, and more friends than she'd ever had. The realization dawned on her as she looked at the steaming food on her plate and the smiles of her two new elvish friends.

"How'd you two sleep?" asked Mae'lin, nearly finished with his own food already.

"I don't think I really did," Firia admitted sheepishly.

Ala'nase answered in a surly manner, "Not enough of it."

Mae'lin looked between them as he finished off his last wafer. "I got so excited practicing spells I made myself exhausted and passed out... I think."

Ala'nase looked over at Firia, then broke into soft laughter.

She grinned in return, looking down at her food before beginning to devour it with relish. Though still, years of eating small made her full far before she was finished. Her thoughts again returned to Varuj, and she wondered if she was starving him again.

She didn't know what was happening to him, or why he couldn't connect with her, but still. She pulled her sac close to her and carefully wrapped up her leftovers, placing them inside.

Mae'lin noticed the maneuver and looked to her. "That's a good idea," he said. "Pocket some for later." He stood up. "I'll be right back. Gonna get more." Despite his own lankiness, he seemed to have no shortage of an appetite.

As Firia watched the elf leave she spotted, off in the distance, the sight of Bran watching her from across the hall. Though shortly after their gazes met he lowered his eyes and focussed on his own food.

"I think I might have offended him last night," Firia murmured to Ala'nase. "Bran, I mean. Not Mae'lin."

Ala'nase looked around with some confusion before following Firia's gaze to the young man. "Really?" she questioned. "What makes you think that?" she asked in a bit of a conspiratorial tone.

Firia shrugged, a bit bashful. "I don't know. Maybe it's nothing." Just that she thought that, being two of the few humans around, they might stick together a bit. Until she had to open her big mouth and embarrass him.

Ala'nase, however, didn't let it go so easily. She squinted her ovaline eyes at the man, studying him intently, as if the mystery would be solved through deep staring. "He probably just has a crush on you," she conjectured after long hard "research", followed by a return to her meal.

"You're just saying that because we're both humans," Firia scoffed, but her face turned bright red and she tried to hide it from her new friend. "And why did you have to stare? Now he knows we were talking about him."

It was hard to refute that, for Bran had lifted his head and noted at least one of them staring at him. Ala'nase averted her eyes, but was far too late for cover-up.

"It's not just because you're both humans," she whispered to her with some urgency, just before Mae'lin returned. "Mae'lin's probably no different either," she said without the slightest hint of hiding it.

Firia's brows furrowed and suddenly she felt like the same shy girl she was all through school. She'd been doing so good to suppress that side of herself! But her throat was dry and she just wanted to run away once more. "I don't know what you're talking about."

Mae'lin looked between the two women. "What's going on? Did I miss something?" His eyes were wide with curiosity. Or was it confusion?

Ala'nase opened her mouth about to talk, but then glanced aside and saw Firia's embarrassment. "Oh nothing," she said in a very blasé manner. "I was just saying I bet you're hot for me, like all the rest." She gave a dramatic sigh and brushed her hair back over her shoulder. "It's a burden I carry," she said like a hammy actress.

To which Mae'lin stared between the two of them a while. "Uh, okay," he remarked, returning to his own thoughtfully disinterested pose.

The playful elf giving Firia a smirk and a "told you so" look, as if the young man's disinterest in her was somehow proof that he must be into Firia.

Firia rolled her eyes and grabbed her knapsack. "Well, I'll leave you two to that, then. Did… you two want to meet up later, maybe? Check out the library?

"Sure," replied the two of them almost in unison, though before another word could be said the tolling of that great bell happened again.

"Oh crap," muttered Ala'nase, while Mae'lin made a point of grabbing his own satchel up and shoving the food in quickly.

It was time.

She was almost knocked off her feet by the excitement, the need to go experience everything. The schedule felt so stifling but at the same time, she couldn't help but crave it.

Her next destination surprised her, however, and not all in a good way. For she appeared next before some of the powerful sorcerers that held her fate so callously in their hands naught but days ago, while standing in the middle of a great chapel-like auditorium, full of fellow students.

The raised platform, surrounded by great coloured crystal statues that towered high, were many senior-looking wizards and professors. She even noticed the aging human who had netted her a right to compete, and then her second chance.

"I can't wait for that to end," came a voice beside her, and Firia turned to see it was Ala'nase, with Mae'lin not far off. The three had been transported near one another, it seemed.

"Me too," Firia whispered back. It was kind of rude, and made her feel a little more than violated. Especially when dragged to a torture chamber.

"I kinda like it," said Mae'lin. "It's like a taste of the power to come!"

Ala'nase gave him a strange look, but before more could be said the rather severe-looking elf that had nearly cost her her place in the academy began to speak.

"Welcome students." His voice carried out over the room to everyone, as if spoken at a normal, conversation tone, by aid of magic. "For those of you joining us for the first time, you are perhaps having a period of adjustment."

His hawkish eyes scanned the room almost predatorily. "Note that Gaul'di-mere is famed amongst the magical academies, and it is because our students graduate as the best in their fields. And why are they the best?" He went on with little preamble, "Because we don't coddle them. They have to figure things out for themselves, and those who don't make the cut? Who can't decipher the mysteries of living at the academy? They eventually go home in failure, leaving only the best to graduate."

Firia had already assumed that much, since she couldn't even get to the academy without solving a riddle. Still, his condescending words made the hair on the back of her neck bristle and more than anything she wanted to show him up. To make sure he knew how wrong he was to brush her off.

"All of our professors come from amongst the brightest and most ingenious of sorcerers and sorceresses in the wide world. Most of them graduated from these very walls, but all went on to do great things, and now stand ready to pass some of that on to you.

"I won't waste a lot of time on introducing you to them now. As I said, Gaul'di-mere is an academy in which you sink or swim. And we embrace that," he declared with a broad grin. "By the time you leave here, you shall have your class schedule for the upcoming semester. Do not lose it. Nobody shall mark your attendance, but the first time you fail an exam, you shall be removed from the academy."

He paused for just a moment to look around at the students with a hard gaze. "Once you are removed from the academy, we recommend to the state that your magical ability is untamed, and should be restrained, for the good of all. Make no mistake, you were all brought here because you have aptitude and promise. But without proper training, those are two things which are a disaster for the wider world."

As he spoke she felt her stomach begin to knot and twist. The idea of being… restrained. Of having her power revoked…

Firia started to feel a bit queasy and regretted bothering with breakfast. She knew it was just a scare tactic, a way to motivate everyone to do their best, but failing one exam and that was it?

She'd had more grace on her entrance competition!

"You'll notice on your schedules that you have a great deal of empty time slots. Make use of it," and those words sounded almost grim. "Perhaps you got here because you were tutored in magic by a very regimented instructor who kept you on task. That is not our role. We are not your parents, and we don't need to particularly care if you succeed or fail. Your first day has been full of regimentation, as spells have zipped you about. You'll overcome that in time if you're a capable magic user.

"Let that be your first lesson: magical restrictions like that are for those too uneducated to overcome them. The only rules that matter are spoken or written down. Heed my words.

"Use your time wisely, visit the library, study, learn. Become better mages. Form questions and seek answers."

On a somber note he ended, "Now head out there. We shall give you all the tools one could possibly need to succeed. Make use of them, for if you fail, you shall have no one to blame but yourselves."

The great doors opened behind them and light flooded on in.

It was gut wrenching and terrifying and motivating all at once, and Firia's body felt almost stiff as she digested it all. She'd been staring so intently at him that when the doors opened she had to blink away the brightness.

She wasn't sure entirely how she felt about the school's policies.

One thing she was certain of, though, is that she refused to fail.

124

CHAPTER 20

Class let out, and Firia couldn't help but be annoyed at the chatter between Bran and Ala'nase. The two never shut up from the moment the aged professors ended the lessons to the start of the next. Every day the same thing.

It wouldn't have been so bad, except she was utterly lost. The first day of classes had been a complete wash for her, nearly. The professors had mostly made such sweeping assumptions of the students base knowledge on magic that it was all two or three steps ahead of where she was.

As the two chatterboxes continued on, she noticed the rather sickly look upon Mae'lin's face. For a second she might've thought she was looking into an emotional mirror.

It made sense. She figured he had to have come from a background more similar to hers than the pampered upbringing of the other students. He seemed just as lost and confused as her, and didn't have the knowledge to read those mystical words either.

It was the first time she ever had actual friends, and she didn't know how to handle it. To try to tell them to be quiet.

To admit how utterly lost she was.

She shimmied closer to Mae'lin, leaning up to whisper in his ear. "Want to hit the library with me?"

The tall, lanky elf looked to her a bit wide-eyed and lost but nodded all the same. "Yeah, let's go." She knew just how powerful and talented he was; after all she'd done magical battle with him, of a sort. Together they'd wowed the academy scouts, so they deserved to be doing better.

Before she could get away though, Ala'nase caught sight of her leaving. "Where you going? We're gonna go practice. Not coming?"

"Ah, no, not tonight." Why did she feel so sheepish about her lack of understanding? She was used to always being bright. Promising.

Exceptional, in her own way.

Now it was sink or swim, and everyone else already had the lessons.

The library was massive. She could tell as much upon first sight, but she really had no idea just how sprawling it truly was. It seemed to dwarf even the towering facade, as if it defied reality itself to encompass so great a repository of knowledge.

Such as it was, despite how many students came to partake of the knowledge there, she never had any issue finding a quiet corner. There were many private study nooks, and Mae'lin and she were able to settle in together.

"I had no idea they would expect us to know so... much," he said with some disbelief, as if his life were crumbling before his very eyes upon his palms.

"Me neither," Firia lamented. "And it feels like we're the only ones that can't understand every other word we're being told. How did they have the time to learn so much growing up?"

Mae'lin ran his hands over his hair, shaking out the blonde spikes, but only making it a little more erratic and wild-looking. It looked good on him, truth be told. "I don't know. I was always working in the fields, making sure the harvest was in on time. My mother basically handed it to me completely until my brothers grew up." He sighed a little. "Are we too far behind, Firia?" His emerald eyes looked to her hopefully.

"I'm not going to give up magic, are you?" Firia retorted, her voice taking on a hard edge.

There was a moment's pause as what she said sunk in, then he shook his head firmly. "There's no giving it up. If I don't make it here, then I'm…" he blushed a little, "I'd have to go back home and be a farmer for the rest of my days. That'd be the best thing I could hope for…"

"I'd be a groundskeeper, so we're both just going to have to suck it up and catch up, alright? If we didn't have the skills, we wouldn't be here, right? So we're just going to have to, once more, struggle to get what the rich kids get for free."

She was surprised by how determined and strong she sounded, for she felt defeated. She couldn't even contact Varuj with all the latent magic in the air and whatever spells they'd used to bind them. She was surprised by how lonely and quiet she felt inside.

Mae'lin went quiet a while, the two of them nestled in their nook together. "How do we learn this stuff though? I mean… if it were that easy…" He furrowed his smooth, fair brow in thought as he stared off. "We were amazing together," he abruptly stated, quickly blushing thereafter as he looked to her then away. "I mean… our magic was. At the competition."

Her skin tingled with warmth and her face began to pinken but she nodded all the same. "It was one of the best things I've ever done. And I don't want them to take that away from me. So I don't know how I'm going to do it, but we'll figure it out together, alright? We won't sit with them tomorrow."

Somehow that made the worry drain from his face before her very eyes. The curiously handsome face took on a pleasant demeanor as he smiled to her so warm and genuinely. With a nod he said, "I'm glad we've become such good friends, Firia. This place…" he took a glance aside, "It'd be too intimidating to go it alone, I think."

"Yea, I'd probably be having scheduled panic attacks," she agreed with a wry smirk. "I'd say since we can't even read the word 'read', that that's probably the best place to start. After all, it was our mini-entrance exam."

Mae'lin laughed softly at her, his whole demeanor back to a more usual glow of pleasantness thanks to her. "We'll grab us some books on translation and practice together," he said, rising up and looking determined. "We'll catch up to them and in no time we'll put them all to shame," he extended a hand out to help her up.

She took it and her eyes widened at the shock that passed between them. Her breath hitched but she quickly recovered. "Damn right, Mae'lin. They'll chat so much that they won't know what hit them when we're casting circles around them. I'd say our first goal should be lifting these stupid spells."

With a chuckle he grinned. "Already skipping past the learn-a-whole-new-language part in your head, huh? You do move fast." He flushed a little after saying it, then realized he was still holding her hand despite pulling her up to her feet.

She bit her lip as she slowly withdrew her palm from his. Her head felt so light and airy as her blue eyes met his emerald gaze. "It's just a language. How hard can it be?"

Mae'lin couldn't help but laugh.

CHAPTER 21

Time was of the essence; Firia knew that. She hadn't been able to speak with Varuj in so very long, and classes continued as she worked with Mae'lin to catch up. The two of them were working hard to learn the arcane symbols that the others took for granted, and they'd been able to glean enough to start making *some* sense of the classes, at least. Though she knew there was still so far to go.

As she headed off to meet with Mae'lin again, Ala'nase stopped her, the dark elf slipping in front of her, books in arm. "Where are you sneaking off to?" she asked with a curiously raised brow.

Firia noted the tomes her friend held and wondered if it was wise to be truthful. She paused as she thought it over before she finally shrugged. "To the library."

Ala'nase scrutinized her with that sceptical look that seemed like it might bore holes through stone once her magic prowess increased. "You're meeting with Mae'lin again, aren't you?" she asked.

"We…" Firia paused. If it was one thing she learned about the upper class elves was that they hated hearing that their fortune was given to them by luck and not prowess. "We're falling behind."

Ala'nase tipped her head back, those piercing eyes of hers locked on Firia as she continued her deep study of the young woman.

"I don't buy it," she said. "I think you two are rushing off to go make out in some corner of the library and do all those things you never could back in your farm town school house," she said brazenly.

Firia's eyes narrowed and for the first time she felt truly disappointed in the other woman. As if she was so heavily policed that she couldn't do that if she wanted to! She summoned and bound an entire demon and no one was the wiser.

"I'm being serious. I'm not... I don't have as much experience as you or Bran."

The elvish woman's head tilted to the side and a grin was slow to form there. "Yeah right," she said with humour in her face. "Run on then. But you know? We should make time to hang out and chat more still. Doesn't do good to ignore the rest of your friends for Mae'lin," she said with eyes wide as she backed away at an increasing pace.

"I just don't want to be kicked out," Firia called after her, loathing how whiney her voice sounded. Still, she hated to have her new friend feel neglected and all the way to the library she felt distracted and forlorn.

She missed Varuj. If he was around he could help speed this all up.

The faint tingle of his presence within her reminded her he was there, but she'd still not been able to find a way to circumvent whatever magic seals kept him from being able to break out again. Was he starving, trapped as he was? Lonely? He had to be frustrated with his position. She knew she was, and she was free to wander.

She came upon Mae'lin in their usual spot, already engrossed in the work. He was copying some of the runic letters into his own pad as he smiled up at her. "We're making good progress I think," he said with such glowing optimism. He'd never let her down by surrendering to defeatism again after that first time.

She plunked herself down and even though she felt miserable, she endeavoured to lose herself in her studies. To work as hard as she could.

To free the demon once more.

"I hope so. It's getting tiring being yanked home just when things are getting good, though," she lamented and then paused.

She'd called it home.

Mae'lin seemed to have caught that remark too and he smiled at her with his head tilted. "You're really liking it here, huh?" he asked, never ceasing his work as he jotted down the notes. Her study partner was almost as diligent and dedicated as her; she had to give him credit.

"Well… sure. I mean, it's not like living back there was ever easy or stress-free. And I've always put this kind of pressure on myself, so not much has changed except now I actually have a chance. I never figured I did before."

The tall elf studied her a while, seeming to have found some deeper appreciation of her and who she was. "I didn't realize it had been that hard on you," he said softly. "I mean… I always struggled, but never quite like this. I just…" he looked around, "I just wanted something more *me* than being a farmer."

"You already are." She smiled at him. "Not many farmers around here. And not many elves that have as good of attitude as you, so be grateful you weren't spoiled."

He laughed, but it was slightly bemused. "If I was like them I'd be able to just teach this stuff to you," he said, holding up the book briefly. "Would be much easier going than having to learn it with you. Or… more accurately, struggling to keep up with you," he said with a wry smile.

"If you were like them, you wouldn't want anything to do with me," she corrected, not looking up from her book.

Those green elvish eyes of his lingered on her. "I can't see how that could ever be true. You've always been the talk of the class, and… I've always wanted to get to know you. I doubt that would change if I were a little snootier. Didn't stop the others from craving information about you."

She stopped, her brows furrowed in confusion as her blue eyes finally rose from the page. "No one cares about the groundskeeper's girl. They just thought I was weird."

With a crooked smile he shook his head and lowered his gaze to his book, but not entirely. He still stole glances at her now and then. "They thought you were mysterious. Clever. And very pretty. They just didn't like to admit those things, so they'd try to hide it by poking fun."

Her nose crinkled.

She'd spent all her years growing up on the outside, feeling isolated and alone. She had so little support, especially after her mother died, and never did she feel like anyone cared about her. About her wants or desires.

She figured they'd sooner watch her fail than help her succeed.

She was just about to argue when she realized he'd said they thought she was pretty and immediately she shook her head. Lowering her gaze to the book, she muttered into it, "You're just saying that."

Things went quiet a moment, but he piped up again. "They'd always tack on 'for a human', but you could see what they meant. I mean… they'd blush or stammer their words after." He laughed. "I called them on it once. Told them to either start treating you nice or simply get over their crush and stop obsessing. They didn't speak to me for weeks after that."

She barely knew what to say. Instead she stared at him and hoped that she wasn't gaping.

Her heart beat faster and she didn't even really understand why. It wasn't like she cared about the people in her class. She'd been with them for so many years and barely talked to any of them.

But the way Mae'lin was looking at her made her flush deepen.

The elf cleared his throat and lowered his head to his book again. "I wanted to talk to you too," he said after a long silent gap. "But I was just too shy," he confessed. "I figured with how cruel the others could be you wouldn't want to speak with me anyhow." The red in his cheeks obvious even with his face ducked down.

"You spoke to me at the competition, though."

With a shrug of his shoulders he said, "I didn't know if I would ever see you again. And… and after the last day of classes when I…" He struggled then said, "Never mind."

"You can't start then expect me not to want to know the rest," she pressed, though she wasn't certain. Did she want to know the rest? Her body felt so warm and prickly as she stared at him. She needed to know. That was why she was here. She needed to know everything she could.

She licked her lower lip, finding it so dry.

His eyes flickered to her, but he couldn't maintain the gaze before he stared back into his book. "I determined that I would approach you on the last day of classes, and ask… and try…" he coughed, clearing his throat. "I would talk with you. But… I chickened out," he confessed sadly. "So when I saw you at the competition I knew… I knew it was my last chance, for real. That I couldn't blow it. And I guess… with all the courage I had summoned up for the competition…" He trailed off and licked his lips, his own seeming so dry. The two awkward youths trying to talk so.

Her lips quirked at the side, her eyes narrowing, "And you were still willing to kick my ass to get in here."

Mae'lin raised his head and stared at her with shock. "I couldn't throw the competition! My dreams all rested on it!" He cleared his throat. "Besides… it'd be insulting to you if I did," he added as he lowered his head.

She smiled, feeling a bit more comfortable as she gave him a stern nod. "Well, that means that we're going to have to both work as hard as possible so we don't get kicked out, huh? I mean, I'm the one that ended up assaulting you to get in here, right?"

With a grin he nodded to her slowly. "I knew we were alike the day you nearly burned me to ashes to get into the academy," he retorted with an attempt to hide his smirk.

"If what you said is true, it's probably less dangerous for you to be burned than for me to be a drowned rat. It'd ruin my image."

Mae'lin's eyes widened then he laughed and shook his head. "I don't know that you could've done anything that would make you seem less mysterious to them," he remarked, smiling so happily that his mouth hung open.

She didn't know where she got the courage to even banter with him, and it was almost as though recognizing that made her clam up. She felt so warm and sticky under her clothing, and there was an excited buzz that she couldn't quite place.

"Get to work," she managed, but she almost felt like floating!

With a grin, Mae'lin nodded and gave one of those peculiar elvish salutes. "Yes ma'am." He couldn't help but smile though, and look over at her once more before returning to his studies.

CHAPTER 22

The grass fields were so full, it was nearly time for harvest. Firia could recognize it, as she'd lived in that country long enough to tell by the simple feel of the air alone. It was where she was born and grew up, after all.

The warm wind washed over her face and she heard, in the distance, a curious sound of approaching feet. When she opened her eyes again she saw it was Mae'lin. Bare-chested and wearing his work pants, she could see every outline of his leanly muscled physique. He'd just come from working his farm. There was a sheen of perspiration on his body, and the way his muscles bulged from a day of strain and effort were so pronounced.

"What are you doing here?" he asked, and instead of feeling awkward or out of place, it felt so incredibly… right.

She wasn't sure she spoke. Not really. It was almost as if something was passed between them, said without the need for words and she smiled. She felt so much lighter than usual, as if her worries had dissipated and left her free of the burdens of reality.

She didn't realize how much they were weighing her down.

Lowering himself down onto the field with her, Mae'lin rested on one side right next to her. "I was hoping you'd drop by," he said so casually. "I was thinking about you all day. And some of the guys dropped by, they were asking about what was going on between us," he said with a bit of a grin as he reached an arm over her waist with a certain familiarity and closeness that felt so natural.

She felt a buzz of excitement and realized she wasn't wearing the usual heavy, hand-me-down robe she was so fond of. Instead it was something lighter, more suited to her mood, and it ruffled against his hand. "What did you tell them?"

The grin on his face grew as he leaned in closer. "That I was going to propose," he stated so warmly, so boldly, "but that you would probably refuse me." It was like the words, though so exciting, were expected. It made her heart beat faster, her skin flush, but it felt… right, and he closed the gap between them and pressed their lips together, his tongue dipping into her mouth as their eyes shut and the world vanished.

Her arms went around his neck, and she his body pressed against hers. He tasted so sweet, so warm, and she felt that spark of electricity travel between them once more.

It only increased as he moved tighter to her, his hard, hot body so primed from a day's labour pressing against her as he moved down atop her form. It felt so right. His kiss so skillful, so… passionate! It grew in intensity and she felt him grind down against her until their mouths broke and…

Varuj looked down upon her. "Have you forgotten me, Firi?" he asked, sounding a little hurt. Wounded.

She blinked, startled from the pleasantness of her surroundings, of her company.

Instead it had warped and she suddenly felt wracked with guilt.

Why?

She shook her head, but words wouldn't come. It wasn't the free flowing sensation she had with Mae'lin where she knew he understood her. This was the silence of shame, of trying to hide from the questions the demon posed.

There was still the heat and hardness of his body pressed against her, his bare chest upon her in her light dress. "I can't hold on forever, Firi," he said sadly. "I'm counting on you to get me out," he pleaded.

She looked away in her shame. She'd wanted to help him, but failed. Then to be caught in such a private fantasy...

He kissed her again upon her neck, soft and pleasing, so caring and romantic. "Use what I taught you," he husked lowly. "I gave you the tricks you need to free me. Just... use what I taught you. Please. I miss you so much," he confessed in a low voice. "I long for your company."

She missed him too. The isolation was so great at night, when she was trapped in her room. Yet when she was out and studying, she couldn't bring herself to think of him. Of the loneliness she was so desperate to escape.

"I don't know how," she whimpered, but the feeling of his body was so pleasant. She could feel every bit of him, every thud of his heart, every breath.

"I'm trying, but I don't understand."

His sweet, hot lips moved across her neck to her ear, and she felt him suckle upon the lobe. "You have what you need, you don't need to know," the words a bit raspy but full of desire. She felt his strong hands move across her form, touch her thigh and slide up it, taking the dress with it. "You have the key to free me, Firi. Don't let me down when I need you most." The curl of his tongue took the bite off his words, the sensuous movements of his hand and mouth so mesmerizing, so pleasurable...

She'd been making it so much more complicated than it needed to be. Figured she needed to learn a spell, a way to unbind herself from the academy's bondage.

Yet even those thoughts began slipping away as she felt the demon's hands and lips move against her flesh. Her body was on fire as she whimpered beneath him, half-heartedly trying to move away but she didn't want to. Not really.

"I miss you," he rasped as his hand moved beneath her dress and across her thigh. "I need you," he added with a husk as his fingers rubbed over her panties to such glorious effect, the other hand clasping her petite breast and squeezing ever so pleasantly.

She squirmed and a moan escaped her against her will. "No," she breathed out but she didn't want him to stop.

She simply didn't want to like it so much.

To feel so uncomfortably warm, a heat emanating from her core and igniting as his fingers moved against her clothed sex.

He didn't stop, but the sensations, the touches, only got more pleasurable. The swell of heated man flesh only more appetizing. The press of his body only greater... and she trembled before opening her eyes and seeing him as he was when she'd first summoned him: giant, hulking, and terrifying. "I long for you, Firi," came his growling voice. "Don't betray me..."

She nearly fell out of her bed as she gasped awake. Her skin was burning and she threw off the blankets, needing the air, but it wasn't enough. She had to throw off her nightgown too, yet that somehow only made it worse. Her flesh felt so alive with sensations, with needs, and she whimpered as she begged her body to calm down.

She'd woken with such desire a few times before but never to such intensity. It felt so overwhelming and no matter which way she turned, she couldn't get comfortable. She was so confused by the dream, by what it meant.

Was that really Varuj?

Or just another of her fantasies?

The thought occurred to her that realistically, it was likely a mix of both.

Varuj had been seeming so much weaker inside her since she'd arrived, and his warming presence within her had only seemed to fade more with time. Did he even have the ability to influence her dreams like that anymore? Or had she waited too long to act?

Her thumb ran across the ring as she lay in her bed, staring at the ceiling. She mulled over what he'd taught her, what she'd seen, and wished he wasn't always so cryptic. Though the books had a habit of hiding their secrets as well, and she deciphered them in time.

There had only been time for him to teach and do for her a few things. He had bonded the ring to her, which had saved her at least once. Then there was the familiar... He'd taught her some tricks with it, how to command it...

She remembered searching the old civic building on her trip to the academy. She'd simply asked the familiar to search out some sense of magic, then to find the flaw in the stone she needed. Could she command the ethereal minion to find whatever wards were keeping Varuj at bay and dispel them?

Standing up, she immediately did the motions bringing forth the conjuration, its shimmering light filling the room as the magical fox looked to her with swaying tail.

It was harder to concentrate, in some ways, because of her dream. Because of the way it made her feel. She only wore her panties, but of course, Luka was a part of herself and she felt no shame around it. The idea of putting clothes on her sweltering body was simply too much.

"Luka. Find what's keeping me in here."

The diligent familiar went to the task, and she watched as he snuffled about the room, seeming to pinpoint one place, then another. And another.

It wasn't until he had found several such points of interest that he yipped and turned to her, giving that subtle sign of affirmation that a job was complete.

She went to the last one he'd found, her hand moving behind his ears before she knelt to inspect it. A little security system. It made sense there'd be multiple points, she supposed, though she had no real knowledge of these things. "Good boy," she purred, stroking him tenderly.

The shimmering fox nuzzled against her arm and hand, the creature so closely linked to her own soul it craved her affection and approval it seemed, eagerly twining itself up against her ribcage.

She still didn't quite know what to do, to get rid of those invisible spots that kept him trapped.

For all others' talks of cleverness, there were times she felt like she couldn't be more daft.

Varuj had taught her how to command the fox in many various tasks, how to retrieve things for her, how to change its shape so that it could better perform certain duties. He had told her the options were near limitless for her dear pet, and it'd help prove that by finding the wards so effectively.

Luka raised its front paws onto her knees and brushed its nose up against her collarbone trying to get her attention.

It occurred to her then.

"Remove the wards, Luka," to which the fox immediately yipped and bounced down from her lap.

It was a curious sight then. The familiar sat in the middle of the floor and before her very eyes seemed to begin to unravel. The strands of light coming apart as he swirled and increased in size, but not density. She could feel the magic all around her, Luka versus the academy's defenses.

It swayed and shifted, but only barely. The wards were strong for the poor fox, and she could sense it wouldn't be a short or easy struggle.

As she waited and watched, it occurred to her that it would be awhile yet before Varuj rejoined her.

CHAPTER 23

The morning was going slowly. Firia was anxious to know when the seals would be broken and Varuj could return, but her obligations to study were unavoidable. She couldn't let anything interfere with that: not her tiredness, or her confused feelings from a night of curious dreams. Though as the elderly wizard demonstrated at the front of the class for them, one thing that began to draw her attention was the feeling of being watched.

She drew her focus from the lesson for a moment and caught Bran, a row ahead of her and to her right, watching her with as much rapt attention as she gave her lessons. Unlike Mae'lin, however, he didn't look away shyly, or appear embarrassed. He smiled to her, confidently, the expression standing out amongst a sea of elves. He was, after all, the only one like herself she ever saw on a regular basis.

Her brows raised at him curiously, not sure what to make of it before she turned back to the teacher. Still her skin prickled with the sensation and she let her dark hair partially shield her face as she tried to take her notes.

It was hard concentrating, knowing you were being watched. It was an odd sensation of being out of control, of awareness of just how visible she was, and it made her heart race.

Once the class ended, Bran met her as she exited the room. He was a big man, not quite so tall as Mae'lin, but a bit broader, as human's normally were. "You never let anything pass you by without studying and absorbing it, do you?" he remarked as they walked, a smile on his face as he looked to her.

"I try not to," she agreed, her lips turned up gently as she glanced to him. "I can't imagine it's that interesting to watch."

He was very different from Mae'lin, he didn't flush or shirk her looks. He seemed to embrace her attempt to embarrass him. "You're the only other human I get to see regularly," he remarked. "And you're very special. You'd have to be to get in here, after all. So that means we have some major things in common," he pushed open a door for her in a gentlemanly sort of fashion, leading out into the sunny day outside.

She laughed lightly. "Well that must mean you think you're pretty special too. They couldn't wait to get you enrolled, after all."

With his chin up he moved back beside her as they went. "I am," he remarked with full confidence. "Like I said, we're both very special. If we weren't, how could we have gotten here, huh?" He brushed his arm up beside hers, walking so closely beside her as they went. "It makes sense to stick together. Two magically-inclined humans, with the ability to show up elves much older than us. That's noteworthy."

She was partially just glad he wasn't holding it against her that she'd been so bitter about him at first and so gave a quick nod. "Well yea. Though if I don't study my ass off, well... they'll have no trouble getting rid of just another stupid human who couldn't make the cut, I'm sure."

With a derisive sneer Bran looked off ahead for a moment. "Well we won't let that happen, will we?" he remarked so firmly. "Firia," he said looking to her as he took her arm and pulled them both to a stop. "We should make an alliance. You and me, sticking through this together. I can help you," he stated, looking at her with his confident gaze. "Ala'nase said you don't have the kind of formal training the rest of us do. So I could give you a boost while we're at it."

She bit her lower lip, her eyes narrowing a bit. "Ala'nase was talking to you about me?" It wasn't like it had been confidential, but still she was embarrassed that anyone knew she was struggling, let alone having it talked about behind her back.

With a nod he said, "I asked her why you were spending so much time with that elf, Mae'lin. She assured me it was just to try and catch up." He smiled confidently and reached out, taking her arm by the wrist and lifting it gently. "Meet with me at lunch. I know a quiet place off behind the library. I can help you a bit," he said with such calm authority.

She stared up at him, scrutinizing his face as she thought it over. She was so far behind, but her pride was holding her back. Making her want to not admit to her struggles.

"Mae'lin and I usually study during lunch," she shrugged.

"But what can he teach you that I can't?" he remarked with a raised brow, sliding his fingers down to her palm, holding her hand. "There's no way he can understand what it's like for one of us." He bent down and kissed the back of her hand in a gentlemanly fashion. "I'll see you behind the library, Firia," he said with a confident smile, turning and heading off.

She sighed, resisting the urge to roll her eyes. She shouldn't be so ungrateful to people willing to help, she reminded herself, but it was still no less embarrassing.

At least she'd be able to teach Mae'lin whatever Bran taught her.

CHAPTER 24

With the first exam of the semester fast approaching, Firia couldn't afford to turn down help. Especially since she didn't know whether Varuj could be freed in time.

So as planned, she went to the back of the library as instructed by Bran. There was nothing of note there, just a few bushes and trees near the wall. Was it truly where he wished to meet?

When her classmate emerged from betwixt the bushes he gestured for her to follow before vanishing back between.

It was one of the most curious sights she'd seen in a while, and she'd been at a magical academy for some time.

Following after him, instead of the strange little hidey-hole on the other side of the bushes she'd expected to find, she instead found herself standing in a beautiful grove, at the heart of a lush forest. Flowers everywhere, birds chirping and…

"Welcome," came Bran's voice, as he stood by a lovely little picnic setup. Blanket and basket at his feet, a great assortment of food ready for her.

Firia was impressed, she had to admit. Her smile spread across her cheeks as she placed her books down atop the blanket, shrugging her bag off after it. "Alright, this seems a little more than what I figured for some homework help," she grinned.

"It's a nice time together with the only other human you know anymore," he said with a cheerful smile, gesturing to the blanket. "I figured if I could share this secret with anyone, it'd be you, Firia."

"Well, thanks," she said as she sat down, crossing her legs beneath her heavy robe. She'd been fretting about it all morning, about what he knew. About how much she could admit to him. Everyone kept saying she was so special, but coming here had made her feel anything but. She was struggling just to understand things that the other students had been taught since they were kids.

"I mean, it is really nice here. How'd you find it?"

Seating himself beside her, he laid out the offered food. "I knew where to look," he said with a wry grin. "Though, might I add, you look lovely today, Firia," he remarked with a confident smile as he looked to her.

Unlike those she grew up with, Bran had a certain air of formality about him, something that seemed to come from training, or at least practice.

She suppressed a self-disparaging laugh, pulling her book into her lap and opening it up, even as she looked to the food with interest. She was surprised how much her appetite had grown since being surrounded by food. She still couldn't eat a lot at once, but she felt like she was constantly chewing something.

"You really went all out." She ignored his complement entirely, seeing it as just another nicety.

"It's nothing," he remarked without hesitation, beginning to snack. "Fortunately I had the apprenticeship of a magician before I came to the academy. It helped prepare me for the trials we face now. And as you know, our kind need all the help we can get, or else those elvish bastards will never let us live it down." He gave her a broad grin.

Her shoulders softened and she nodded gently. "How'd you manage to get that?" It was so beyond her reach growing up she'd never even considered it an option.

"A wizard took interest in me when I was young, I was told. So tutoring was covered for me, and I was placed in a magical immersion program. I was surrounded by elves, but everyone except us children were magicians of a sort. You can pick up a lot that way."

"I can only imagine." It sounded amazing, and she felt that dark jealousy turn in her stomach. He tried to act like they were the same, that they had to stick together, but she had far more in common with Mae'lin in that regards. Bran was just as pampered as the other elves, and the envy made her squirm.

They ate in quiet until Bran finally broke the silence. "You're still learning the arcane syllabary I see?" he asked, indicating her book.

"Uh..." she glanced down and felt her face redden. "Yea. It wasn't taught to me. Obviously, or I wouldn't be learning it now," she replied, flustered.

Bran looked a little surprised but then took her notepad from her and studied it. "Aha, here," he said, taking hold of her pen then correcting something. "I know technically it means 'consume,' but in practice it really means destroy. It's an important distinction," he said with a genuine smile. "I can help you learn this. It's like a second language to me now."

She studied the letter, pursing her lips to the side. "Well... good, because I'm pretty sure it needs to be a second language to me, like, last month. Or six months ago." It was so frustrating how far behind she was, and she took a deep breath.

With a laugh he got up then shifted across to sit beside her, shoulder to shoulder. "Well, I don't know if I can be that quick of a teacher, but... with some extra time and effort, I can get you there soon I think." With his strong jaw jutted out, he gave her a confident smile. "Now let's run through some practices," he said.

He was speaking *her* language, and she nodded eagerly. If there was one thing she excelled at, it was studying. Still, she had a lot of years to catch up on.

Lunch was too short for her liking, but as they finished up he smiled to her, handing back her book. "Meet me again tonight. We'll have a late dinner, just you and me," he stated firmly. "We can squeeze in a nice bit of time together before curfew kicks in."

She didn't argue, just gave him a nod. She felt like she was making some headway at least, and it was better than the blind leading the blind. She couldn't wait to show Mae'lin what she'd learned, and she smiled broadly at Bran. "Sure, alright."

Bran put a hand on her shoulder and guided her out the exit. Before rounding the corner he smiled and said, "We're in this together now. Remember that. I'll help you, and together we'll rise to the top of this place. The first human pairing to truly make a name for themselves in magic, that could be our future." He gave her a broad smile and a wink as he headed off, "See you tonight."

He really believed it. She let out a soft laugh of disbelief. Did his desire to see more humans represented in the Academy really mean that much to him? Still, it was quickly forgotten as she ran off to her next class, filled with excitement that she hadn't felt in far too long.

CHAPTER 25

The final class of the day always ended up being so trying. Firia paired off with Ala'nase for the practice assignment, the immense court giving plenty of room for the pairs of young magicians to work.

"Be warned, I have some practice at this," cautioned her friend as she held up her hands. The practice for the day was with telekinesis, and using it upon another sorceress. "It's kind of like arm wrestling. We practice our strength against one another, except the goal isn't to win here. The goal is to push ourselves as hard as we can without overpowering the other."

Of course Ala'nase would have practice with this. It was getting so discouraging being surrounded by people who had so much more experience and knowledge than she. Part of her found it inspiring, the push she needed to keep trying so hard, but the other half of her was just getting so frustrated by what a gaping head start the others had.

Even Bran.

"Well… thanks for the heads up."

"That's what friends are for!" she said with a smile, just a moment before Firia felt the invisible pressure begin to build and she had to press back with the spell she had only just learned. And barely.

"Easy now," cautioned the elf as she adjusted her own spell. "You're a powerful sorceress, for you this'll be about control, not force."

Perhaps Firia was better than she realized at this.

She thought back to the competition with Mae'lin and felt a small rush of panic. She couldn't control that, but now she had developed her skills. Gotten more training. Surely she could control herself – and the magic – better now.

Firia felt her own power radiate out in uneven waves, whereas Ala'nase's was so controlled, directed. "I wish I had your talent for this," explained the dark-skinned elf, exhaling a bit as they tested themselves against one another. "We'll be in for a bruising once you're caught up on the basic stuff," she said with a playful smile.

Firia felt pride begin to well up inside her, the warmth flooding through her. Confidence slowly edged into her consciousness and she stood a bit taller. "Hopefully it won't take too long to catch up on a lifetime of learning."

With a sweet smile – that happened to twitch a bit at the corner from her struggle to keep up – Ala'nase said, "I could help, you know. I… would've offered sooner, but…" she laughed a bit awkwardly. "You're such a promising sorceress, better than me, and I didn't want to embarrass you." She added on quickly, "Not that you should be!"

"What are you talking about? You don't even need to pay attention in class. You're always ahead of everything," Firia retorted.

Ala'nase gave an awkward laugh, trying to carry on the conversation as they maintained their delicate balance. "Well that's the thing. I know this stuff, but… that doesn't mean I have the potential to use it as well as you do, Firia. There's more to sorcery than just memorizing instructions and spell patterns."

"But without that, then they could have me reported as being dangerous." She thought of her dad for a brief moment, wondering if he was still trapped in some jail cell. He'd helped her get to this place, and she wasn't going to screw it up by being deemed a danger!

"I know," replied the elf with a sigh. "That's why I want to help you if you let me. I'd hate to lose my best friend, and have to go it alone at the academy day in, day out from now on. So what do you say? I can help you study. Heck, our rooms aren't even far apart so there's not much of a commute."

"I'd like that." She paused. "Hey Ala, are you any closer to figuring out how to break curfew?"

"I wish." She grimaced. "That's something that takes both finesse and power, I'm afraid. Apparently most students don't manage to do that until year three. So it's a long haul ahead for me I'm afraid," she said with a sigh.

Firia's nose crinkled. "That's just cruel." She didn't really have that long to wait, so hopefully Luka would be able to... zoom past three years of intensive training and study. Varuj had given her such a head start, and she felt like she could really use another boost.

Though quickly she tried to push away the thought, for as soon as she was reminded of him, she started to turn red from the memory of the dream she had. It felt so real...

More than that, her powers had flared up and Ala'nase looked about to pass out in her effort to resist. "Firia!" she squeaked out as she wavered beneath her telekinetic assault.

Firia gasped, staring wide eyed at her friend. "Sorry, sorry!" She had to get control of her thoughts, and she took a deep breath before biting in her lip. "Are you okay?"

"How about we take a break?" she managed, and she looked about ready to pass out as they both released their magical tension. "Wow," she said with a sigh, her chest heaving. "I need to help you get caught up just so you're not a danger to me!" she said with a laugh, not aware of how close to home that joke struck until it was said. "S-sorry."

Firia's face fell and she looked towards the ground sheepishly. "I'm really sorry Ala. I got lost in thought..."

"C'mon," she said with a sigh as Firia came and helped her along. "Let's duck out. I'll help you with that some more later. For now I think we've gotten about as much practice as I can handle," she remarked.

Firia swept her black bangs from her face, a nervous habit she'd almost kicked since coming to the Academy. Now she just felt like she wanted to hide into a hole. Why'd that dream have to make her so... unstable? She'd barely been able to look at Mae'lin, but that was only half the problem.

Was it actually Varuj intruding upon her dreams?

152

CHAPTER 26

Despite Ala'nase's generous offer, Firia had an appointment to meet with Bran. She stopped at her room on her way out.

Immediately the light show that was her familiar spilled out of the room and she had to slip inside and shut the door. She could feel the magic, its presence and the ongoing battle rippling out. She immediately noticed one of the wards was no longer present, and then – with a thunderous crackle – she witnessed the flash of arcane energy as another gave way to Luka's assault.

Excitement flooded her. Maybe this was really it. Luka was getting closer, and it wouldn't be long before they were all taken care of. She wanted to stay, to watch, to try to help, but she knew that it would still take a torturously long time if she watched.

"Way to go, Luka." She smiled brightly at her familiar.

There was no response from her embattled familiar, just the undulating lights that threaded about in a war of sorcery.

As she worked her way through the student's lodge, she passed off the smiling Mae'lin. "Hey Firia," he said softly, approaching her so enthusiastically. "I know you said you had to do something else today, but I was thinking tonight while I study I'll put together a little exam for you. I figure that way we'll both benefit from it even while you're away."

For a moment she tried to shy away, to go unseen. All she could think of was the way his hands felt against her, the way his mouth tasted. Her pulse quickened and she had to stop herself from just running by him.

That was what the old Firia would have done, but that wasn't who she was any more.

"An exam?" He'd proposed in the dream. Or at least said he was going to. She fidgeted to her other foot. "What kind?"

"Just some questions about the arcane syllabary," he said so pleasantly. He didn't have the calm composure that Bran did, so he fidgeted a bit with his hands. The tall, lanky elf glowed positivity however, in a way she could never quite imagine her fellow human doing. "I'll really grill you. So make sure you don't forget what you've learned, okay?"

She'd never seen Mae'lin without his shirt on, yet after the dream it was spectacularly easy to imagine it.

Another rush of excitement teased her veins and her loins and she nodded a bit too quickly, trying to move past him as she spoke. "Absolutely! Make it hard..." She nearly choked on her own words.

As she exited into the night the rush of cool air was a welcome calmative.

Firia set off to find Bran. She was barely outside the building when he took hold of her arm and spun her about to face him. "There you are," he said with a broad smile. "Ready for dinner, m'lady?" he asked with that curious air of charm and grace that seemed so out of place on another human.

She gasped when he touched her, her heart nearly stopped from the fright. She'd been so lost in thought and her face flushed as she nodded. She just hoped he couldn't see what she'd been thinking of.

She'd brushed her hair back into two pigtails and dressed more casually than her day robe, though it wasn't saying much. She was still stuck with second hand clothes and few at that, but her smile was bright.

She needed to learn to control her thoughts, and him catching her in a daydream was another reminder of that.

In the looming evening shadows he guided her along, "I trust I didn't catch you before you had time to prepare," he stated, glancing to her as he guided her to the same secret hiding spot he'd shown her before. She was slow to realize he'd changed his clothes. No longer wearing his fancy wizard's robes, he instead had on a rather striking suit. Black boots, pants and jacket, with a high collar.

Did she not look prepared? She looked down at the worn outfit and frowned, wishing she had something nicer. It was just another thing that made her stand out among the sea of elves.

"I'm ready." She brushed her bangs out of her face, as if that would make her feel more confident, but as usual it didn't work. "You… really didn't have to get dressed up for me."

The glade was even more beautiful at night, and silver of the moon reflecting off the flowers, the grass and surrounding trees. She saw then another beautiful spread upon a very spacious blanketed area, and he took her there, helping her down. "Nonsense," he stated so pleasantly. "A gentleman should look good for his lady."

His lady? Her nose crinkled. This was… a study appointment, right? She thought they'd been clear in making plans. Still, when she tried to open her mouth she felt flustered and unsure of herself, afraid that she was reading into it too deeply.

"Well… a lady," she finally managed, but it was choked out.

Bran paid her words no heed, but offered her some of the food as he smiled. "I was training this afternoon with fire. It made me think of that performance you put on at the competition, which I sadly missed. How I'd love to see you do that again someday," he remarked.

"I'm not sure I'll be up for it any time soon," she admitted. "Not until I get more control over it, anyways. I mean, Mae'lin really could have been hurt…"

Bran merely laughed as they continued to eat. "Oh well, I've been made to feel more than a few lumps by overzealous elves in practice. They just love to make us upstart humans hurt," he said with a flash of his brows and a grimace.

"I don't know. I've never been hurt like that." She'd been the one far more out of control, and then earlier with Ala'nase … She was getting worried that if she didn't get Varuj back, and fast, she'd never be able to make it through her first year.

"You're lucky then," he said. "In the magical immersion program the elves were always ganging up on me with their newly learned spells." With a shrug he said, "It forces you to toughen up to survive. And I got a few scars to show for it," he remarked as their meal continued.

"Sounds like it kind of… sucked. No offense."

With a brush of his hands he nodded to her before pouring up some cups of drink from a decanter. "It did. But it made me a stronger sorcerer. I figured something similar had to have happened to you to get so far, with so little training. I mean… by all accounts you're pretty amazing, Firia," he said with a charming smile as he handed her the cup.

"You keep saying that." She took a sip of the tea thoughtfully before she shook her head. "I just always knew this was what I wanted. It's always been what I've worked towards, before I even knew it was a goal."

Bran sipped his drink as he watched her. "You're determined," he said after some thought. "That's important. It's what matters most. And to have held onto that determination for so long? So many let it die out before it really matters." He smiled and lowered his free hand, resting it next to her leg so that his finger brushed her knee.

"Yea, well… Being a groundskeeper isn't exactly what I wanted for myself. And it's not what my dad wanted for me either. So I guess what kept me motivated is just wanting to do something…" She didn't want to say better, because it wasn't necessarily better. It was just better for her.

Cozying up beside her, Bran rested his cup down then placed his arm around her back. "You didn't want to be chained to mediocrity," he stated. "You've a great deal of promise with magic, it would be a crime if that were to happen to you," he stated confidently, a thin smile on his face illuminated by the moon.

"Still… You look so comfortable with it. Like nothing bothers you." She felt him press around her and it felt so safe, like when her dad would hold her after a long day. And she'd had so many long days, filled with so much excitement and worry.

And loneliness.

What was comforting suddenly changed and her body prickled as she shifted away from him a smidge. "I just hope I could get to that level."

Bran didn't back off though, for he reached up and trailed the backs of two fingers along her jawline. "Together we'll go to levels no human magic-users ever have before, Firia," he said in a husky, firm voice. "I've always known I was destined for greatness." He lowered his hand back down to her knee, resting it atop it this time, "But now I realize that together, you and I? We could surpass even my dreams. We'll be the envy of all others."

Her skin was electric to his touch, and she felt such intense need. To be close to someone. Anyone.

Yet Varuj's voice rang in her memory and she stood up instantly.

Had she forgotten about him?

The thought haunted her, but what bothered her most was… Should she care if she had? The thought of the demon's body pressing against hers, kissing her neck and feeling so right was horrific, and she looked down at the confident Bran. They had so much in common, didn't they? The only two humans at the school, in the same year. Both so determined.

"Sorry," she apologized, though she didn't know why. Was she afraid of offending him?

Why did Varuj have such a hold on her? No matter how she tried to organize her thoughts, they kept coming back to him. *He's a demon, damn it!* she cursed herself.

Bran stood up with her, a look of confusion on his face. "Are you okay?" he asked, "I don't understand what happened," he struggled with the words, for the first time seeming to have lost his intense feeling of control over all situations.

"Come sit again," he pleaded, reaching for her hand, "It's too early to end the night already."

She looked up at him with her blue eyes, and she wasn't sure what happened either. She just… panicked.

"Do you like me?" she asked, her voice skeptical.

The look that crossed his face was something of relief, and the most pure expression of joy she'd ever seen the stoic sorcerer exhibit. "Absolutely," he said. Though from there it did not go as she anticipated, he lunged for her, arm around her back, the other on her arm as he pressed their lips together in a passionate kiss.

Bran was much larger than her, stronger, and he held her in such a tight hold, pressing her to him as he tongued her lips beneath the silver moon.

She couldn't believe what was happening. She was simply shocked into inaction, and she didn't even protest. Couldn't!

Was she sure this wasn't another dream?

Suddenly she was both afraid of and hoping for Varuj's interruption, for him to imply she was selfish. That she'd forgotten him and got lost in her interest for another.

Yet the kiss wore on and there was no demonic presence, no shift in perspective. Just the taste of his hot, spiced mouth on hers.

Bran was such a strong presence, so confident, and he took control of her then and held her petite frame against his chest. She felt like he might never let go as that smug young wizard pushed her to the grass and…

A gasp broke the moment, and Bran tore his lips from hers to twist his neck around and looked behind.

There, Firia and Bran saw standing behind the bushes a gaped-mouth Ala'nase and a terribly sullen-looking Mae'lin.

"What are you two doing here?!" insisted the shocked Bran, still holding onto Firia.

"We didn't mean to intrude!" Ala'nase looked both shocked and apologetic in equal measure.

For a long moment Firia wished she could simply disappear into the grass. She couldn't even get up and flee with the weight of the man on top of her. She gasped for breath and squirmed beneath him, but that only made it so much worse.

What was happening to her body? Why did his weight on top of her feel so damned good when she should be feeling ashamed?

She didn't want her friends to see her like this. To get the wrong idea, but it was far too late for all of that.

"It's not what it looks like," she pleaded with them, but what good would that do? Mae'lin was already gone, she noticed, and Ala'nase was holding up her hands and backing away.

"So sorry, Firia!" the elvish woman called out as she receded back through the bushes. "I am so, so sorry!"

Bran, filled with irritation at the interruption, finally looked back to her, clutching her hand. "How did they find us here?" he lamented, but squeezed her hand and leaned in. "Now they all know about us anyhow," and he kissed her lips again.

She pulled away and shook her head. "Bran, I have to find them. This... I'm so not ready for whatever this is," she finally managed as she struggled free.

The confident young wizard looked simply confused by that declaration. "What do you mean...?" he muttered, still lying there on the grass, supported on one palm as he watched her go. "Firia! We're partners now, you said..." he struggled for the words.

She didn't know what he thought she'd said but she grabbed her book. She hated having to crush him so, but what other option did she have. "Look, we'll talk later, okay? Thanks for dinner," she shouted over her shoulder as she ran towards the exit.

"It's good that they know!" she heard him call out as she left.

She ran through the bushes, but no sooner had she come out the other side of the secret entrance did she go crashing into Ala'nase. The two went sprawling with the impact, and Firia's satchel spilled its contents about the grass behind the library.

"I said I'm sorry!" Ala'nase cried out as Firia lay atop her slender, elvish form.

She couldn't control her magic or her bumbling form, and she rolled onto her back to free her friend. "Listen, it wasn't what it looked like. We were just talking and he grabbed me and... it just happened so fast, I didn't know what to do."

It would be different if she felt for Bran, wanted it to happen. But it hadn't even really occurred to her, and the surprise had made her slow. And embarrassed.

Ala'nase, for her part, rose up onto her palms and began her own hurried explanation. "No, you don't need to explain! It's my fault, I saw you get grabbed from one of the upstairs windows, and I thought you were in trouble! So I ran out to get you, Mae'lin saw me in a panic... and as soon as he heard what I saw he refused to give up. So the two of us went searching for you and... It was a big mess! I'm so sorry for barging in like that. I shouldn't have let my imagination run away."

Firia felt so flustered as she pushed herself up off the ground. "Where'd he go?"

"He's back inside, isn't he?" she said with some confusion, slower to brush herself off and get back up.

"I don't know," she admitted. "He just... Damn, he looked really hurt."

I was going to propose.

The dream with Mae'lin popped back into her mind and she couldn't help that it made her heart pound, despite what Varuj wanted. Regardless of his interruption.

"Bran look hurt? So why'd you leave him then?" she asked with confusion. "Or you mean... Mae'lin?" Ala'nase looked about, slow to catch on to the complexity of what had really just happened. "I don't know, he was really concerned for you. He's probably gone back to his room," she explained.

"Look, we'll talk later, okay? Just... I need to find him." She didn't wait for a reply, though. She didn't need one right then.

She just didn't want for Mae'lin to hurt a second longer than he had to over this.

Night had sunk its claws into the sky deeply, it was very dark on the campus, and the moon was hidden behind one of the buildings wherever she went, it seemed. She went back to the dormitory and up to Mae'lin's room. She knocked on it there. But no sound emerged.

"Mae'lin?" she asked, knocking again fruitlessly.

It wasn't long before one of the other male students looked to her curiously and she asked, "Have you seen Mae'lin?"

He shook his head. "Not in a while," he remarked.

Damn, damn, damn.

The only other place she thought she might look and actually find him was their study corner in the library.

Or maybe she was just hoping he might be sentimental enough to be there.

The library was so labyrinthine, the endless corridors; up and up she went. Only the convenience of the air tunnels the arch mages put in made getting around it take less than hours. Though still, she was breathless when she reached the proper section.

She headed down, passing off row and row of book shelves. She knew exactly where their little hideaway was, but all the same, she checked each row as she went by to see if she could see him.

As she neared her destination however, she saw something…

It was a bag of some sort. It was dim and hard to see, but there was something there – someone! – in the section. She hurried towards it faster when suddenly that now familiar bell tolled so ominously.

She tried to call out but instead she found herself calling out "Mae'lin!" into her own bedroom, the shimmering light show of her familiar as bright as ever as she stood alone.

The tears in her eyes made the glitter even brighter and she fell to the bed, frustrated. Tossing her books aside she lay back at the mattress, staring at the ceiling as she sobbed herself to sleep.

CHAPTER 27

The sound of thunder reverberated all around her, the heavy pelting of rain beating upon Firia's form as she pressed on through the rocky hills. She knew the place, knew it well. She'd explored the hills to the west many times growing up, the lonesome treks through the woods up into the hills to see the valley below were another lonely experience of her time growing up.

She'd had good times doing it, discovered curious wildlife, played with magic. However, it was dark and the storm was biting through her, the thin clothes she wore not enough to keep the chilly fangs of ice from biting through her.

She cowered from the first two strikes of lightning, but on the third she managed to keep her head up, and in the dark of the night she saw the outline of something ahead.

"Something" was about as specific as she could get, for it could've been a person, a monster, or merely a pile of rocks. The flash of light was too brief.

What wasn't too brief for her, however, was the sense of terror. She was alone. Abandoned.

With desperation in her veins she took off as fast as she could, but the way was rough going. The stones jagged and uneven, though as the lightning flashed again and she looked behind and saw it closer, gaining ground!

All her friends had abandoned her; she was on her own. Even if she got away from that thing she'd probably freeze to death, the realization sank into her deeply.

The panic of that thought made her trip, her ankle twisted and she fell, a rock gouging into her leg as she landed.

While over her it looked. It's silhouette large, ominous. Terrifying.

She tried to remain still and quiet, hoping that it couldn't see her shivering form. There was no fleeing or escaping, not with the sharp pains that traveled her ankle and calf. There was nothing left, nothing she could do to escape the thing that threatened her.

As he bent towards her, its great visage blocked out the rain, and she was able to see clearer. The ruddy-dark flesh of Varuj as she'd first encountered him entered her view as he picked her up in his mighty arms. The heat of his body was so prominent and soothing as he cradled her against the storm.

"I won't abandon you," he said in his deep, rumbling voice.

Her arms went around him and she wasn't sure if it was the rain or tears that streamed down her face. She couldn't recall ever feeling such relief, such warmth flood over her. He saved her from the rain, but also that crushing loneliness and her fingers clutched him almost painfully tight.

Cradled against that massive, broad chest, only the heat radiating off his hard muscles to warm her, she was carried through the storm by the giant demon. The pelting rain was blocked from her by his form, and the more she saw his broad, masculine face, the less terrifying it seemed.

The prominent horns in his head and chin, so pitch black, were less and less intimidating as he brought her to the shelter of a cave, the howling of the wind behind them. "You're safe now," he said in that gravelly voice, a warm little smile formed on those thick lips of his, the fiery eyes less like pits of hell and more like warming flames.

She just wanted to be close to him, to feel not only the physical heat but the emotional as well. She hadn't realized how frail she felt, how lonely she was. She'd managed for so long on her own, with her friends, but they couldn't understand her.

Not like he could.

With tender care, the giant fiend knelt down, holding her in his arms as he sat back, sheltering her even from the cold draft that emanated from the cave entrance. With a soft kiss to her forehead, he nuzzled against her clammy face, the unearthly heat so pleasant as he rubbed his hands along the length of her calf and thigh, her forearm and bicep.

"All might leave you, but I wouldn't. The world might fall apart, but I would snatch you up from it and save you, Firi," he husked to her lowly in such a loving voice, so ill-fitted to his demonic rumble.

Just the reverberations of his words soothed her and she nodded against his body. It felt so right, so natural. So peaceful.

Nothing else mattered except for this moment.

The radiance of his hard, muscular body, the tender friction of his strong hands. The sweet kiss of his lips as they pressed to her forehead, her nose. Her lips. It all warmed her so deeply, and he squeezed her a little tighter. "I love you," came his words.

She awoke then to a loud snap, a terrifying crack, her familiar battling the wards at a greater intensity than she had seen it ever before. It was almost frightening to behold, if not for what she knew it portended.

Her breath was so much faster and she pulled back on her bed, curling into the corner. She still managed to feel so loved, despite the alarm she felt. She tried to slow her pulse, to calm her mind, but her entire body screamed with desire.

With a near blinding flash of light she heard the last of the wards give way and cave in. The burst of magical energy made the little hairs on the back of her arms stand on end.

It was done. The wards were gone…

Her familiar swirled faster, and she felt it subsuming the excess energy in the air before reforming back into the familiar fox she was so used to. It lay down immediately, looking weary. Exhausted.

The darkness that took over the room then was so complete. The room had been so excessively bright since she'd started assaulting those wards, but…

She heard something move. A small little flicker of light from the corner of the room lit up, and shed just a smidgen of light upon a man's visage.

The orb of reddish light grew, and as he stepped closer she saw the familiar sight of Varuj. Not as he had been in her dream, but youthful, lean. His smooth chest on display from beneath his robe as he smiled at her lightly. "I've missed you so badly, Firi."

How could she have forgotten how much she enjoyed his presence? His company?

She swiftly jumped from the bed and leapt to his arms, hugging him tight. The first day, when she realized she hadn't felt him, she'd been so afraid but she pushed it down. Hoped for the best.

Now that he was back with her, though, she was surprised by how badly she needed his comfort.

Varuj released the orb to float by itself and put his own two arms around her, holding her up off the floor as he squeezed her tight. His natural heat radiated through her, though only a fraction of what it was when he cradled her in his original form in her dream.

"It's okay," he muttered to her in that charming accent, kissing the side of her head, her hair. His one hand stroked over her black strands down her back and he took her back to the bed, lowering themselves both down to it, but not parting from her. "It has been too long, sweet Firi," he murmured.

"Are you hungry?" Her voice was still hoarse from sleep, but it was the first thing that occurred to her. He'd been lost so long, within her body. Within her soul? She didn't quite understand it but she knew that he was trapped inside her.

He pulled back from her just enough to rub his hand over her cheek and smile at her longingly. "Yes," he said, "but it can wait. I am just so glad to be back with you. I long to hear about all your trials and tribulations without me. To know all I have missed about you, sweet Firi." He leaned in and kissed her gently upon her cheek, just lightly touching the corner of her lips.

The touch of his mouth was so sweet, not like Bran's. It was so warm, loving, and... invited. Not like that young wizard's had been.

Yet it still made her breath hitch and her cheeks turn pinkish as her face dropped. "I didn't realize how much I didn't know until I got here. I've been... struggling."

With a smooth motion Varuj moved back to the corner where her bed met the wall and cradled her against him so comfortably. Her head rested to his chest and he stroked her hair with loving repetition.

"If only we had more time for me to show you the things I know. But we shall… sweet Firi, I shall show you."

"Now that you're back." It felt like she was at home now. At peace. Like she was somehow complete once more, and she clung to him like a child as she began telling him about her studies. Her issues with the professors, how dire it was for her to pass.

Yet she never mentioned the vivid dreams, nor her experience the day before with Bran and Mae'lin.

She just couldn't bring herself to express what she was feeling about all of it. She could barely make sense of it in her own mind, let alone verbalize it to him.

To Varuj.

Her demon.

It must have nearly been daybreak by the time she finished her long story of life at the academy, and he had listened to every word of it with rapt attention, combing his fingers through her hair again and again in such a soothing manner. Showering her head and face with soft, caring kisses from time to time throughout.

"You have struggled so long and hard, yet it has only just begun with your entry into the academy," he said with a soft sigh. "You have been brave and diligent without me, sweet Firi. But you no longer need go it alone."

His words filled her with gratitude and reassured her of what she already knew.

He'd never abandon her. He'd never misunderstand her.

He was a part of her, wasn't he?

With gentle care he tilted her face up towards him, showed her his dazzling, handsome smile before placing a soft kiss on her lips. "We shall take pains not to be 'separated' again, no?" he remarked before pressing his mouth to hers once more, lingering there in warmth and closeness.

Perhaps it was the drowsiness, the excitement of having him back. Maybe it was all of the stress and anguish that simply made her body more responsive, but she didn't pull away from him. It wasn't with the shock and surprise as it had been with Bran.

This time it was because it somehow felt right and natural. Welcomed.

She trembled in his arms and tugged herself closer before her lips left his and she stared at him with lidded eyes.

What am I doing?

Varuj had the looks of a dashing foreign prince, his sleek black hair framing such handsome, smooth features. Yet when he smiled at her then, it made him look so caring – no, loving – rather than suave. "Go and get me some food, sweet Firi. I am famished after so long." He stroked his hand over her cheek and along her jawline, "Do hurry back, please."

She scrambled from his arms, and it was only then she realized how little she was wearing. The light nightgown was so much less proper than what she usually wore but she'd been so excited. So desperate.

Quickly she threw on her robe and she was grateful for a chance to get away from him, even if she longed to be with him. She felt like she was being torn into pieces, uncertain of what to do next. For so long she'd been alone, and now she was being forced to choose between three men.

Well… two and a demon.

She exited her room, the night's curfew ended it seemed, and she confirmed why when she exited out into the light of morning outside.

The eating hall was open, as she'd been told it was round the clock, and she was able to go in and beat the lines to retrieve a rather generous assortment of meaty foods to Varuj's liking. Only a couple people out of the whole of the academy occupied the great dining hall, and none seemed to pay her any mind as she made her way out, pockets and satchel stuffed with food.

When she returned, she took a deep breath then pushed open the door, heading back into her room. What she saw then, stole her breath, however.

Absolutely bare, the ruddy-brown demon stood with his robes hanging down from his elbows as he inspected himself in the mirror. The fullness of his nude form on display in profile, from his lean, hard chest which she'd become so familiar with, down across the firm abs and beyond a small, neatly trimmed tuft of pubic hair to a gorgeous piece of manhood.

He wasn't even erect, but it looked so large to her eyes, and rested above powerful thighs that looked like they belonged to a long-distance runner.

She stared, dumbfounded. She knew she should apologize, close the door. Hide her face. Maybe never even tell him that she'd intruded.

But she couldn't do any of that. She was transfixed, and it felt like hours passed as she watched him inspecting himself.

It was very nearly hypnotic, for he was the picture of male beauty. She saw as he licked his own full lips, ran his fingers down over his chest, across his abs and…

It twitched. That organ swelling with life and growing so fast before her very eyes.

It distracted her, and she didn't notice anything else until he pulled his robe back closed, covering the thick organ before it reached its fullness. He turned then as he knotted his cloth belt and smiled. "Ah, welcome back," he said as he approached her so casually. He didn't know she was watching. Did he?

Certainly he could figure it out by how red her face was, by how she refused to look him in the eyes as she brushed past him to lay out his breakfast. "Thanks." She felt like slapping herself. Thanks? Thanks for what? For the welcome back?

Or for the titillating show?

She was so lost in thought she didn't even detect him move beside her, rest a hand upon her hip. "You brought so much," he said with his curious tone of excitement, "and it all smells so good, my sweet Firi." He reached around her, plucking up some and taking a bite. "Mm, to go without real, material food for so long…"

"This place has a lot of food." She should know, she was already softening in the hips a bit, and his hand felt so nice against it. It seemed more sensual in some ways.

It was probably the fact that she'd been gawking at him so recently that made it so.

"If you need more…"

Varuj sat himself down and pulled her onto his lap with his strong hold upon her hip. "Eat with me?" he asked softly, offering her a tiny morsel upon his fingers as he smiled. "I have missed the little things. Like company while I eat. Even though… we got to experience it so little together as is," he lamented.

She accepted the offered food but squirmed on his thigh. She knew what lay beneath it, so tentatively hidden from her, and it made her adrenaline rush. She didn't know what she wanted, of him, of anyone. But she couldn't deny how seeing him nude made her feel, and being so near to him – to it – thrilled her as much as it frightened her.

Her motions had an effect she didn't intend however, and she felt him stir beneath her, and she could see the light flare of his nostrils that went with it. "You are anxious?" he asked softly, taking another bite of food himself, squeezing her hip as he took up yet more to offer her, such a small bite she had to use her tongue to take it from betwixt his digits.

What was the right response?

What was the real one?

She chewed thoughtfully but it tasted of the salt on his fingertips and instead of disgusting her it made her yearn for more.

Somewhere in the back of her mind she pictured Mae'lin, looking so hurt and betrayed by Bran kissing her. Yet this man… this demon. He posed such a larger threat to the sweet elf.

"I have to get to class," she finally managed.

With a slow nod he said, "I know. But we have a moment more, do we not? I would treasure savouring it with you," he said so sweetly, though that contrasted the thick throb of his manhood beneath her that signified so much that confused, frightened and aroused her.

Her breath was quick and shallow, but she didn't want to leave. Or, at the very least, she didn't move away from his body. It felt so comforting, so inviting, and her blue eyes fluttered closed. "What if someone catches you?"

"I will set about measures to protect the room," he said, continuing to eat and feed her at intervals. His smooth motions were so suave, his tender rub of her side so pleasant. "We will need such privacy when we begin anew our training, sweet Firi. The academy is swimming with magic and the magicians who wield it. We must be careful for the time being," he moved in towards her, pressed his nose to hers, their eyes locked. "I will look out for us."

"Well, you better, because it took long enough to break those wards and I don't know how to make new ones yet." Her nose felt so small against his, and it was a struggle to keep her gaze on his. She kept picturing him, naked and staring at himself in the mirror.

A corner of his lips crooked upwards and he gave a low laugh. "Those wards did us no good, don't fret. I will handle everything. And someday teach you how to do the same. For now, however, we do not have the time to wait." He gave her rear a squeeze and kissed her cheek, right at the corner of her lips again. "Rest assured at your classes."

Her mind went hazy as his mouth touched hers, and she inhaled his scent.

She'd missed him more than she thought possible.

"I have to go," she whispered and slunk off his lap.

Varuj stood up and brushed his hands off. "I know. I shall miss you all the same," he said with a resilient smile. "Do hurry back to me though, yes? We have much to do if you are to be prepared for what's to come. And I do not care to leave anything up to chance when it comes to your future." He reached up and cupped her cheek, stroking his thumb over the soft flesh. "Sweet Firi."

She took a quick step back, needing to be away from his touch. From his flesh.

He felt so good, so warm, and she was greedy for it and that frightened her. "I'll see you tonight," she promised as she reached for her bag. "Please be careful."

"I shall," he said, a hand upon his belt as he turned sidelong to her and plucked up yet more food. The pose was so similar to when she'd walked in upon him that it was nearly dizzying to think of how he'd looked beneath that wizard's robe…

Her body buzzed with the fantasy and as she exited her room, the air felt so much cooler on her scorched cheeks.

CHAPTER 28

Classes went much the same as usual, which is to say a lot of complicated jargon that Firia was only beginning to grasp. Though something she couldn't help but notice was the absence of Mae'lin from the day's lessons. Neither he nor Bran were present that day, and the only response she could get out of Ala'nase as to their whereabouts was a shrug, a smirk and a teasing: "Off fighting over you, no doubt."

"You're not helping," she muttered back ruefully.

She didn't know which she sought distraction from more. The two men, or the demon that awaited her back in her room. Either way, it was becoming too much, too quickly, and it fogged her mind from what she should have been focusing on. School.

Her one chance for success, to leave the life of drudgery behind.

So why was it so damn hard to focus?

As the two young women made their way down the hall out of the building the gentle melodies of some hypnotic music carried to them, and before she even realized it, Firia had detoured off her usual course a ways and found herself outside a crowded classroom from whence it came.

"What's going on?" asked Ala'nase, looking as entranced as Firia felt. The pair were compelled to prod at the students clustering about the doorway to take a peek inside.

It was there she saw a familiarly unfamiliar sight. For sat upon the stool at the front of a classroom was the devilishly handsome and fiendishly tricky Gway'lin. He looked serene as he played upon his flute, all the students seeming summoned to him as he swayed and bobbed his head with the haunting melody.

Firia had, of course, listened to many a musician over the years. Music making and song playing were great pastimes of the humans back home, but nothing they had ever done approached the curiously unworldly tunes that came from the elf's playing.

It was almost as if the music itself warped reality about him, his long, billowy black sleeves seeming to lift up and dance with the sounds. His hair rising up like numerous pythons out of some story book, entranced. Yet the moment she tried to focus in on any one of these things she saw it was not so. A trick of the eye? No, it had to be magic that empowered his playing. That made the whole world seem to spin to his whim, that made the lights dim for all the world but its very core: Gway'lin the musician magician.

Firia had been struck breathless, though it didn't dawn on her until he finished playing and reality seemed to return to normal. Applause was quick to break out.

She joined in, though her blue eyes went to Ala'nase. Since when was she concerned with what others thought of her, or what she enjoyed?

It was so foreign to her, all the changes she'd been struggling against since coming to the Academy. She had friends. People she actually cared for, outside of her father.

She was letting herself open up. Just a little.

From out of the crowd, the musician himself came up to her, the students slow to disperse as the lingering effects of his playing dissipated. "Ah, there you are, young madam," he said with such glowing warmth. "I was hoping to attract you to me this afternoon and spare me a trip."

The look of envy Ala'nase gave was palpable.

Oh firecrackers, this was all she needed. Another person for Ala'nase to make sly jokes over.

Firia was glowing red and she tried to hide behind her black hair. She'd been growing it out, slowly, and it finally covered most of her jaw and part of her neck successfully. "It seems a bit excessive, if you ask me, to summon an audience just to save yourself a trip."

"Perhaps," he said, his handsome face still practically glowing as he stood before her, hand on hip, looking as confident and sure of himself as ever. "The message was marked as urgent, however. Though it arrived by mundane means." He reached into his robes and pulled out a scroll. "It's marked as private, so…" he let his eyes trail to Ala'nase before going back to Firia, "I suggest you read it alone."

With that he extended the scroll out to her, smiling pleasantly.

She didn't share his enthusiasm and tried to still her hand from shaking as she took it from him. "Well, thanks." She tried to force a smile, but dread pitted in her stomach.

There was only one person outside of the school who would contact her, and she prayed for it to be good news. "Ala, I'll meet up with you later, okay?"

The young elven woman nodded, then quickly swooped in to Gway'lin's side. "Hey teach, what was that class you were just instructing anyhow? How to make the ladies wet their knickers?"

That and the instructor's joyous laugh was the last she heard as Firia rounded the corner and headed straight back to her dorm.

Upon opening the door, she saw an empty room. Though once it closed, he seemed to take form out of the shadows itself, his exotic, striking figure standing before her. "What's wrong?" he asked, though she hadn't been aware that she'd betrayed her distress. Some subtle cues in her behaviour and appearance betraying her to the charming devil that knew her so well.

Her lip twitched in annoyance as she walked past him, settling in on the bed. She didn't want to open it.

Why was she even dreading it so much? She didn't have reason to.

Well, except for the fact that it was marked urgent. What good news is ever urgent?

She took in a deep breath, feeling out the parchment, trying to will herself to simply rip it open and get it over with, but terror stilled her hand.

Very gently, Varuj settled in beside her upon the bed, his curiously masculine scent tickling her senses as he put an arm around her. "Here," he said smoothly, sliding both of his hands up to hers and helping prod her along to open the message.

The scroll unrolled with the help of his guiding hands, and she saw the very obviously human scrawl written upon it.

She didn't need to read it all, couldn't read it all. For when she saw that her father was being tried as a rebel and a saboteur, her heart skipped a bit and her vision failed her.

"No, no, no, no," she kept repeating, and she was only vaguely aware of it. This couldn't be happening. The man she'd spoken to at the station, he'd seemed so kind. Like he would take care of it. Didn't he promise her that?

She felt Varuj's arms wrap around her, but instead of being a comfort, it was confinement. Confinement like this stupid Academy.

She was trapped there, kept away from her father when he needed her most!

It was like her whole world was caving in on her, crushing her under its tremendous weight. Not even the handsome demon's comforting grasp could take away its awful bite.

Her father. Her lone family. About to face trial for treason. And wrongly so. She just knew it.

He lived a simple life, and though he was not a simple-headed man – she knew that for certain – he was not a violent or conspiratorial man. He remained focussed on their life, on getting her out of their cycle of mediocrity, enforced by rigid social standards.

"What does this mean?" asked Varuj curiously.

Her lip trembled and even as she tried to form the words to let him know, she couldn't. Her mouth simply wouldn't let her say such horrid, terrifying things.

How could she say it?

Instead she looked away, down to the floor, slumping in the bed lower and lower.

"I have to do something," she finally managed out between sobs.

"But what?" he asked, his arms moving about her waist, supporting her, keeping her from slumping down too low. "You have your exams to be concerned with. We have not even begun our training as of yet." His voice laced with concern for her, though her own mind was worried for her father.

"And what's that all matter, huh? When dad's..." She couldn't say it. "I'm just supposed to forget about him and move on?"

"You would throw it all away to go to his side then?" he asked so calmly, though the implications weren't necessary to state. Her father had gotten himself into trouble just trying to give her an edge in the competition so she could one day be an independent sorceress, and not a groundskeeper.

But it didn't matter.

All the stress, the pressure, the confusion, it was all too much to handle. She thought back to the simple life she could have led, and it seemed so much sweeter for that moment. To give it all up, to throw it all away, to retire herself to mediocrity.

Would she do that for her father?

She pulled away from the demon, rolling onto her side as she curled into a fetal position.

Even then she could see through the haze of torment and know she didn't want that. She didn't want his life.

But that didn't mean she didn't want to *save* his life.

Silence hung in the air, and finally Varuj stood up. "You're going to do it, aren't you?" he asked with such certainty. He had such an ability to see right through her. See her true feelings, sometimes even before she did.

It was getting obnoxious, and she kept shifting so as not to look at him. "I'm going to do what's right," she agreed. Her father had sacrificed so much to get her in here, but she wasn't going to let him sacrifice everything.

The calm charm upon the demon's face shifted. He was distressed; that much was obvious.

He bent one knee and came close to her. "If you do that, you will destroy yourself. All he worked for. And set us both back so far, Firi. Do not act hastily, please." Normally his charms could cut through her so deeply. And he poured it on thick as he pleaded with her then, but when it came to her father...

It was her only weak spot. The only thing from her human life that she truly loved and cared for.

She knew her father wouldn't want her to sacrifice the Academy in order to save him. She knew it.

Yet in her grief, she didn't care.

"Then find a way for me to do it without destroying myself."

Varuj rose up and turned away from her, his long, glossy black hair swaying behind him as he clasped his hands and began to walk up and down the length of her room.

He looked for all the world like some dignified foreign ambassador, struggling over some matter of earth-shattering importance, rather than the decisions in the life of one human girl.

"If I go in your place to save him," he began as if each word were a dangerous blade, "you risk being unprepared for your exam." Failure of an exam meant being kicked out. She knew that.

"I could surprise you," she retorted bitterly. "I've worked quite hard to get where I am in your absence."

He looked down to her and nodded. "I know you have. But so much hangs in the balance… each risk—" he cut himself off then gave her a soft smile. "I will do this for you. If you promise me one thing, Firi."

She sat up, her skeptical gaze upon him. "And that is?"

Kneeling down before her again, he took her hands and stared into her eyes with his own, almond-shaped gaze. "Promise me you will focus on naught but success, and succeed in this test whatever the cost. We have so much more to do together, and we must not falter now upon our first steps together, Firi."

His plea sounded so heartfelt.

She stared for a long time, trying to find the hidden meaning. Even when he seemed to speak plainly it always felt as though there were layers to his words. Something hidden and cryptic that she wasn't knowledgeable enough to understand.

"I won't be leaving this Academy willingly, if you will take care of my father."

Squeezing her hands he nodded. "I will see to it that he is freed from custody. One way or another, I swear it to you." Before she knew what was happening, he swept in and pressed his lips to hers with a passionate kiss.

Her mind was buzzing with so many thoughts that he took her utterly by surprise. The taste of another person's mouth on hers was so foreign, yet so welcome. She needed comfort. She needed something simple, yet logically she knew this was anything but.

He was a demon.

So how did he manage to chase away all her fears and insecurities, just with a kiss?

She forced herself to back away, but her eyes were half lidded as she stared up at him, aghast.

"You have to go now," she managed to murmur softly, concern for her father winning out.

Varuj pulled back and gave a lopsided grimace. "I will have to take Luka with me," he said grimly. "He is made from your soul-stuff, and I will require that to mask my departure from the academy. There is no way around it."

She tugged in her lower lip, her brows furrowing.

She wouldn't admit it. Not then, not to him, but the prospect of having them both gone from her would be like missing a body part. Something so important.

Yet still she nodded, for there were no other options. Sink or swim, she'd be getting her father free.

"I need to be able to trust you. That you won't lie about his safety." It sounded so silly. She needed to trust a demon. A demon she no longer had control over, no less. A demon she gave freedom.

Her blue eyes were wet and she blinked it away. "Just, please do this. I'll feel a lot better knowing he's safe."

Pushing his shoulders back, Varuj grasped his rope-like belt in both hands and nodded to her firmly. "I will see it done. But don't you fail us both while I am away. So much counts on you, Firi. The future. Our future." It was slow to occur, but the striking demon gave a soft smile to her. "Do whatever it takes. You've come too far to stop now."

Reaching behind him, he pulled the hood of his robe up over his head, hiding his horns and much of his face beneath its shadow. "Come, Luka," he said, the spectral familiar looking to Firia as if in silent request of permission.

She hesitated before her fingers moved between the fox's ears, giving it a farewell before nodding.

"Hurry back, with my father's life assured, and I promise that I will pass this test."

The spectral fox moved to Varuj, and the demon held out his hand, touching it. The swirl of light created a near-blinding flash as Luka was absorbed into the dark-skinned demon, swirling about his fingers, his arm, before settling in beneath his skin.

Without another word the demon turned to the door and opened it. He gave a final look back to Firia, his exotically shaped eyes tinged with glossiness before he quickly vanished out into the corridors, the passing women seeming not to be able to see him. At all. As if he were invisible to sight.

Firia took a deep breath and held it. Was he truly sad? Lamenting that he had to leave her? It startled her how much she wished that would be true, and she took a step back before plunking down on her bed.

She couldn't let herself become distracted. Rationally, she knew that, but with everything that had happened the past couple of days her head was spinning.

And she still hadn't seen Mae'lin. Her study partner. Her... What was he?

What did she want him to be?

She tried to take a deep, calming breath, but it just made her feel more agitated and she swiftly moved to the door. She needed to study.

CHAPTER 29

Awaking with her face in a book was not uncommon for Firia, though she couldn't help but lament lost hours of study due to falling asleep. The insistent knock on her door was more pressing however, and she had to get up, straighten her sorceress robes and go to answer it.

When she opened the door she saw someone she wasn't expecting. Gway'lin, the strikingly handsome elf, stood there in his resplendent instructor robes, the gold and emerald blue seeming to shimmer even in the dull hallway.

His broad, usual smile seemed to falter, and he looked her over curiously as if noticing some profound change that wasn't simply seeing her dishevelled after a late night of study. It took him a moment to recompose himself. "Ah, morning." He hesitated again. "How are you?" His whole demeanor awkward, not at all as she was used to seeing the elf.

Her brows furrowed. Lack of sleep must have been doing things to her mind, though she suddenly wished she'd glanced at a mirror first.

How was she? Terrible.

Hopeless. Despondent.

"At a disadvantage," she finally admitted. "Couldn't you have just played your flute to make me come to you?"

The stunning male cracked a smile at that. "Who says I didn't? Maybe you were just in too deep a sleep," he remarked with casual humour. "But the real reason I am here is somewhat urgent, miss Firia. I could use your help."

She cocked her head to the side. "I have an exam to study for. You remember, the do or die one?"

He leaned in towards her and spoke quietly. "As I said, it's urgent." He peered over his shoulder, the hallway empty outside. "Some of your friends are missing, and I need your help to find them before it's too late. As you say... do or die." His luminescent eyes locked onto hers, glowing bright like the morning sun.

Wait, was this the exam?

She tried to blink the grit from her eyes, even as she grabbed her bag and pushed past him into the hall. "Alright, so what are the clues or whatever?"

She felt like a ragged mess, but it didn't matter. She'd do everything she could to succeed.

Though honestly she was a bit curious who he thought were her friends any longer.

Gway'lin put his hand at the back of her shoulder, the warm touch gently guiding her along as he lead her down the hall and out of the building. "Two of them, Mae'lin and Bran, were last seen fighting on the roof of the library. An unsanctioned magic battle," he added ominously.

"Wait, is this the exam?" Were they actually fighting over her? She felt some heat of rage and pleasure rising within her, the sick emotions wrapping around her heart. She shouldn't take such enjoyment in needless violence, but she'd never had anyone who cared about her.

None except her father.

Her heart panged with worry but she tried to forget it. Forget it all.

"Focus here, Firia," the elf said to her as they walked across the campus grounds. "I've checked the scene atop the library, and didn't find anything, but I've my own leads to follow. But being close to them as you are, I thought you might be able to discern something I couldn't.

The markings of magicians can be hard to decipher for those not familiar with the caster." He looked to her seriously. "You've studied with them both, I need you to do this. If they're missing much longer it'll be impossible to keep secret, and their time here will be over. Regardless of anything else. You understand?"

"I'll do this." Test or no test, she understood that it was important. Still, a shiver went down her spine as she tried to recall all she could about the two men, about how they used magic.

They were both powerful, but Bran had the advantage of wealth and class. He had access to knowledge that Mae'lin and she were still trying to discover the basics of.

Suddenly she was desperate to find them both, safe.

Gway'lin took her to the front door of the library, finally releasing her of the touch of his hand. "The door to the roof is unbarred. I removed the glyphs of binding so you could access it and examine the scene. I've got to go, so do what you can." He gave her a serious stare before he turned and left in an obvious hurry.

Firia ascended the great library through the series of tubular tunnels, using the magic imbued in them to levitate up, the whole time her mind reeling with thoughts of what was really going on.

The access to the roof was normally barred, but true to Gway'lin's word, when she got there, she found it open to her.

So high above the academy, the sun seemed brighter, as if the grey clouds were thinner, or that she was above them. Though she knew that couldn't be, rationally.

When she looked around, she saw no immediate sign of a spell fight. Nothing.

Carefully she began to inspect the place. Though as she began to run out of rooftop, her memories took her back to the government building back home. How Luka had sniffed out signs of magical influence on such an undetectable scale.

The familiar would've been an incredible asset to her in the search, yet he was off and away with Varuj. Seeing to the safety of her father.

She nearly caved to despair as she finished her search with nothing seen. Was this why Gway'lin had called on her for this task? He knew how she had performed back then. He was there, albeit in disguise to monitor them. He likely assumed she could trace magical trails with ease. And she could, if Luka were there.

The morning was passing by, however, and she knew time was bleeding away, both for her and her two friends. So she began the process again, this time focussing her senses further. She'd been at the academy a while now, and she could sense magical power, albeit crudely. She just needed to hone that ability further.

It was a hell of a time to have to do so, but as she made her fourth survey of the rooftop she finally felt something. Like seeing waves of heat over a hot stove.

Her excitement caused her to lose sight of it. She had to calm herself, focus her awareness and search again.

This time she kept herself composed, and she could feel the strangely familiar scars of magic use. She knew instantly that it meant they were cast by someone she knew well.

Mae'lin was responsible for most of it she realized. There were only a few, faint trails of Bran's casting. Though, she regretfully admitted, her ability to interpret the marks was not so great that she could figure out exactly what spells were used.

The shifting placement of the battle scars did leave her with the distinct impression of motion, as if the fight had shifted in a certain direction. Though once she realized what direction that was, her heart skipped a beat.

The last signs of their encounter that she found were as if spells themselves had grappled, the two combatants entangled before taking a plunge. Directly over the side of the library roof to the waiting tower, at least a hundred feet below.

When she looked down she saw evidence of the truth to that: the ceiling seemed dented, and a small steeple atop that mini-tower was broken. Undoubtedly from one or both of them landing.

With that realization she rose up and dashed for the door. She had to get news to Gway'lin or someone else to help. Perhaps follow the trail, for they did not stop there at that tower. They either survived and moved on, or rolled over the edge.

Her excitement to help further became panic when she realized the door wouldn't open.

It was sealed. And not by any mundane lock, but a magical one.

Gway'lin had opened it for her to get up, but it had been set to reseal afterwards, it seemed. Was this a test then?

She forced her calm and tried to gauge the magical aura there as she had the battle scars. The magical syllabary came into view, and the first of the words she recognized clearly. How couldn't she? Gway'lin himself had been there to teach her.

Read.

Easy enough. The incantation below it was something much more complex, however.

Her heart was pounding, but she wouldn't give up. Her choice was to figure out this lock or tumble through the air and possibly kill herself on the spire below.

And Firia didn't care much for pain or broken limbs.

Her eyes narrowed as she focused on her breathing, thinking back to the time she'd spent with Mae'lin in the library. A soft smile turned up her lips, though she immediately felt guilty. What did that mean, that she'd have such tender thoughts of someone and they'd make her feel so horrific?

Her thoughts were getting away from her, but she kept refocusing on the task at hand.

The words were slow to take shape. She could make out the first couple of words in the script but got stuck after that. She trailed her eyes along the beautiful lettering, remembered the nights with Mae'lin, poring over the sorcerous language together, catching up on what they'd missed.

The tall, lanky elf was such a calm and steady joy to be around.

She remembered being stuck on a symbol for the fourth time, and him patiently smiling at her, trying to help her out...

That was it! She had it, and immediately the rest of the words fell into place with it. She intoned the incantation and the door opened for her easily. She was free to follow the trail downwards, and so she went.

When she reached the outside she thought to go find Gway'lin, but time was short. She'd spent so much of the morning just figuring out how to detect their magical trails that the exam period grew closer. If she didn't do it before then, either them or her, or all three, would be banished from the academy.

Going around the side of the library, where she estimated the two would've landed, she opened her senses and traced their magical auras. She'd been right. She could see the distinctive signs, the two having been using their spells right down to the ground, doubtlessly to save themselves. Though they did not save a bush she found, crushed beneath them or their spells; it was wet and crumpled.

It occurred to her, one of Mae'lin's water spells! He must've used his control over water to take some pool atop that tower above to help cushion his fall.

She was on the right trail, she knew that for certain, and followed it off.

To her surprise, the signs of spell casting did not end. The two must have been insistent, for they seemed to have continued their struggle to the bitter end, right around the back and towards…

The secret grove.

She ran to it, pushing through the bushes and then…

A trap.

The moment she passed through, she realized it wasn't the quiet, secret grove she stood in, but a magical snare. A dark chamber lined with so many doors, each with its own arcane words scrawled upon it, and – she sensed – a powerful glyph, the likes of which had once barred her into her room at night.

The likes of which it had taken her familiar days to beat down, and she had little inkling of how to even try. She had… hours to not only reproduce that task but firstly to decipher which door she had to begin with.

Her stomach churned.

CHAPTER 30

The Night Before...

Ancient and immortal, Varuj had powers beyond the reckoning of most. Once free of the academy's influence, he travelled across the world by some mysterious arcane means to Firia's home.

His tall, athletic form strode from the constables quarters. Her father hadn't been there. He'd been moved to a higher security facility closer to the capital.

With another great burst of magical energy he tore through the air to appear at his destination. Though exhaustion nearly overwhelmed him. It had been too much of an exertion for so short a time. Two long distance travels in one night would've been beyond the abilities of most mortal sorcerers after all.

The dark-skinned Varuj kept composed however, and headed along the sleepy town's street to the prison. He'd feed his hunger later and make up for the lost energy.

The constables offices were quiet, rightfully so. It was late. Though moments after he slipped in through the door, officers pushed past behind him and he had to slip around a corner out of sight.

"Those damn mundane rebels are at it again," cursed the elvish officer. "But this time, we'll stop 'em."

He could hear the sound of at least three sets of boots moving through the office towards the armoury. "Shouldn't we be making our way to the Guild Hall then?"

"Not until we've armed up," replied a third voice. "They might not have any magical ability, but there's bound to be a lot of them. And armed with weapons of some sort."

"Don't be fooled by these sorts. They're dangerous, like any animal, when backed into a corner."

With that they were gone again, vanished into the other side of the law enforcement building. Varuj pondered for a moment and conjured up Luka from within him, the swirl of lights announcing the creatures presence.

Go, came his voice psychically to the creature, *follow those men and report back to me where they're going.* He had a plan formulating already.

Obediently, Firia's familiar dimmed then pranced off to follow the constables on their mission.

With that done, Varuj was free to find her father and –

"What are you doing here?" came a woman's voice, and he turned around to see the sight of a female constable at the end of the hall he had been hiding in, standing outside an open door with her arms folded over her chest.

He'd been caught. Cursing himself inwardly for allowing such a slipup – thanks to his depleted magical state – he forced a smile to his face. Those devilishly handsome features shone through from beneath his dark hood as he stepped slowly closer. "I was hoping to find a constable that might help me," he said in his silken voice.

She didn't look swayed, however. "Awfully late to come sneakin' around here." Her blonde hair was pulled away from her face and pinned at the nape of her neck, revealing her strong jaw and full lips. "You look more likely to be a thief."

With a broad grin and a deep, smooth chuckle he said, "Would be the wrong place for a thief to show up, no? The heart of law enforcement itself." His curious accent rolled off his tongue so deliciously as he approached the elven woman, a triangle of chest bare from his foreign robe-style. "I am Tieq. A visitor from afar." He gave a deep, gentlemanly bow that surpassed the grace of the most noble of elves.

Her eyes narrowed at him, her suspicion not allayed. "And you decide, of all places to act the tourist, to come here in the middle of the night?" Her voice was a bit husky but calm, even though her motions spoke to being apprehensive.

Rising up, he reached beneath his hood and stroked back some of that thick, lustrous black hair. "In my land, the law is caretaker to all. An aid to lost travellers, a…" he hesitated, his almond-shaped eyes brightening as he stood but a foot from her then. "Comfort to the lost man," he said in manly husk, the subtle influences of his spells lacing his every word with such powerful persuasion.

It gave her pause, and she held her breath for a moment longer. Swallowing, she looked him over once more, taking him in and considering the truthfulness of his story before she finally nodded. Even in his exhaustion he managed to make her agree, and her arms unfolded from beneath her chest.

"What is it you're lookin' for, then?"

"Well," he began, a wry smile on his face, showing those white teeth of his, so flawless. "I was looking for a man I heard to be arrested, but…" He looked her over with obvious interest, his hand moving up, then trailing down the center of his chest, drawing the woman's eyes to his hard pecs, then down along the trail between his chiselled abs as he parted the robe lower with his touch. "It is hard to think on such things in such beauteous presence."

She shifted, watching his hand intently as her lips parted. It was a natural and subconscious response to his teasing, but the woman was clearly trying to fight it. She swallowed hard, but when she spoke again it was breathily. "What type of man?"

"Human, somewhat tall." He described her father in as great of detail as he could, ending with, "He was arrested for treason, I hear. Nasty sort of accusation, no?" He stepped in close to her, his scent, so masculine, so exotically foreign, so alluring in her nostrils as he hovered near. "'Tis a shame I must concern myself with such a fellow, when I stand before a woman every bit more worthy of my attentions," and his free hand rose, touching beneath her chin. That warm stroke of her flesh was scintillating, filled with magical influence.

Her head tilted into him, her lashes descending downwards. She looked so peaceful and calm except for the heat that radiated from her cheek. She was luxuriating in his feel, his smell, his presence. It was as though she were dazed by him, struck by his strange attractiveness.

Varuj moved in so that his nose grazed hers: "You wouldn't happen to know where such a man is held, would you, hm?" His voice such a deliriously pleasant husk as he stroked his fingers from her jawline along down her neck.

He felt her swallow again as she nodded. "He's in the interrogation cells." Then, obviously remembering he wasn't a constable, she added on, "At the end of the hall take a left, then a right. Go up the stairs five flights, then take a left until the end." She rubbed her cheek into his palm, forcing him to stroke her like an affectionate cat.

Varuj smiled so approvingly, and it was enough to make her blush. "Thank you, darling," he cooed so affectionately. "You have been a tremendous help," and he leaned in, head tilted as he pressed his lips to hers, letting his tongue penetrate her full lips and whorl about her mouth so sensually.

He could still taste some lingering sweetness, as if she'd stolen away for a snack. Her mouth was so warm against his, and she was so receptive. So sweetly enthralled by his magics and charm.

With subtle grace he brought his other hand to her side, grasped her hip and pulled her in tight to him as he kissed her so deeply. So passionately, so…

She was unconscious, as he had intended with his soothing spell, and he held her body in his arms as he dragged her into the room she'd come out of and set her down in the chair. "Rest well," he said with a smirk, heading off back into the hall and following her directions.

It took him a while to make it to the interrogation cells, as he had to be careful to not be seen again. Conserving his remaining magical energy was vital to his plans.

So when he approached the cell containing Firia's father, the man didn't even hear his approach.

"Firia sent me," came his voice so quietly, though it stirred the silence.

"Firia?!" came the excited and confused voice of the middle-aged man. "H-how?" He came to the cell door and grasped the bars. "Who are you?" he asked, seeing the strange man staring in.

"A friend of hers. From the Academy," Varuj replied. "I came in her stead, for it was the only way to convince her not to throw away her future on your behalf."

A half smile teased the man's lips before he shook it away. "Well I'm glad to see she still has some sense left. I told her before I left, giving her what I did…" The man took a deep breath. "Still, it's too late for me. I'm already guilty in their eyes, and I won't apologize for what I did."

Varuj stared in at the man seriously. "You know that will not be enough to satisfy her," he retorted immediately. "If I do not free you from here, she shall never be satisfied, and will throw her entire future away in restless pursuit of your freedom. That is an unavoidable fact of the situation."

Varuj wet his lips as he peered up and down the hall before speaking next. "I can get you out of here. But not without a price. I have already paid greatly just to get this far," he intoned.

The prisoner grimaced. "I gave everything I had for Firia. Everything."

"Not that kind of price," he said grimly. "I can free you. Bring you to people who may shelter you. But it will take a heavy toll. And I need you to sacrifice something far more valuable than coin to make that possible." He softened his gaze and asked, "You love your daughter, no? And you crave freedom from this prison? I can give you both."

Kanfa continued to stare skeptically at the man before finally he nodded. "Fine, yes. Whatever it is to keep Firia on her path. Just, we must be quick. The guards will be checking me before sunrise."

Varuj brought his dark, neatly manicured hand up to the window slot and reached through. "Take my hand then," he intoned, and the two men joined their touch. "You've volunteered a great sacrifice for your daughter. You're a grander father than I could've imagined. I only hope you remain half as much minus your soul."

The middle-aged human had little time to react, barely passing the stage of confusion before he felt the very essence of his life leach out of him in spiritual pact.

It was a more horrific experience than one could've imagined, and Kanfa would've cried out if he had the ability, except for that moment there was nothing but the anguish of his soul pouring out of him and into the demon.

When it was done at last, Varuj had only to touch his hand to the door and intone a single spell word for it to swing open. Kanfa stood there, looking the same as before, although the warmth and affection seemed drained out of him.

"We must go," stated the demon softly. "I know some people who should take you in. With some persuading at least."

Kanfa nodded somewhat dispassionately and followed after him.

It wasn't until they were out in the night air again that Firia's father could really sense the emptiness, the notion of having lost something so precious. He would've mourned, but he didn't particularly feel that strongly about it. "Where to?" he asked.

"This way," said Varuj, pulling back his hood and revealing his stunning yet changed features. No longer did horns grace his head, and his masculine beauty, not diminished in the least, seemed somehow more natural. More of the world he was in. He looked like a dark-skinned elf from afar rather than a suave demon.

Most importantly, he no longer felt fear of being detected for what he was. After all, he now had a soul of his own.

CHAPTER 31

They approached great hall at the center of the craft district in the dead of night. From nearby came trotting Luka, the spectral fox reporting to Varuj in silence.

While the rest of the city slept, the place was clamouring with constables ringing it, the raised voices of people squabbling inside, orders being barked and chained humans being hauled out.

"Your salvation," exclaimed the "reformed" demon, casting a sidelong look to Firia's father.

"Hardly looks like much," he remarked in return a bit listlessly, little hope in his voice.

"Not yet," agreed Varuj as he looked to the fox. "Go. Return to your mistress, she may have greater need of you than I, and time is of the essence. Hurry."

As if he were caught in the wind, the fox swirled and wafted up into the air, taken away into the sky, vanishing into the night.

"Now stay close," remarked Varuj. "I'll need to earn you a place in this group, so they can hide you."

Kanfa could only study the strange man with some detached curiosity, unsure of what to expect.

Varuj simply strode forward into the cordoned off area, one of the constables approaching him. "Turn around! You can't enter here, this is official –"

The elf went flying, striking against the stone wall with a loud crunch, with only a finger laid upon him.

With each step, Varuj swelled in proportion, his muscles bulging as more attention was garnered from two constables herding captives along. "What in the –"

"Stop right there!"

With massive fists, Varuj broke their jaws then kicked a third that came at him from behind, knocking him into the hall's door and breaking the mighty wood.

It was like a bee's hive disturbed then, and the rest of the constables began to swarm upon the towering monstrosity. He showed no fear, batting them away like flies.

A constable came at Varuj from behind, but Kanfa picked up a baton and struck him with it in the back of the head, saving the brute from a stabbing.

Varuj noticed and grunted. "Free them!" He gestured to the staring humans, chained up and given reprieve from imprisonment.

The fight was slow to wind down, until the other humans were freed and they joined in.

When all was said and done, the hulking not-demon breathed heavily, with his robes tugged down, revealing a sweaty, heaving chest. "You owe your freedom to his man," he said, pointing to Kanfa, who looked lost in events bigger than him.

From out of the crowd of freed men and women came one. She looked a bit blackened and bruised, but bore the countenance of someone accustomed to leading. "He was sentenced to death for treason," she declared. "And after tonight we'll likely be no better off. How can we shield him?"

Kanfa looked to Varuj, the great hulk of a man licking his lips before answering. "You are rebels. Your own fate was sealed before we came along. You were going to let this man take the fall for your acts," he announced, though truthfully he was taking but a stab at the truth of the matter based on but a sliver of divined truth.

Though judging by the looks on some of their faces, he had predicted right. They were the true traitors, plotting rebellion against the civil order. And they were going to let Kanfa take the fall for it.

"After tonight the people will know you defeated the constables, and freed one of your own from a death sentence. Use this opportunity well." With that, Varuj turned and began to stride off, though from behind him a voice rang out.

"Why should we trust you? You're no human, and you obviously use some... sorcery." The word was spat out by the woman like venom.

The great, dark giant turned and looked back at them. "This man bartered for his freedom, and I care naught for what you do against the order of this land. Refuse him if you would and sabotage your own interests if you're enough of a fool." He shrugged and strode away. "I have business of my own to return to, far away from here."

With that, he vanished back into the night as dawn broke, plans of his own in the making.

CHAPTER 32

Deciphering the sorcerous writing upon the countless doors was painstaking, and Firia was only fortunate to have brought pencil and paper to take note.

She'd figured out the words, their meaning, even cracked the riddle to decipher which would lead her to her friends! Or so she hoped. Though as she focussed her magical powers upon the glyph and sought to unravel its energies, she could feel the sweat form upon her brow from sheer strain of anxiety.

Firia had never dispelled a glyph before, only even understood it in the most basic of abstract terms. She barely fathomed what had happened with Luka when he'd done it to unleash Varuj.

Varuj.

Thoughts of the curious demon wafted back into her mind and made her concentration waiver. She cursed herself silently, she'd have to start again, but then…

That first night with him. When she had brought him to the world, it had been such a curious experience. He had been intimidating, gorgeously masculine but alarming. She'd freed him from–

She'd freed him. Freed him? No, she'd summoned him, hadn't she? But… thinking back on the ritual, it had been unlike any other summoning.

That was why she had been drawn to him as her goal in the first place. Unlike other summoning spells, his was more complex. He was obviously a being of great power, for she had to perform complex preparations unlike anything else she'd encountered, she'd had to…

Her eyes flew open at the realization. She'd had to break through a binding glyph before she could even begin the summoning. A powerful wizard of some sort had sealed him away so that he couldn't be summoned, she realized.

Yet most importantly at that very moment, she knew she'd done this before. It wasn't so mysterious as she'd thought.

Excitement made her pulse quicken, but it was no longer one of nerves and uncertainty. This was something she understood, but it wasn't at the Academy that she'd learned it. It was on her own, hidden in that library back home.

She cursed herself for pushing away her initial studies, but it didn't matter. She had it, she was positive!

It took careful patience to work through the magic of the glyph sealing the door, but she understood it, finally. And better yet, compared to the glyph that was used to seal Varuj on another plane, this glyph was child's play.

It was just time she needed, the increasingly dwindling resource that threatened her future. Yet she couldn't let those thoughts interrupt her, cause her to stress or panic. Anxiety would be her enemy in facing this barrier. A calm, collected demeanor would be essential to cracking it.

The afternoon wore on, and she fought off the stray worries. The thoughts of missing her exam, of whether Varuj could save her father or not.

It all slipped away as she became more and more involved with the casting.

For the first time since she'd arrived at the Academy, she finally felt like she belonged there. That she wasn't some stray pet taken in out of pity or selflessness. She deserved to be there, but more than that, she knew she wanted to be there.

She'd gotten so wrapped up in the instructors and their worrying statements, so frightened at the fast pace and how outmatched she was by some of the other students, that she'd forgotten how much she loved this. How much of a thrill she got from just the act of casting a spell. The excitement she felt when she knew it would work.

Startling her, the door crackled and the glyph flashed. Then vanished from her perception. She'd done it.

The door swung open, then all around her the black chamber faded, as if disappearing into the beautiful surroundings of that familiar grove. Though before her she witnessed a strange sight.

Mae'lin and Bran were frozen in place, enclosed within a magical cube of pure aether. Like insects frozen in an ice cube.

Firia didn't know quite what to make of it until she heard applause, and saw Gway'lin dangle his feet from over the top of the cube. "Well done," he said with a soft smile, looking not quite like his usual cocky self. "Took you longer than I thought it would, but... you did it, fair and rightly."

Her nose crinkled at the elf, mildly insulted. She still wasn't sure what to make of him, but then, he seemed so untouchable. So beyond her understanding and experience.

She'd always been the serious sort and didn't have much time for pranksters, though. Perhaps that was all her trouble with him. "Thank you, I suppose?"

Pushing himself forward, he slid off the aether-cube and dropped to the ground. It was a long fall, and should've been a tough one to make, but he fluttered down slowly, as if his robes were a parachute easing his descent. She knew it had to be some sorcery, however.

"Seeing as you're the only first-year student to have cracked the glyphs on their room in many decades, I just figured you'd have blown through the mystery and got here promptly," he said, smiling warmly at her. The tricksters-look in his eyes had melted away somehow, and he looked like a totally different person. "But I guess you still struggle a bit on the syllabary. No fault of your own," he added.

"I like to ensure I'm doing things right. Perhaps I'm just more cautious than you give me credit for?"

Despite the calm words, she felt anything but. Her face was flushed and her hands trembled beneath her robe. "Does that mean this was the exam? Or… just a fun distraction?"

"Neither really," he said with a light shrug and a smile. "What I told you was true, your friends had fought against the rules. They had disappeared. What I didn't tell you was that I had already found them and punished them by locking them in time here." He glanced over his shoulders at the pair, "Quite the pair they make."

"So… you just wanted to see if I could do it?"

"No, that's not all it was," he said with a wry smile. "You see, any student who manages to crack the seals on their room so early has to be tested. To ensure they didn't cheat by receiving outside help," he explained calmly. "It just so happened that the two instances lined up nicely, and… well, I think you earned your friends a waiver on this indiscretion of theirs, don't you?" He arched a brow.

She looked to them, and once more that guilt rolled in her stomach over their fight. Over the fact that it thrilled her for a few moments that she was so important to them.

"I think the Academy would be losing out if you discarded them this early."

Firia was trying to push down the shame and embarrassment that Luka had been truly the one to break the room's seal. She would loathe to have it show on her face, and Gway'lin seemed to see far more than most.

Those bright azure eyes of his bore through her before he nodded. "I agree. I'll let them go so they can take their exam then," he waved a hand behind them and the two young men unfroze, looking startled and confused.

"Run along gentlemen," called Gway'lin in his musical voice. "Or you'll miss your exam."

The two were slow to soak in the words, but Firia could see the panic on their faces the instant they each determined that their futures were on the line. Bran took off fastest, though Mae'lin gave her a sort of wounded look first before following.

"No more fighting," called Gway'lin casually, not feeling it necessary to threaten.

Why did Mae'lin have to be so stupid and blind? Why'd he have to come across her at just the wrong time? Her gaze fell towards the ground and she felt such embarrassment even though she knew she'd done nothing wrong.

But she'd hurt her friend, and that was difficult to handle.

"I guess me too?"

Gway'lin walked around her, stopping at her side and resting his hand on her shoulder. "Go rest up. I think you've proven the test is below your abilities. I'll see to it you're exempt," he said with a warm look and a gentle squeeze of her shoulder. "You look like you need a bit of time to yourself anyhow."

She tilted her head and looked at him. For that moment, she felt like there was a real connection and understanding between them, but then it was gone and she simply nodded. "Thank you, Sir. I appreciate it."

"Sir, huh?" He smiled unevenly. "Working on inflating my ego already, are you?" He slipped his hand from her shoulder and gestured to the exit. "Go rest up. You looked like you had barely slept a wink when I came to get you. Sleep well, Firia."

As she turned to go, she saw sitting there Luka, the spectral familiar, staring at her, its fluffy tail waving against the leaves with its barely suppressed excitement at seeing her again.

Relief filled her. Certainly Varuj wouldn't send her pet home if…

She paused, just for a moment, before forcing herself to continue on, recalling the familiar into her.

Varuj had told her that he'd needed Luka to get him out of the Academy unseen. Was he back already?

She nearly ran back to her room, dread and excitement filling her mind with endless possibilities from the morose to the miraculous.

Her room was empty.

CHAPTER 33

It had been the better part of a week since Firia had last seen Varuj. Her familiar had returned in light spirits, and some days later she had received a simple note from her father. All it said was, "I'm safe, but must hide. Thank you."

It had arrived in an unmarked envelope in the usual mail delivery. In fact, the only reason she knew it was her father was the handwriting she recognized.

Yet still, no Varuj.

He'd abandoned her. He couldn't get back into the Academy, not without Luka. He needed it to shield him, and now he didn't need her fox anymore.

He wasn't coming back.

She hated that it bothered her so much. He was a demon that she didn't have under her control any longer, and that should have been almost a relief to have him gone. Instead she missed him terribly, and though she was grateful that he'd done what he'd promised and freed her father, she still couldn't help but lament his absence.

Still, she pushed the thought away as she went back into the library, once more trying to find Mae'lin to apologize. To explain.

Over the past few days she had checked for him repeatedly, but he'd never been there. This day proved no different, for their usual spot was vacant. Firia resigned herself to a lonely time studying, when abruptly she felt a hand on her shoulder.

Turning about she saw the familiar face of Mae'lin. He looked more himself, though still bore a bit of a pout. "Firia... I wanted to apologize," he said softly. Sounding genuinely contrite.

She smiled so brightly. Her anger and annoyance and shame all dwindled away at just being able to see him again. To hear him speak with her.

Firia shook her head. "Mae'lin, you're so dumb sometimes. Why did you keep running off? I could have explained."

He reached a hand up and stroked his palm back over his hair. "You don't need to explain to me though, is the thing. And... well I felt so foolish after. I wanted to apologize, but then... the thing with Bran. It was so... dumb. And embarrassing." He swallowed and peered down at her, the lanky elf so much taller than her. "I feel like a fool."

"Why'd you even fight him?" Firia shook her head, "Look, he only likes me because I'm human. Because he thinks that's all that matters." She wanted to be mad at him, to tell him he had no right to treat her like that, but she'd softened so much since her younger days. She didn't want to be alone anymore.

Especially not with Varuj having abandoned her.

"I know!" exclaimed Mae'lin. "Look... it wasn't like you think. Not exactly." The pale elf looked flustered. "I didn't start anything with him. He came to me and started shooting off his mouth about how you and he were the same kind, and I was sick for even hanging about you, and... on and on. It just got so disgusting, and when he said you were his 'territory' I just kinda... lost it." He screwed up the corner of his mouth. "It wasn't right for him to talk about you like that."

Her nose crinkled and she had to drop her gaze. Her entire body felt so hot beneath her robes and her hands kept balling into fists as he spoke. It was far worse than even she'd thought. There was no joy or pleasure in this.

"What a jackass," she finally managed. "Why didn't you just come to me?"

"Well, I did! Just now..." he rubbed the back of his neck bashfully. "I know I should've come sooner, but I felt like such a fool.

You're a powerful sorceress in your own right, you don't need me to stick up for you, and you certainly didn't ask for it. And I wouldn't have butt in, but… he was just such a jerk. I… lost control."

It was hard to imagine Mae'lin losing control. For as long as Firia had known him, he'd been so quiet and peaceful. Though as she looked him over, she saw his fists clenched at memory of Bran's behaviour.

"You didn't come to me before the fight either," she reminded him.

"Well," he began, wetting his lips, "I thought you and he were… y'know… going out." He looked so mortified to be speaking to her so, and he moved aside and sat down in their usual spot, head hung in shame. "I figured I was giving you your space to do that, but… no, really I was hurt and… and…" He cleared his throat and looked up to her, eyes a bit glossy. "But once I heard how he spoke of you, I knew you couldn't have fallen for a guy like that, Firia."

"Of course not!" She plunked down beside him. "Hell, when he was studying with me I was so excited to come back and show you what I learned. Hopefully you didn't need it for the exam," she teased lightly as she tucked some of her black hair behind her ear.

Mae'lin gave a sheepish smile to the side at her. He didn't have the looks or charm of an elf like Gway'lin, but she knew him to be a pure-hearted sort, and so his smile had a penetrating effect.

"I did well enough to stay at least," he said with a sigh. "I understand you did so well they threw out the test for you," he remarked with good humour.

"Well, I was busy rescuing you so I couldn't get those last few hours of study in," she said dismissively. It was so nice just to be back with him, and she was surprised how much she'd really missed him. Her heart thudded harder in her chest and she had to look away. "Just… talk to me next time, okay? I'll be honest with you."

A weight seemed to lift from Mae'lin's shoulders and he reclined back into their nook with her. "I just didn't want to be clingy and possessive. It's not like… we're dating or anything," he remarked with a noticeable red tinge to his cheeks.

Her lashes fluttered and she looked down, nodding. "Still. At the very least we could have studied together. Like always."

"Yeah," he responded, and his hand came to rest beside hers. "I wouldn't want to lose that, Firia," he said softly, a gentle smile on his bashful face for her.

"Me neither," she agreed breathlessly. Her pinkie finger extended, touching along his so gently, so bashfully, and yet still she had to look away. She'd been so confident back in school, but that was because she simply didn't care to know anyone. Now she couldn't do this by herself, and Mae'lin had been such a rock for her to lean on.

Other than when he thought she was seeing Bran…

She knew it must have been hard, and embarrassing for him. To think she was with someone else.

She couldn't help but forgive him.

Very gradually she felt his larger hand reach over and encompass hers with such a gentle touch. "So our study dates are back on?" he asked with a hopeful smile that lit up his face, making him look so much more striking to her eyes.

She nodded, her motions so slow and careful. She'd never been in a situation quite like this before, and it made her stomach clench and feel so tight and fluttery all at once. "Well… yea. We'll have an exam coming up before we know it."

A smirk formed on his face, such an uncharacteristic expression for the pure-of-heart Mae'lin. "There's always an exam around the corner," he mused in return, leaning in closer towards her, dipping his head as he spoke lowly to her. "Thank you for forgiving my foolishness, Firia."

"I don't want to lose you over something so silly." It was honest, and she bit her lip as if to silence herself before blurting out more truthfulness.

Mae'lin's spindly fingers squeezed her hand tighter and the tall elf moved slowly in, closing the gap between them in that quiet moment. Their lips met in such a cursory manner that it barely felt like a kiss at all compared to what Varuj had done in times past. Yet the simple touch was so perfectly Mae'lin, gentle and careful, yet driven by an inner passion that few could appreciate. Other than her.

She swallowed, and for a moment it was almost as if her lips were filled with sensation and devoid of it. She could taste him, lingering there, and she pushed back against him, harder and with all of that anger and tension she felt coiling through her body.

Her enthusiasm surprised him at first, but then he squeezed her hand back and pressed into the embrace tighter, lifting his free hand to touch at her back as they kissed.

It wasn't the fiery passion with which Firia and Varuj had embraced, but it was its own uniqueness, its own special flavour. She could savour that as they pressed their bodies together in their private nook, feeling the tension melt away over what was and wasn't between them. Their lips locked together, there seemed so much less to worry about.

Her skin tingled and burned with prickly heat, but she wouldn't pull away. Varuj had left her, and now there was no question, no guilt. She hadn't realized just how strongly she'd felt for Varuj until he left.

Yet by the same token, she hadn't admitted just how much she liked Mae'lin as well. With the demon out of the picture, it was almost as if he'd freed her in a manner, and her tongue gently pressed along the seam of Mae'lin's lips.

They parted for her, and the curious elf met her tongue back with his own, so moist and warm, yet tentative. He didn't have the experience of Varuj, and in fact it was his first kiss, his inexperience showing.

Though he stroked along her back and gave a soft little moan of pleasure as they made out. He enjoyed her touch, her press so intensely, and that innocent pleasure eked out of him so plainly.

She felt so in touch with him. With Varuj and Bran she'd always been surprised, confused about their motives. With Mae'lin, she understood them. He was so much easier to read, and her fingers went into his hair, massaging his scalp with her nails.

It was so pleasant, so relaxing, and she shifted closer into him. The heat was growing so intense beneath her robes, but it didn't matter. She just wanted to feel more of him.

Time was lost, and she had no idea of how long they were locked in their embrace. Mae'lin's furtive touches, his cautious excitement were such a contrast to what she was used to, though he never seemed to grow tired of it. Of her.

The moment was only spoiled when the sound of books slipping off the shelf onto the floor and feet retreating jarred them from the illusion of privacy, and they jerked away to look around.

Firia's cheeks were flushed bright red, and she squirmed away from Mae'lin more out of concern for embarrassing him than anything. He tasted so... nice, and she licked over her lips unconsciously.

Though for every bit of embarrassment she showed, Mae'lin seemed to show double. "Sorry for getting carried away," he murmured to her. "I don't know what came over me."

Such innocent words from him, when compared to how she'd seen other men behave.

"It's fine," she managed to breath out, fanning herself with her hand as she pushed herself up. Her lips were numbed from the kiss and she kept licking them, hungry for more. "I mean, it was good." *Not fine, Firia. Nothing about that was as benign as fine*, she chided herself.

"You... you think?" he asked, his pale cheeks tinted rosy, his lips looking puffy and full from their making out. "I mean, I'm not... I'm new... I just haven't... before I mean." He struggled then broke into a soft laughter. "Sorry, I feel so silly. Giddy!"

He was so adorable sometimes. She couldn't help but smile, her gaze dropping to the floor. Her heart was still racing and she nodded again, feeling quite the same. "Yea. Yea, it was good," she reiterated.

CHAPTER 34

The days at Gaul'di-mere Academy were long, yet short. So packed full of activities, so exhausting, but never enough time to do all Firia needed. Certainly not enough to do all of what she wanted.

Though free time was given, those who didn't use it to hone their abilities and enhance their knowledge sank in the sea of competing sorcerers and sorceresses. So many of them eager to crawl over the backs of the slothful to claim the fruits of success, including appointments to senior instructors and advanced degrees.

So despite their initial interlude, the days went by with little more than time spent studying with Mae'lin. Though she cherished those moments.

"Snap out of it," said Ala'nase, snapping her fingers quite literally in front of her face. "You're in a complete trance," she remarked as they walked along towards the dining hall for dinner.

"Sorry, Ala," she apologized to her friend for what was surely the dozenth time. She kept drifting off, smiling at those hidden glances and forbidden touches that she and Mae'lin now shared. It was so simple, and so enjoyable, all at once. It didn't feel complicated or frightening. And despite them being different races, it felt quite right.

"You're a real aether-case these days," mused the dark-skinned elven woman as she clutched her own books and walked along. The sun was out in full force and she was enjoying it, "Classes keep getting tougher. There's no easing up here, is there?" She mused aloud.

Firia began to notice, people seemed to be rushing about a bit more than usual.

"There's always something on the go," she said with unease. "Why do you think they're all in a hurry? Did I miss something in my, ah, daze?"

For all her chiding, it seemed Ala'nase was no less lost in her own world, for she hadn't even noticed the growing furor amongst the people. "Hey," she remarked with some consternation, "is it just me or are they all heading away from the dining hall?"

Firia had little time to ponder that, for as they were but a few meters shy of the great doors to that hall, they burst open – quite literally – with a shower of splinters sent flying.

Before the two young sorceresses loomed a giant beast, with hooked-talons for claws, long spindly arms, and a beak-like snout. Though far from resembling a bird, the hideous monstrosity loomed over them more like a ravenous bear, and a great, skull splitting shriek tore from its gaping maw.

"What the..." Firia gasped, taking a step back. Her instinct wasn't to run, though. Somehow it was as if everything at the academy translated into a test, and her first response was to succeed. Completing the game to save Bran and Mae'lin had ignited that love of magic in her once more, and instantly she called Luka to her side.

Normally summoning forth Luka was such a beautiful process, though calling him out so abruptly, it was like a tear in the air as the light burst forth in a crackling fit to form the spectral fox.

It was scarcely a moment too soon, for the great beast lashed out with one of its taloned hands, and Luka dove before Firia to block its blow.

The crackle of light that erupted from the display was both beautiful and startling, and Luka lost form as a fox and spiraled about the creature's almost human-like hand to fend off those claws. For its part, the beast recoiled, then shook its limb to try and free itself of the tendrils of light that burned and constricted about it.

"We should run!" cried her friend at her side, grasping Firia's arm and tugging.

But Firia wasn't going to back down from any test.

"We can do this, Ala!" she shouted, even as she felt that ring begin to tingle as she summoned its powers, falling back on her element. Fire. Everything was weak to fire.

Wasn't it?

Regardless, the surge of heat that coursed through her set her hair to dancing behind her head. She watched flames lick up around her arm as she conjured forth fire to her palm.

So great was her display it drew the attention of the beast before her, and it lunged forward onto its forelimbs and snapped its beaked maw at her.

It was only the quick thrust of her arm and the surge of flame that thwarted the beast's ravenous attack. It shrieked in agony as the fire burned its face and set its furry hide to smoldering. Though it was not quite as effective as she had hoped.

As Luka slipped away from the creature to dash to her side again in the form of a fox, the beast retaliated quicker than either of them could hope to counter.

Those giant, raking talons tore through the air faster than anything Firia had experienced, and were enough to easily cleave her in twain.

By sheer good fortune, Ala'nase finished her own spell, and the stone and earth beneath them rose up in a sheer wall that caused the creature's talons to rake upon it instead of them.

Stone rubble fell about Firia's feet, the wall that had appeared so mighty shattered to bits and the creature little more than surprised.

Why weren't the other students helping? They could defeat it if they all joined together...

She ran backwards, but never did she stop conjuring that flame, willing it to burn brighter and hotter than anything she'd worked with before. She'd given it her all to get into the school, but she felt that relaxed calm flood through her.

For the first few months school had seemed overwhelming and complicated. The theories. The studying. Learning a new language.

She wondered if she hadn't been overzealous thinking this was her calling.

But in the moments that she was truly working magic, bending the world to her will, she knew this was her calling. She'd never felt so passionate about anything in her life.

Well, aside from surviving the day.

"Fight!" she cried desperately to the fleeing students.

Though she was so wrapped up in her own battle, she failed to realize there were no fleeing students left. They were all long gone but for Ala'nase, clinging to her "coattails" as it were.

The great beast was in pursuit, down on all fours as it barreled towards her again and again.

The heat from her flames was so intense, the waves washed over her and sent her robes billowing back behind her, the cloth moulded to her shape.

She continued to build that heat to such an intensity, and Luka bought her time to hone the spell while Ala'nase chipped away at it.

Chunks of stone flew from the ground to peck at the creature, doing it little harm but distracting it and making it wince on occasion. Its great bulk was able to take the brick sized stones like mere annoyances.

Luka darted about so spryly, at times slipping in beneath it when it let its guard down to nip at its great ankles and cause it to stumble.

Upon one of those stumbles, its head impacted the ground, and though it looked ready to lunge forth once more, Firia took her opportunity.

The concentrated fire in her palm glowed blue rather than red, and it struck forth like a missile rather than flame. So powerful was it, that caught in its wake, both her and Ala'nase were knocked back a few feet further by the heat waves as they missed the moment of triumph when flesh and fur were seared and the tower of looming death let forth a mournful cry.

All before swaying and struggling to its clawed hands before slouching forth and collapsing in heavy, laboured breathing.

Firia didn't take the time to celebrate, though. Instead she began conjuring again, feeling that magical ring burn her finger, but she suppressed it. She wouldn't be caught off guard.

"Where are the professors?!"

She didn't need to wait long for an answer, for Ala'nase pointed to the side, and right there was a familiar sight.

Several instructors rushed forward, looking surprised. Amongst them she recognized the haughty elf who had nearly cost her admission to the academy, Gway'lin and the old human who had stood up for her.

"Petulant child!" cried professor Yae'ra, the one who had tried to steal her dream. "Why did you take on an aviard beast instead of fleeing?!"

The looks upon their faces were a mix. Some aghast like professor Yae'ra, others shocked, while the two most important to her were quite different. The old wizard looked impressed beneath his beard, while Gway'lin looked equal parts frightful and joyful. For her.

She gasped and let the flame dissipate, looking to the fallen beast. "I couldn't run! It was... instinct." Her heart was thudding so heavily, and with the three of them staring at her suddenly she did want to flee. From them.

Ala'nase still tugged at her sleeve, as if the two could still simply run off and escape any trouble.

"You are far too inexperienced to take on such a threat by yourselves! The danger you put yourselves and others in by attacking and enraging that thing are–"

Gway'lin stepped out in front. "You both are unhurt, I trust?" he asked with concern, his melodic voice so heavenly as he looked to Firia with those wide, round blue eyes of his.

"I think so, and to be fair, sir, it was kind of already enraged when it burst through the doors and started trying to attack us..." Her voice kept getting softer and softer at the attention, and she moved a bit closer to her friend.

Maybe Ala knew of a spell that would let the ground swallow them up.

The other professors moved to contain the still-breathing creature, but she retained the attention of those three.

"For this outrage you'll both be–"

"Given a special reward," interrupted the aged human, arms folded across his chest.

The other two elves looked to him with surprise. "You can't seriously mean to reward these two for their reckless behaviour?!

Think of the example it shall set for the whole of the academy!" cried Yae'ra.

Gway'lin butted in again, "Surely we can handle this in such a way that word does not get out to encourage all the students to tackle such issues beyond their abilities." He was pleading on their behalf, and his melodic voice was so convincing.

Not, however, to the two powerful sorcerers he contended with.

"It is already too late for that," intoned the old human whom Firia had thought was on her side. "We tell these students that everything is a test here. That they must solve the many puzzles we put before them to succeed." The wizened wizard arched a brow. "Do we really intend to feign surprise that they take this to heart even in the face of mortal danger?"

"And how could they even be absolutely certain it was mortal danger," added Gway'lin again. "They may have thought it was merely an apparition. A test!"

"Isn't it, though?" she asked, her eyes furrowing towards the beast. "I mean… how else did it get in the cafeteria?"

"Of course it's not!" snapped Yae'ra.

Gway'lin looked to the creature, which the other professors had bound and were in the process of having suspended in the air and taken away. "I'm afraid it wasn't a test. Not at all. But likely someone at the academy dabbled in powers beyond their ability. It happens from time to time. Despite our best efforts to temper people's enthusiasm."

Firia's eyes widened. Throughout it all she'd half assumed she wasn't in real danger. That the professors were able to keep this world safe and controlled.

Knowing that wasn't true made the very real fear chill her spine, and she clutched Ala's arm tightly. "I.. thought it was just a test. To… see what we'd do in the face of danger, without planning. It all happened so fast, that was just my first… thought."

"You see?" murmured the aging wizard as he moved forward and watched the giant aviard towed away by the other professors. "You're free to go, ladies. You'll receive an appropriate reward later."

Yae'ra fumed, and Gway'lin turned to them, speaking softly. "You two should run along now, there shall be some tidying up to do."

They were both too eager to disappear, and the moment they were out of earshot, Firia was apologizing to Ala. Luka rubbed against her leg and she dipped down, giving him a rewarding stroke between the ears as they fled towards their rooms.

"I've never seen anything like that."

Ala'nase looked quite pale, a strange state for the dark-skinned elf. "I hope to never see another one of *those* things for as long as I live," she murmured. Though Firia couldn't help but marvel at the fact her friend had stayed with her through it, regardless of her state of fear.

She'd never had someone she could count on. Not like that.

Not even Varuj, she thought bitterly.

She was content in her life, happy with what she shared with Mae'lin, but still she found herself thinking of the demon and wondering what she'd done to make him abandon her like that. He'd saved her father, and then just... left.

Had she asked too much of him?

"Thanks for sticking with me, Ala."

"I was too terrified to do anything else," the elvish woman said, breaking into a bit of laughter as Luka coiled about Firia's calf like a kitten rather than a fox.

"Me too! I don't even think we could have run away if we wanted to. Did you see how fast that thing was?" Firia's voice rose with excitement as she, too, tried to laugh off the terror. "I was certain Yae'ra was going to kick us both out. I would have felt awful if I did something like that to you."

Ala'nase batted a hand at the air and took a deep breath. "I'll manage that on my own before too long, I'm sure," she said with wry humour and a crooked smile.

"I wouldn't be surprised if Yae'ra sent that after me just to get me kicked out. He hates that I'm here," Firia lamented. "He tried to ignore me and not let me enter the competition, then he disqualified me because of what happened with Mae'lin..."

Mae'lin. The lanky elf popped to mind and she realized they were to meet with him. In the dining hall. The kind-hearted elf had always managed to get there before either of them somehow, doubtless in no small part due to those long, fast legs of his.

Ala'nase continued on, however: "I doubt he'd resort to *attempted murder* though, Firia."

Firia paused in her steps. "Mae'lin," she whispered, looking to her friend urgently. "Ala, I was supposed to meet him in the dining hall!"

The elf's eyes went wide. "You don't think... he's still in there?" Though judging by the expression on her face she thought the prospect very real. And very alarming.

They took off, racing back towards the dining hall as their robes flowed in the air behind them. The great doors were battered, barely hanging from their hinges as they hung loosely, great chunks missing.

Running inside, Firia saw that there were a dozen or more students about, and some of the staff and senior students were tending to them.

Moving past the terrible mess of the hall, where the tables were overturned, askew or destroyed, she eyed the injured seeking out the familiar face of Mae'lin.

Again and again each one proved a different student, and Ala'nase said behind her. "Maybe we should check outside; he probably got away in the panic."

Before Firia could respond, she saw him.

Sat against the wall, one of the senior students tended to him, his arm hanging limply by his side as he grit his teeth together in apparent pain.

"Oh no," Firia murmured, but it was mostly to herself. She was already sprinting away from her friend, her eyes wide. Both apprehension and relief warred within her.

It could have been so much worse than pain.

"It'll take a while to heal properly," remarked the woman tending to Mae'lin, though both the elves turned their attention to Firia as she ran up.

Mae'lin's grimace melted away as he looked up and saw her. "You weren't hurt were you?" he asked, worried for her despite his own condition, obviously the more pressing.

"Of course not," she scoffed, kneeling at his side, her hand going to his uninjured shoulder. "This is what you get for being early, Mae'lin."

The lanky elf couldn't help but grin as the student finished tying his arm up in a sling. "Usually it just gets me the first pudding, right off the top," he replied as Ala'nase came up, joining the other two.

"Nobody likes a man who comes too early, Mae'lin, take notes now ahead of time," replied the nearly out-of-breath Ala'nase.

Firia rolled her eyes as she pushed herself off her knees. "I don't know what they're going to do about exams with so many people injured…"

The senior student finished her job then rose up, brushing down her sleeves. "Only one student was injured so bad it seems he'll have to leave the academy for the time being," they remarked before peering about. "And it seems he was the one responsible for the fiasco to begin with." With a roll of their eyes she said, "Foolish first-years," as she began to walk away. "Dabbling in things they don't understand."

As Firia's nose crinkled she stared down at Mae'lin. "Hey, did you see who did this?"

With some help from her, he rose up a bit shakily. Though the tall elf seemed more anxiously startled than physically injured. "Only a glimpse. He wasn't one of the students I knew," he remarked, his damaged limb dangling in its sling as he cradled it. "Soon after the creature rose up, things went flying, people went running and… well, someone tripped. I tried to help him, but then I got hit with a table," he remarked with a wince.

"Could be worse," remarked Ala'nase, "could've gotten hit by the thing itself."

Remembering the claws it sported, that did indeed seem the more serious threat, and Firia nodded.

"Well, you're safe now. Ala and I took it down." Firia grinned mischievously.

Mae'lin looked at her with humour in his eyes, until… "You're not serious."

"Oh, she is," replied Ala'nase. "She's got a real death wish."

"I thought it was a test," Firia responded, her body pressing in against the larger elf's form, her hand surreptitiously slipping into his.

"Some test," he remarked, looking at her with wide eyes. Though when he squeezed her hand and smiled, she could see the pride there, if tinged with a bit of fright. "That's amazing though… wow. Wow!" He shook his head. "I wish I could've helped."

"It wasn't all it's cracked up to be," interjected Ala'nase, quite blasé about the whole thing.

"Yea, we… kind of almost got kicked out because of it."

Mae'lin actually recoiled at the news. "Almost kicked out for… saving everyone?" He seemed rather disbelieving as they began to move along. "That's insane, Firia! I mean… I understand not wanting to encourage everyone to follow in your footsteps and tackle giant, roaming monsters, but…"

"Well we're not kicked out, are we? So just be thankful for small favours and some kindred spirits who would rather I not fail in this place, I guess." Firia clasped his hand tighter, her body subtly moving against his. "I should get you back to your room."

Mae'lin pressed back against her, and she noticed he couldn't help but smile affectionately. "Thanks," he said softly. "I heard mention they'd give us the rest of the day off to recuperate… generous, huh?"

"Yeah, they're practically saints," said Ala'nase, pushing on ahead. "I'll catch you two lovebirds later then. No point in being a third-wheel!" She waved over her shoulder as she headed off outside.

Firia thought she'd never leave and a smile graced her lips as she began tugging Mae'lin towards his dorm room. "I'm really glad you're okay, but you know… we're going to have to study a lot harder to make sure you're up to snuff."

With a laugh, Mae'lin grinned a bit bashfully as they made their way to the residences and climbed their way up. "If it wasn't for you, I don't think I could've kept my enthusiasm going this long as is. It's a little scary how much work it takes to succeed here. Especially after all the work it took just to get *in* here," he said as they opened the door to his room.

"Just another benefit of being poor, I guess," Firia teased as she closed the door behind them. Her heart thudded as she looked over him. He was like an injured fawn, and she just wanted to coddle him. Nurse him back to health.

She didn't know why. She'd never truly felt an emotion like this prior, and even her fear for her father's life wasn't entirely comparable.

It was as if she'd been shown just how fragile her mortality is.

How fragile his mortality was.

She had no way of knowing the future, of knowing what might happen to them, but she knew of the genuine affection she had for him. The true excitement he made her feel. He was her friend, someone she could trust and rely upon, but he was something more.

Something she never figured she could have.

Firia lifted herself up on her tiptoes and pressed her lips to his, her arm snaking around his neck and pulling his head to hers. Passion poured out of her as she reveled in the fact that they were both there, alive and alone.

Mae'lin had but the one arm to wrap around her in return, but he held her tight with it, meeting her lips with his own intensity.

He was such a gentle, considerate man, yet she could feel the heat of desire beneath the surface as their lips met. Feel the excitement that ran through him as they shared the private moment in his bed chambers that they'd never had before.

Academy life had consumed them whole, devoured all their time, their energies, so it was such a sweet relief to take the little moments for each other. To steal away from the nonstop race through the ranks of the academy and revel in one another.

It wasn't the sort of fire she had with Varuj; it was its own thing. Different, but she dared not contrast them.

This was the affection she should crave and seek out. The innocent and honest lust between two students of the Academy. Even though he was an elf, even though there were some that looked down on him for being with her, he didn't care.

All he wanted was her, and her blood began to warm to him.

With each passing moment she became more and more wrapped up in his body, in the sensation of his mouth toying with hers. All of the sweet, youthful seduction made her heart patter and her body squirm.

Without realizing it, she had put so much of her weight against him, her squirming causing the lanky elf to fall back atop his bed with her in tow.

Far from being a hard landing, they hit upon the soft mattress comfortably, and Mae'lin gave little more than a soft "oomph" of a noise as he held her with his one good arm.

It did, however, break their kiss, and she looked into his wide, elven eyes. The sparkle of affection so prominent, unmistakable. There were no lies in his gaze; he was true and honest, and his affection for her was no less so.

"People will be so upset when they find out about us for sure," he remarked, a hint of amusement in his voice just before he kissed her lips again with a moist smecking sound.

"We're used to being social pariahs," she reminded him between the flurry of mouths and tongues. She didn't give a shit what anyone would say about them.

This was something real.

Something good.

Something more than she could ever hope to have with Varuj.

She shifted uncomfortably at the unbidden reminder of the demon, trying to force the dark thoughts of his abandonment away. They couldn't interfere with her relationship with Mae'lin anymore. She was finally free to like someone without being torn in five directions, so why couldn't she just enjoy this?

His hand rubbed over her back, through the magician robes she wore, stopping above her waist. The curiously handsome Mae'lin paused though, gave her a few more soft kisses then asked gently, "Are you okay?" He'd sensed her turmoil somehow, and looked to her with those big, elvish eyes of his to try and discern what was wrong, as if reading tea leaves.

She was always flushed, but now guilt twisted with her arousal.

She wanted him. Surely she did. He made her feel loved. It was a safe and comforting feeling that she craved, but she couldn't deny her longing for the absent demon.

Her eyelashes fluttered down and she forced a smile, enjoying how numb her lips felt from his mouth. "Yea. Just worried we'll be caught is all."

Mae'lin gave her an understanding smile as his hand stroked comfortingly along her spine. "It'll be okay," he remarked, his voice a bit lower from their long make-out session. "We should get back to studying if we want to keep doing well anyhow."

He shifted, and she could feel it, the bulge of arousal in his loins. She'd felt it before with Varuj, and felt it again then with Mae'lin, though he was so gentle and understanding as he shifted so they could both sit upon the bed. "So where should we start today?" he asked with a bright smile.

How could he so easily shift focus? Even she was having issues with her hazy thinking, and she licked her lips thoughtfully. She tasted him there and she longed for more, but something stopped her.

Why couldn't she just get over Varuj? He was gone! She might never see him again, and she'd be better off because of it! All he did was confuse her and make her feel things she never wanted to feel.

"Probably at something that doesn't require much writing," she finally said with a sigh.

"That probably means we should work on more writing," he said with a cheeky grin before breaking into a laugh as he pulled out one of their books with his good hand.

CHAPTER 35

The days were going by so quickly, despite her conflicted feelings for Mae'lin, the nonstop treadmill of classes, coursework, and study keeping Firia busy both day and night. Though the growing companionship between her and Mae'lin was a balm to her, soothing the stresses and anxieties of the academy.

After the first class of the day, Firia was surprised to find herself walking alone. Neither of her usual companions had joined her afterwards, though for Mae'lin it wasn't particularly odd.

The eager elf often went ahead to secure them study materials, a seat in class, or lunch quickly so that they'd have no waiting to be done. She couldn't figure out how he did it even, the tricky fellow.

As she wound her way through the campus, however, she came to a spot where she heard something odd. The sound of whispering carried far, further than a lower tone, though whatever conspirators chattered away seemed unaware of that fact.

Firia was not, by nature, a nosy individual, though something seemed so familiar about the two voices, and they came from the all-too-familiar nook in the gardens where so much had happened in her time attending the academy.

She held her breath as she moved nearer, simple curiosity edging her forward. Her hair had grown long since she started the Academy, and it was pulled into a high ponytail, letting her hear a bit better.

"What do you take me for?" came a sharp voice, and Firia recognized it instantly after drawing close. It was nearly impossible to mistake Ala'nase for anyone else when she was scolding someone. "No way, find someone else for your twisted little–"

She was cut off by another, gruffer voice. "Think about it. You know we work well together, remember–" The male's voice, so familiar, yet she couldn't place it right away, was too cut off as Ala'nase interjected again.

"I remember a lot. I remember how you cast me off pretty damn quick after we got here. So you can think about me kicking your ass if you try this shit again!"

Firia heard her friend stomping off, and had to scurry to get back onto the path to avoid getting discovered. Though when she rounded the corner of the building again, she saw Ala'nase approaching, book clutched to her chest as she looked perfectly fine. As if nothing in the world were wrong.

"Hey," she said, her usual voice, her usual manner.

That was... odd. "Hey. You disappeared after class," Firia chided, though she kept trying to place the man's voice.

"Elf-lady troubles," she said in that same dry-humour she always remarked. "You wouldn't understand." Her bright eyes travelled over to the center of the courtyard and she remarked, "Another big gathering. Wonder what it is this time?"

Any sense of alarm Firia might have felt instantly faded, when she saw the people weren't running or looking alarmed at all. Instead they seemed to be interested in something going on by the main gates.

"I really, really hope it's not another trick to lure us in, only to kick us out when we prove how awesome we are," Firia quipped as she moved closer. "And you know you can talk to me, right? I mean... you know all about my human troubles."

Ala'nase simply gave her a quiet look for a moment before starting to nudge her way through the people with Firia. "What's going on?" she asked to someone in the crowd.

"They're bringing in some new student," said the elven male to her.

"Now?" she asked with surprise. "It's the middle of the semester!"

The man shrugged his shoulders, "Beats me. It's never been done before as far as I know. But with the empty first-year spot after that dining hall fiasco, I guess they thought there was room for more." His eyes darted back to the front. "Oh, watch! He's showing off!"

"They've never replaced any of the others that got kicked out," Firia murmured to Ala, her eyes narrowed in suspicion. "He must be something special."

Pushing ahead of her, Ala'nase saw him first, her eyes widening in surprise then narrowing in a certain sort of seductive trance. "Oooh, I'll say he is."

It took a bit longer for Firia to get a good look. All she saw were fleeting glimpses. A brown, black, gold and red robe fluttering through the air. A shot of glossy obsidian hair as it swept behind the man. A flash of light as he cast some spell she couldn't even make out from her lack-of-vantage point.

A brief look to Ala'nase let her know whatever she was missing was quite captivating, however, her hand clutched to her breast as she stared open-mouthed. The crowd around them ooh-ing and ahh-ing.

With a bit of force as Ala had done, she pushed her way through and saw the man. Her heart stopped.

He was different. Yet there was no mistaking him, not in an elf's age.

Sandy-brown skin, sleek, long hair, a handsome, cocksure smile, all exactly as she remembered them. Yet no horns. No sign of him being anything but a man – an elven man perhaps – from some far off lands, blessed with exotic male beauty.

The robes even, were so similar. Cut low in the front over his chest, though beneath he wore billowy red pants and curved satin shoes that looked almost like slippers.

His almond-shaped eyes found her out of the crowd, and though he gave little away, she could see it: a tiny little sparkle in his hazel-coloured eyes that was all for her, just moments before his latest casting was complete. The earth exploded before him, a spiral of rock and vine shooting up into the air as he leapt upon it, lifting him up over a story into the air where he sat, cloak billowing in the air as the students below applauded. Ala'nase more than any.

He's back.

She couldn't believe it. Not wholly, and she pushed herself away from him. From the crowd. From the swooning Ala.

What did it mean?

She struggled until she was free of the tightly packed mob and she swiped her eyes. She didn't truly know why she was crying, but there was such an intense sensation of relief and gratitude and anger that swirled within her heart.

Besides. She didn't need to be there for him to find her.

If he still cared.

CHAPTER 36

The last class of the day was come and gone, and Firia walked off out of the building when Mae'lin approached her. "You up for our usual study date?" he asked with his cheerful smile, unpresuming as always. The tall, slender elf was a constant comfort, and she was glad to see his arm was out of the sling.

"Absolutely," she agreed as her hand ran along his forearm. "All healed up, hm?"

"Just about," he responded happily, the two of them striding across the campus. "Your place or mine?"

They'd gotten into the habit of studying in one another's room as of late, only going to the library as needed as their familiarity grew.

Varuj entered her mind, but she'd not seen him again that whole day since witnessing his show at the gates.

"Yours. Mine's a mess."

She hated the fact that she expected Varuj to be waiting in her lonely dorm room. At the same time she delighted in the idea that he was and that she would force him to wait for her. So long she had gone without him, but knowing he was back made her anger at him all the more apparent.

More than one time that night, Mae'lin asked her, "Is there anything wrong?" Her focus wasn't there on the work as it usually was. She realized that. Though the smiling elf before her was simply all optimistic concern.

"Yea… Maybe I'm just coming down with something. It's probably nothing."

It wasn't nothing. Her heart was in her throat and her stomach was twisted in knots. Guilt and hope kept dancing with one another and she didn't know how to stop it.

Mae'lin was perfect for her. She kept reminding herself of that, over and over.

So why did she want so, so badly to find out Varuj was waiting for her?

Leaning in, he kissed her on the lips softly, tentatively.

"If it's nothing you want to talk about, we can just end things for the night. It's about time for curfew to kick in anyhow." She'd lost track of time, and was reminded that she'd not shared the fact she can bypass curfew, first and only amongst the first-years so far.

She kissed him back and felt some tears begin to form beneath her eyelids. *Get it together, Firia,* she chided herself. She cared so little about others back in her former school, but now she couldn't stand the idea of breaking Mae'lin's heart.

Grabbing her bag, she quickly hid her reddened face from him. "Rest up and I'll see you tomorrow," she said with all the mustered calm she had.

The trip back across the dark campus was quiet. Few other students still traversed the grounds, for though more senior students often had means to buck the curfew, they were often too wrapped up in their own increasingly tenacious struggle to succeed to waste time.

Climbing the stairs, she could feel her excitement build as she saw her door at the end of the hall. The answer to whether he awaited her lay just beyond that familiar door. It made her afraid for the answer, and she delayed.

Leaning against the doorway she swiped her finger beneath her eyes and took in a deep breath. It was torture to wait, but her heart couldn't handle the disappointment.

Besides, if he was there, she wanted to seem put together. Unfazed by his abandonment.

Yet pushing in, there was nothing. Just air. Just her room, as lonely and as messy as she had left it.

She couldn't have imagined a greater disappointment, and nearly sank into immediate melancholy, except...

There was a knock at the door, soft and gentle, barely audible.

She composed herself, straightened her hair, cleaned up her face, but went to the door and opened it. Opened it onto an empty corridor.

Her heart could scarcely take anymore let down, but when she felt the familiar touch of that damnable man-demon, she knew he had been waiting.

"I've missed you," he husked into her ear, his arms moving around her waist as he embraced her from behind, the door slowly closing shut as if of its own accord. She could even smell that all-too-familiar scent of his, so exotic, such a pleasant musk.

Her emotions were sweeping her away. In her youth she had been so stoic, so collected. She hadn't cared about anyone but herself and her family.

Yet these new needs and desires muddied her mind, and her breath grew shallow. This is what she wanted. The pain, the anger, the fear, it all melted away and left only lust in its wake. The demon, the cruel tease, the damnable fiend...

He was tearing her apart, away from all that was right and good in the world. Her life should be so simple, so blissfully rewarding, and yet he tormented her.

"Then you shouldn't have left me," she shot back. "I never thought you'd come back and face me again."

She felt him still, her words biting into him more deeply than she'd ever managed before, and he pulled back ever so slowly. So gently.

"What do you mean?" he asked, that same curious accent on his voice, that familiarly odd way of speaking. "I saved your father, did all I could for you," he remarked, looking to the back of her head with an expression of hurt confusion.

"And then you ran off! If you remembered, you told me you needed Luka to get back in here undetected!" All of the strange emotions kept brewing to such intensity, and the only one of them she truly understood was anger. It felt good to be mad at him, to make him hurt.

To have control.

Varuj recoiled ever so slightly from her verbal assault, stunned by her anger. "You were facing a test all by yourself!" he said, his own emotions rising, she could see it in his expression. That handsome, flawless face of his, so strikingly gorgeous. "I sent Luka back to you as soon as I was done, so that he might help you in my stead should the need arise." His dark, deep voice tempered, his own emotion repressed as he explained himself.

He reached out for her, turning her about to face him. "I could not risk seeing your dreams and mine go up in ashes when I could find another way to return in time."

"And now you have! Showing off, finally, to an adoring crowd. Making sure everyone knows just how powerful you are. How did you even manage getting in, huh?" Her eyes were wide with fury and it was so cathartic.

His brows furrowed. "I had to impress them to get in! They wouldn't allow a late student in without a great deal of showing off, bribery and persuasive talk," he pled with her. Though he did his best to calm himself, reaching out and taking one of her hands, clasping it between his two warm palms. "I worked hard so I could return to you, with your affairs in order and no more worries to distract you from our life and goals."

Tears burned her eyes and she tried to fight them back. Her face was red and she had no way to express what she wanted. What she hoped to achieve with her anger.

It would kill her to lose him again, yet she wished he would disappear at the same time. She could be so, so happy without him. Without his complications.

Firia was at a loss for words and her body trembled as the anger dimmed.

Varuj slammed a hand to the door over her shoulder and leaned in. He was so close she could feel the heat radiating off him. Feel the warm wash of his breath as he pressed against her. "I longed for you," he said, his voice nearly a hiss. "I missed you dearly. What I did, I did for you. For us. To take care of your father, see him safely secured, that I might return here and be by your side forever more."

She could make out the dim glow of red in his eyes, and as she gazed at him she saw it wasn't anger. Not exactly. The passion that ran through him was conflicted, like hers, but she saw it clear as day: desire. "We're bound together. And I love you, Firi," those last words a low husk that reminded her of her father's sweet words and Varuj's fiery passion.

Biting in her lower lip she stared at him intently. The anger had ebbed and left something far more dangerous in its wake, and she pushed forward. Her mouth met his as her hands went to his hair and she tasted him with all of that pent up longing and rage.

The fire and intensity with which he returned her kiss nearly bowled her over. It wasn't like the sessions with Mae'lin, muted passions of two young, inexperienced students. There was anger and longing the likes of which Firia couldn't even truly understand, and Varuj didn't have the elven man's composure.

Two arms went around her, his tongue thrust deep into her mouth, and he nearly crushed her between himself and the wall as he let loose his own pent up feelings. His body was so hard and burning against her, loins so swollen in what seemed like a mere heartbeat of kissing her.

She hated herself. Hated what she was doing.

But she knew there was no going back. She didn't want to. Not then.

The long nights, dreaming of this man, of this demon... It tormented her, truly, but the lust it had awoken within her belonged to him. No matter what reproductions she could try to have, it would never be able to compare with the raw passion she felt for him.

She couldn't change that, no matter how she wished it to be different.

Instead she embraced it all, the nip of his teeth upon her upper lip, the digging bite of his nails as he rubbed his fingers through her hair so that her ponytail was undone and her dark hair came flowing down.

He had none of the shyness or reticence of Mae'lin. His hand moved from her hair, across her neck and in under her robe as he grasped her shoulder with his nearly searing touch. That raw physical contact was so sweet, so burning, she felt him grip her side with his other hand, as they gasped for breath whenever they could in their frenzied make out.

She'd never felt so alive, and her body ached for him. For more. To feel his touch all over her and fully be able to appreciate it.

She admitted she was terrified. Horrified, really, of what she was doing, but she wanted it so badly. She thought back to the night they met, to the way he had touched himself. It was his way of expressing interest: That was how he had explained it, and the reminder sent a shiver through her nerves.

He was a beast. Huge and terrifying. The mask he wore of the good-looking man was a farce, and she was the only one who knew it.

Firia had summoned him, and she had seen what lay beneath the surface, and still her arousal beat out her terror.

She moaned as her hands felt him out, exploring his body in a way she'd never dared to before and she was surprised by how powerful and alive it made her feel.

Her mind was a haze, but she could swear she felt the mental image of him match what she felt, and when her lashes fluttered, eyes flicking open a moment, she swore she saw him big. A hulking monstrosity as he was when she first summoned him. Looming over her as they kissed and touched... her hand slipping inside his robe, which came undone so very easily, letting her roam about the smooth, hard muscled flesh.

All the while his own powerful grasp did the same to her, letting her robe slip down over her shoulders as he reached in and touched her bare stomach. She heard his deep gasps for breath, the low grunts and groans of excitement and pleasure.

She should stop. Her brain was addled and fright balled up in her abdomen, but she couldn't let go of him. She wouldn't move away from him as he slowly peeled her clothing off of her.

She'd never been naked in front of anyone since she'd developed, and the baggy robes did little to reveal her form. Embarrassment crept into her, some modesty making her want to cover her small chest, the slim curve of her stomach, the swell of her rear. The robe pooled around her feet and left her so near to nudity.

Nothing but a sheer top and light pants hid her from his hungry gaze. It was as near to nude as she'd been, but she reminded herself of the weeks he'd spent with her...

She had no idea how much he'd been able to see. She had tried to fight that curiosity and ignore the worries all together, but now there was no denying it. Her pale flesh prickled under his touch, but her own exploratory hands didn't still.

They roamed across his hard, ruddy dark flesh, felt the firm abs, the edge of his own satiny pants. Even grazed the bulge of his manhood, so hot and pronounced, throbbing so thickly.

He didn't relent, didn't stop and ask her if it was okay, as Mae'lin would have done every step of the way. Varuj knew what he wanted, knew what she wanted intuitively, and just ran with it. Letting his own large, strong grasp roam over her without hesitance or pretense. He didn't skirt or brush against her bust; he cupped her breast, squeezed it firmly, with such passionate desire.

Varuj kissed and explored her in such a way that she was left with no doubts as to how he thought her the most gorgeously stunning woman in all the world. His every touch, every squeeze, every caress spoke of his unchecked male desire as she found her hand rested upon the string that held his pants tied closed.

She couldn't even think any more. She didn't want to.

For months, all she had done was think. Was study. Was worry and ruminate and learn. Her intuition and her confidence had been shattered over and over by the Academy's rigid rules, and this was her escape.

Him.

A demon.

For a while she felt like she might burn up, her body contorted as it begged him for more. He gripped her so firmly, so securely, she didn't feel afraid or insecure. He was guiding her, and that made her more comfortable, even as she tugged that string. Her heart stopped in her chest as her gaze fell downwards.

Somehow it looked bigger than she even remembered it. That long, slightly curved shaft, bulging with veins – bulging with lust for her – so ruddy and dark against her pale skin. Perhaps it was just the juxtaposition, of seeing it so close to her, not against his hand, but against her stomach.

It was a moment like no other, and she had made it happen when she tugged that drawstring. Yet it was all him that hoisted her up so firm and securely in his grasp, carried her with such ease to her bed and laid her out as he bent down to one knee over her, his mouth hungrily devouring her cheek, her ear, her neck. The hot, moist kisses insatiably unending as she felt one of his large hands roam up beneath her shirt and touch her teat bare and unhindered, squeezing her supple young flesh so that her nipple protruded out between his thumb and index finger.

It hurt, but somehow, it was a good hurt. Her body arched, and she wasn't sure if it was into the pain or away from it, but in the end it didn't matter.

The feel of his hand on her bare flesh, testing out her pert breasts...

She never figured it could feel like this. Never thought that it might be something so amazing. Her mind hazed over and her eyes fluttered open, looking over his body with such urgency.

He'd not appeared before her in such a manner since the day she'd summoned him from his realm. She'd thought it reassuring to see him in that more human-like form, yet to have him hovered over her, his body so big and bulky, the muscles hard and well-defined...

Though he was demon, his physique was all man. Pure masculinity, from the bulging pecs and biceps, across the ribbed six-pack of his abs, the thick, throbbing cock, with the dangling, heavy sac beneath, all nestled over thighs that could've crushed her.

Yet his face... those large horns, the fangs, the fiery eyes. She heard her bed creak beneath them from his great heft, but nothing stopped him from touching her, kissing and groping her. His dick bobbed with his excitement, smearing sticky pre-cum over her lower stomach, followed by his free hand raking its sharp claws over her flesh towards her waistband to tug them down.

She was so scared. He was massive. Huge! She wanted him to go back, to be a simple elven man again. To be that man that comforted her in her bed and knew her deepest secrets.

Her body arched as he tugged down the only thing that protected her untouched sex. It sent a shock of fear and anxiety through her, but lust addled her mind.

His size was so intimidating, but she couldn't stop touching him, whimpering as his hands were all over her body. Feeling out soft skin, exploring her nubile form, and she couldn't stop herself from making soft, kittenish sounds of need.

She felt his fingers return to her body after discarding of her panties. Those sharp claws of his tracing upon her stomach as he lifted his mouth from her neck to gaze longingly over her towards that waiting quim.

There was no denying that whatever desire she felt was at least equalled in him. Not with the way his fiery red gaze locked onto her slit, soaked in the sight of her laying beneath him, nude but for her flimsy white shirt pulled up over her breasts to reveal them to his fondling touch and fiery gaze.

Firia saw as his dick swelled again, that massive organ so intimidating as it disgorged yet more sticky pre-cum that smeared itself over her inner thigh and outer labia as he leaned down and suckled a teat into his mouth with a growl.

It was all happening so fast, yet not fast enough. All of those pent-up and repressed emotions, the fact that she pushed aside so much in favour of success at the Academy, bubbled over as her breathing grew heavy and loud in the small room.

"Varuj?" she whimpered, but she didn't know what to say.

She just wanted to hear him.

The hulking demon, several times her own size, taller than anyone else she knew, suckled her nipple before tugging it up and letting it snap back so elastically. He let loose such a growl of desire, unmistakable even in her inexperience, and she felt him reposition, the tip of his slick, bulging cock prodding her pussy as he licked and kissed up to her ear, that rumbling voice so dark and ominous, yet every bit the reassurement she craved.

"I need you, Firi," he said with a fire of unparalleled passion. "You're mine for all time, and I'll watch over you to the end of all things." His voice had transcended to something else. It was possessive, it was protective, it was... fatherly in a way, so rich with warm comfort as he nudged to her virginal canal.

"It won't fit!" She squirmed, and she knew it had to be true. They were so mismatched in size, and her body was so small compared to his. She wanted it, wanted him, so bad. More than she'd ever desired anything else. It was irrational, but she didn't care.

She just wanted to feel him become one with her.

Varuj, that hulking demon in his true form, moved his face up over hers, placed a hot kiss upon her lips and gravelly husked, "I'll make it fit. I need to be inside you. I need it right now." She felt the urgency in his words, his two strong hands sliding down to her thighs, grasping her legs.

He had little trouble encompassing her thighs in each hand as he bent back her knees and spread her open wide. He left enough of a gap between them that as his hungry lips moved on to devour her neck, that she could look between them, watch as that oversized dick pressed in against her cunny, causing her lips to bulge out around it, the labia embracing its dark, throbbing crown.

The tension in her hymen rose sharply then, that thin sheath of skin strained just on the cusp of breaking as he released a leg to roll back his foreskin and angle himself just perfectly at her too-tight hole.

Her eyes widened as she had second thoughts about this. About all of this.

The stress on her body wasn't pleasant, and she shuddered to think about how much it would hurt. She writhed beneath him as her thigh muscles were pulled taut, but her body was so slick. She was so turned on, and that was her only real saving grace.

Clamping her eyes shut she shook her head, the pillow ruffling her long, black hair. "Varuj!"

Whether she called his name in fright or desire, Varuj answered with passion, and thrust into her forcibly. That unholy girth ripped her innocence asunder and battered its way into her narrow little canal by sheer force.

The pain shot through her instantly, yet in equal measure that mighty demon arched back his head and let loose a loud cry of deepest satisfaction and most sincere of lust. The feel of her tight, virginal cunny wrapped about his oversized dick fulfilled a long held desire of his that he'd harboured from the moment he saw her.

Tears pooled beneath her eyelids, and she let out a squeal before biting it back. She couldn't stand it if anyone heard them, but it hurt so bad.

And so good.

The dull ache was combined with something she didn't have words for as her heart raced beneath her small chest. Her pink nipples were so tight, poking off towards the ceiling as her legs strained open for the demon.

Yet the pain and struggle hadn't yet ended, as that beautifully sculpted demon from the abyss began to rock his body, pumping that thickness into her deeper. She felt her poor little unused quim stretched and delved into like she'd never imagined. Like no elf or man ever could've done to her.

Certainly not Mae'lin.

To hear Varuj's husky breathing as he rutted into her, that harsh, deep voice cut through. "You're mine, my sweet Firi," his battering ram of a cock thrust so roughly, jarring her cervix as he plumbed her utmost depths. "I've waited so long to fuck you, and I'll have you forevermore. Mine!"

Punctuating his harsh claim, he grasped a breast and clenched it tight as he let loose his low, noisy grunts and groans.

His tone should have terrified her, but her mind and body were so overstimulated that everything was received through a haze. A frightening, delicious, wonderful haze. There was no end to pain or pleasure, they simply overlapped and combined into something new. She wanted him to stop, to keep going. To slow down, to speed up. Her mind was filled with contradictions and all she could do was whimper and pant dumbly as her hands gripped the bed.

His hands gripped her: her breast, her neck. His hand tightened about both as he tilted her head up and to the side, bearing her slender stalk of a neck to his mouth, which he devoured amidst his rutting. Each pump of that thick girth was able to be felt through her so intimately as it strained the limits of her youthful flexibility with each throb.

The lick of his devilish tongue across her neck was exquisite as she felt his hand tighten and squeeze, his dark voice so filthy and harsh. "I've longed for this from the moment I laid eyes upon your nubile form, sweet Firi. I shall rut you through oblivion's end."

It was a side of him she'd never known, and she shivered despite the growing sheen of perspiration between them. Her breath grew heavier, and finally she managed to open her eyes to mere slits.

His face was so devilish, like the things young girls have nightmares about. But not Firia. Firia had summoned him into her world, bound him to her. She had been so reckless, so brave, and now things had changed so much.

Her body felt like it might break under the strain, but her arms went around him as much as they could, clasping him tightly.

When he relinquished his tight hold upon her breast, it was but momentary relief. That towering demon clawed his thumb down over her belly until she felt the hard pad of his digit fondle her folds and then… he found a sweet bud of sensitive flesh even she had never dared toy with.

Through the pain of his oversized cock ravaging her, the sensation of him circling and rubbing that tiny little clit of hers was overwhelming. She only needed glance at his wickedly grinning face to know he intended every bit of it: the pain, the intense pleasure. Varuj held her in place through it all, his hand still at her neck as he refused to let her wriggle free of his control.

It was unimaginable. Never in her life could she have believed she would feel… this.

The sparks of pleasure shot off in her body as she writhed beneath him. Gone were her apprehensions of making noise. Gone were her fears and anxieties. It was as if he'd stolen her away from her mind, forcing her to turn it off for a blissful few moments.

For once in her life she was able to enjoy a perfect minute in time when her body sang and her brain didn't hinder her enjoyment.

All thanks to surrendering herself to the lustful ambitions of a demon.

Varuj's fiery eyes rolled back into his head, his own neck arching as he tightened his grip upon hers purely instinctually. He let loose a mighty roar of satisfaction as he plowed into her, never letting up on his torturous use of her body, of his exquisite ministrations on her sensitive bud.

Even in her carefree state, she felt the abrupt shift in his thrusts. The erratic nature that took hold as he swelled repeatedly within her, and she knew – instinctively – that some great moment was approaching fast.

"You want it, my sweet Firi," he growled out amidst his howls, "you want it, don't you?"

She couldn't speak. Not with the pressure on her throat.

And it was bliss.

Nothing but physical sensations. Nothing but the tremors that pulsed through her body. Nothing but the blinding ecstasy that started at that small bud and branched out.

She gasped in, her throat constricted, but her grip on his sides tightened. Her nails dug into his flesh as she bucked and writhed in a pleasure she never dreamed of.

Then it came. Then *he* came.

The flood of inhuman seed upon the crest of his bucking cock, that bestial thing that was too large for her pummeling her insides as he loosed his loins fully into her fertile young quim. His dark, ruddy body held a shimmer of perspiration as he arched his spine and spilled every last drop of his essence into her waiting depths.

He rode atop her like an unholy monster claiming his mate, those final moments all loud, noisy and full of the wet slaps of their groins as they struck each other. Every last drop of his seed squeezed out of his large balls and into her waiting, fertile womb.

Tears slipped from her eyes, the intensity of what she'd just experienced unlike anything else. Her body was sore and exhausted, her muscles crying out in agony, her throat feeling squished, and her cunny…

She groaned, but the aftermath of her own orgasm lingered with her, soothing her pain through the last few bucks Varuj gave her in his spent state.

When at last he came to a complete halt, he loosened his hold upon her neck and lowered his massive form atop her.

Firia was nearly crushed beneath him, but that warm, hard flesh was a comfort as he held her. Kept her filled with him as his tongue trailed up her neck to her ear, where he suckled her lobe and mewled his dark, unearthly voice to her. "Perfect. You're perfect." That broad chest of his swelled with his heavy breathing, causing her breasts to be pressed down hard against her with each intake.

It was difficult to breathe, but she didn't want to part from him. Not yet.

She was sure she looked a mess, her face red from the heavy breathing and the heat that had built up in the room. Still, as she panted for breath, it somehow felt right.

It felt like what she'd wanted and never realized before.

CHAPTER 37

At some point through the night he must have shifted back into his more mortal form, for when she awoke in the early hours of the morning, she found herself entwined comfortably with his dark-skinned body. The ravenous demon now simply appeared to be a stunning man, lying beside her on his back, arm about her.

As she realized that, it dawned upon her: if he was still there when the dormitory awoke, she'd never sneak him out without others noticing. And more than mere gossip hung in the balance. It could raise questions as to how this new student from far off exotic lands could possibly know her.

"Crap!" she hissed. The warm body holding her felt so sweet. She thought back to the times in her old home, feeling so comforted and loved by him. It disturbed her no less now than it did back then, but still she craved it.

And the comfort was ripped away from her too quickly as she shifted and felt her body flare up in new pains. Firia groaned as she pushed Varuj's shoulder, but she loathed to do it.

She'd rather lay in his arms all day than have to move again.

Varuj stirred beside her, his eyes fluttering open before he turned that beautifully masculine gaze upon her. "Morning," he said so deliciously, his hand stroking down her side before he leaned over and kissed her shoulder with his full lips.

It was such a contrast to the beast he was the night before when he'd fucked her, took away her virginity. The smooth, gentle caresses, the soft kisses. The fact that – though still much bigger than her – he was of normal proportions as he held her near-nude form.

It all felt so good. Even the dull and throbbing pains beneath the surface, if only because it was caused by him. How had she let herself fall in love with such a beast?

Guilt and shame slowly began to brew in her stomach. Mae'lin…

He'd been pushed from her thoughts almost as soon as Varuj walked back into her life. He was so sweet… He didn't deserve this.

Her gaze broke from Varuj's and she pulled away. "You have to go before someone catches you."

The dusky demon lifted his head, the silk sheet of black hair flowing behind him as he wrapped both arms about her. "We've still a bit of time, sweet Firi," he husked in his dark morning voice, the searing hot flesh of his member brushing along her thigh as he stiffened. "We were apart for so long." A hand slid up over her stomach and in beneath her shirt to cup a breast again. "But never again."

And just like that her worries were replaced by early morning lust, her eyes lidded as she stared at him with such longing.

She could never have guessed how strong her feelings were for him. She tried to ignore it, the taboo desires, but it was impossible now. With his dark body pressed into her pale flesh, all she wanted was to be surrounded by him.

"I feel sore," she murmured truthfully, readjusting herself into a more comfortable position.

Those strong arms of his pulled her to him, beneath him, the seductive demon sliding over her as he kissed her neck, licked his way up to her earlobe. "It'll help you remember me – and what we did – the whole day through," he remarked of her pain in a lust-filled rumble. He wasn't the hulking behemoth of the night before, instead looking so much like a being she knew and could understand, yet she knew it was not quite so. It was a facade, no matter how appealingly crafted it was.

She shivered, and even though her body pleaded with her just to say no, to force him out the door, she couldn't help but want him to stay. To feel that warm lust pour over her again, and her lips found his. At first it was softer. Exploratory.

Quickly, though, it grew hungry and ravenous for more. She wanted him. She wanted him more than she ever thought imaginable, and it completely erased all of the terrible feelings that being with him would give her.

There would be time for that later, she was sure.

He was inside her. It happened so fast, so easily compared to the night before. His size was so much more manageable after being split asunder by that inhumanly large organ. Though the ache of its previous violation still made his entry a painful affair.

Though he wasted little time, lifting himself up on one palm, the other still clutching her breast as he began to pump his length into her warm, wet, puffy quim. It wasn't like the night before, thanks to his smaller size, yet there was still that passionate vigor, that lust-let-loose which drove him to plunder her more ravenously than she imagined a normal man would.

And she couldn't stop kissing him. Tasting out his lips and his mouth, feeling that wet warmth against her. Firia's arms wrapped around him, begging for his touch. The feel of his skin on hers.

Her legs wrapped around his back and she gasped and moaned, but still he didn't slow, and she didn't want him to. Caution was thrown to the wind, and all she cared about was being with him. Being one with him.

This was magic.

She'd never been exposed to such things in all her life. Devoting herself to study had left her sheltered in some ways, and the powerful demon that thrust within her so raw and savagely had introduced her to a world she scarcely knew existed.

And he introduced her with little ease or gentleness. His pace quickening as he went, the slap of their bodies filled the room as his hard flesh wetly struck her soft, yielding form.

Firia felt him swell within her, not nearly to the proportions of the night before, but still so big. So virile. His chest on display for her as he arched his shoulders back and broke their kiss to pound a little deeper, giving her such a stunning sight of brown skin over hard muscle, curtained with long black hair.

He was gorgeous. She hated admitting it. She had always hated to admit it.

That first time she saw him in the library she had been so disgusted and curious, but when he'd changed form...

All that remained was interest and desire.

Yet last night, it was his immortal form she'd craved and received.

The thought sent a chill down her spine, but it was laced with taboo pleasure.

She should've been concerned for practical matters: for not being exposed with him, for what would become of her and Mae'lin thanks to her careless passions for Varuj. Yet there was only the grind and thrust of their two bodies, their sweet intertwining forms as she locked him into her with her legs.

Her poor, aching quim received his ceaseless pounding until she felt the shift in him. She was still so inexperienced, and it was but her second time, yet she felt the growing erraticness of his thrusts, the swelling of his member that strained her lust-slick canal.

She didn't want it to end. She knew what it signalled, and she felt such dread well up within her.

Not because she was afraid of being exposed. Not because she was afraid of Mae'lin finding out. Not then. Not at that moment.

She simply hated the idea of not being with the demon any longer, and that feeling was so overwhelming.

Varuj drew the moment out, for his pleasure and hers. His hand squeezing, kneading her breast, teasing her nipple as he coaxed such fiery sensations from her body with his cock. Until at last, it happened, and she watched his gorgeous male form spasm as he spurt his unholy seed into her yet again, heedless of everything but the satisfaction they drew from their act of breeding.

The last thrusts after that came slower, until finally he bucked into her one final time, his leanly muscled physique glistening as he emptied the last of his load into her nubile young body.

She whimpered as she lay back on the bed, her eyes partially opened as she looked over him. He was so stunning. Beautiful.

She didn't know if it was love. Not really.

She loved Mae'lin, and this felt nothing like that. This felt primal and wrong and crass.

So why did she want more?

It took all of her willpower to finally say the words: "You have to go now."

Finally relinquishing her breast, he lifted his hand and combed his fingers through his thick black hair before letting the strands fall slowly back into place. "We should play it safe for a while," he said in agreement. "Suspicions would do neither of us any good." He pulled out of her, his stiff, dark cock leaving her gaping and drooling his pearly white seed.

It felt so empty and alone to have him leave her, the fiend she craved pulling his clothing off the floor to get dressed.

She nodded in agreement even as a part of her burned with need. She didn't want to play it safe. She wanted to be reckless and revel in what she'd finally found...

But she knew that it couldn't be. It shouldn't be.

She shouldn't want him.

Pulling down her top she hunted for her pants, finding them discarded near the bed and quickly tugging them on. She felt as if she'd aged a decade in the last few hours and suddenly nothing else seemed so important as sex. As him.

But she shoved those thoughts aside. Rationally she knew that, to her, staying at this Academy was her priority.

Yet to see that feral man, his still-turgid cock tenting his pants as he stood topless, it was hard to acknowledge it.

He looked to her from the corner of his view, and she saw him grin, his eyes giving a light twinkle as he pulled his robe from the floor. "Don't worry," he said, pulling it over his shoulders then placing a hand upon her pert rear as he leaned in and nibbled her earlobe. "There shall be so much more time for us," he husked in a whisper to her, squeezing her ass.

Excitement and dread combated within her and she nodded before pushing him away. "Please don't let anyone see you, Varuj."

With a smug smile he tied his robe closed then said, "Don't worry, I shall be as quiet as the mouse." Though the final look he gave her before he left spoke of such smoldering desire still lingering in him. Lingering in him for her.

She felt horrible. Dirty and sullied and like a void had opened up within her.

As soon as he was gone she had to grapple with the concerns that his presence had quelled, and as she went to the bath, her stomach was like a lead pit.

Mae'lin loved her. And she loved him, didn't she? That affection, that adoration she felt for him couldn't be faked. The way he smiled at her, the covert brushes of his hand against hers, the glee in his eyes when she kissed him…

This would break his heart in two. She'd seen what happened when he thought Bran and her were together. He'd withdrawn.

Sure he'd said it was out of respect, but she knew it was something more, and as the warm water caressed her sore muscles she felt the tears begin to flow.

She really did love him.

So what was this thing with Varuj? Why was she so inexplicably drawn to him? Even though he'd battered her body, her fingers still grazed against those tender areas, and it brought about a pleasant feeling. It brought reminders of him, just as he'd promised.

Firia let out a sound of annoyance in the empty room, and it echoed back to her.

The frustration was palpable.

CHAPTER 38

Going about her normal routine was arduous, for she saw Mae'lin without delay. The tall, lanky elf greeting her as they made their way to class.

"Good morning," he said cheerfully to her, not a shred of understanding or suspicion in him for what she had done. How could he? The poor man reached out and let his fingers brush against hers as they walked.

Her heart fluttered and her stomach constricted. She touched him back, just a fleeting, exploratory thing. Could she have the same passion with Mae'lin? Would it always be this quiet, calm, sure thing?

She thought of what her first time could have been like with him. Gentle. Cautious. Enjoyable and tepid.

How cruel was she to compare the two? They were different and both spoke to different parts of her soul. Mae'lin was her rock, her comfort, her confidence. Varuj... he was her passion, her fire, her drive.

How could she be without either one of them?

"You okay?" he asked at her silence as they walked along, the reassuring yet concerned smile he gave heart-warming. And heart-breaking. "You seem to be miles away this morning," he remarked. "Oh, I bet you're already worrying about the next exam, huh?"

"There's always one right around the corner," she agreed. It made as good of an excuse as any. "Hey, have you spoken to Ala lately? She was a bit off when I saw her the other day."

It occurred to her then how odd it was not to run into her on the way out. She lived in a room so close to hers, after all, and they walked out together most every day.

Mae'lin shrugged, however, his warm fingers grazing hers as they approached the class building. "I saw her yesterday, but she seemed fine to me."

"Well, she always seems fine. I mean… she's brave. Strong. I think something's going on but she won't tell me." It felt so insignificant, but worrying about her friend distracted her from her crippling guilt. For the time being, anyway.

CHAPTER 39

When lunch came, Firia wound her way to the dining hall, and as she joined a smiling Mae'lin at the table, she saw Ala'nase at last. The tall, shapely elf was on the lookout for someone before she wound her way over to them.

Taking that time to study her, Firia realized the other woman looked different, then realized why. Her blonde hair was more studiously cared for, her clothes obviously freshly cleaned and pressed. In fact, the usual robes she wore were exchanged for an outfit Firia rarely saw her in. A pair of tight pants with high boots, and a tunic worn beneath a cloak that hung from her shoulders, the neck undone low so that it gave a peek of décolletage.

Firia's brows rose, then her face fell.

Surely. Surely no.

She couldn't be dressed like that to impress him, could she?

Firia shook her head free of the thought, but she couldn't stop glancing at Ala'nase whenever she got a chance, watching her astutely. It must be a coincidence. Maybe she found someone else. Maybe whoever she was talking to in that hidden clearing…

Mae'lin took hold of her hand beneath the table, squeezing it. "You looking for someone, Ala?" he asked their mutual friend, making idle chitchat as they all sat to eat. Only Ala'nase hadn't even bothered to fetch a lunch for herself.

"You could say that," she muttered, her bright blue eyes still scanning the room.

"You... going somewhere?" Firia probed.

"Only if I'm lucky," she responded, her gaze locked on the crowd.

Then it happened. Firia watched as Varuj entered into the hall, and not only did *Ala'nase's* eyes lock on him, but so many more, too. The seductive demon drew so much attention as he strolled on through so casually.

"Wait," said Mae'lin, "you're not obsessed with the new guy too, Ala, are you?"

Their friend didn't seem to hear, as she was watching Firia's dusky demon walk with rapt attention.

Damn it all to the void.

It was bad enough breaking Mae'lin's heart. To have to break Ala's as well? To alienate the two people she actually liked?

It was that simple. She just had to... not see Varuj anymore.

"You still with us, Ala?" came Mae'lin's voice, snapping their friend out of her stupor.

"Huh?" she looked back to them, wide-eyed and confused.

"You're hung up on that new guy too, aren't you?" he asked.

"Who? That dreamy hunk of a luscious foreigner?" she retorted. "No, why would anyone care about that stud?" Her sarcasm dryer than ever. "I'm just gonna head on off to get some food," the timing impeccable as Firia noticed Varuj headed in that same direction.

Firia let out a soft sigh. "She knows what she wants, doesn't she?" Her friend had always been so blunt before, but now that Firia knew she was hiding something from her she wasn't certain any longer.

It wasn't fair, of course. Firia had more than a few secrets from Ala. From Mae'lin. From everyone.

Secrets that could destroy her.

Still, knowing that Ala was hiding something made her uncomfortable.

Watching her walk up to Varuj in the lunch line and feign bumping into him was more uncomfortable still. Ala laughed, though she was too far away for Firia to hear, though she could see with crystal clarity. The way she smiled, stroked her hand along Varuj's bicep as she apologized.

The ways – both subtle and not – that her elvish friend set about seducing the demon she had summoned. Her demon. The one whom not but a few hours ago she'd coupled with. Twice.

She felt her body begin to burn with possessive anger, and her hand squeezed Mae'lin's under the table. She'd barely touched her food but still she forced a smile at him. "Hey, let's get out of here, okay?"

Always accommodating, Mae'lin smiled and set aside his as yet unfinished meal. "Sure," he said, squeezing her hand back as they pushed out of the booth and made their way towards the door. Though in her effort to watch Ala'nase, she saw the demon turn his gaze towards her just before she left. And saw her holding hands with Mae'lin.

"I didn't figure Ala would like his type," Firia admitted, though she didn't know why. She just felt so hateful towards both of them for that moment, the jealousy and rage completely irrational. It would be better if they *did* get together! Then she could be left alone to her simple, busy life.

"Him?" Mae'lin remarked, glancing back even though the doors were already shut behind them by that point. "He looks to be exactly her type, if you ask me," he remarked. "I think she has a taste for the different."

"I guess." Of course he was right. That just made it worse.

"Hey Mae'lin, did you want to just... go study somewhere today?"

"The whole day?" he asked, brow raised curiously. "You mean skip classes?"

"It's as good of time as any, and I think we'd get a lot more done." Truly she just couldn't stand to be around anyone else. She wanted to be alone with him, which is the last thing in the world she figured she'd want that day. Maybe it was her guilt or her jealousy, but she just wanted to see...

To see if what they had was real? If she could feel that passion with him? She wasn't certain.

Ever agreeable, Mae'lin smiled and nodded. "Sure. Your place or mine?" he asked, giving her hand a squeeze as the midday sun lit up his fair skin and wheat coloured hair. He was handsome in his own way, peculiar for an elf, different. Nothing like Varuj, yet he had a charm all his own. Just more subtle.

"Yours." Hers was a wreck. Even more than usual.

She was surprised by how easily he agreed, though not really. Mae'lin had always been happy-go-lucky. She was the reason they never skipped class or did anything daring. Even then her stomach clenched with fear at what she might miss, but she simply couldn't take it anymore.

So why did she want to be alone with the one person she should be trying to avoid?

Mae'lin's place was immaculate, as always, and he welcomed her in familiarly before shutting the door and resting down his satchel. "I think we're doing pretty good with the syllabary now. It's probably time to move onto more advanced stuff," he remarked, the two of them alone and away from the outside world at last.

How could she exist without him?

She moved to his bed and sat down, resting her bag to her side. She hadn't realized how little she knew about him, personally, as when she tried to speak about something other than work. Other than the Academy.

He knew next to nothing about her as well, but then, for the past year she'd thought of almost nothing but magic.

"Sure. I think we can handle it."

The two of them had grown up in the same quiet farming area, had both attended classes together most of their lives. But knew so little of each other.

How was that? The answered dawned on her as they worked away: because there was so little to their lives other than their aspirations to become mages. Their yearning to master magic and get away from their humdrum lives consumed them both.

When he wasn't studying, he had been tending to his family's farm. She knew that. She remembered him telling her, she remembered… she had dreamt of him before. Of the two of them, back home, her coming to meet him at his farm. Seeing him working, engaged in that physical labour, bereft of shirt.

He wasn't blessed with as impressive a physique as Varuj, even in her dreams, but he was striking then, nonetheless.

She remembered, too, how the dream ended. How just as Mae'lin told her he was going to propose, just as they began to kiss, his form had shifted. How he was no longer Mae'lin.

Varuj had taken over her dream, begging her not to forget about him.

It wasn't fair.

Now he was doing the same thing in her waking hours.

Shut off from the outside world, it was only when supper approached, and their hunger disturbed their studying, that they had to face reality again.

"I wish we could've started studying together like this years ago," remarked Mae'lin with a smile. "I think we'd be far more prepared today if we had."

Who knew the path she'd be on if that were true. She might never have gotten in to Gaul'di-mere, if not for Varuj.

"I wish we had," she finally admitted. "Mae'lin... You know I really like you, right?"

He looked to her, his elven eyes alight with tenderness. That unmistakable twinkle of affection in his gaze. "I know," he said gently, bending to his knee and taking both her hands in his. "And I really like you, Firia. I've..." he hesitated, but continued, "I've liked you long before I ever met you. I watched you from afar and somehow felt from a young age you were so very special. The one for me, if I was ever so lucky to be with you one day."

She felt the tears begin to build up and she forced her gaze away. "I never want to hurt you, Mae'lin." *But I will* went unsaid.

Gently he stroked his thumbs over the back of her hands and leaned in, kissing her cheek tenderly. "Don't worry," he said softly. "I'm tough. Remember the last time you nearly burned me alive?" he said with gentle humour.

"Yea, next time I try to kill you publicly I'll have to try harder," she teased back, but her heart wasn't in it. "Just... There's some things that I've done. That I'm not proud of. But that's all in the past, and I'm going to try to be... better, okay?"

The starry-eyed Mae'lin didn't quite know what to make of what she said, but he nodded tentatively. "We did what we had to to get here. All that matters now is getting through the Academy. Together. So we can start our lives together. Free."

Her lips pressed to his but it was chaste, and her smile was tight when she pulled away. "I'll be better, Mae'lin. For you."

"We'll head out and get some supper together, don't worry about anything else for now but getting through this," he reassured, tugging her up to her feet with his hold on her hands. Giving her a sweet kiss in return, his whole face lit up.

She was a horrible person.

How could she do something to such a sweet and honest elf? An elf that adored her and had faith in her?

"Lead the way," she breathed out.

CHAPTER 40

It wasn't until they had finished their meal and Mae'lin excused himself to the washroom that Firia saw Varuj again. The suave demon slid into the booth across from her with a smile. "There you are," he said in his charming accent. "I was on the lookout for the most beautiful girl in all the academy, and thought I might never track her down."

"Cute," she murmured, sighing audibly and looking around the room cautiously before she leaned into the table. Her voice was quiet as she stared at him, "I don't think we should be seen together."

The dashing devil leaned forward onto one elbow, cupping his chin in his palm as he murmured back to her. "What's wrong with the new student trying to make a new friend, hmm?" He gave a wry smile and a waggle of his brows as he let his eyes dip over her momentarily. "Nothing suspicious about that."

"It's not about you and this… new student thing. This is about you making my life so complicated. I know you saw me with Mae'lin. If he sees you here…"

Varuj's dark eyes narrowed just slightly, and she swore she saw a flicker of flame, as if his true nature coming through. "So it is true. You and him…" He didn't say it, he just seemed to fume in silence as he watched her.

"You and I aren't meant to be." Firia was trying to stay strong, to be confident about her decision, but she hated it. Every second that she spent looking at him, telling him the truth, it killed her.

But Varuj could take it. Mae'lin said he was tough, but she knew the truth.

Varuj, on the other hand… he'd find someone else instantly. Someone to replace her.

It made her lip tremble and her gaze fall.

"Meant to be?" he repeated derisively. "We make our meaning from life, you and I," he ground out with some anger. "When I helped you get into the academy, we made our own fate. When I saved your father and brought him to safety, we did it again." She could see his free hand was clenched into a fist. "When we mated we made our own fate, intertwined," he said, his voice raising almost dangerously high.

Her eyes went wide with fear as her face burned with embarrassment and anger.

It spilled out, before she could stop it. The truth. The utter, whole, absolute truth. "I can't hurt him, Varuj."

"And what about me?!" he said angrily, jabbing his thumb into his chest as he drew attention to them. To make matters worse, Firia saw Mae'lin returning, walking down the aisle back towards their booth.

"You have… others. Other options. Other people. Please, you're powerful and charming and you will have no problems… no problems with anything. You have the world. He…" She shook her head, glancing frantically towards Mae'lin. "Please."

"I have *you*." He leaned over the table towards her, his eyes burning. "You are *mine*," he stated firmly, and Mae'lin was so close. She knew she could say no more without him overhearing.

She had to get Varuj to go immediately or it would all come to a head.

"Listen, if you want someone to catch you up, I can do that, I just don't know why you're so insistent it be me." She was disgusted by how easily she changed the tone of her voice, disguising the anger and pleading. "I'm usually really busy studying, but… I can try. Meet me in the library tonight, I guess, and we'll talk about what you need."

Varuj glared angrily, then rose up. His movements were so elegant as he swept away, leaving Mae'lin to look baffled as he returned to her.

"What was that all about?" he asked her, looking completely bewildered. "Normally he's all smiles and pomp when he's flouncing about the place."

"He's upset because I told him I already have a standing study date," Firia lied. "I told him I'd see what I can do tonight to get him caught up to speed. Since you and I studied more than our fair share today." She hated this feeling of dread in the pit of her stomach.

"Oh," he said, looking off after Varuj curiously. "Well... did you want me to come along too? I mean, I wouldn't want you to feel awkward with the new guy alone," he remarked with a sweet smile.

"Hey, if he tries anything funny, I'll just practice out some new spells on him. Don't worry about me, Mae'lin." She tried to smile, but it was half-hearted as she pushed out of the bench and kissed his cheek. "Maybe you should spend some time with Ala. It might be good for her to have someone to talk to."

He returned the kiss, even though they were continually getting an increasing number of looks the more frequently they showed such affection publicly. "If I can find her," he remarked, "but if you need me, I shouldn't be hard to find. I'll take a look for Ala then head over to the residence."

"Thanks, Mae'lin." He was just being protective because of Bran, she reminded herself. Because of what he'd walked in on.

Still, as she went to the library she felt her skin prickle with agitation. Why couldn't Varuj just... make this easier? Why couldn't he accept her feeble protests?

Why did he have to feel the same way about her as she did about him?

She'd never said where in the library to meet her, but she got the feeling after entering that he was close by and following her. She wound her way up the building, and almost found herself going to her and Mae'lin's usual spot. Instead she detoured, going to a different floor she knew to be quiet.

Before she could settle on a location, he grabbed her shoulder and spun her about.

Firia found herself looking upon his stunning facade, his gorgeous face gazing down at her intensely. "How could you think to cast me off?" he hissed. "I go away to save your father and secure your future and you find another?!"

"You abandoned me, Varuj! I didn't go looking for someone else. It just happened. You even knew it was happening! You knew I'd been dreaming about him. You knew my feelings, you said it yourself." Firia was shocked by how angry she was getting at him, again, after how much she'd loved laying in his arms, feeling his body all around hers.

The thought made her blush and she hoped she could pass it off as rage. "You knew how I felt, and you never told me that you'd be returning, so I moved on, Varuj!"

He grabbed her neck, and instead of her first reaction being fear, it was a reminder of how he'd done so the night before. When he'd first entered her, and their bodies became one.

"I did not abandon you," he growled at her in the dark corner of the library. "I did everything in my power to help you pass your test as I saved your father." His chest heaved with his breathing, and she could smell his musk, his very excitement, upon the air. More than that, she saw in his eyes what lurked in her mind: the anger, the lust. "I would never abandon you," he added harshly, his lips but a hair's breadth from hers.

"I know that now! But I didn't know it then!" Her eyes were burning and she glared at him with such fury. "I didn't ask for... for whatever I feel for him. For whatever I feel for you! The only thing I know is that this would destroy him, but you..."

With his grasp still around her throat, he brought his other hand to such a daring spot. She felt him reach inside her robes and press in over her womanhood, that hot feel of his meeting her own smoldering heat. "What we did last night was no mere pastime," he growled, "it marked a very important turning point for us. For you." He so heedlessly rubbed her, stoking her own fires hotter. "You belong to me now. We have mated. Bonded."

He pushed his mouth to hers, a brutish kiss, not with the flair of his previous lusts, just hard and savagely passionate.

She gasped and a moan passed from her to him. She was trying, desperately trying to end this. To end the lust and the passion and the insanity that surrounded the two of them.

He made it so hard, though. Her body wanted him so badly, even as he made her ache with pain. She'd managed to ignore it as best she could for most of the day, but now it flared up, angrily and with such intense wanting.

"Varuj, please. Please don't make me break his heart," she whimpered, her body trembling like a leaf.

"You're mine," he growled right into her ear, flicking his tongue over the lobe as he slipped his hand into her pants and touched her puffy folds directly. The ache and pleasure he stirred with his motions so pronounced. "Say it. Admit it," he commanded.

"Don't make me do this," she whimpered, but with every word her protest became less and less certain. He made her feel so good. Her heart was racing, her body surged with adrenaline, but that gnawing guilt wouldn't easily subside this time.

Furious, he yanked his hand out of her pants, his fingers glistening with her wetness as he glared. "You'll regret this," he said. "No matter how hard you try to resist, you are bound to me now. And if you can't admit that now, I'll make you in time. I'll make you regret resisting me," he licked along his glossy fingers after his ominous words.

She watched with such rapt attention, her thoughts stolen from her as she took in his daring display. Her hands went to his wrist, tugging it towards her body as she stared up at him. Everything was red. Her passion, her fury, her need, her hate.

"Don't do this, Varuj."

"I can teach you so much more," he said to her, their eyes locked. "I can give you power beyond reckoning. Make you become the greatest sorceress to have lived. Together we would accomplish such things, they would tell of our union forever more." He pressed his forehead down to hers. "And I could fuck you into a delirium every night of your life should you just confess you are mine." He pressed that hand to her breast over top of her clothes. "Say it," he growled.

Her pulse raced and her breathing was so shallow. She didn't even realize she was doing it as she ground into him, offering her body to his greedy hands. Firia wanted him so badly. Burned for him.

The words were entirely unbidden. She tried to bite them back, to swallow them before they could ruin her, but it was useless.

"I'm yours."

Varuj didn't care that they were standing amidst the book stacks of the academy's library. At her words he grabbed for her, tugged at her clothes as he kissed her so passionately. He opened her robes completely, undid her pants, and was tugging them down before she could make any sense of it.

He was going to take her, then and there, she knew it. Wanted it. Feared it. He tore their lips apart and forcibly twisted her about and bent her over with his powerful grasp.

She felt like a doll. A mindless object, robbed of thought or will.

And she was grateful.

Sure, practical concerns bothered her. Someone could stumble upon them.

The moment she thought it, she moaned, and it surprised her. Was she that twisted? That she'd risk it all, that she'd allow him to have sex with her in public? Just for the thrill?

"Wait," she gasped, but it lacked oomph.

It was also too late. For she had nothing to do but brace her palms to the wall as he grasped his own fiery manhood and speared her upon it. To brace herself and bite down upon her lip to stifle her cries, that was all she could do as he took hold of her hips and began to pump his cock into her with a ravenous hunger that would not abate.

Even the slaps of his heavy balls striking against her wet clit threatened to give them away, however.

Damn him for making her so foolish. So reckless.

So needy.

She was so sore and it was hard to bite back all the soft whimpers, the little winces and murmurs of pain and pleasure as they combined. She was fast growing addicted to this, to the anger and the passion, as they came hand in hand.

He felt so good in his mortal form, though. It wasn't the fear and agony of the hulking demon. It was just the smooth, hard body that made her senses tingle with delight.

One of his hands left her hips, and she felt his fingers coil her dark hair about. The tug he gave back on her head nearly made her cry out, each strand straining her scalp as he fucked her and pulled her hair.

The way his hard body struck against her smooth, pristine flesh. The way his heavy, heated sac slapped her moons again and again, how she dared risk it all for this tryst with a demon. Not just Mae'lin or Ala'nase, but her very place in the Academy. Her whole life's work. All put on the line when she handed control over to that vile demon.

It made her body shudder and she was surprised that it wasn't another bout of tearfulness. The intense, searing pleasure struck through her like lightning, her silent gasp filling the air. She'd never felt something so powerful as her muscles and nerves coiled and sprung loose.

As her body exploded and her loins flooded about Varuj's stiff, hard cock, he tugged back on her hair, eliciting more of that sweet pain as he growled into her ear. "You're mine. Say it." He thrust into her hard, not easing up through her exquisite climax, even as his own thrusts grew erratic and his release became eminent. "Say it," he insisted louder, the threat of him yelling for her obedience implicit.

"I'm yours," Firia whimpered pathetically, her voice breathy and dark. She hated him and she lusted for him all at once. It was torture.

He rewarded her obedience – if not her emotion – with a sharp final thrust, hilting himself inside her as he erupted. That stiff member twitching and spurting its seed inside her, coating her tight, abused canal with his creamy essence so completely, until her loins were naught but a slick, sticky mess of their fluids.

For so long she'd ignored this part of her, and now it was overwhelming her. Her sexuality had always been a muted background noise, but he'd ignited something within her. Something she wasn't sure she liked.

Something she wanted, all the same.

262

CHAPTER 41

Her days with Mae'lin. Her nights with Varuj.

It was such a precarious balance, and it left her torn inside. Torn with guilt. Torn by dual passions. Torn by possibilities.

She felt – no, knew – Mae'lin and she could get through the Academy together on their own. Yet Varuj had proven already he could offer her so much more than merely passing.

They had coupled. Fucked, as he'd said, but moments before, yet seeing him stand before her, nude in all his glory, displaying a new spell for her, it was hard to focus.

"Telekinesis, so useful." He held out his hand, lifting a book from across the room with only magic. The sinew along his arms and shoulders shifted subtly as he manipulated it carefully. He'd shown her the method, the intricate casting, now it was up to her to imitate it.

"It's hard to concentrate with you like that." She still was partially clothed, him having torn down her pants but leaving her shirt intact for their latest session.

Still, she tried her best to focus, to imitate his motions. She was feeling so exhausted lately, and she knew why. Leading two lives was so stressful, and she never felt truly rested any longer.

"Do you expect the world to behave conveniently for you when you cast?" he remarked, brow raised as he slipped in behind her. One hand sliding along her figure until he was guiding both her hands through the motions. Even with him out of sight, however, she could feel his hard body pressed to her. His still partially turgid manhood nestled against her rear.

He had marked her his again and again since he'd returned, tainting her with his sticky seed, leaving it to roll down her inner thighs even as she practiced the magical spells to her.

Her breathing was heavier and she willed herself to concentrate, feeling herself grow more familiar with the intricate motions.

Magic was her life. Her passion.

So why did she keep getting distracted by so many more earthly matters?

More than once over the past few days, it had occurred to her to try and shake him off. If only a little.

To get Varuj's attention elsewhere that she might get things into order. Or maybe…

Her newly kindled urges were driving her down a road she feared. And more than that, she worried of hurting dear Mae'lin.

Mae'lin…

She thought if only she could find physicality with him as she had with Varuj, then it might all sort itself out. Firia could be with him, content and focussed.

The touch of those devilish hands made it so hard to think though… to try and come up with a more rational plan.

"Rest up for the night," he said abruptly, pulling away. "You need to practice this. I've given you the power, but now you need the ability," he remarked, picking up his clothes and getting ready.

Disappointment and gratitude. Her emotions were becoming such a strange mix of polarized feelings. "Fine, Varuj," she sighed, but still she looked at him with longing.

She needed to break his spell over her.

His pants hanging low, revealing the edges of his dark pubic hair, he reached out, robe open as he cupped her chin. "Remember," he said in that smooth, suave voice of his, "you are mine, Firi. We are bound eternally. But my tolerance for your daily activities will not last forever."

Her pulse quickened.

"Varuj…" Her breathing was shallow as she forced herself to meet his gaze, but what more was there to say? She could promise nothing.

He was gone without another word. Her lover from hell.

CHAPTER 42

Each new day began in a daze. The pressure of school, approaching final exams, her feelings for Mae'lin and Varuj colliding, and all the while her head swirled with the new spells she was learning.

For all his wicked nature, Varuj was an excellent teacher. Though it wasn't just his teaching, she suspected. Whatever infernal arts he mastered, and whatever their connection, he was able to pass to her spell casting ability beyond her station.

"You're awfully quiet today," chirped Ala'nase, and Firia became aware of the woman's presence right beside her. How long had she been walking right with her? She was getting so carried away with it all she was losing her grip on reality! "Say, I've gotta tell you something," she remarked in a secretive manner, touching her hand to Firia's arm and leaning in conspiratorially.

Firia tried to look excited for the news, but it was hard enough just getting her mind back into the present. Still, she was forever grateful that Ala had been such a loyal and good friend, so she urged her on.

"What is it?"

Little seemed to phase Ala'nase for long, and the beautiful elven woman smiled, a twinkle in her eyes as they walked along and spoke. "You know the handsome new guy?" It was then Firia noticed again that the woman was dressed rather well, beyond her normal attire and with a generous dollop of dark crimson lipstick and eye shadow.

No. No, no, no.

Firia smiled thinly. "Yes, I remember him."

The woman's long lashes descended as she narrowed her eyes and looked about almost suspiciously. "I'm going to ask him out," she said with a wry smile, oblivious to what that meant for Firia herself.

No, no, no.

Firia's heart lurched, but it was two-fold. One part was fear for her friend getting turned down and broken-hearted, but something darker lurked beneath it. Jealousy.

What if Varuj said yes?

It would serve her right for continuing to see Mae'lin despite Varuj's... disapproval of it. But she couldn't bear the thought, even as she longed for a way out.

"Oh?" was all she could manage.

"Of course," she responded, flipping her long blonde hair back. "How could he resist my charms, hm?" The elven woman's confidence resonated off her as she walked along beside her in the cool morning air.

"I don't know, Ala. You're beautiful and clever." It was true. "It's just..." Firia trailed off, but she had nothing. No reasonable excuse why her friend shouldn't ask her crush out.

Except for the fact that he was a demon that Firia had summoned and was making love with every night.

The elven woman looked surprised by her reaction, staring at her with some confusion. "It's just what?" She asked, though Firia could detect a certain oddness in her voice. Was it just confusion? Or was it something worse, insult?

Firia's face began to flush and she slowed her walking momentarily, "Well, just... I don't know, I couldn't imagine asking someone. With Mae'lin it just happened. Naturally."

Ala'nase stared at her a while then swatted her arm. "Yeah well, I don't have eternity," she remarked with some amusement. "There's about a million other harpies with their talons ready to sink into this guy, Firia. If I don't strike while the iron is hot, he'll be snatched up by someone more shameless than I."

"Well... you know I'll always be here for you, Ala." Firia started walking again, faster. She needed to get away, to find some way out of this tangled web.

She didn't need to go far, for as she rounded a corner she nearly stumbled into Gway'lin, the dashing elf quick to place his hands upon her shoulders and prevent a full on collusion. "Firia," he said with some surprise. "Just the lady I was hoping to see," he remarked pleasantly, his thick mane of golden hair glimmering in the morning sun.

"Uh, I'll catch you at class then. Got some hunting to do anyhow," remarked Ala'nase with a wave.

Firia waved back, but her mind was swimming. She could barely even focus on Gway'lin's handsome face until she finally realized his palms were still rested on her shoulder and a flush went through her. The thoughts were totally unbidden and she stepped back, bashfully, as her gaze fell to the ground.

"What's wrong?"

"Wrong?" he said with some surprise, then laughed softly and shook his head. He had such a musical voice, even his laughter was like a beautiful chiming. "No no, nothing wrong. In fact," he looked about then gestured towards one of the little private garden areas strewn about the campus. "Care to take a seat on the bench with me for a moment?" he asked cordially.

"Sure, though I have to get to class soon," she said with a soft sigh. She couldn't help but feel that the humdrum of class was hindering her growth rather than helping it. It was making her thoughts too linear and small, forcing her to get away from taking large risks, and that made training with Varuj more difficult.

Though truthfully, training with him would never be easy.

With a gentle yet firm hand upon her shoulder, Gway'lin guided her to the bench and sat beside her. "Lessons are nearly at an end for the year, Firia, and as your orienteer–" he said with a bit of a wry smile, "it's up to me to give you a bit of guidance for what's next, since I'm quite confident you'll be passing and carrying on."

"Well, that's a relief," she admitted. She always felt like she was skating on thin ice, especially with some professors she knew who thought little of her "kind".

With a light chuckle he continued on. "It's still too soon to look for a professor sponsor," he said gingerly, his beautiful voice reminding her of lovely songs, even as he spoke in such a casual manner. "And I wouldn't presume that you'd want to choose me as your professor sponsor when the time comes anyhow. I'll still be a very fresh and new one, with little influence to help you, after all," he explained with a gentle smile.

"Still, you seem to actually want me here, which is more than I can say for some professors." She shrugged. "Who did you choose when you were a student?"

Gway'lin couldn't help but give a bit of a toothy grin to that. "Well, truth be told, I was such a troublemaker none would have me for the longest time. Not many of the senior sorcerers are willing to let themselves be questioned by a subordinate," he said with a chuckle. "You don't know her, but when she finally chose me, Mistress Trae'vana plucked me from the jaws of my own self-sabotage."

Firia grinned and, for the first time since Varuj came back, she felt some of that bitterness and worry begin to melt away. She leaned back on the bench, folding her legs in under her thighs. "Well, now I kind of wish I did know her. She seems bright enough to spot talent behind your mouth."

With a tinge of sombreness to his smile he nodded and patted her knee. "But nonetheless, you won't have to deal with that quite yet. However, starting with next year, you'll have some choice about what classes you can take, Firia. And as I told you before, I'm a new professor myself, so..." he rubbed his palms together then opened them up skyward, "I'd like to see you in my class on mysticism and illusions."

Her eyes widened a bit and she stared, a bit dumbfounded. "Wow, really?" It was one thing for her to be an adequate student. Even a good one! But to be recruited for a class by anyone was flattering in and of itself and she smiled, quite genuinely. "I'll be honest, it's not really my strong suit."

"I know," he said gently, smiling brightly at her acceptance. "It's still a pretty introductory level course for the two arts, but maybe if I teach it well enough, and you like the subject matter, you'll follow after it through the ranks and become a true sorceress of the arts eventually."

"Well, fine, but you can admit it. You just want to make sure you have at least one person in your class that won't use their newfound skills to pull pranks on you."

He threw back his head and gave such a musical laugh, his thick, golden hair barely budging in the display. "Oh, I don't know about that. After having been subjected to mine so much maybe you'll bite back," he remarked with a playful wink that lit up his stunning face. It was so hard to get away from the fact he was the most stunning male – well, non-demonic at least – that she'd ever laid eyes upon.

Firia bit her lower lip, watching him intently before she finally tore her gaze away and forced herself to stand. She felt a buzz of excitement rush through her and she forgot entirely about Ala'nase and Varuj for those few, blissful moments. "I'm really flattered you asked me, by the way."

Sliding up to his feet, his own long robe flowing about him so gracefully, he gave a warm smile and a light bow of his head. "It shall be my pleasure to have you in my class, Firia. I truly hope I can inspire and invigorate you to greater heights with my tutelage." His beautiful emerald eyes shimmered before her. "Goodluck with classes."

"Thanks, sir," she teased with a small crook of her lips.

It was so easy with him. So carefree.

Why did it have to be that everyone else she loved gave her such heavy feelings of guilt?

Because you're a liar, her subconscious reminded her quickly and those light, airy feelings slipped away.

CHAPTER 43

Mae'lin.

She'd been classmates with him years before she got to know him, and that seemed such a shame. He'd said it to her himself as they sat upon the grass in the private little sanctuary, taking some time to escape the bustle of the academy to eat.

It had been his idea. "You've seemed a little over-stressed lately," he said with concern in his eyes, and still as he ate some carrot sticks he smiled over at her, his irrepressible concern and determination a buoy through the storm.

And yet it only made her feel guiltier. Guilty that she didn't feel that burning hot passion for him. Guilty that she'd made love to another.

Guilty that she'd told another man that she was his. Whatever that meant.

Her hand rested on Mae'lin's knee and even though she tried to smile, she knew it faltered.

She wanted this, so bad. This kind, considerate, calm relationship. This sweet, caring elf that was so smitten with her in an adorable, boyish way.

"You're always thinking of me," she said breathlessly.

He rested his hand upon hers, his long, spindly fingers warmly embracing hers. "We're going to make it to the top of this place together, Firia," he said so confidently, smiling at her widely. "You've been improving so quickly, leaving what little advantages I have in the dust."

His hand gripped hers so tight before he rubbed her smooth skin and knuckles, a different sort of air about him she was finding hard to place.

It confused her, but she squeezed his hand back, breathing the fresh air deep into her lungs. She hoped it would clarify her mind, but nothing did these days. She looked to him, studying his face in a quiet, contemplative manner.

This was her boyfriend. The innocent boyfriend that a girl like her should have. Someone that makes her a better, kinder person. Someone that cares for her and accepts her.

She leaned in and kissed his cheek softly, rubbing her nose along his skin. She'd been less giving with her token affections lately, pulling away from him, and she hated it.

Mae'lin received her little sign of affection with a sweet kiss of his own upon the corner of her lips. It was so unfair, comparing such a sweet and loving man with one so fiery and… demonic. Though when she felt him lean in further, nuzzle and kiss her earlobe, she almost felt for a moment like he was someone else, a more daring man.

A soft moan was his reward, and her lashes fluttered with some contentment.

She was conflicted because she didn't want to be without Mae'lin, just as she didn't want to be without Varuj. She loved them both, and her fingers squeezed the elf's knee tighter. "You're always thinking of me."

He was a hot-blooded male; she knew that. She knew he had to think of her in those compromising positions she now knew so well. Didn't he? She'd felt his arousal pressed against her when they'd made out. The heat of it. The hardness.

Brushing their cheeks together, he placed his other hand upon her thigh and said, "Always. We're in this together, Firia. And I've never had that before. A partner to face the world with." He kissed her ear again, then took the fleshy lobe into his mouth to suckle ever so lightly.

She was going mad. All of this fear and anguish kept knotting her stomach and she knew she had to do something. She had to let one of them go.

And Varuj was so powerful and insistent.

Yet instead of doing the right thing, instead of doing the thing that could spare the elf so much pain and hurt, she moved further into him, into his lap. She twisted about, her chest pressed to his as her robe pulled up around her thighs, straddling him so eagerly.

She just wanted the guilt to go away. She wanted to make him feel good.

She wanted to see if she felt something for him. Something raw and animalistic and wild.

The lanky elf was taken a bit aback by her abrupt pounce, but he made room for her atop his lap, and she felt the now familiar press of manhood hardening beneath her inside his britches as he put his arms about her and held her close.

The increase in his heart rate and breathing was noticeable, and she didn't need to guess if he thought of her in his quiet, private moments.

"You're so beautiful, Firia," he said breathily, though a bit embarrassed as he kissed his way down her neck, throbbing beneath her.

Her hips ground into him, instinctively, and she silenced his complement with a kiss. She didn't need his sweet words, his kind consideration. Not now. All she needed was his body pressing into hers.

She had bruises, little love marks on her arms and hips and legs from when she and Varuj got carried away, but now she craved new ones. Ones from Mae'lin.

She wanted him to cut loose in a way she didn't know he was able to. Her hips circled rhythmically, putting pressure on him before teasing it away and her moan filled his ear.

Mae'lin's moans were unmistakable, and she felt his manhood throb so exuberantly beneath her, swelling with such intense desire as he kissed and suckled her neck softly. It took her by surprise when he broke the seal of his lips on her and in a panting voice murmured, "If you keep that up I'll..." he blushed a fiery red, and she didn't need to guess too hard as to what he meant. He twitched so frequently beneath her.

She was surprised, nonetheless. She desperately tried not to compare him to her more experienced lover, but she slowed the rocking of her hips. Her breath was quick and shallow, but she knew she was wishing Mae'lin could be something he wouldn't be.

Not without her guidance.

Yet with it, she knew he'd do anything for her. Try anything. Fulfill any request she had.

So why was she so hesitant to tell him what she wanted? It was something more than just her fear of being thought of as too experienced.

She was afraid that if she told him what she wanted it would lose its effect when she got it.

Her slowed rocking wasn't enough to save him however, and still he twitched and tensed, perched so precariously to an early climax as he bit his lower lip. With a shudder he squeezed her, then forced his lips to hers. "I love you, Firia. And I want you," he confessed in his sweet, caring voice, those eyes of his lit up with such adoration. Yet tinged with desire.

"I want you," she whispered back, truthfully. She swallowed as she stopped her hips, keeping him teetering on the edge as she kissed him back, slowly and passionately.

With his arms around her, with the silence of the world outside of their private getaway, she felt safe and protected.

Loved.

His shaft throbbed, as if sorrowful that she had stopped grinding upon him, and Mae'lin himself kissed her back so tenderly. He held her long before finally breaking away to look her in the eyes, his own gaze narrowed by his drooping, lusty eyelids. "I don't want to pressure you," he said, swallowing, unaware of the odd circumstances, "but whenever you're ready… I want us to…"

It was a greater difference than night and day between the two men she cared for. Greater by far.

"I'm ready."

Screw Varuj and his controlling manners. His dominance and possessiveness. Screw how much he'd taught her, and how passionate he was for her.

Her answer surprised him, though she wondered how it could with her behaviour. "You're sure?" he asked, but she made no uncertain terms of the fact that she was.

Tall yet so very trim, Mae'lin still had no trouble lifting her up and laying her down upon her back on the lush grass.

Gazing up at him, there was no mistaking the nervousness on his face as he leaned in and kissed her so warmly. Yet there was no missing the throb of his erection as he began to undo his belt, and strip away his robe over top of her.

She pleaded with herself to be kind, to not compare the two men, but she knew it was futile. Still, watching him she was... enchanted instead of annoyed. Happy instead of nervous.

She did want this. She did want him.

The sweet smile, the excited tug of his pants, it all endeared her to him as she began to shimmy down her own trousers beneath her robe.

It was so different, and he was so shy, looking absolutely red-faced as he took off his robe and exposed his stiff manhood to her, the organ throbbing with an excitement the bashful elf couldn't display any other way. A tuft of pale wheat hair above the organ as he leaned down, kissed her and confessed, "I've never done anything like this before."

She stared, a bit lewdly at that, taking him all in. He was beautiful, in his own way, and her breath quickened. Her gaze travelled his entire body until his kiss stole her attention away, and her fingers went into his hair, feeling the silky strands. She wouldn't lie to him, and she silenced him with her mouth as she began to edge up her robe, baring herself to him quickly.

She was a slim woman, her breasts perky and her nipples stiffened as she exposed her pale flesh to the elf.

With his long, pale shaft in hand, he guided it down to her cunny. He was so slow and gentle about it, nothing at all like Varuj. Yet his excitement was palpable. Even as he fumbled to find her entrance, not knowing the workings of a woman's vagina as the more experienced demon had, he simply felt about, prodding her clit, her vulva.

"You're so beautiful, Firia," he said in a breathy, lust-laden voice. His eyes opened and he looked down upon her with such awe.

"You're far prettier than any elven maiden," and it was high praise indeed.

She couldn't rightly put into words what she felt then. It was a combination of so many things, but all she knew was she wanted to protect him from any harm. Any horrific thing that could happen to him, he didn't deserve.

And that included her.

Briefly she thought to tell him to stop. To not allow herself to take his innocence.

But how could she? Firia loved him. Deeply. Cared for him more than she could say.

Things were just too complicated, and her hand moved between their bodies. She grasped him, edging his hand away as she guided him towards her warm, waiting entrance.

"Ah," he gasped as his organ felt that warm, wet kiss of her quim, enveloping the swollen crown atop his elven shaft. His firm, hard stomach rising and falling with his increased breathing as he hesitated pushing in any further beyond where she'd brought him. "Is it okay?" he asked, swallowing down his excitement, his cock swelling within her. "I don't want to hurt you."

"Mae'lin, you won't hurt me. Trust me."

She was so excited. Firia wanted him, wanted to make him feel good.

Selfishly, she wanted to be his first. Even if everything fell apart after, she needed to give him this pleasure. To share it with him.

The boyish elf did trust her, and though it wasn't rough as Varuj might have done, he slid the fullness of his length inside her warm folds until he was nestled completely inside her. Though more intense than anything she felt, was the look of complete ecstasy upon his face. The way his eyes rolled back into his head, the lewd, low moan he gave, all as she felt – so intimately – the swelling of his loins within hers.

She inhaled deeply and felt so at peace. The worries and fears slipped from her as she pulled him in, holding his naked body to hers. They were one, and for those blissful moments, nothing could tear them apart.

"Mae'lin," she murmured so softly it was barely audible.

Her name upon his sweet lips was uttered back to her, and she felt his whole body tremble a bit with the excitement of his first time. It was cute and sexy at once, as if there were some greater fury beneath the surface that waited to bubble over, but he kept it in serious check.

When he tugged back his hips, beginning to thrust his cock into her, it was inelegant but so very eager. She could tell how deeply he wished to make the moment something special, despite his inexperience, pumping his shaft into her as he mewled and moaned, barely able to place his soft kisses upon her.

She whimpered back, her body arching into his. Her stiff nipples grazed his flesh as her body took on a light sheen. Excitement ran through her spine and she placed a quick kiss on his neck. "I want to do so much with you," she breathed.

There wasn't the smooth rhythm of when Varuj "fucked" her, as he put it. It was somewhat erratic, and the young man shook as he pumped his dick into her, his balls slapping against her wetly at a slow pace.

She began to realize he was already about to climax, but struggled to resist. His face was screwed up and he was gasping and breathing irregularly in his attempt to restrain his release to make the moment last longer. "I can't..." he gasped out unfinished, but she knew what was on his tongue.

She didn't want for it to end, but she clung to him tighter, needing the feel of his smooth flesh against hers. She wanted his scent, his sweat, to cover her. To drown her in that sweet, tangy odour, to mark her as his.

To make her his, as Varuj had claimed he'd done.

It was abrupt and intense, his whole body convulsing over her, his groin grinding into hers. His chest crushed down atop her breasts as he buried his full shaft to the hilt inside her and loosed such a flood of thick, creamy seed.

For all the negative contrasts she might've made between the two men, to see him so enraptured – so blown away with his first brush with carnal pleasure – inside her, there was no comparison. For his first time, Mae'lin had found a depth of satisfaction Varuj could never replicate. He was far too experienced to be so swept away by the simple act of gentle love making as Mae'lin was.

The elf just kept endearing himself to her.

She tugged him close, their hearts both pounding between them, and as she pressed her head to his chest, she smiled. She didn't know what would happen in the future, but then, for that moment, it was perfect. It was true love.

A true love so satisfying she didn't hear the rustle of the bushes nearby, nor the sound of retreating footsteps.

CHAPTER 44

Earlier that day...

Ala'nase sighted him leaving class, his own exotic robes flowing about his shoulders so beautifully, its gold stitching shimmering in the light. Nobody had anything on him in the entire academy, she thought. He was unique, confident, and obviously both talented and powerful, after the display of his she saw.

The glittering rings and gems on his fingers drew her attention, and she knew he must have quite the collection of magical trinkets to augment his abilities.

She straightened her shoulders and flipped her long hair off of them. She felt her stomach flutter with butterflies, but it was good. It made her feel alive, and her eyes widened with excitement. She was finally going to do this!

Ala'nase walked right towards him, not wasting any time as her smile grew. It was such a natural and joyous expression that made her seem so much prettier as she reached out to touch his arm. "Hey," she whispered, moving in towards him. "Did you notice the professor's robe was totally translucent today?"

The devilishly good-looking man turned his dark face towards her, a brow crooked high as he laid those curious eyes upon her. A slight smirk teased his lips and he came to a stop, rolling back his billowy sleeves as he looked to her full-on. "I would wager it a prank if she were more shameless about it," his voice so rich with a curious accent she couldn't quite place.

Still, it was enchanting, and it made her grin widen. "I knew someone as keen as you couldn't have missed it," she purred, touching along his arm. Her pulse was racing but she knew she wasn't blushing. She'd luckily never had much of an issue with wearing her heart on her sleeve.

"I got a bit distracted though and kind of stopped taking notes. Do you mind going over yours with me? I know of a place we could go," she added on, her voice taking on a seductive lilt.

His almond-shaped eyes dipped down over her, and very shamelessly he checked her out. It was the kind of moment she felt her preparations that morning had all been for. There was no way he couldn't be impressed with what he saw, but when he smiled back at her and spoke again, it was with a curious shift in topic. "You are the human girl's friend, no?"

Ala'nase tried not to sound offended. "Who, Firia? Yes. We met before, though, don't you remember? In the cafeteria on your first day. We went up to the line and bumped into one another." Anger started to boil beneath her skin, but she kept it under tight control.

She popped her hip, her slender hand grasping it and drawing attention back to her body, "Ala'nase."

He repeated her name, the syllables rolling off his tongue so seductively. She never knew it could sound so good, though her own not-so-subtle motions didn't fail to draw his attention, she noted successfully. "My apologies, madam Ala'nase. Of course I remember such a lovely elven maiden." He reached out, took her free hand in his smooth grasp and bent forward. He put other elves to shame with his graceful motions as he kissed the back of her hand. "Varuj, at your service."

Her hand tingled underneath his touch and she smiled brightly at his affection. He was gorgeous! And so gentlemanly. "Well that's more like it!" she teased.

With a low rumble of a chuckle he rubbed his thumb over the backs of her knuckles. "I am on my way somewhere right now, however. Perhaps..." he looked aside, then back to her with a pleasant smile. "Would you care to meet with me later that we might compare notes, hm?" A singular brow arched at her quizzically.

"How do they say 'hell yes' where you're from?" Ala'nase's chest puffed up and her cheeks went a bit round with her proud grin. "Maybe after supper, before curfew?"

Meeting at night was always a good idea, she thought. It made everything so much more romantic and passionate.

"Sounds lovely," he said with his deliciously masculine husk, and he brushed back some of his long, glossy back hair. "Shall I come meet you outside your dormitory?" he asked, and she noticed he hung a free hand off his curious silk belt, thumb tucked inside it as he studied her.

"I think that sounds great," she agreed, quickly telling him precisely where to wait for her. She couldn't resist letting her gaze trail along his body, drinking in that delicious form before smiling once more. "I can't wait to see you again, Varuj," she purred.

CHAPTER 45

Later that day...

The rest of the afternoon had been an utter slog, and that excitement in her stomach didn't dwindle. She could barely sit through her classes, and she completely skipped dinner. Her nerves simply wouldn't allow her stomach to settle enough to eat!

Instead, she washed her hair with a dab of the rare oil she'd managed to secret away from home, and put a bit of berry stain onto her lips. it made them darker against her fair skin, and she thought it was quite fetching.

Pulling on her elaborate top and pants, she checked herself in the mirror once more before leaving her room and walking down to the main entrance. She wanted to be seen on that handsome stud's arm and could only hope there was a crowd coming in from dinner to gawk at her prize.

Surprisingly, she found the dashing young sorcerer waiting for her, a furrow on his flawless brow as he looked about, as if something troubled him deeply. The scowl only added to that impression, which was odd, as she'd never seen him do anything but smile so handsomely about the academy.

When he caught sight of her, though, it all but vanished. "Ah, madam Ala'nase," he said so enticingly, and she caught a whiff of his aroma, like fragrant foreign spices. "So good to see you," he remarked in the dim evening.

"What, did you think I wasn't going to show up?" She grinned as she leaned in, her hand resting atop his forearm.

He gave a curious smile, then extended his arm for her to hoop hers through. "Women can be enigmatic like that," he remarked as they began to stroll along, "at least where I come from." She got her wish, as he didn't shy from the main thoroughfare as they passed through the academy, the tall, dark man leading her along so confidently. "I trust your afternoon was as annoyingly dull as mine, hm?"

"No more see-through robes or handsome classmates," Ala'nase agreed. She was just so thrilled to be next to him, to feel his touch on hers, but still her wit didn't dim. Thankfully.

He smiled beside her, then let his gaze trail along her, up over her form so suggestively before returning to the path before them. "Unfortunately," he concurred brazenly.

She noted that he was leading her towards the private, hidden grove. Something she barely knew of, and was amazed to find he had already discovered it on his own.

Her heart pitter-pattered in her chest. This was going even better than she hoped! Her hand wound around his forearm a bit tighter, feeling out the muscles beneath that exquisite robe. "I save those robes for the second date, I'll have you know. I'm not some slattern!"

It was a bit slow to appear, but the smile and low laugh came as he guided her into the moonlit hideaway. She couldn't possibly fault him for being anything but gentlemanly as he helped her through the bushes.

"Tell me," he asked, guiding her over towards a worn, fallen log, a lovely little makeshift bench of sorts. "What is going on between that friend of yours and the gangly fellow?"

Ala'nase's eyebrow knit and she looked at him curiously. Why did he want to talk about Firia again? Her free hand balled into a fist, the nails forming little half-moons in her palm before she forced the tendons to relax. "They're dating."

There. That'd be the end of that. Firia was unavailable, it was as simple as pie.

"So why don't you tell me a bit more about yourself?"

There was something a bit off about him. He didn't seem his usual self, or at least what she could judge to be his usual self. She'd only encountered him briefly on a couple occasions, after all, but she'd gotten the impression of him being focussed, and always collected. Cool.

He sat her down then did the same for himself right beside her. "A young fellow with aspirations to greatness," he said plainly, giving her a smug smile that was only partially kidding. "I'm here to climb my way to the top, crush my competitors, and then claim the world for my own. What else is there to say?"

"Well, when you boil it down to the basics, I suppose not much!" She crossed her legs, her arm pressed into the log and arching her torso towards him rather blatantly. "And I like an elf with drive and ambition."

Something seemed to be bothering him, yet he showed no reluctance when he put his arm about her, touched her lower back and held her close. "I stumbled upon your two friends fucking here in the grass like rabbits earlier today," though there was no humour in the way he said it. It sounded rather mean, instead.

Ala'nase's nose crinkled. "Ew, poor you, I guess," she responded lightly. She didn't know how to take his strange, sour mood, but she loved the warm hardness of his body. "I guess we don't get a lot of privacy around here..."

She thought on it a moment longer before giving a brief laugh. "She never even told me they'd done it! I was wondering why she wasn't in our last class."

He took his time, mulling something over before he spoke to her again. Even then it was only after eying her over a few more times, holding her in the cool night air, "You and her are – safe to say – the two finest female specimens this academy's novice classes have to offer."

"Well... thanks?" She smiled a bit, but he was being so strange. Why did he have to keep bringing Firia up? Why did he bring her to the place he'd caught her friend having sex with her boyfriend? It was rather unsettling, and she shifted a bit from her brazen pose. "Did you bring your notes, then?"

"No," he said simply, just before moving his hand over and resting it upon her thigh. "Why bother? The real appeal is in you and I being here alone, is it not?" he remarked a bit crassly, stroking her inner thigh then squeezing it. He was leaned in so close it was hard to ignore the obviousness of his intent.

It was hard to ignore that fact no matter how good he looked, how good his hand felt, how much she wanted more.

But it was harder to ignore how wrong this felt.

It wasn't at all what she'd expected and she couldn't even really put her finger on why. Maybe it was just his strange behaviour, his obsession with her best friend. Whatever it was, she felt uncomfortable, and swatted his hand away. "Hey now. I don't do that on the first date either."

He looked down over her again, that expression of desire intense, but without the pretense of charm from before. It was a hard gaze, and he refused to budge his hand from her thigh.

Instead he leaned in, so close to her ear as he spoke lowly. "Why?" He inhaled through his nose, his nostrils flaring, "You're ovulating. You're quite primed and ready, in every respect," he remarked so obscenely.

"Ew!" she groaned, pulling away and trying to push his hand off of her thigh. "Why would you even say something like that?" she almost shouted, all of her cool, seductive confidence stripped away. Alarm rose within her as she realized just how isolated and alone they were and she began to panic, her breath coming out as shallow gasps.

He let her thigh go and she was able to get up and away from him. "Where are you going?" he asked. "We haven't even had an opportunity to get to know one another quite yet." He inhaled the air around her, "I know you and that elf she was fucking had something at one time… some feelings perhaps?" He asked, dredging up memory of an old rebuffing that had hurt her ego.

It so flustered her she didn't notice his fingers moving subtly in a spell. Though it was too late, and instead of reacting to him with fear or anxiety, she instead could only physically feel deep attraction to him. As if her every action was now divorced from her inner thoughts. "We still need to get to know one another deeper, don't we?" he asked, and his words were delectable to the ears, no matter how much she felt otherwise.

She stepped closer to him, even as she tried to pull away. It was the strangest sensation she'd ever felt, and true fear began to knot her stomach. She didn't tell anyone about Mae'lin, and surely… surely he couldn't have been gossiping about her like that. He didn't seem the type… she didn't figure.

But then, she would have run from Varuj as well. Chalked it up to some weird, foreign custom and blown it off.

So why did she keep moving closer to him?

It dawned on her that it had to be the spell she caught him casting. But spells of seduction and manipulation of this sort were well beyond any first year magic student. It was the sort of stuff masters at the academy would've struggled with! It was near impossible to imagine this foreigner having such control.

"That's a good girl," he husked to her, his darkly delicious voice so ominous. "You were turned down, it's hard to believe, hm?" He curled his fingers in the air, ushering her closer. "Turned down by a simpering, gangly fool like him, when you're clearly both a luscious and powerful sorceress with more on the horizon than he could ever hope for."

He was right, of course, but now that he said it she wanted to disagree. If this was a seduction spell… Her stomach turned at the thought, but she couldn't move away from him. Not with that masculine, husky voice saying such delicious things.

She moved closer but she willed herself to run, to flee. To regain control of her body.

Instead she walked right into his arms. Those warm, welcoming arms coming up in under hers as he smiled toothily. She swore she saw fangs, but wasn't sure what senses she could trust anymore. "You need a strong mate," he mused to her, brushing some of her luscious hair away from her forehead. "A powerful one, who can see your value. And ride to the top with you, yes?" and the words were so overwhelmingly enticing. Not even in just a spell-tinged sense.

"Mate?" What an odd choice of words…

Yet isn't that what she wanted? Someone strong, someone that would appreciate her… someone who would stand by her?

She tried to shake her head, to free herself of the disturbing thoughts, but it was no use. Whatever he had done to her was strong, and panic made her heart race.

"That's right," he said as he tilted his head, leaning in close, their lips about to meet. "And there is no stronger here at this academy than me, I assure you, Ala'nase." Each word rolled off his tongue as such a husky growl of lust and desire.

She was helpless to his charms. Powerless against what magic he wielded, and regrettably, with his former charm somewhat returned, she felt much of the attraction was genuine. Not forced.

She both yearned for and dreaded the touch of his lips, and just as their mouths were about to meet...

The gong. It was her saviour. It carried even to the secret grove, and the powers of the academy whisked her away, back to her own room. The safety of her own private room.

Ala'nase gasped, spinning around and feeling regret strike at her very core. How could fate be so cruel as to yank her away from him? Her pulse was racing and her entire body seemed tensed and primed for him. For his mouth on hers.

She threw herself onto the bed, allowing her sullenness to seep in.

CHAPTER 46

The deep regret had its claws in Ala'nase, so much so that she nearly missed the sound of her door opening. Though so odd of an occurrence it was, that she managed to look her bleary eyes up and see the bizarrely out of place silhouette.

No student could've entered her room. Only a professor at the academy could've had the authority to breach the wards on her room. And they would only do it in moments of extreme emergency. Yet…

The door shut, and the light dimmed to a reddish hue as she saw who it was.

"We were so rudely interrupted," came his seductive husk, and she saw as he nimbly undid the golden strings that held his tunic's front open, revealing the dark, hard chest beneath.

Glee and terror combated within her as she stood from the bed. How could this be? She swallowed and even though she knew this wasn't right, that he shouldn't be here, she was so grateful. She wanted him, and her gaze followed his fingers, her tongue glancing across her lips nervously.

Ala'nase knew, deep down, in some untainted part of her, that she'd never do this. Never behave this way.

Yet she moved closer, all the same.

As he undid his tunic, exposing himself on down to his smoothly contoured abs, he reached his other palm out, cupped her cheek and trailed his thumb along her chin and lower lip. "I'm going to claim you as mine tonight," he said to her with such confident assurance. "And from there forward, you'll never need worry again." He gave an almost gentle smile, though tinged with a bit of something else. "You'll be tethered to me. Mine," he repeated the word.

What was that supposed to mean?

Her frown deepened as her brows knit and she tried to take a step away, but couldn't. "Tethered?" She didn't like the sound of that. She didn't want to be tethered to anyone! Not even... especially not... him.

"Don't be like that," he said, though she betrayed so little with her physical exterior, which he held so powerfully in sway. "I know you want it," he remarked, tugging open his trousers, letting them fall down, revealing a member larger, more thickly veined than any she had ever seen. "Self-denial is a foolish thing." He traced his digit down from her chin, along the center of her shirt, the buttons coming undone by some force of telekinesis, exposing her flesh to him with such a simple gesture. "With me you'll never need deny yourself any pleasures, no matter how minor or petty." He traced his digit over her stomach and she shivered.

"No," she whispered, but her skin prickled with excitement, her nipples stiffening beneath the simple shift. He was so gorgeous, so masculine. She didn't want to fight it anymore, but a part of her screamed that she had to. That this wasn't her.

That she was under his spell.

Yet she couldn't help but inwardly admire that power. Some part of her craved a strong partner, just as he had said. Her first love... he had been strong. Powerful. Cruel.

In the end he had cast her off when they should've been climbing to their greatest heights, yet instead... she was alone. Vulnerable to the dark foreigner's 'seductions'.

"You're gorgeous," he said, the sharp prick of his nail as it made such a bizarre tracing upon her belly. "You want to part your thighs and welcome me inside, don't you?" he remarked, and she saw his stiff cock throb before her, beneath a patch of short, dark pubic hair. "Do it," he said with a smile.

Even without the spell those words would have sent a thrill through her spine. She was so used to being in control of everything - of her emotions, her power, her friends - that it was almost freeing to have it stolen from her. To have her body respond no matter what she wanted, no matter what she desired.

Varuj took hold of her shoulder, and with a rough shove, he pushed her down onto the bed, letting her body fall back atop it as he stalked after her, like a stunning predator.

With a quick tug, he yanked the pants from around her ankles and discarded them to the corner of the room before prying her thighs open. "You smell as ripe as a harvest plum," he rasped, lowering himself down over her, pinning her arms to the bed as he grasped the shirt that still wound about both of her elbows.

It had been so long since she felt someone's body so near to her, and the power and force he had over her was incomparable. The way she responded, her body tilting towards him as she tried to back away was as though an intense war were going on within her. For, of course, it was. She was battling with him for control: control she desperately needed, and still wished she could shed.

Her full breasts bounced as she tilted away, her blonde hair trapped beneath her shoulders and pinning her head awkwardly. "This isn't right," she tried to protest, but it came out so small, so forceless.

"I know," he said to her so simply, even as he cupped her full breast and squeezed it so roughly, so pitilessly. "But it will seem but a minor evil in time." His masculine scent filled her nostrils as he leaned in, let the bulging crown of his large dick trace her vaginal seam, nudge her vulva as he positioned himself, his whole body arched and on stunning display as he prepared to violate her so raw.

The impaling came hard and fast, a single thrust that shoved the biggest cock she'd ever seen deep inside her. The throbbing veins pressed against her vaginal canal as he ground himself against her cervix hard and rough, giving a growling groan of satisfaction.

She couldn't believe it was happening. It was almost as if it were some strange dream, some weird fantasy that she was having in the dead of night.

But to actually feel it, to actually have him inside her, sent her mind reeling. He felt so good, but at the same time it was so wrong. So terribly wrong.

Ala'nase gasped and tried to push away from him but all she succeeded in was taking him deeper, making her eyes bulge. How? How could this be happening to her?

"You're mine now," he growled out in his increasingly ragged voice, the hard thrusts coming on fast as he built up momentum, his heavy sac slapping noisily against her, filling her former sanctuary with the noises of her violation by the gorgeous man. "And you're lucky to be chosen, bitch," he snarled, biting her neck as he clenched her tit in hand, letting the hard nipple dig into his palm as he rut into her like a ravenous animal in heat.

She wanted to scream, but instead it came out as a gurgled whimper, a softer protest than he deserved. The word, that word, was almost worse than anything. The sex, his body, some carnal part of her wanted that. Craved that. Had dreamed of that.

But the cruel and hurtful word, it stunned her and she tried to push him away.

He bucked into her harder, and noticed her shying away, her pathetic attempts to escape his carnal violation. He ground his teeth together, then it happened. Quite surprisingly, he slapped her cheek, left it stinging and reddened with the heated blow before clutching her hair and tugging it hard, wrenching her face up towards him as he pounded into her, setting her breasts to bounce and jiggle.

"You were tossed away, rejected," he growled, his dark eyes seeming to light up in the red tinged room as he met her gaze. "But you'll be mine now. And through listening to me I'll make you something greater." He grunted, and she felt him swell within her, his dick throbbing with excitement. "You'll be a good girl for me," he purred, his voice so seductive again.

The contrast, the hot and cold, the cruel and seductive set her head pounding. Her eyes watered as they widened with fear and anger, her struggles becoming more furtive. The spell, however, kept them weak and muted. Still, the fury building within her was steeling her heart to him, her resolve building.

He seemed to see that deep within her, that crystallizing resolve. And he tugged her head to the side, the strands of hair prickling upon her scalp from his rough handling, and he whispered into her ear.

It was difficult to hear the words over the resounding slaps of his hard body striking her amid the savage fucking, but what he said was unmistakable. She felt her eyes water up, her barriers break down, and were she not still under the sway of the spell she would've broken down into immediate sobs.

Instead she could only meet his gaze as he moaned and swelled within her, showing signs of his impending release. "But if you obey me loyally," he husked in his dark voice, "you'll never need fear betrayal… abandonment… ever again, sweet Ala'nase." The words struck at her so deep, to her very core. He needed no spell to win over her mewling obedience then.

His hold on her head tightened, his spine arched and she knew the tell-tale signs of what was coming. She murmured meekly through the tears, "Not inside… please."

His motions continued, and he thrust deep inside her with such increasingly erratic force. "Yes inside," he rasped. "It has to be that way," and with that she felt it, the final pulse that travelled up his shaft, pushing her slick canal open wider as his climax tore through his flesh and poured forth in a torrent of virile, pearly white seed, flooding her as he ground himself to her innermost depths and revelled in it noisily.

Everything about her felt as if it'd been torn up and reassembled, hastily put back together again. All within the span of what had to have been less than a half hour. How was it even possible that her entire world could change so quickly?

The woman shuddered beneath him, trying to push him away, to free herself from his hold, from his cum.

He refused her that though, clutched her tight until her resistance ebbed, then smiled and released her, pulling himself away and leaving her drooling his seed. "Rest up," he said to her as he stood and got dressed. "You're mine now, pretty girl," he cooed from across the room.

CHAPTER 47

It was amazing to behold, the entire academy seemed to go into overdrive before Firia's very eyes. People bustling about, not a single one in anything but the biggest rush of their lives. She'd never seen so many flowing robes lifted up on the air as the conjurers that wore them bustled about.

The one's that weren't panicked were either simply anxious or just going about their business in as best a way possible. So it stuck out to her that her friend Ala'nase walked along in a slow meandering pace, her books clung to her chest as she stared at the ground.

Firia had an idea of what happened, so she moved to Ala'nase's side and matched her stride, a small, sympathetic smile tugging her lips. "Hey, Ala. Are you okay?"

It took the young woman a moment to lift her head and look to her friend, "Huh?" She seemed confused, but shook it off. "Y-yeah, I'm fine. Why do you ask?" she looked about, somewhat suspiciously, seemingly afraid of giving away her vulnerability.

"You're not yourself is all. Ala, if you ever want to talk to me..." Firia reached out and placed her hand, lightly, on her friend's bicep. "You just look so upset." It broke her heart because she knew why. Varuj had turned her down, and even though Firia wasn't sure she could handle all the gory details, her friendship with the young elven woman was very important to her.

She averted her eyes from Firia, still clutching her books as they began to walk together, the only two slowpokes in a sea of busy students. "How are things with you and Mae'lin?" she asked, shifting topics entirely. "You two seem to be doing great."

Firia smiled as her gaze dropped, her stomach fluttering at the mention of him. "Yea… yea, I think so." She didn't want to pry into her friend's business if she wasn't comfortable, but she licked her lips, trying to think of what she could say. How would she like to be treated if she was rejected?

Firia didn't really have the answer to that question. She'd probably like to be left alone to ease her bruised ego. "Are you ready for exams? You'll probably whizz through."

She gave a rather noncommittal response to that, and looked off. Firia followed her gaze and saw Mae'lin coming. He looked even cheerier than usual, his cheeks dimpled with his broad smile as he approached the sole human in their small group of friends.

"Morning ladies," he said, reaching out to take Firia's hand subtly as they walked.

Her fingertips tickled his palm, the glee shared between them pungent in the air as Firia glanced back to Ala'nase. She felt uncomfortable with her friend being so sullen, so dejected, and was afraid her happiness was only going to make her feel worse.

"Ala, did you want to do supper tonight? Just you and me. Maybe I could come to your room and you could help me on a few things I'm stuck on?"

"I…" she hesitated, glancing to her then about. "Well maybe. I'll see, okay? I've gotta go look into something right now. Exam preparations," she said, waving to them before scurrying off in a hurry, immediately lost in the crowd.

"Is she okay?" asked Mae'lin, squeezing Firia's hand and pressing in close to her side.

"I don't think so," Firia admitted, looking at the direction she ran off towards. "She's been weird the past little while. She won't tell me what's going on." She sighed, her lips pursed to the side. Ala'nase was keeping secrets from her, she knew, but who was she to judge?

She squeezed Mae'lin's hand and felt the pang of desire and guilt make her stomach flip.

The adoring elf squeezed her hand and smiled brightly. "We should get to practicing. It won't be enough to simply pass these upcoming tests," he explained casually, unfazed by the challenges they faced. "I'm told passing the trials is but part of it. In the final event we'll be facing off in displays of magical prowess against other students. And not all will make it."

"Well, hopefully if I burn you to death, you won't hold it against me this time," she teased, but she was distracted. "On second thought… practice might be good."

Mae'lin broke out into a hearty, good-natured laugh. He never once held it against her, the mistakes of their first bout, and he squeezed her hand and tugged her along, picking up pace. "Better hurry then, because I wanna survive this test so I can continue to study with you next year!"

CHAPTER 48

The whole of the academy was abuzz with activity, but Ala'nase was milling about a quiet nook, pacing along the stone floor beneath an overhang. The rain was falling, an odd occurrence for the academy, but she was shielded from it.

Her emotions were conflicted, but when she saw the physique of the dark, foreign sorcerer approach her, the sensation that won out was relief. As frustrating as that was for her to confess.

When he stepped in beneath the overhang with her, she saw not a sign of dampness in his robes, or upon his flesh. It was as if nary a raindrop had dared touch his glorious physique, and he quite casually helped himself, reaching out and touching his palm to her cheek.

"Good girl," he husked in approval at her showing up. Just as he instructed.

Her breath quickened, her gaze falling demurely. It was so unlike the brazen elf to avert her eyes of anything or anyone, but part of her didn't want to see him. Didn't want her to lust for his gorgeous body or handsome face.

Yet he pressed those hot lips to her forehead, and it nearly made her delirious. The most painful part, however, was knowing that he no longer used a spell. That it was all how she felt, truly felt, without any force.

"I need a favour of you," he husked into her ear as he kissed his way across her face. "Something you can do for me. For you too. And then we can prepare together. I will show you things you didn't dream of knowing so soon," he said, that delicious voice making such promises.

Her heart was in her throat as she nodded, her light hair framing her delicate features. "What is it?" She barely realized that she had agreed before she asked, but what more was there to do? The things he'd said, the sweet words... He knew her. Down to her very core.

"There is someone who has stolen a great deal from you," he said so persuasively, his rich voice making each word sound delightful and convincing. "She made your former lover leave you, so that he might pursue one of his own kind," he explained to her in that tempered, fatherly voice. "She caught the eyes of that elf Mae'lin so that when you went for him, his heart was already claimed."

His words rang true. So true that it overwhelmed her shock at the realization that he spoke of Firia. Her friend.

The lump in her throat thickened and she couldn't speak. She didn't well up with tears, she didn't start trembling in fear. The time for that was past, and despite the gnawing discomfort within her body, she nodded again.

Even though she'd not held that against Firia, even though she cared for the human woman, he was too right for her to disagree.

"I'll get you your revenge, sweet girl," he husked, nuzzling his nose to her cheek before rising back up and looking down to her. "And you'll get rid of two more competitors that stand in our way for this final trial," he added with a smile that was somewhere between tender and wicked. "You want that, don't you?"

"I... I guess." Her voice was so soft, still uncertain and conflicted. It was one thing to agree, but all the pain she'd been caused, ever since she got to the Academy... it was all Firia. All her best friend.

She could have moved on from Bran, could have so easily found another with Mae'lin. But instead, she was left alone while Firia taunted her. Holding hands in public, those sweet little kisses... that should have been hers.

Neither of those two men were her equal. A human and some gangly elf from the country? Yet she'd been spurned by them both. And for what? A lowly human girl whom she had done nothing but be nice to.

Varuj kissed the corner of her lips and gave a pleasant smile. "You do," he assured her. "You're a powerful witch at heart, and the truly powerful do not suffer such injustices. Do not suffer the weak stepping upon their toes with impunity." His dark eyes lit up as he met her gaze, "No woman of mine would suffer it and let them get away."

"So what do I do? Firia has caught the eye of some professors, and if they wouldn't kick her out over that… beast, then what can I do about her?"

His masculine touch brushed her pale hair back and he smiled as he leaned in so near to her lips. "Just relax and do as I say." He kissed her mouth so faintly, then slipped back towards her ear, whispering his dark words there.

Ala'nase's eyes widened in shock at what he said, but when his free hand dipped between her thighs to grasp at her loins she couldn't help but gasp.

She was in so far over her head. The past twelve hours had turned her life on its axle and she was spinning out of control.

"I can't," she whispered, even as she subconsciously ground into his hand.

"You can and will," he murmured back to her, his hand rubbing at her harder, stirring up such a heat in her loins. "I'll give you what you need and you'll make it happen. Now tell me," he licked along her cheek with his moist tongue, "Who do you belong to?"

He was so possessive. So powerful.

She was a stranger to neither, and it made such conflicted, confusing, terrible feelings to rise within her. "You," she muttered back, and her eyes fluttered shut. Yes. Him. He'd protect and take care of her. He wouldn't leave her. He'd make it all right.

"Good girl," he husked approvingly, and his hand slipped inside her trousers, and she felt the firm touch of his heated flesh upon her folds. Her sweet reward.

CHAPTER 49

Firia awaited her friend at the dining hall as they'd planned, the note reaching her that she'd make it just before the end of class. Though when someone slid into the seat across from her, it wasn't her dear friend, but another face altogether. One more familiar still.

"We need to talk," he husked in that deep, demonic voice of his, sounding so much like that first time she'd spoken with him. Before he took on the pleasing form before her.

She glanced around for a moment before leaning in, her brows furrowing. "About what?" She'd brushed her hair, letting the black strands fall over her shoulders. It was growing out really quickly and was almost down to the bottom of her shoulder blades. More and more she was leaving it down, the dark strands contrasting her fair skin.

"Exams are here," he said like the death knell of a tolling bell. Plain and simple. It reminded her that they hadn't trained together for some time, and he'd last left her to train her new telekinesis spell all on her own.

"How could I have forgotten, Varuj?" She leaned back, annoyance tainting her expression. He was risking outing her just for this? He could have come visited her as usual.

"Remember what we spoke of last?" he remarked to her, reminding her of just how long it'd been since he'd last came to visit her in the dark of night when she was all alone. Too long, part of her thought.

She pushed the thought aside. "I've been practicing, Varuj." She didn't add on, *'You'd have known if you visited,'* like she wanted to, though. Her blood warmed just with the thought. She'd been trying so desperately to forget him, to just... make him disappear from her life, but she couldn't ignore the attraction she felt for him.

"Not that," he remarked bitterly, his handsome face contorting in distaste. "My tolerance for wasting your time with that fool is up, Firi," he said like a father scolding his child. "You waste too much of your focus and attention on him." He leaned forward, his eyes lighting up red as he glared into her gaze. "You are mine," he said, that last word a snarl on his lips.

"Varuj," she whispered, leaning in. "Can we talk about this somewhere else? I don't want to fight with you here." Why did he insist upon this? He knew her. He knew what was in her heart, in her soul. He'd been a part of her for so long, and she admitted that she missed that absence of his presence. Of his calm reassurance.

Ever since he'd gotten back, he'd been so possessive and borderline cruel to her, and it frightened her. She longed for the days back in her home when she'd slept in his arms, feeling so safe and protected...

Loved.

Her eyes met his and she didn't see it anymore. Instead there was something darker than she'd ever been able to fathom.

"I claimed you as mine," he growled to her lowly in their booth. "Don't you remember that? I took you, your innocence, and made you mine. You accepted it. Became my mate!" He raised his voice so high some people from a neighbouring table looked over. "You must end this ridiculousness now and remain faithful," he demanded with a deep intensity to his eyes. "That's the only way we can go on as before. A pair."

She hissed back at him, anger tainting her voice. "I summoned you. You were mine before I was yours, and I released you. I trusted you. I'm not some... some... possession, Varuj! I'm a person, and I have feelings! You told me that you were better than that hellish place I stole you from, but you don't even act like you care at all for me! You just want to… to… what? For me to do whatever you say?"

"I was never bound under your control, you foolish girl," he growled quietly. "I was free the moment you brought me here. I just didn't want to frighten you!" He was breathing heavily, and looked enraged. He looked… hurt, she realized. A strange hurt, unlike what she'd seen from him before. "I tested you. To see if you could be trusted. And you agreed to 'free' me. It was a test! To see if I could trust you. And I thought it worked!" He clenched his fist. "You said you were mine!"

Her eyes hurt as she desperately held back her tears. He couldn't be telling the truth. He was lying to her. Manipulating her somehow.

She's summoned him! He'd been bou—

Just like that, she remembered the fumbled words, the hesitation, the uncertainty. She'd been so excited that it'd worked, so terrified of the beast she'd pulled to her… She hadn't remembered it all, the more complicated incantations that were still beyond her…

Her face fell with the realization and she pulled back, staring at him through those blurry orbs.

Varuj's anger seemed to abate somewhat as he watched her recoil, her eyes water. He reached across the table to her. "We have a special bond," he said in his suave voice, as smooth as caramel. "We've worked together. I got you into the academy. I saved your father." He licked along his full, ruddy lips. "I made love to you. Claimed you as my mate. You would throw all that away for this… fool of an elf?"

Her mouth trembled and she had to look away as he stroked her fingers with his. "What we have isn't love." She felt so distant from him, and she didn't know she could ever get back those lonely nights that he'd comforted her. He needed so much from her, so much control over her life, and it scared her.

Even through her lust, her attraction and need, there was something that felt so hollow at the centre. She didn't even realize she was saying it, her brows knit and her voice a whisper. "Every time, every single time it just feels like we're trying to cram back together. How it used to be."

Varuj wrapped his fingers around hers and held her hand tight. "It can be like that, and so much more," he promised her, "If you just give yourself to me, like a true mate – a true partner – should." His almond-shaped eyes widened, and she could see the dim flicker of fire within them as he gazed upon her. "Be true to me, Firi. And I shall be true to you. Together we'll rise to the top of this academy, then the world. We've shown each other we can be trusted before this… this fling of yours."

"It isn't a fling, Varuj. When you left, after I thought you weren't returning… You know I feel something for him. Can you still… can you still even feel me, or have you cut that off too? Severed that tie with this new form of yours?"

"I feel it deeper than ever!" he pleaded with her insistently, eyes wide, almost manic. "When I was away I sacrificed much for you. For us! I made myself more human. More like you!" he insisted, and she felt him clutch her hand painfully tight. "I gained a soul of my own, so that I could be a true partner for you when I returned. Does all I've done – all I've sacrificed! – mean nothing to you because of a few months apart?!"

"No, but it does mean that I had time to develop feelings for someone else," she pleaded. "I don't want to hurt him. He cares about me, Varuj, and I care about him!" Her voice was raising and she desperately tried to keep it in check. "I don't know what to do. I want…"

She paused, licking her lips and swallowing the lump that was lodged in her throat. "I love both of you. In different ways."

That got his ire, but she watched as he fought some inner battle, his chest heaving as he stared across at her. "You have to choose one of us, Firi," he said in as delicate a voice as he could muster. "You cannot string us both along forever. And which of us do you think could make you more powerful? More successful? More…" he licked his lips and hesitated, "which of us could make you happier? More satisfied," and the final word was laced with such hidden meaning.

Him. All of those things, all of those promises, those were ones he could keep. Months ago, they would have been the only ones that mattered.

But thinking of the sweet Mae'lin, of the kindness and affection and quiet adoration… that meant something. It wasn't powerful, it wasn't strength, but it made her look forward to waking up in the morning. Didn't that count for something? Wasn't that satisfaction?

"Varuj," she whispered softly, but her voice trembled and she had to stop. To try to get herself back together as she swiped a tear from her cheek. "Varuj, I love you. I do. I don't want to lose you. I…" she swallowed a sob. "I'm so grateful for all you've done for me. For my father. I wouldn't be here if it wasn't for you. But I don't know how I can… I don't know what to do."

Her voice was barely audible, but she forced herself to continue, to be honest with the demon that had somehow stolen her heart and her virginity. "Varuj, ever since you've gotten back… you've been so hard. So cold."

"Because you've broken my heart," he said to her. "You gave your love to another when I was out giving my all for you." He steadied his breathing, staring into her gaze. "I am what I am, Firi. I care for you. I want us to be as before. But I cannot do that while you waltz about the academy hand in hand with another man. When you shoo me away in public, instead of embracing me." He narrowed his gaze at her slightly, as if inspecting her for the truth, like the answer to his upcoming question would be written on her face, and not said in her words. "How would you feel in my place?"

"Devastated," she whispered, her shoulders slumping. Yet what was she to do? Tell Mae'lin it had been fun, and that even though she loved him, she was going to date a new guy that no one even knew she knew? It would look like she'd been… cheating on him.

She exhaled deeply, leaning back in the seat and staring at him intently. "Ala would be so broken if we started dating. Ever since you first came back she'd had her eyes on you."

Varuj's hard, hurt look melted a little, and he took her hand in both of his, smiling just faintly. "Don't worry about her. I'll help ease things. Everything will be fine… the world will be perfect, as long as you're mine, Firi. All mine." He lifted her hand and kissed the back of it tenderly. "Together we are bigger than the world's problems."

"We'd be breaking two people's hearts just for the sake of our own," she protested, but her resolve was weakening.

He brushed the back of her hand against his cheek, his smooth, dark cheek. The contrast of their skins – light and dark – such a pleasant mix. "I would see the world burn for you, Firi, and judge it worthy."

She looked up at him with such sweet, innocent concern that no longer suited her. "I did something so horrific," she whimpered, looking around the room briefly as shame rouged her cheeks.

"I know you have," he said solemnly. "Why do you think I hurt so badly, Firi?" He looked to her watery eyes with such disappointment. "But I can forgive you your... infidelity. As long as you come back to me. And be mine: heart, body and soul."

Her mouth dropped open and she inhaled sharply. How could he have known? She'd not told a soul about it, and she wondered if what he was saying was true. If he still felt that connection to her, even if she didn't any longer. That strange, emotional tether that bound them.

Yet in the end, she knew. She loved Mae'lin.

And deep down, deeper than she even knew, she understood she had to leave him. Varuj was what he was, but no matter what happened with them, she wasn't right for Mae'lin.

She, like Varuj, was too cruel to the ones she cared for.

"Say you'll do it. Say you'll leave him and be mine, only mine, and I will forgive you your sins and take you back into my arms and heart, just as it used to be." He gave her a hopeful smile. "Say you will do it, and I will handle all the rest, as I handle all your problems for you, sweet Firi. It shall be that simple."

"Handle the rest? What does that mean?" Her head tilted to the side and she stared at him. She knew the demon that lurked beneath the surface, the cruelty he could bestow on someone.

But was he any better than she? She took Mae'lin's innocence, knowing that she wasn't faithful. That she was lying to him, constantly, and hiding so much of herself from him. He didn't deserve her terrible treatment, even if he was ignorant to it.

"Do it your way, my way, you can wait until exams are finished, just agree. Tell me you'll be mine, Firi. Tell me you'll forsake that elf, that you'll pledge yourself and your undying love to me, and all will be right with the world. And more importantly, with us," he pleaded. "Do it."

It took her a few moments, her gaze dipping to the table as she sighed. "I will let him know, after exams, that I can't see him any longer." *That I can't keep breaking his heart and living with this guilt.*

Pressing her hand together between his two palms, he lifted it up and kissed the tips of her fingers. "You are mine, Firi. All mine. Say it," he pled, "say it again, as you truly mean it. And make me happy and whole once more."

"Varuj, it feels weird to say it." She was exhausted with his constant pressure. "Can't you just accept that I love you? That I'd hurt someone I love because of it?" It was hard enough for her without having to say those words.

"It needs to be said, Firi," he murmured so softly, no longer any fear of them being overheard. "After what I've been through… after what you did… I need to hear it. I need to feel the words and their sincerity. I need to feel your warmth about me."

Firia inhaled deeply, sighing out the words, "You have my heart, Varuj. You have for a long time. Longer than you know."

He gave a gentle smile. "That'll do. For now. Thank you, Firi my love. We are meant to be on this journey together."

CHAPTER 50

Bran strode through the academy as cocky as ever. Exams were nearly upon him, but he looked more than prepared. He refused to rush about as the other students did, refused to show any weakness.

So Ala'nase found him like that and touched his arm, tugging him towards the dark alleyway between the dormitory and the wall. "Ala?" he asked, his brow furrowed in some confusion. "What are you doing?"

"Inviting you to continue our discussion from last time, silly," she said a bit saucily. "You *do* remember it, don't you?"

Of course he did. He'd proposed the two of them reuniting again. She'd have none of it, and never thought she would. So it surprised him to see her even mentioning it. Though he followed into the dim alleyway none the less. "Of course I do," he said, looking a bit confused as he tugged at his mage's robes, straightening them. "You've reconsidered?"

"I've thought about it a lot, Bran." Her voice was low, conspiratorial but tinged with something else. Something dark and seductive. "Things aren't the same without you. We could go so far together, you were right about that."

A faint smile tugged at the corner of his lips. "I thought you might never forgive me enough to realize that, Ala'nase," he said, still holding his robes in both hands as he looked her over. "And it's a great time for it too. The final test shall be a free-for-all event. All the first-years pitted against one another. A secret alliance could give us an edge over the others."

She smiled back, her own hands strategically straightening the front of her robe. The dim light still managed to catch the little sparkles of embroidered silver, and she traced over her form, drawing his eyes down. "I will consider it, Bran, but only if you do something for me."

The human male's eyes dipped down to that area between the shimmering silver, and he said gruffly, "A favour?" He swallowed, wetting his dry throat. "Name it, Ala'nase. It's only fair I do something nice for you, after our little misunderstanding."

Misunderstanding. What a joke. He had tossed her aside in the hopes of finding someone more "suited" to him at the academy.

"I need you on my side this time, Bran. Besides, I think you'll like this favour."

She stepped towards him, her hand brushing her hair off her neck and letting the long tresses combine over her shoulder. "We need to get Mae'lin out."

Bran's eyes widened in shock and surprise. "Mae'lin? Why him? What's there to worry about that bumpkin?" He looked her over, the obvious desire mixed with complete confusion.

"I'm surprised you're not more interested. If he falls, don't you think someone else may fall as well?" She reached her hand into a small pouch at her hip, running over the glorious curve before handing him a small item. "Just do it, and do it first. Once he's gone, we'll take out the others. Together."

The tall, brown haired human eyed the trinket with confusion. Though he didn't hesitate overlong before he said, "What if I'm caught though? I would be expelled myself, Ala'nase," and she detected his worry as the one thing that mattered to him was on the line: his own advancement. It was such a tough obstacle to overcome with the stubborn Bran.

"So wouldn't that be proof and more of your devotion to us? Come on, Bran, you didn't think it would be that easy to win me back, did you? You know what a hot commodity I am, but I was too broken up after you to even entertain all those others that were interested. Now I'm here, giving us another chance, and you won't even take a little risk for it?"

His brows furrowed, and he stared at first the trinket, then her. Then back again. "How do I know you're serious? And not just trying to use me? You know I'd do anything for you, Ala'nase," she knew no such thing, of course, "but I need to be sure this is genuine. That you're ready to forgive and be my girlfriend again."

Her fingers trailed to his chest, flirting above his heart. "Then know it, Bran. You know me better than anyone, and you stomped on my love. So you're just going to have to trust that this will make up for that."

She was unsure if that would be enough to sway him, but Bran gazed down at the crystal trinket as he thought before finally wrapping his hand about it. "Very well, Ala'nase. I will do this for you. And then we can go back to being lovers again," he said confidently. "Just like before."

Just like before he ruined everything.

She leaned in, brushing her lips tenderly against his jaw, a little bolt of electricity passing between them. "Just like before," she agreed, her warm breath washing over his skin.

CHAPTER 51

All the preparation with Mae'lin over the months prior had made the initial portions of the test a breeze for Firia. A relative breeze, she assured herself. It had still been tougher than anything she'd fared prior to trying out for the academy.

She'd had to put her spells to use in trial after trial, finding creative ways of using the most basic spells. Solutions to puzzles that she scarcely fathomed could be made, let alone solved.

Through it all, she'd persevered, and yet...

Mae'lin walked up beside her at the edge of the great ring at the heart of the academy grounds. A broad, warm smile on his face as he reached out and took her hand in his. Nary a word spoken, just that quiet pride in her, in them, for succeeding so far where those far more prepared – far more privileged – had done much worse.

There was no time for words, however, out over the courtyard the voice of Professor Yae'ra boomed out, amplified by some magic.

"For the final test of your abilities – and your worthiness to continue here at Gaul'di-mere Academy – you shall all enter into the Grim Jungle. There, you shall face a free-for-all competition. A hunt to find your first awards as students here, your finest accolades thus far." The fancily dressed wizard stood atop a hovering platform, far above the courtyard, his golden robes not even able to billow in the chill winds, it was so heavily inlaid with precious gems and metals.

"Once you enter into the Grim Jungle, your only rules are thus: No harmful spells against one another. You may inhibit, stall, or slow your opponents, but outright assault that causes or seriously risks life threatening danger shall not be allowed. Anyone in violation of this shall be expelled."

Mae'lin looked to her, a reassuring smile on his face as he squeezed her hand.

"Go into the 'arena', novices. But emerge as genuine mages on the track to greatness. This is your great chance to prove yourself, for take note: The masters of this academy are watching, observing. Making note of who shall be their apprentices someday."

"Good luck, Mae'lin," she whispered, and she meant it with all her heart. She was excited for herself, but she wanted, more than anything, for him to succeed. For him to have joy in his life, true value and meaning, and she squeezed his hand back.

She'd worn her lightest robe, the one that fit her bodice tightly and didn't trail much. The last thing she needed was a minor snag to slow her down. Her hair was pulled back into a bun, out of her face, and she'd been practicing all night.

She knew she'd get this.

"Be one with the arcane," came the final words of the dour professor, and no sooner were they said than Firia felt herself pulled through reality itself.

When she reappeared it was not at Mae'lin's side. Nor in any place like she had assumed she would end up in with the title of "jungle".

All alone, she stood beneath a great mushroom, as big as some houses where she was from. It lifted up into the air over her, sheltering her from the sky… sky?

Stepping out along the alternating rocky, spongy jungle floor, she looked up and saw only stone above her. Whatever sort of jungle it was she was in, it was within a cave of some sort.

There were more than simply giant mushrooms about, though; strange flora of various sorts were all about. Great purple blooms, some of which were bigger than her. And more disturbing still, they undulated and moved of their own accord, more like an animal than a plant.

She took the time to study her surroundings, to become more familiar with the strength of the floor, the way she breathed. All of the little things could affect how quickly she moved, how fast she'd finish this, and she didn't want to rush off willy-nilly.

Be one with the arcane. She didn't know if there was a hidden meaning, but she tried to obey, opening her mind to the unseen.

It came to her, albeit gradually. She could feel the flow of the magic about her, and realized it permeated the whole of the cavern. It was strong there, even more so than at the academy. Though there was something odd…

When she reached out with her ethereal self to the cavern walls, she was immediately forced back away. The walls were barriers, not just against the physical, but the magical.

Slowly Firia began to make sense of it. The immense concentration of magic, it was all contained there by those stones. It was no ordinary cavern, but hewn out of stone with some sort of anti-magic properties, which kept so much arcane energy bottled up inside.

It was as she pondered those mysteries that she felt something else so very odd. The giant blooming flower beside her emitted some odd aura, it–

She jumped back away from it, scarcely a moment too soon.

The great plant had moved closer! It's great fronds reaching out like an abductor in slow motion. And within its great, pitcher-like bloom she saw something that looked like hard teeth. Razor thin and sharp near the entrance, but others for gnashing deep within.

Her heart beat fast with the close encounter, but then something more dawned on her: there was something else in the mouth of that plant. It was a scroll, and must have been enchanted, for its papers looked pristine, as if straight from the scribe. Yet it sat in a murk of mucousy goo.

She could do this. Varuj had taught her, and though she struggled with it, her confidence was renewed just knowing what to do.

The other students would have to find more creative ways to get at such a clue to the test, but she was able to hold out her arm and draw out the magical energy within herself and manipulate the object from afar.

It resisted the movement, the arcane energy that imbued that plant-animal not giving up the possession within it. Not without a fight at least.

Firia had to twist her fingers and augment the spell as best she could, funneling her energy through the ring she wore to amplify its power. Her brow creased, the plant-animal shuddered, but she saw the scroll drag along its gooey, fanged maw.

The creature tried to bite and gnaw on the scroll, to keep it from getting away, yet whatever magic that kept it pristine also kept it from harm.

She had to take a step back to avoid the approaching thing, but at last the scroll popped free of its hold and then careened towards her before landing upon the rocks and rolling to her.

With a deft grab, Firia scooped it up then moved away, back to the relative safety of the sheltering mushroom she'd appeared under.

Undoing the seal upon it, she rolled open the scroll and saw but a simple drawing there. It was a great tree, not like the ones in that underground "jungle", but more like those she knew above. Yet not, all the same.

She didn't understand, and her fingers traced over the strange scroll as if reading it another way. She was still so excited at having figured out the first test so quickly that her mind was racing and she had trouble slowing it down, focussing on the next piece of the puzzle.

There was nothing for her to do but calm down. Explore.

Rolling it back up she moved through the curious underground jungle, avoiding the slowly lurching plant-creature as she wound through the giant mushrooms.

The ground had such a strange feel to it. At times hard and rocky, at others spongy and soft, like the fungus around her.

It made for such bizarre footing that she almost didn't notice it when the ground gave way entirely and she very nearly toppled over a cliff.

Desperately she reached out and clung to one of the mushroom stems beside her, heart thudding at an incredible rate as she stared down the rocky incline. The jungle continued down it at a steep angle, and she found herself worried how she would climb it safely. Jagged rocks stuck out of the fungus at weird angles, and she knew if she missed her footing even once, it could be the end of her. Or at least the end of the test.

As she mulled it over she saw one of the great mushroom tops beneath her. The bizarre purple pattern of a star there, seemingly growing naturally.

Storing up her courage she took a few steps back, checked her footing and... ran!

She ran to the edge and with a great leap sprung out over the cliffside.

There was nothing but air beneath her cloak as she moved towards her destination. Though as she began to arc downwards, panic nearly set in.

She wouldn't make it.

Calling upon all she knew of magic, Firia reached out with both hands, the telekinetic force she expelled digging furrows into the spongy fungus.

She never made contact with the bloom, but the invisible grasp of her arcane magic kept her dangling from its edge none the less. She hung there, swaying back and forth with not but the force of her magical power saving her from crashing down below.

They were torturers at this academy! There was no room for failure, and she was so grateful to the adrenaline pumping through her. Without it, she was sure she'd break down in fright, but instead she took a deep breath, cleansing her body and her mind.

She could do this.

"Firia!" a cry came from below, and she instantly recognized it as Mae'lin's.

From the jungle below he was clamouring up the cavern side, grabbing onto every rocky outcropping he could with his hands and rushing forth. His cloak even snagged on a stone beneath him, ripping a big tear down its backside as he pushed on heedlessly. "I'm coming for you!"

She didn't need his help though. She slowly pulled herself upwards, the telekinetic grip she'd formed hauling her up at great effort. Her brow sweated, face turned red, but she pulled herself up further and further. She'd make it, and avoid the fall below, just another –

From out of the underground jungle a ball of fire hurdled towards her, and only the deft attunement of her mind to the arcane from before alerted her to it in time. Yet there was nothing to do, but drop...

She did, with no other choice before her.

Firia plummeted downwards, the searing heat of that fire blast narrowly avoiding her, but singing and cuffs as she fell. Smoke billowed from her as she fell to her abysmal failure.

There was no telling how he did it, how Mae'lin had climbed up that rock face so fast, but when she fell into his arms she could only be grateful as the lanky elf swayed and nearly fell over from the force of her impact.

Her eyes went shut and her arms were around his neck, clutching him desperately. How? She didn't care. All she knew was immense gratitude as she clung to him. "Holy hell, what was that?"

Mae'lin moved back then crouched down, hiding them behind the mushroom trunk as he breathed heavily. "It had to be another student," he said after but a moment's thought, the words a struggle to get out, he was so weary. Though once he laid her down on the spongy ground she saw how he'd managed his rescue in so timely a manner, his trousers were torn at both legs, and both hands and knees were bloody from his climb over the jagged rocks.

"Had to be," she agreed, grimacing. How many enemies did she have here anyways? "Listen, have you seen anything like this?" She grabbed the scroll, quickly unfurling it for him, her pulse racing. Even if she had nearly just died, she needed to succeed.

Mae'lin studied her scroll a moment, "It's not quite the same as mine, it's... a bit different." He unfurled his own, then put it beside hers, though it made no more sense.

However, once she looked up, she saw in the distance over the jungle canopy several great trees spiralling up above the fungal forest. They were each different, but she immediately found one, then another, that resembled the images they were given.

Mae'lin followed her gaze and said, "That's them then!" And a big smile crossed his face, their goal in sight already.

"We have to move, before whoever just tried to fireball me to my death catches up. Do you see a good route we could take?" She was in charge, detached, and she'd never felt so sure of anything. It was wonderful to have something to take her mind off what she had to do to the sweet elf who had, quite literally, saved her life.

"I think I saw a better way down then the one I took up," he stated, standing up again and offering her his hand. "C'mon," he said with a smile. "We're gonna do this, no matter who tries to stop us."

"Damn right," she agreed, and she moved so quickly and with such confidence. Together, they were unstoppable! They'd been able to work together, studying almost daily for months now. They knew one another's strengths and weaknesses and at his side, there was no doubt of their success.

324

CHAPTER 52

Ala'nase cursed at herself for missing the woman, her prime opportunity lost because of that love-struck fool, Mae'lin.

As she climbed down over the cliff face, she touched the stone upon her necklace, the glow getting brighter as she approached the holder of the other, matching one.

Bran came into view, looking up to her in surprise. "Oh, it's you," he said with some relief, a spell upon his fingers. "The stone you gave me was indicating he was this way," he remarked, pointing off exactly to where they'd gone.

"That's where he went, definitely," she muttered to herself in irritation. "But he's got company now. He somehow managed to luck upon Firia," she remarked bitterly.

"Firia?" he said, his voice laced with some strange emotion.

"I'll have to distract her so you can handle him," she asserted.

"She can't know it was me," he said, eyes wide.

"Don't get your nuts in a knot," she said irritably. "I said I'd distract her."

Seeing her fail and be cast out would be the utmost distraction, she determined.

CHAPTER 53

The cavern was humid, and getting more so as they went further down into the valley. Mae'lin had to keep wiping the perspiration from his brow as he went, but he never lost his smile.

Firia never lost her alertness.

As they neared the giant trees that were their destination, a disturbing reality started to come to the fore: the trees themselves rested upon an island.

In the midst of a great underground cavern, in a jungle of mushrooms, lay a lake of tepid, dark water. Worse still, even if they waded or swam across, the island itself seemed to have sheer cliff faces, that would be near impossible to climb, if not utterly so.

"What'll we do?" Mae'lin bemoaned, resting against one of the fungal trunks with one palm, the great mushrooms continuing out into the lake even.

"I do not feel like taking a dip in there," she agreed, and she knew there must be a way around it. A way that didn't involve getting soaking wet. This entire place reminded her of something Gway'lin would have loved. A trickster's paradise, filled with riddles.

Any thoughts of swimming across would've been quickly dashed, as Firia noticed nearby a ripple in the water. When she pointed it out to Mae'lin, he looked and together they saw some fanged fish-like creature rise above the surface, two beady eyes upon the flat top of its head looking about before diving back beneath.

"Yeah, let's not go for a swim," he remarked, then with a snap of his fingers he grinned toothily. "I've got it." He patted the thick fungal trunk by him and said, "These things go right across the lake. We just gotta get across by using them as jumping platforms."

"As long as no one lobs a fireball at us," she retorted, even as she stood and looked at the "platforms". "It's going to be dangerous, Mae'lin. And you won't be able to catch me. And I won't be able to catch you either." Well... maybe. She could try her telekinesis, but that was asking a lot of her abilities.

Firia thought on it a while, but then she remembered her search for the missing Mae'lin in his altercation with Bran. "You can manipulate the water to lift yourself up!"

A light went on in Mae'lin's head, and he grabbed her, sweeping her into his arms and giving her a big, passionate kiss, the likes of which he had never done before. "You're brilliant," he said, eyes glittering. Then pressed their mouths together again in his excitement.

Her heart broke.

It wasn't before. It wasn't when she had sex with him, knowing it couldn't last. It wasn't when she'd made her promise to Varuj.

It was then, and it took every ounce of strength she had to persevere and not break down, utterly. Instead she gently put her hand on his chest, pushing him away with a sheepish smile. "We have to hurry before someone finds us."

Undaunted, Mae'lin smiled and nodded. "We'll have a lot of celebrating to do after we win this contest," he remarked, and immediately began to work his own magic.

Since they'd first faced off together, Firia knew he was masterful with his control of water. He had an affinity for it that was quite impressive, and he brought forth the murky liquid into a spout. "I'll send you up first," he said.

Firia nodded, and gathered her robes about her. She'd get wet she figured, but perhaps not if she used her telekinesis right.

Hesitating, she focussed her abilities before she leapt onto the water spout. A field of telekinetic energy shielded her from the damp spray, but up she went all the same. The force of the jets sending a spritzing of water all about until she was sent up high, on the level of the mushroom peak.

She tried to reach out for it, but its spongy, slippery surface was awful for grasping hold of, so instead she had to leap across.

Her boots nearly failed her when she back stepped after her landing, but a heartbeat later and she was secure. Safe.

With a laugh she looked down and saw Mae'lin smiling up at her. "My turn now," he said.

It was all going so well, just according to plan, though she got an odd feeling that she couldn't quite place.

"Firia!" came a familiar voice, and she turned about, seeing Ala'nase a few mushrooms over.

The nimble elf leapt closer, coming nearer still. "Wait up!" she cried to Firia. Though the feeling of discomfort only grew the stronger.

The gasp and cry she heard from Mae'lin's direction sent her spinning back around, just in time to see the lanky elf's spell go awry. Or rather, him to go awry.

He jumped as if into the spout, same as she did, but his leap was off. Oddly so, he had far too much wherewithal to mess it up so badly. It caused his own jet of water to flip him over and send him careening into the inky water of the underground lake.

"Mae'lin!" Firia cried out as the elf sputtered to the surface, spitting water and flailing about. Something about it all sat so badly with her, and she was reminded of the curious display of misdirection that Bran had done during his trial to get into the academy.

She looked back to Ala, searching some aid or help, but that off feeling didn't dissipate. She didn't have time to understand it, and instead she desperately tried to cast her magic, to tug Mae'lin out of the infested lake.

As she nearly finished her casting, Ala'nase tumbled into her, knocking her over and ruining her casting. "Sorry," she muttered.

But Firia was only concerned for Mae'lin. She got up to resume her spell casting, but saw the outline of that bizarre underground fish moving towards him on the surface of the water. "Mae'lin! Watch out!" she cried.

The elf saw the danger, and began to move away with the aid of her spell helping him.

That feeling of wrongness only grew, however, and just as Mae'lin reached safety he went flying up and back as if struck a blow on the chin. The mystery made sense as she caught a flicker of something; a dark augmented spell had made Bran invisible to their eyes by some illusory magic.

It was a competition. They were being turned on one another in their pursuit of the prize.

"Mae'lin!" she cried out again, but this time she was casting something different. Something more her speed. Quickly she summoned Luka, her fox familiar, and sent him towards Ala'nase. She needed protection from her friend, though she had little reason why. With that, her fingers began working again in an intricate frenzy, her sights instead set on the glimmer of the attacker.

"Firia! Why?!" cried her friend as the fox slammed into her, knocking her over onto her back.

Though beneath her she watched that fish thing rise up out of the water. Firia had little time to act, and her telekinesis was not strong enough to pull Mae'lin out of the water.

It was however, strong enough to knock someone in.

With a deft sweep of her wrist, she sent Bran tumbling into the murk directly before the monstrous fish-creature. It took the bait and lunged for the human.

Before she could do any more, however, she heard the yelp of Luka being knocked away and the force of some dark magic.

When Firia looked behind her, she saw the spectral fox upon its side, the victim of some sort of magic amplified through a dark crystal which Ala'nase held on a chain. "You–"

The elven woman lashed out, but not with spells, instead it was a swift kick that set Firia off balance and took her quite by surprise.

They were mages, not brawlers, the physical blows seemed too off. So very wrong. But most importantly, unexpected.

"You stole everything from me that crossed your path!" cried the elven woman, and she was upon Firia's back before she could get up, twining her dark hair about her caramel fingers.

It was such a savage maneuver, but Ala'nase yanked back on her hair, and the sharp move – though painful – gave her a brief glimpse of below. The fish-monster had ripped a large piece off of

Bran's robes, and the human sorcerer tried using his dark crystal to ward it off.

Before she saw more, Ala'nase slammed her face down onto the mushroom top. "You had to have it all!" cried her former friend in a shrill voice, slamming her face down again, giving her another brief glimpse of Bran tossing the amulet away. But why?

The third slam of her face into the mushroom brought her another reprieve and she saw the creature lunge for the crystal and snap it up out of the air. It *was* drawn to whatever magics inhabited that trinket.

Firia was dazed, her mind reeling upon things other than breaking out of her former friend's assault in the confusion. Though it passed; the spongy, flesh-like material of the fungal bloom was not hard enough to cause her any serious injury.

She hardly had any idea what Ala was talking about. She knew that the woman had been upset and withdrawn, and that Varuj had likely told her that Firia was the reason they couldn't be together. That would cause her friend pain, but not like this.

She began casting, her hand growing warm though not hot enough to scorch. Just enough to let a spark of flame fly toward Ala's face as Firia rolled onto her back.

The spark sent the elven woman back screeching. Despite her efforts to not seriously harm her friend, the fire did ignite a few strands, and she rolled about trying to douse them.

Firia, however, was already turning her attention back to the struggle below, her worry for Mae'lin outdoing her own troubles in her mind.

And what she saw troubled her deeply. The fish-creature was bigger, more freakish than before. It had sprouted long, hideous limbs, and was growing in size. She didn't need to wonder what was happening, as she felt the tainted arcane magic warping its structure. Perhaps some combination of the dark crystals and the curious makeup of the cavern itself.

It slashed out with its claws and struck Bran, the human falling into the water face down.

Mae'lin, however, went to his own attacker's rescue. He dove back into the deeper water, and grabbed for the human. He pulled him out of the water, gasping for air and bleeding from his revealed chest through several claw marks.

"Mae'lin!" cried Firia, but it was too late. She saw it all unfold.

Heroically, when he saw the monster coming for them both, he shoved Bran to the shore with all his strength, and the monster got him and him alone. Its long, dagger-like fangs sunk into the lanky elf's shoulder and he let loose a terribly cry just before vanishing from the testing area in a burst of arcane energy.

He had failed.

He had been betrayed.

Sabotaged.

Attacked.

Firia's fury grew at what had happened to the noble man she loved, but before she could unleash it, the blow to her back knocked her forward.

She went spinning, and should've careened off the side of the mushroom. Yet somehow she came short, and slid to a halt just along the edge, able to look up and see the approaching Ala'nase in a rage of her own.

"Why won't you just go away?!" Ala'nase cried, and the smell of smoke in the air was too pungent to be the small singing Firia had given her. She'd been hit by a fireball! The same sort that had been flung at her earlier.

Yet, when she looked back, she saw no signs of it, but a light blackening of the fabric on her robes. What had happened?

"You're done taking from me," Ala'nase reasserted, and Firia watched as the woman struck out with her long, shapely leg to kick her in the face.

Firia's eyes closed in anticipation.

Yet the blow never came.

Instead a yelp filled the air, and when she looked up she saw the elven woman in a pair of dark arms, confined.

Varuj held her restrained, and with a prick of his nail and a muttering of an incantation, he caused her whole body to go limp and unconscious before letting her fall to the spongy mushroom top.

She'd not been so relieved to see him in so long. Her head felt so full, so heavy, but she smiled tentatively at the demon before looking at her friend with concern. "She hates me…"

If it had been nearly anyone else, she wouldn't have been too surprised. But the friends she made, she was dedicated to, and Ala is... *was* her best friend.

"She'll get over it one day," he said to her, striding over to her purposefully and taking her by the arm before helping her to her feet. "We have no time to mourn lost friendships, however. There is still a contest on, and we shall make it together. As we always should have," he said, giving her a faint little smile that said more than his many other wider and more charming ones.

She nodded, simply, for what else was there to do? She recalled Luka back into herself, feeling him nestle within her soul, as she looked forward to their destination.

"Let's get this done, already."

Varuj took her by the hand, and together they ran. He made the leap so easy, she could feel his powerful sorcery projecting them higher and further, carrying them from one mushroom to the next. Though something caught his eye.

"Competitors," he said, and she saw them, two others doing something similar, sorcerously controlling the wind to propel them forward on their robes. "I'll take care of them," he said, and with a subtle flick of his wrist he sent them one off course, causing him to land back where he came from. The other lost his footing just before take-off and crashed onto his bottom.

Neither was hurt, nor out of the game, and the demon who held her hand abided by the rules perfectly, she had to confess.

Though his own focus on the game meant he didn't see the slimy, googly-eyed monster climb over the edge of the next mushroom towards, its fangs and claws ready to gouge them both.

Firia used the telekinesis she was quickly becoming a master of, and knocked the thing from its precarious perch back into the murky waters below. The splash let her know her job was well done, but Varuj's appreciative grin did the trick too. "Well done," he remarked as they carried on.

"I told you I studied," she shot back, pride resounding in her tone.

When they landed upon the stony island, she saw none of the spongy fungal growths at all. Instead there was the oddly out-of-place trees, as if a real jungle lurked at the heart of the underground fungal version.

Together they walked to the center, and amidst the greenery a light began to grow stronger.

They had to squint their eyes against it, but looking up, Firia saw that it came from a hole in the cavern itself. It was sunlight from above.

With a blink of their eyes, they felt themselves being lifted up into the light. Hand in hand, together.

CHAPTER 54

The great dining hall was decked out for a celebration, curiously glowing lights in the shape of the first students to arrive – Varuj and Firia – graced the center, while gorgeous streamers and all sorts of other magical displays lit the place up. Yet the mood was anything but celebratory.

A great disturbance had filled the hall, and all the occupants clustered around a central area.

Firia immediately thought of Mae'lin and pushed her way forward.

Before she got there, the booming voice of Professor Yae'ra demanded her attention. "Someone will need to explain what has happened to this young man."

Someone.

CHAPTER 55

The words of the healer still rang in Firia's ears.

Mae'lin was unconscious, and nothing they'd done had changed that. They were out of ideas.

She saw his pale, sinewy form wrapped in bandages and bed sheets before her. Treated with potions and elixirs, they did what they could, yet the venom from the creature that had bit him had been altered in some way they couldn't place. It never should've happened, they assured her. The entire cavern was enchanted so that any serious harm would've been extracted, just as any students that suffered it would be extracted.

"Bran has been expelled," came Varuj's voice as he rested his hand upon her shoulder.

She somehow didn't feel mollified. Mae'lin had tried to save the man, his attacker, and she'd gotten him kicked out. Even after what he did, how forceful he'd been, she did feel an odd kinship with him that wasn't easy to shake.

Getting him in trouble had been difficult, and she'd tried to paint it as innocently as possible, but how could she? She had to tell them about the strange amulet, hoping desperately that it would help them cure Mae'lin.

She'd spared Ala'nase, though they hadn't spoken since. What was there to say?

Varuj and Firia had finished in a tie for first place. Yet there had been no celebration. Not on their end.

Some of the assistant healers came in, jabbering about violent upheavals throughout the countryside, but she couldn't handle it.

"Come along," Varuj said, as if reading her mind. He took her hand in his, and guided her out of the room.

"I just don't understand," she sighed, not for the first time. "They were supposed to be my friends."

"Trust in others is risky," he said to her in that deep husk of his as he guided her through the building and out into the crisp air. "I have invested my all in trust of you, Firi," he said with some fondness, the two walking hand in hand through the center of the academy. The hustle and bustle all gone, the students now took their time and enjoyed their break. "I pray you don't let me down," he said, looking to her fondly and squeezing her hand.

She was worn out, and his presence was reassuring. Comforting. "Varuj, thanks for saving me from Ala'nase."

The demon lifted her hand and kissed the backs of her knuckles for all to see as he came to a stop. "I am glad I was there to do so," he said smoothly. "Had I been further away I might not have been in time to see us both through to the finish."

She withdrew her hand, though gingerly, as she looked up at him. "Varuj, I'm not going to let him find out by some drama monger. I want to tell him myself."

"You worry too much," he said to her, his smile fading a bit. "But I have a solution for you. The year is at an end. A brief break is upon us. The wealthier students are off to visit their families. You cannot do that." He gestured with his hand around at the others who walked about. "However, you can come with me on a trip away from your worries."

His full lips spread wide into a warm smile. "You need the rest to prepare for the upcoming semester. Or you shall be good to no one. Come with me, Firi." His proposal so enticing as the handsome demon brushed back some of his ebon hair from his smooth, masculine face.

Yet she didn't want to. Couldn't.

How could she leave Mae'lin to wake up alone, and without anyone to care for him?

If she stayed, though, would that make things better or worse? He'd saved her life, and now she had to break up with him. Because she didn't deserve him. Didn't deserve that amazing, wonderful elf.

Firia looked to the handsome demon, the one who knew all her secret joys, and pleasures, and pains. Who had visited all of those things upon her. Who had caused her more hurt and more bliss than anyone ought to have been able to.

Mae'lin would never understand. Part of her hoped he one day could, though. When he woke up.

CHAPTER 56

In all her years, Firia had only been to two places. Her homeland in the fields of farm country, and the academy.

Varuj had changed that.

They had little time for enjoying such things; classes would resume before long, but when she walked to the open balcony door and smelled the sweetly warm air of the desert night outside, it was breathtaking. The curious black fruit that grew on the trees, with their beautiful pink blossoms, gave off such an aroma of decadent sweetness that wafted across the river and the oasis, mixing with the dry scents of the desert beyond before coming to her.

It was such a pleasant place. Even at night she felt comfortable walking out onto that window overlooking the private garden in only her tunic. The loose, untied garment barely covered her bottom as she revelled in the place. The sights of the curiously triangular buildings, their steeples gleaming copper even in the moonlight.

As she bent over the railing, the feel of Varuj's heated presence came up behind her. His arms embracing her as the fullness of his hard body greeted her. He was so much bigger than her, his ruddy flesh so comforting, in such a bizarre way.

"Avoiding the bed?" came his ethereal voice, reverberating so darkly. So deliciously masculine. He was himself. As when she first met him. Well… almost. She thought him changed somehow. Not quite so… sinister in appearance. It seemed like proof of what he had said: that he had sacrificed some of who he was to be more human.

"Always," she agreed, even as she leaned back into him. She'd shirked all of her responsibilities, put her heart on hold. She had no idea what she was going to say to Mae'lin, but she dreaded it. It was the only dimmer on the vacation, and she tugged Varuj's arms around her tighter. She'd deal with it when the time came.

Until then, she'd promised herself that she'd relax from the hardest year she'd ever suffered through.

His thick arms were a great comfort, the hard, broad muscles a shelter from the worries of the world, it felt. Each bicep seeming about as thick as her waist.

The villa Varuj had got them was away from the city, away from all others. Just a private getaway in a foreign land, where both of them were free to be themselves. For her to enjoy. For him to be the hulking fiend from another realm.

She felt the stirring of his loins, that oversized shaft rising up, and up, brushing betwixt her smooth thighs as he licked, suckled and nibbled her ear. "That's fine by me," he growled out in that otherworldly voice that should've scared any normal woman. But only made her cunny moisten.

Maybe she had always been a bit messed up. She thought back to the fateful night in the library, about how excited she was to summon a demon. How she'd specifically looked for a male demon, for someone like him.

Maybe she'd always known, deep down, that this is what she wanted, though it'd taken her so long to reconcile. Life would never be the same after she realized it, though, and she pushed back into him.

"I'm not going to be able to walk if you keep this up."

The brush of his horn against her hair sent a shiver through her spine, but his cock jumped at her words, and when it slapped against her slit with its eagerness she felt her knees weaken. "Maybe I'd enjoy that," he growled into her ear, his tongue teasing just inside it before he pulled back his hips, dragging his veiny girth along her moist cunny, teasing the bulbous crown to her engorged clit.

It wasn't fair how easily he made her body his, even if her mind and heart remained more... non-committal.

Her nipples were so stiff against her top, her skin prickling with desire and arousal. She'd never felt like this before, so brazen and free. She couldn't help but moan, her ass pressing into his hips as she stood up on tiptoes. "You're a bad influence on me." What an understatement that was.

She couldn't see his devilish grin, but she felt his large palm press about her tit and squeeze it rough and hard. "Good," the singular word a bestial growl just before he impaled her upon that unholy shaft of his.

He'd taken her virginity upon that monstrously sized dick. He'd taken her again and again since then with it. Yet still, every time, it was such a shock to be filled so completely, so close to the breaking point by that veiny girth.

She had to reach out for the balcony to save herself from careening forwards. The force, the depth, it made her head spin with pleasure and all of her protests and smart-ass comments dissipated. The year had opened her up to so many experiences, so many new bits of knowledge, but the carnal intimacy she'd found had been something unexpectedly delightful.

She'd finished her traditional schooling as an outcast loner, and yet her first year at the Magic Academy had been filled with more friendship, more love, more passion than she'd ever known possible.

Her hand squeezed the balcony as the other reached for his hand, digging her nails into his demonic flesh.

"Yes!" She gulped for air and felt her body undulate against his.

She'd played with fire, got burned, and she liked it. Wanted more.

He gave it.

Tugging back his hips, her tight quim gripped his shaft so fully her whole body was yanked back with him before his grip tugged her back into place and he slid out of her. The thrust back in was more exquisite still, the pendulous swing of his heavy sac, the slap of those hefty balls against her clit. It was all such sweet, debauched pleasure, and he gave it to her in full, picking up his pace and pumping his shaft into her faster. Harder.

The low, gravelly husk of his breathing in her ear, his hot breath washing over her skin as he took her again so soon after her bath. She could never remain clean for long with him nearby. Part of her felt she'd never be clean again. And would never want to be.

He'd seduced her body, wrenched her heart in two, and expanded her mind. He'd bedded with her soul, saved her life, and shared a connection deeper than either of them could put into words.

It was as she said. Every time they made love, every time they touched, it felt like they were two parts of the same, broken whole. Desperately trying to make one another a full person again.

She loved him. Deeply. Wrongly. But with every thrust, every gasp, every groan, her desire for the demon mounted.

As he clutched her breast, his other palm went to her lower stomach. She felt his hand there, not tracing a pattern as before, in that way that elicited such a tingle of pleasure. Instead it was a slow circling, a tender sort of caress that belied the powerful, hard thrusts he was giving to her.

Varuj was a creature of contradictions, she realized. Yet she found it hard to resent him for it when he was bringing her to such heights. Powerfully manhandling and fucking her body so expertly.

"You're mine, Firi," he growled, though the words weren't said so badly, she thought. They sounded more loving than possessive. Or at least, more so than they had in the past. She couldn't be sure. But he licked, sucked and kissed his way down her neck as she felt him swell inside her, causing her to gasp at the increased pressure, the increasingly erratic nature of his motions.

Her body tingled and her legs strained as she angled herself to take him in, to let his hands wander and play with her flesh.

"I love you," she whimpered, her spine arching as her pussy clamped down on that oversized, demonic member.

The feeling of his massive, rough hands all over her flesh, mauling up her tunic, her body. The sound of his deeply satisfied groan as she milked him so intentionally. It all drew it from him, those gravelly, heartfelt words rumbling out from his deep, barrel chest as he came. "I love you," the words said so harshly in the throes of his pleasure, but meant so sincerely, she just knew.

Each long spurt of virile, demonic seed up into her was another reminder of that as he clutched her breast and held her firm stomach.

"Firi…" he called out, his sac tightened as it drained itself of every last bit of his essence.

She pressed into him, encouraging his orgasm so wantonly. She'd gotten to know his body, his demonic pleasure so intimately, and her hands clutched at his, pressing them to her. Her breathing was so heavy and her heart was racing, but the trysts made her feel so blissfully alive.

His every touch enhanced it. The way he caressed her in their post-coital closeness. The gradual softening of his inhumanly-sized dick. The slow drool of his seed out of her battered folds and down her inner thighs, until at last he lifted her up in his mighty arms and carried her inside.

There was no comparing his strength to any other. She was but a feather to his muscular might, and he laid her out on the lavish, silk and satin bed with care. The smile on her demon's face brightened her heart as he plucked up a cherry and dangled it down to her lips.

She accepted it, her body burning with the pleasant after effects of sex. Spitting out the seed she exhaled, the sweet scent on her breath. "How much longer do we have here?"

"Leave those worries to me, sweet Firi," he assured her on his deep voice, her flesh still tingling with the fire of their coupling as he plucked another cherry from the bowl beside them and fed it to her. His endless pampering and savouring of her never seeming to end.

She accepted it with a soft smile, relaxing into the surreal paradise so far from home and her worries.

NOTE FROM THE AUTHORS

Thank you so much for reading and purchasing our story! We hope it made you squirm. Once you recover, sign up for our newsletter at http://jmkeep.com/newsletter and check out the rest of our catalogue at http://jmkeep.com.

Did you enjoy yourself? Take a quick second to tell your friends in a review on Amazon and Goodreads! Reviews are a great way of helping other readers to find our work and make it so we can write more frequently!

We love connecting with our fans! You can find us here:

Website: http://jmkeep.com/

Twitter: @jmkeep | @jekeep

Facebook: http://www.facebook.com/jmkeep

Remember, though. The best way to find out what major projects we have in the work is through our newsletter at http://jmkeep.com/newsletter! You'll get a free book just as a thanks for signing up.

MORE BY J.E. & M. KEEP

Erotic Novels:
The Vixen Torn
The Vixen Arises
Magic Academy
When Dreamers Wake
The Warlord's Concubine
The Mistress
Vile Wasteland
Forgotten Thrones
Erotic Novellas:
In Her Dreams
Brutal Passions
Brought the Stars to You
Bound as the World Burns
Her Master's Madness
Led Into Temptation

Outcast
Outcast 2: Her Survival
Bound by Forbidden Love
Bad Wolf, Be Good

Collections:
The Ultimate Erotic Horror Collection – Contains Her
Master's Madness, Bad Wolf, Be Good and Led Into
Temptation

BIOGRAPHY

Joshua and Michelle Keep combine fantasy, scifi, horror, romance and mystery into exciting and titillating books.

As long term, loving partners in a very happy relationship, they love to torture their characters. Dark romance wraps its way around all of their stories, corrupting both characters and readers alike.

Some of their work contains dubious consent and erotic pain, so it's not for the faint of heart. Their stories are often called twisted and arousing — at the same time.

Joshua and Michelle have been writing fantasy erotica for over 10 years from their home in St. John's, Newfoundland Canada. They are the owners of Darknest Fantasy Erotica, a forum dedicated to adult fantasy and video games.

Newsletter: http://jmkeep.com/newsletter
Patreon: http://www.patreon.com/jmkeep
Facebook: http://www.facebook.com/jmkeep
Youtube:
http://www.youtube.com/user/JMKeepSFF/videos
Twitter: http://twitter.com/jmkeep |
http://twitter.com/jekeep
Email: admin [at] jmkeep [dot] com